THE PALE SURFACE OF THINGS

HOPEACE PRESS
Victoria, British Columbia
www.hopeace.ca

THE PALE SURFACE
OF THINGS

A NOVEL

Janey Bennett

PUBLISHED BY HOPEACE PRESS
Victoria, British Columbia

Copyright © 2007 by Janey Bennett
All Rights Reserved

Set in 11.5 point Bernhard Modern Standard
and 36 point Lithos Pro type.

Canada Library Cataloging-In-Publication data
Bennett, Janey, 1938-
The Pale Surface of Things / Janey Bennett.
ISBN 978-0-9734007-2-4
1. Title.
PS8603.E55953P35 2007
C813'.6
C2007-900122-X

PRINTED IN CANADA
on 100% post-consumer recycled paper
and vegetable-based ink.

For Carol Bly and Fr. Michael Pappas,
whose help on this journey was a true blessing.

THE PALE SURFACE OF THINGS

1

It was ten o'clock. The cathedral bells thudded through the hot, still air. Tourists emerged from their hotels to buy mementos of their holiday in Crete before the day grew so hot they could do nothing but lie on a lounge chair near the hotel swimming pool. The lucky ones landed at Big Kostas's taverna at the top of the old city for breakfast.

Three Danes, shaky from the night before, were drinking their breakfast: several lagers with a chaser of *tsikoudia*. Singly and together, they asked Kostas, "Where's the Amerikan?"

The American they wanted was Douglas Watkins, who traded free room and board for chatting up Kostas's tourists every night. Kostas was also wondering where Douglas was. The boy was late for his own wedding.

August 18th. The wedding party that assembled in the mayor's office lacked only the groom to proceed with the ceremony. The hour of the wedding was linked to the departure of the cruise ship the couple would take for their honeymoon.

At one-minute intervals one guest or another went down the black-and-white-striped marble stairs to the foyer to look for the groom. The guests were the entire staff of the George Hanson Institute of Minoan Archaëology, based in Chania but supported through Laronwood University, a small, private college in the outskirts of St. Louis, Missouri. The waiting bride was Denise Hanson, daughter of George and niece of Les Hanson, Dean of Laronwood U. The tardy groom had been in Crete for ten weeks on a student fellowship with the Institute, digging for signs of a missing Minoan palace.

At that very moment, he was running toward Kostas's taverna from the seawall.

Kostas yelled at him, "Hurry up, you're late."

The Danes yelled, "Come and talk to us!"

Douglas yelled, "I can't. I'm late," and he ran up the wooden staircase to his third floor room. As he went, he yelled down, "Hey, Kostas. Call the Institute and tell them the truck got towed, will you?"

"What happened to you? Where you been?" Kostas yelled up the staircase.

Douglas's voice came back down, muffled by the clothing he was putting on. He came clumping down the stairs in new leather shoes. He was nearly into a new tailor-made summerweight worsted suit, grey, very nice, white shirt, not yet buttoned at the collar, turquoise and grey silk tie in his hand, short hair damp, and face red.

"You go to the digging place today? Why? She'll be mad. You know?"

"I know. I had to check the gate against goats. I forgot yesterday." He paused in front of an Irish Stout mirror to tie the necktie.

The Danes lurched to their feet and toasted him. "Skaal! Douglas!" They sank back into their chairs in a cascade of laughter.

"Where's the truck?"

"Take me to the mayor's and I'll tell you."

The morning grew hotter. The two men ran to Kostas's red Honda minibike. Kostas kickstarted it and they were off, down Theotokopoulou Street crawling carefully between the tourists and then bumping down the sloping steps the Venetians built for their donkey-carts.

"Did you reach anyone at the Institute?"

2

"Nobody home. Too late. What happened to it?"

"Highway construction. Big hole in the paving. No barrier. The axle broke."

"You got to face them cold. Just say 'I do and I broke your truck.' Here you go."

He pulled up in front of the *Dimarchion*, the City Hall. Douglas leapt off, said, "Thanks for the ride," and ran to the door.

In the mayor's office upstairs, the mayor of Chania stood to one side, regarding the wedding party. He knew it was a bad idea to have an American wedding in his lovely office. He murmured a prayer to the Holy Mother of God that she should see to it these people would not spill that sweet punch or the soft goat cheese onto his beautiful deeply padded blue carpet, especially that soft cheese, or if they did, that they wouldn't grind it in.

He had decorated the office himself, covered the walls with chrome-and-glass bookcases which he enhanced with photos of himself with celebrity visitors and his collection of crystal paperweights.

He should have never agreed to this.

The bride was a perky young blonde in a backless dress the color of mustard flowers. Her substantial parents were taking up most of the air in the room. The bride's father was in some big clothing business. The mayor guessed that was why the bride and her parents looked so unwrinkled, as if their clothing had just come from a shop instead of in suitcases flown half way around the world.

The bride's mother was in lime green linen, a well-bred dress and jacket, with a single strand of large pearls at her throat. Her hair was smooth, like sheet plastic. The father, Mr. Big Shot, paced back and forth in a lightweight blue blazer and white slacks with a red and blue striped tie.

The rest of the guests were wrinkled. A number of young men were milling about, wearing the only clean clothing left in their backpacks. Were they workers? Mr. Hanson's staff? Of what? Which one was the groom? The bride seemed to ignore all of them.

There was one older man who was wearing a khaki drip-dry travel suit. He spoke Greek with a strange accent. Hovering around him was a Cretan woman who seemed to be his caretaker.

3

Every few minutes the bride checked either the wall clock or her wristwatch. Her smile froze on her face, and frown lines appeared on her tanned forehead.

Her mother talked to the guests. She explained to some of them, *sotto voce* so the mayor wouldn't hear, that they had found this adorable young Orthodox priest who was from San Francisco—with perfect English too!—and they had wanted him to perform the service, but he'd gotten coy about doing it, so they'd just refused to negotiate. The mayor would have to do.

Denise interrupted her. "I still think if Daddy had offered him a little more money he would have done it. I mean, to be married by a man dressed in an outfit like that, on a windy empty beach, would have been like in a movie. So romantic."

The bride's father had heard this scenario before. He leaned into the conversation and said, "There aren't any empty beaches on Crete in August, Denise. And the priest said no. Then you asked to have the service in those locked Minoan ruins in the center of town, remember? Well," his teeth gleamed, "it didn't work out. So be happy with this wedding, honey. You'll have the big church wedding in October, back home."

She kissed him. "I am happy, Daddy." She looked around again for her groom.

Quarter past ten. The bride asked for water. Someone brought her a cup of punch. The wedding guests stopped milling about and retreated to the space along the walls. A few began nervously nibbling on olives from the platters of local specialties placed out on the conference table. Apprehension settled over the room. George Hanson sidled up to the small man who spoke Greek, and, out of the side of his mouth, said, "Do something!"

Roland Ducor was Director of the George Hanson Institute of Minoan Archaeology. He was Belgian, a small man, dressed, as usual, in his khaki drip-dry travel suit, white shirt, and bow tie. In honor of this occasion, his suit had been pressed by the Chania Dry Cleaners, so he did not, for a change, look as if he had slept in it. He was sartorially respectful today because the bride's father, George Hanson himself, was the principal source of funds for the Institute.

4

There was a slight chance the groom's absence might be, in part, his fault. He'd had a nervous feeling when he'd said yesterday, "Douglas, I've sent Efthikas home sick, so you're responsible for locking the site tonight. Don't forget it."

There'd been a little celebration at the end of the workday, and everyone had some beers and then wandered off to take Douglas drinking on the night before his wedding.

No one would be working at the site for the next week. Those goats got into things, even when people were there. If they got past the fencing and fell into the open pits, they would starve—unless they broke their necks in the fall. He would have to pay the shepherd.

It might have been better if Ducor had gone out to the site to check the fencing himself and left Douglas to his pre-wedding preparations. But Douglas was a responsible person. Mostly responsible. Ducor felt stifled by the heat.

He could not help acting officious every time George Hanson was around. The man made him nervous. Now something had gone wrong and Douglas was late. Ducor's stomach fell and his skin felt crawly. He knew it was not the flu. It was fear.

He approached the mayor and asked to borrow the telephone. When he dialed the taverna where Douglas stayed, there was no answer. His breath began to come in short, irregular gasps. Another asthma attack. He looked for his secretary, Athina, who caught his signal and fished a puffer out of her purse. He shook it and sprayed it into his throat. She found him a chair to sit in, then stood by, watchful.

At that moment, a form appeared beyond the obscuring wire-glass door. The door burst open and a guest-sentry appeared, saying "He's here, he's here. He'll be right up."

The guests livened up. Ducor's asthma attack stopped. People straightened their clothing and attended the door. Denise looked at the wall clock. Her face changed color. It went dark and her eyes flashed sparks. She stared at the empty wire-glass in the door.

A shadow crossed it, the door opened again, and the groom appeared.

His eyes searched for Denise. At first, he couldn't focus. Then he saw the color of her dress. He jumped out of the way as a glass sphere

5

came at him. It hit the door jamb and rolled elliptically to a stop. It was a rabbit. No time to think why a glass rabbit should come at him.

He said, "Denise, I'm sorry. The truck broke down. I couldn't get back."

Another glass thing came at him. He jumped to one side. "It had to be towed…"

"LATE! You're LATE!" Denise was sweeping the bookcase with her arm, reaching for another missile.

"But listen! I had to get a taxi and the tow yard is way out of town …nearly to Rethimnon, I think."

The mayor placed himself between Denise and her target, and tried to pry the third paperweight from her hand. He was speaking sternly to her…something in Greek.

Denise was yelling, "LATE! LATE! LATE!!!"

Her mother's hands were flapping.

The guests flattened themselves against the far wall.

George Hanson appeared next to Douglas, whose arm was suddenly in a grip so tight his hand began to throb.

"You promised you wouldn't be late today, Douglas," Hanson said, in a dangerous tone. "You've been late for every goddamned event since eighth grade."

His hand closed tighter on Douglas's arm. "Let me explain something to you, son…in case you didn't get it before now. Mrs. Hanson and I have sunk years into grooming you because Denise wanted you. I made you into someone who could marry my daughter and take over the business."

His face got larger and redder. It filled Douglas's field of vision.

"We've done everything for you and you've dragged along like a goddamned cork on the water. Couldn't you do your part—get here on time? Just once?"

A swirl of movement, green and mango, flew past. It was his bride and her mother, moving fast around the room. Denise was howling. Guests scrambled out of their way.

"I went to all your goddamned track meets. I sponsored you for the Junior Executive Training Corps. I was there for you. I was the father your dead father couldn't be. Wasn't I?"

Douglas was frozen to the floor. His eyes were open but he saw nothing.

"Wasn't I?"

Douglas managed to nod. He was aware of the sound of constricted screaming.

"And what about Mrs. Hanson? That poor woman has cared about you! She cooked for you. She taught you to drive. The Hanson family has been good to you, Douglas.

"You pay us back like this! All along you've been forgetful. You're late for everything. The only thing we asked was that you be on time and you still came late.

"Today is the wedding, *your* wedding, AND YOU'RE LATE! It's not like you didn't know when it was. We're all here on Crete so you could do your archaeology thing. We could have been back in St. Louis!

"Now you have hurt Denise. Look at her!"

Douglas saw Denise and the mayor in a struggle for a large crystal paperweight.

"If I ever hear that you have hurt her again, Douglas, I swear I will kill you—and not quickly, either. I'll kill you slowly, with a lot of pain."

Denise let go of the mayor's paperweight. She looked around for something else to throw. The guests scattered.

Douglas's feet began to jog in place. Trouble stretched ahead of him, as far as his eye could see.

From some part of Douglas's spirit, a small voice spoke to him. It said, Run. Run! Turn and run out of this office! Run! NOW!

So he did.

7

2

Father Dimitrios rode down the mountain on his ancient Vespa 150 Sprint Veloce. He wore his cassock and *kalimavki,* no helmet. His *sakkoula* rested on his left hip, the strap diagonal across his chest. His pectoral cross bounced against it as he rode, and his beard was flattened against his face. The sakkoula was from Kyria Ariadne. She said it was not seemly for a priest to wear a backpack. Sakkoules are traditional. She made him a black one, with traditional tassels at the corners. Black tassels.

Although he loved the routine of his daily life in Vraho village, he still looked forward to Thursdays. That was his day to go down-mountain to Chania.

He had three stops on his list today: First, he would go to the post office for the parcel he'd been waiting for. Then he'd see his metropolitan for his weekly report on the parish. And finally, he'd check for e-mails at the internet cafe. If there was time, he might stop by the bookstore down by the harbor and see what fresh books the tide of tourists had beached there this week.

The post office was crowded as always. The line spilled out the door onto the sidewalk. He parked his Vespa in a small space between two cars, on the good chance that neither car would pull out before he was through at the post office. He took his place in line. The sun soaked into his black cassock. He counted the people ahead of him until he would be in the shade of the building.

When he reached the counter, Fr. Dimitrios presented a notice and was given a large cardboard parcel with mashed corners. Tape and cord bound it. He thanked the clerk and moved over to a table by the wall. He slipped the cord off the parcel and used his Vespa key to break the box open. He lifted the contents out of the box and wrapped each item in a piece of newspaper from a stack on the table. He put the bundled things carefully into his sakkoula: a jar of Rhoplex AC33, some microcrystalline wax, a half-dozen needle-less syringes, and a package of swab sticks. He didn't stop to read the instructions. Time for that when he got home to his church.

Back on the Vespa, he wove his way through the crowded traffic on the summer streets to the cathedral. He parked at the side of the building, in the shade, and went in the door of the cathedral offices.

Ioannis, Metropolitan of Chania had been his official mentor for these three years he'd been a village priest on Crete. The role of the church in the traditional villages was changing. How a priest lived his life in full sight of his village could make the church there stronger, or bring it down—especially if the people saw the priest both as one of them and as an intercessor to the world of God's grace. It was difficult to find that exact balance when the older people of the village remembered him when he was a little boy. They told stories about him and his parents and even about his grandfather when he was village priest here, before his father had taken them all to America. He had not seen these people since he was six years old, more than twenty years ago. He didn't remember them, but they told him endless tales from when he was small. He had to work hard to earn their trust as their priest. Metropolitan Ioannis had been very supportive to him.

Kyria Ariadne was his other mentor. She called herself the mother-hen of the Ano Vraho priests. She had cooked for his

9

grandfather, the widowed Old Fr. Dimitrios, and then for the unmarried priest who followed, Fr. Theodoros, and now for Young Fr. Dimitrios. She brought him dinner, the same meal she and her son ate. She kept his house organized, partly because it was her job and partly in memory of his grandfather. She watched out for him in little ways, too, and kept him from making big blunders. He had learned to trust her judgment about people.

The door to the metropolitan's office was open and Metropolitan Ioannis smiled and said, "Come in, my son."

"I'm late, Your Eminence. Please forgive my tardiness."

Metropolitan Ioannis smiled and flicked away the injury with a sweep of his hand. His secretary, a pale, reedy man, made a point of looking at the clock as he left the room.

"And how is Ano Vraho this week?"

"The village has been quiet, Your Grace. The most quarrelsome men are up in summer pasture on the *madares* with the sheep. We haven't heard any reports of problems from there, and the villagers left behind are busy with their kitchen gardens, so all is peaceful."

"And you?"

"I had to stop taking whitewash off the mural because the plaster began to crumble beneath it. Last week on the internet I found a company that sells materials to stabilize plaster," he rummaged into his sakkoula and pulled out the newspaper-wrapped jar of Rhoplex, "and here it is." He handed a parcel to Metropolitan Ioannis, who unwrapped the newspaper and studied the jar curiously.

Fr. Dimitrios explained the process of bonding the plaster back to the wall. Together, they examined the Rhoplex label and the instruction sheet that came with the microcrystalline wax. The metropolitan seemed very pleased. His Eminence said the diocese would pay for those materials.

"I find it admirable that you spend your free hours working on the church walls. Most priests need a break from their parish duties. You seem to live in your church."

"I promised my grandfather I would uncover the murals he had to cover over in the war. It's important to me."

"I see that. Well, I hope you find the answer you are looking for." The metropolitan smiled. "You have done a fine job there for three

10

years now. I think I'm ready to ask you to check in with me only once a month."

Fr. Dimitrios's heart sank. "Oh, no," he said before he could stop himself. " …Your Eminence."

The metropolitan's smile grew wider. "You need the trip to town, don't you?"

Fr. Dimitrios gave a small nod.

His metropolitan continued, "Perhaps it will remain necessary for you to come to Chania to meet with me every week. I am pleased with your industry. May God aid your effort for the wall." He rose and extended his hand for Fr. Dimitrios to kiss, as is the custom.

Fr. Dimitrios bowed and said, "Let it be blessed."

"Go, now, with God, my son. I'll see you next week."

Fr. Dimitrios let himself out of the metropolitan's office.

The internet cafe he liked was not far from the cathedral. He left his Vespa safe by the church and walked toward the network of alleys that led to Kafe INTER-NET.

As he crossed the small square of Platia 1821 near a favorite bakery, a young man in a business suit ran through the traffic. He didn't look Greek, and no one wore a business suit in this part of Chania. As the priest watched, he ran right into an old woman on a bicycle, knocking her over. The melons in her basket rolled out all over the street. Fr. Dimitrios went over to see what help he could offer.

Something about the young man looked American, even in the suit. He seemed very distracted and in a hurry to run on.

The *yia-yias* who always appear when trouble happens were already helping the fallen woman to her feet. Fr. Dimitrios spoke in English to the young man, suggesting he check the bicycle for damage. The runner was hopping from foot to foot, running in place. He stopped long enough to pick up the bicycle and look it over.

Fr. Dimitrios went on his way.

Why do I always feel embarrassed for American tourists when their behavior stands out? he thought. I spent most of my childhood in America, but my cultural origins are here; I think of myself as both American and Cretan, but I don't feel shame around misbehaving Cretans. Only American tourists can make me blush.

11

Kafe INTER-NET was in a traditional shop down a dark and cool alleyway in the oldest part of Chania. When it was closed, folding metal doors, with rows of small designs punched at the top and bottom, sealed it from the street, but by day, only a low wall separated the computer-users from the strolling tourists outside.

As he approached it, he remembered last week, when he had been tracking down the answer to his crumbling wall. An American woman's voice interrupted his thoughts, saying, "Oh look, George. Isn't this too funny!! Look, there's one of their priests in old-fashioned dress and he's using a computer. You wouldn't think he could. I thought you told me they could barely read or write."

The man laughed. "Do you suppose his donkey is parked outside? Go on in, Wife. Ask him where his donkey is."

"Aw, George, those people don't speak English."

Donkey, indeed! thought the young priest. He knew he was an anachronism with his cassock, his kalimavki, and his American education. He reminded himself that he was a bridge between the old Crete and the new.

He had come to like the cassock and kalimavki and what they represented. When he first came to Crete to take up his parish, three years ago, he had worn a black suit and a clerical shirt, a dog-collar. That's what he wore in the States during his time as an apprentice priest after he graduated from Holy Cross Seminary. He smiled at the memory. When he arrived for the first time at the bus stop at Therisso, he had been met by the *proethros,* the village president, a man named Spiros Kiriakis, and the man's wife, Sofia, as had been arranged. They were looking for someone in a cassock and they didn't even look at him. He had to go up to them and introduce himself as their new priest.

Spiros said, "A priest, a real priest, doesn't wear clothes like that. Are you still a student?" and Sofia, too, looked unconvinced. As soon as they took him to his house, his grandfather's house that was his now, he put on the cassock and kalimavki and wore them for all occasions. Only now, after three years in the village, could he occasionally wear black jeans and a black sweatshirt to work on his roof or help dig out the community water system. The villagers joked about their modern priest, but one by one they came to see that his new ideas for the water system and his support for their health care were making life better. They saw he meant well and they began to accept his strange ways.

So now he's gone from looking too modern to Cretans to looking quaint to Americans. He encountered that American couple again in the bookshop near the harbor. It wasn't a large bookshop, but Dimitrios looked forward to his visits there. Its shelves offered him surprises. The used books blew in with the tourists and left the same way. He was frequently delighted by the changes.

Recently, he'd been trying to read his grandfather's copy of *The Odyssey* in Homeric Greek, but it had forms that he didn't know. Nouns in the dative case. Unidentifiable verbs. Tiny footnotes about the optative mood or the perfect aspect leered up at him from the page. He knew in theory what the dative case was, but demotic Greek didn't use it. It gave him both a headache and the fierce determination to continue reading it. But he thought a copy of Lattimore's English translation might give him a hint where Homer was taking him.

He was only a little boy when his grandfather taught him to recite from *The Odyssey*:

...THERE IS A LAND CALLED CRETE IN THE MIDST OF THE WINE-DARK SEA,
A FAIR RICH LAND, SURROUNDED BY WATER,
AND THERE ARE MANY MEN IN IT, PAST COUNTING, AND NINETY CITIES.

Papou told him there were not so many cities or people there nowadays.

He had grown up listening in Cretan Greek as his grandfather filled his head with anecdotes of both saints and heroes. He liked all the saints on the calendar. Some saints he thought about as he prepared for their feast days. Others he thought about more often. They were his companions. As a boy he especially loved Agyios Dimitrios, the warrior saint. His name-saint. St. Dimitrios rode a red horse alongside St. George, the dragon-slayer, on his white horse.

The community of saints lived with him daily now. He devoted most of the week to serving them, the church, and his parish. That devotion didn't end his curiosity about the other side of his Greek heritage—the Homeric heroes, especially Odysseus trying to get back to his home. Papou talked a lot about mankind's need to go home.

13

Young Dimitrios thought his grandfather identified with Odysseus's longing.

He took old Lattimore down off its shelf.

A sharp voice interrupted his thoughts. "Miss? Would you tell that priest that book isn't in Greek?"

Fr. Dimitrios glanced at the counter. The young sales clerk looked puzzled. The American woman who'd made the comment about him and the donkey came over to him. She spoke slowly and loudly, as if he were deaf. "Greek...books...there." She pointed to the rear of the shop.

It took a minute for the sense of what she was saying to sink in. It is true he was an Orthodox priest, bearded and wearing a black cassock. This woman meant to be helpful, he told himself. He smiled at her.

"Thank you. I do know it's in English. I already have it in Greek."

"Oh, you read Greek and English too, then. You sound almost American."

"I'm Cretan, born here, but I lived in California for part of my childhood."

"Oh, how lucky for you." She looked as if she were trying to catch a wayward thought. Then her face brightened. "Say, could you do a little service in English? I mean, you speak English. You could use it in a service? Instead of Greek?"

He answered, carefully, "What service do you have in mind?"

"A wedding! My daughter and her fiancé are getting married here next Thursday morning, in a little impromptu ceremony, just family and his work colleagues there, you know, and it would be really charming to have you perform the service. So colorful. It would add a real flavor...."

"Is your daughter Orthodox? Is her fiancé?"

"Oh. Oh, I see what you mean. You have standards you have to meet, is that it? Too bad. Well, then, what would you suggest? We just got here yesterday."

Fr. Dimitrios gently answered, "You could check with the tourist information stand. They're up the street. Maybe they can suggest something. I'm sorry. I can't help you."

He took Lattimore's translation to the counter and paid for it.

Her voice interrupted the transaction. "You're buying *The Odyssey*? Isn't that surprising for a priest to be reading? Godless literature and all that, I mean?"

He felt his face redden. "It *is* literature. Excuse me, please," and he took the plain brown bag containing his *Odyssey,* and went solidly out of that bookshop. Or tried to. In the doorway, he collided with a large man wearing a blue and white striped shirt and white linen trousers.

"Excuse me," said Fr. Dimitrios, and waited until he could squeeze past. Over his shoulder came the voice of the woman, "George, this nice priest speaks English!"

George asked the same question, "He does? Say, Father, how would you like to perform a wedding next week? The name's Hanson. How d'you do." He extended his right hand and Fr. Dimitrios shook it. "We'd pay you, of course."

"Your wife already asked. I'm sorry. It's not possible." Fr. Dimitrios slipped quickly out the door and into the flow of tourists. He went across the square and up the stone-paved Halidon Street to the coffee bar he liked.

He ordered a *kafe Elleniko metrio*—that is, Greek coffee with a medium amount of sugar—and sat down at a tiny table in one corner of the open cafe. A dusty branch of oleander stroked his head. He moved his chair away from the branch and arranged himself for a period of reading and sipping his kafe Elleniko.

He took his *Odyssey* out of its brown bag and opened it. The fragrance of the coffee and the welcome friendship of Lattimore's comments about Homeric Greece restored him. He looked up at the strong sunlight coming off the wall across Halidon Street. It reminded him how different the light was in California and made him glad he was here. Pigeons cleaned up the paving nearby, cooing as they moved about, randomly looking for crumbs. The chatter of the passing tourists and the cry of a seagull on the roof opposite lulled him. The sky was very blue. A joy filled him.

15

"Well, look who's here! Taking yourself out to coffee, Father?"

George Hanson's smile covered a determination that must have made him a success in business.

"I thought you might change your mind about doing the wedding if you met the bride. Father, this is our Denise."

Fr. Dimitrios rose. He wasn't sure whether to greet the young woman politely or to bolt. "How do you do?"

The blond bride-to-be looked even more forceful than her parents.

"Oh, Sir, my mother told me such nice things about you." She gave him a big smile. "Are you sure you won't marry us? It would be so…appropriate…to have the wedding conducted by a local priest, especially one who speaks English like a native. I mean, a native American. I mean…"

She looked flustered. She giggled. With her eyes still on Fr. Dimitrios, she continued, "Daddy, if we could have the wedding on that beach where they filmed *Zorba the Greek*, and have this nice man there in his outfit, it would make the most wonderful photos." Now she said, "Oh, please say you'll do it, or at least come for photographs with us. Please."

"If you and your bridegroom have the time and desire to take instruction and convert to the Greek Orthodox faith, I will perform the wedding for you. But it would be impossible by next week and if you are not members of the church, the metropolitan himself would forbid me to perform your wedding." He paused, not wishing to seem unkind. "And no, I couldn't agree to a photo session. Why don't you ask the mayor of Chania to perform the ceremony?"

He sat down and reached for his kafe Elleniko.

Mrs. Hanson had joined them. Now she said, "There's an idea, George. Maybe we'll get the mayor to do the wedding inside those nice ruins behind the Institute."

"Inside the chain link fence? The ones that're supposed to be some Minoan city? We couldn't get in there."

Denise said, "Wait, Daddy, that's a pretty idea. I can ask Douglas whose dig that is. I'll bet Professor Ducor could get permission for us."

The wife laid her hand on Hanson's blue striped sleeve. "George, nothing's impossible. You just have to offer to pay for it as if you meant it."

An idea seemed to strike her and she turned the force of her smile onto the priest.

He caught her eye and shook his head. No, lots of money won't make me perform your non-Greek-Orthodox daughter's wedding. Not on the beach. Not in the ruins.

He took his *Odyssey* and stood. He wished them all a good day and he left.

"You forgot to drink your coffee," Mrs. Hanson cried after him. He waved back in what he hoped would pass for a courteous gesture and slipped in among the tourists on Halidon Street.

Now, another American interrupted his Cretan Thursday, slamming into that old woman's bicycle. It made him wonder about last week's American tourists. He couldn't resist walking to the end of the alley to look over at the fenced Kydonia excavation to see if those Hansons had managed to arrange permission to hold their wedding there. But the ruins were empty, snugly contained by their chain link fence. He went back to the Kafe INTER-NET and logged on to his e-mail server.

3

Douglas crossed the second floor lobby in three long strides, headed down the zebra-striped marble stairs, first with quick small steps (like Cinderella leaving the ball, he thought), then two at a time (dangerous, he thought), then he leapt across the last four steps, dodged right, opened the glass door and was out on the sidewalk. (Free, he thought.)

The sidewalk was moderately cluttered with pedestrians. He dodged between Cretans in business dress, skirted around a few Europeans in tourist clothes, and crossed the street on a diagonal, avoiding cars and motorbikes as he did. On the corner across the street was a bakery that must have been good. People were lined up outside, and those coming out had paper bags and satisfied smiles. He made a note to try it some time.

Busy mind. Busy feet. He circled the line of hopeful clients and crossed the sidestreet against the signal. Nearly to the little park. His eyes were on the park. He didn't see the bicycle coming from his right.

He pitched over its front wheel and landed on his hands and a tangle of feet and spokes. An extremely ancient woman lay on the street in a heap, but her box of melons spread out across the paving in all directions. Everyone stopped to see what happened. People went after her melons for her. Four melons split open onto the paving.

Douglas disentangled his shoes from the bicycle wheel and stood up. He offered his hand to the fallen woman, but three Cretan women were already clustered around her. They helped her to her feet.

The bicycle seemed all right. Nothing obviously broken. Not that he could see. He said, "I'm sorry, Ma'am. I didn't see you." He backed up a few steps and began jogging in place.

At that moment, a voice said, "The word is *sygnomi*. I don't think she understands English. You want to say sygnomi to her. That means 'I'm sorry.'"

Douglas turned around. An Orthodox priest was speaking to him in American English.

"What? Say what?" Douglas turned back to the woman who was brushing herself off, with the assistance of two of the other women. He touched her arm and she glared at him.

"Sygnomi," he said.

She continued to look at him.

He said it again, "Sygnomi." Then he turned back to the priest. "What else do you want me to do?"

"Check the bicycle over for her. Make sure it isn't broken. Then write your name and the name of your hotel on a note, so she can send you the bill for any repairs and for the melons she's lost."

Hotel? I'm a fugitive. I have nothing to write but my name, and maybe I won't do that, either. Douglas looked over his shoulder, afraid he'd see Denise and her parents running toward him, but no one was there except the crowd watching his accident, so he stopped jogging in place and picked up the bicycle. He checked the spokes on both wheels, set it down and tested the frame with his weight, then straightened the handlebars, which were twisted to the right. Now they were straight. He handed the bike back to the woman.

The priest had disappeared into the crowd, and Douglas nodded a final apology to his victim and ran on away from his wedding, without leaving his name.

19

He ran past a row of small tables outside a *kafenion*. Old men leaning against the shopwindow watched him run by. He dodged through a door in a wall, came out near the market hall, kept running, up hill, toward what? He didn't much care. Away from the City Hall and the mayor's office. Time to think about what he had done later. Now was the time to run.

As he passed the market hall and crossed Yianari Street, he ran into the side of a bus. (Damn! he thought. I have to start looking where I'm going.) The bus driver, thinking that the young man in a business suit was running to catch the bus, stopped and opened the door. He looked questioningly at Douglas, who hesitated, then climbed aboard. Busses are faster than feet and he would be less visible inside the bus, in case anyone was pursuing him. He reached for his wallet to pay the busfare and felt only an empty pocket. The wallet. He saw a flash of the wallet in his case at Big Kostas's. Didn't want a bulge in the wedding suit. His credit card and all his drachmas. Damn! His passport was at the Institute. Double damn!

He climbed back down the stairs toward the door. By then, the bus was moving in traffic. The driver gestured to him to hang on til the next stop. Douglas dismounted the bus when he could.

He found himself in a part of town he'd never seen before. To be truthful, most of the town he'd never seen before. He wasn't curious by nature and he had never traveled anywhere. He knew the route he drove in the truck. It went between the parking area by the seawall out to the highway and west to the site of the dig at Rhodopou, with a friendly gas station along the way. Within Chania's old town, he knew his way through the tourist alleys to all the restaurants and he knew one secure path to the Institute offices. The rest of the city and the surrounding areas were like a moonscape to him.

The late morning August sun burned images into his retinas. The hot-lit objects cast strong shadows. The air wavered with the heat. Douglas's head was beginning to pound. He took a deep breath and looked around. In the distance, he saw the mountains. He ran toward them.

From almost any place in western Crete, you can see Lefka Ori—The White Mountains. They form the rugged spine of that end of the island. The metamorphic limestone, scoured and polished by brutal winds, reflects sunlight with a cool brilliance: the mountain surfaces look snow-covered, even in summer. Above the tree line, those mountains are so harsh nothing lives at the peaks. Broken by ravines, riddled with caves, beat down by landslides, Lefka Ori have always provided a haven for resistance fighters, outlaws, and those who need to hide. Douglas headed straight for them.

He was not dressed for running; he was dressed for an informal wedding. He loosened his necktie as he ran. He saw a gas station several blocks ahead. His feet hurt in their leather shoes. He slowed to a brisk walk. Dust covered his gray summerweight worsted wool suit, the new shoes, and his face and hair. The elusive gas station seemed as far away as ever. He began to run again.

The sun was particularly cruel along this road. It turned the black macadam paving silver and bleached the rest of the world to colorless ghosts with shadows. Douglas looked across flat fields of dry grass toward the Lefka Ori and the blue cloudless sky beyond.

At last he reached his goal: a men's toilet in a gas station. He took off his jacket, looked at it for a long moment, then rolled it in a ball and dropped it in the trash bin.

The jacket looked back at him reproachfully from its plastic-lined wire coffin. There it lay, the most expensive item of clothing he had ever owned, custom made just for him, now wounded, dying at his own hand. With it, all the known plans for his life went into the trash, too.

The turquoise and grey wedding necktie followed. He unsnapped the broad white suspenders that tugged his trousers up high, and dumped them into the trash, too. The pants gratefully sank to rest on his hipbones. He unbuttoned the neck of his shirt.

He looked in the mirror, not at himself but at the surprising appearance of the face of the person who had just taken over his life. There was a resemblance to his former face, but something was changed. A young, astonished person looked back at him. This face looked scared and excited. If he is, Douglas thought, I am, too.

Then the familiar voice of his conscience said, What do you think you're going to do from here? He wondered if Denise and

21

the Hansons could sue him for breach of promise. Not in Crete, he supposed. He was probably safe as long as he stayed here. Would they search for him? He'd better avoid the center of Chania for awhile.

He soaked a paper towel in water and used it to cool his face and the back of his neck. He looked around for paper cups but there were none, so he cupped his hands and filled them from the tap. He slurped several handfuls of cool water. One more splash of water on his face and he left the dark coolness of the washroom and went back out into the blazing daylight.

A sign identified the next town as Mournies. An open Fiat and a BMW parked along the curb suggested that this was probably a commuter suburb of prosperous Cretans with businesses in Chania. Douglas had heard of Mournies. It looked as if once it had been a pretty little village. Now it seemed very inviting. Even though the houses were post-war, built of concrete without much charm, the streets were lined with thick-leafed plane trees that softened the edges of everything. Their puddles of deep shade offered a cool walkway along the commercial blocks. Shopwindows displayed kitchen appliances and embroidered clothing, not for tourists but for the residents.

Douglas would have loved to stop for a cold drink but without money he could not, so he kept walking past the tavernas and kafenions of the town.

He thought how limited his experience of Crete had been. Other students working for the Institute had parents to pay for their summer course. The Hansons had given Douglas a special deal—a graduation present, they said. Because the institute was named after Mr. Hanson, he had arranged for Douglas to get the tuition waived for the ten-week program. They'd also paid for his airfare over from St. Louis. He had used up half his savings on food, books, and rent in the first two weeks. Then he lucked into a way to slow down the expenses. He could save the rent money.

Big Kostas owned the taverna at the top of the old town hill. Lots of tourists spent their time there, asking for stories of Crete. Douglas enjoyed listening to the talk. Soon he knew enough to answer questions for the newly-arrived tourists. Big Kostas was afraid his English was not very good, so he asked Douglas if he wanted a job, a barter job, no money attached. Talk to the customers in English. Keep them coming back. Stay in the room upstairs. Douglas took it. He served beers and tsikoudia and conversation to the English-speaking tourists every evening. He told them things about Crete, and he even skimmed the tourist books Kostas gave him, to make sure he had the stories more or less right.

He wouldn't go back there, for awhile anyway, for fear of meeting Denise. He couldn't even call Kostas to tell him not to expect him. He had neither card nor coins for the telephone. He wondered what Kostas would do with his clothes. How many days would he wait before he chucked the things in the trash? Would he give them away? Or shove his bags in that spare storeroom on the top floor? Would he find the wallet? The Institute would probably keep his passport for him. Someday he'd be able to reclaim it.

Someday? He began to see the ways his life was different. No more Hansons. No job, no career, no easy life. It felt principled, somehow, noble, even, to leave all that prosperity behind. But no Chania, either. No Ducor, no institute, no Big Kostas's taverna, no idea where he was going next. His stride slowed, but then resumed its purposeful pace. The rhythm set up a phrase in his head: "The train jumped the track, the train jumped the track." He let it repeat for awhile, then added, "and it's not going back." He smiled to himself.

He imagined a life with unexpected turns, where everything wasn't pre-planned for him by the Hansons. He imagined the possibility of joy in his life. It seemed remote, but he had felt glimmerings of it this summer, when he had lost hours, concentrating on dirt at the Rhodopou dig. Real joy. Losing himself in the work. He wanted more.

He didn't see a clear path from his present circumstances—on the run from Denise—to a life in the world of archaeology, but there was more chance now than strapped into that marriage and that fast-track career in the Hanson clothing business. Any glimpse of daylight was better than total darkness.

Why had he never noticed before that marrying Denise would be the end of his life? He felt annoyed at himself. That in itself was unusual. Feelings were rare and fleeting in Douglas's experience. This

23

annoyance came from a new sense of himself. He was worth saving. He was capable of joy, at least moments of it.

He ran on.

In school, Douglas had been a skinny kid who hung back and was hard to see. He wasn't big enough to hold his own in contact sports and he couldn't catch a ball. In seventh grade, a kindly coach had noticed the quiet boy and convinced him to try running. It was a sport without danger, one he could practice alone. He ran from that day on. He competed in highschool track meets.

Over the next two years, he grew tall and fit. People—girls, that is—found him handsome. They liked him because of his good looks. What he did or what he thought didn't seem to have much to do with their liking him.

He guessed he was just lucky to be nice looking. He sometimes thought they were dumb not to care that he wasn't very interested in what they were talking about. They seemed satisfied with just having him around for his good looks.

When he ran races, always long races, he would pick out an empty seat at the top of the stands and imagine his dead father was sitting there, proud of him. He would nod to the empty seat. Once he caught himself as he raised his hand to wave to his father's imaginary form.

His father would have been a big-shot dentist in town by now if he hadn't died. Douglas would be living in a nice house, with nice things, like the Hansons, well, maybe not that rich, but good middle-class things. He remembered his father's new dental office, opened just before he died. Douglas was eleven. The waiting room smelled like new carpet. It was full of vases of tall pink gladiolas with ribbons of congratulation and cards on bamboo sticks. He could see shapes when people moved behind the opaque wireglass in the doors, and their lives seemed full of promise.

His father's death was not a suicide. His mother said he had always had a weak heart. It's just that people talked.

Douglas tried not to hear them. He knew it was not true that his dad killed himself. Neighbors wondered about big debts from dental school, the cost of the new office. Where had the money come from? Did some loan shark threaten him? Had he been addicted to laughing gas? Dentists often commit suicide, y'know. All this floated around him, in fragments of comments whispered nearby. Douglas shut it out. He shut the world out.

His mother went to work. Douglas grew quieter. He stayed on the edge of things. Then in middle school, that coach showed him about running track.

In eighth grade, a fair-haired girl had chosen him. When Denise took him home to meet her parents, the Hansons said it was too bad he was a fatherless boy. They swept him into their family. From then on, his social life went where she did. She and her parents introduced him to the people at their country club, the Pebble Beach Golf and Tennis Club of St. Louis. He went with Denise to dances there and he was introduced to her father's friends, important men in the business community.

He felt like a rag between two dogs. His mother was jealous of what the Hansons could give him. They wanted him with them all the time. They offered him the perks of wealth. They paid for tennis lessons for him. They took him on vacations to their cabin at the lake, and out to dinner to nice restaurants, and even to hockey games sometimes.

Once they took him to hear a concert with the symphony and a cellist named Yo-Yo Ma. He thought it was great. Denise liked the clothes on the women in the audience.

When Mr. Hanson's friend Roger asked them to come see his daughter Caroline perform in a local production of *The Fantasticks*, the Hansons took him along. Caroline's voice wasn't very good, but seeing live actors on the stage right in front of him was great. Denise hated the show. Denise never did have much use for Caroline.

George Hanson started to come to some of his track meets. It made him uneasy to have him there. It felt disloyal. He still set his father's spirit somewhere in the bleachers.

His mother complained that he wasn't ever home to spend time with her. He tried to keep things nice with her, but time with the Hansons was more fun and pointed to a secure future, too. Like the wedding suit. Made by George's tailor. Gone now.

25

In May of his junior year at Laronwood U, his mother died. At George's invitation, Douglas moved into the servants' quarters over the Hansons' garage. The Hansons took him even further into their life. That had been okay with him until just now, at the wedding. Weird. Where had that voice come from?

The road began to rise toward the mountain range. Hot remnants of spring gardens bravely held up limp blossoms against the sun. The plane trees stopped, the road narrowed, the sidewalk disappeared. Urban dogs barked at him from behind iron fences.

Some instinct made him turn to the right, parallel to the mountains, and go down a shallow hill toward the plain of orange groves. Maybe he could find day work there. Picking fruit. He noticed that the oranges on the trees were green, and that no one was working among the trees. Wrong time of year. What *do* people do in August around here? He cursed himself for not knowing more about Crete—at least to know what would be harvested now. The ancient Greeks knew. Hesiod wrote it all up in *Works and Days*. How did they know that? How did they know when to plant things? He hadn't paid much attention to practical matters, just market economy theories in his dull business courses. He had escaped the tedium by studying what Denise termed "useless" archaeology. He'd taken archaeology first because it fulfilled a humanities requirement, and later because it intrigued him. Besides, he liked the teacher, Professor Ducor, and Ducor seemed to like him. The man even said he'd be a good technical illustrator for archaeology. But that wasn't a career. Denise's father's travel clothes business: that was a career. And a pretty sure one.

Denise had said many times that he was wasting his time, and hers, too, taking archaeology classes. She kept enrolling in them with him, though. Denise took all the same classes he did, even the business classes. He wondered why she stayed so close to him, but he guessed she really liked his company. In the business classes sometimes she would get fired up about some technique or principle and she'd become ferocious (the teacher would be impressed, and Douglas would be surprised), but then she'd sink back into disinterest and do only the minimum to pass.

She never got fired up about archaeology. Douglas spent hours researching a term paper. He would draw a careful, detailed

26

illustration of the ceramic object or piece of metalwork he had written about. Denise would look over his shoulder at the drawing and say, "Boy, it doesn't take much to amuse you."

The small plain of orange groves looked like a loosely-woven carpet. There were several areas of taller, brighter avocado trees, as if the carpet weaver had run out of a dye-lot and had to change wool. Still, it looked like very big agribusiness, despite the film of red dust over everything.

Ahead of him lay the west end of the island. Projecting north, the fingers of two peninsulae reached back toward Europe across the sea. The farther, smaller landform was Gramvousa. It stretched out past Falasarna, where there was a harbor built in the third century BCE. Seven centuries later, it was landlocked by a geological uplift of the west end of Crete. So recent!

The nearer land was Rhodopou, the site of the Institute's excavation. He knew its smells and its feeling underfoot. It was the closest to home for him of any part of Crete. He had worked there. He had poured his effort into uncovering its secrets. In some way, it was his.

The site was not far from a Neolithic coastal settlement, a large cave called Ellenospilo at Potisteria, north of Moni Gonia. The cave settlement was thought to be pre- or proto-Minoan, apparently abandoned for the more plentiful water and easier habitation in the Eastern half of the island. The cave site was excavated in the 1930s by Marinatos, filled in, and not touched again until 1994 when Ducor, sampling the area, found a couple of pieces of surprisingly sophisticated pottery, belonging to Middle Minoan II style. First he thought the peninsula had been used as another port, but then he decided that it must have been the site of a palace. Somehow, Ducor had convinced George Hanson to take on the project.

The George Hanson Institute was well-funded. It was associated with Laronwood University, where Ducor taught and Douglas and Denise had been students. The institute had fancy offices in Chania, and this was its first season of digging. There were four other students from Laronwood still working on the dig (though two of them didn't really do much work. A fifth student broke his foot and went home

27

early), Efthikas the foreman, four experienced Cretan workers, a nice secretary named Athina, and the professor. So far they'd uncovered just the foundations of two storerooms and a typical house off to the side, and a lot of sherds of coarseware, the unglazed stuff. Ducor had assigned the house to Douglas. He'd drawn the plan and a projection of what the house probably looked like. Ducor said it was like other Minoan houses on other sites. Douglas also drew the most interesting sherds, and was in charge of cataloging all of them on a computer.

The back of his shirt stuck to his skin and damp stripes ran down his sides from his armpits. Douglas didn't take pleasure in discomfort. He wished he had a hat, dark glasses, even a tree to sit under. The tree, at least, seemed possible. He turned off the road into an orange grove. As he stumbled over the uneven soil, he looked for a level, shady spot to settle. He went through the rows of trees toward an irrigation ditch. The water in the ditch might help cool the air, he thought. When he got to it, the ditch was dry. The shade under any tree would be the same. He chose one, and sat down.

Ants.

He got up and brushed himself off and looked about again. Across the irrigation ditch was a slope toward a cluster of tall eucalyptus trees responding to some faint breeze. Their leaves hung down, their smooth bark peeled and changed colors from patches of pale yellow-green to dark grey. He went over to them, wondering if there would be ants around them, too. He sank down onto a noisy bed of dry eucalyptus leaves that gave off a fragrance like some shampoo he remembered from his childhood. It was pleasant. He closed his eyes.

For a moment, he felt the shakiness he'd lived with most of his childhood. After his father died, and, come to think of it, even before then, when his father was home, silent or grumpy, Douglas felt like an observer, someone who hadn't paid the full ticket price to participate in life. Now was different. From the moment he ran, he was participating, all right. He just wished he had some idea how to do that.

He felt an ant crawling across his hand. He slid a careful finger under it and set it down on a leaf.

But I was always a nice guy, he thought. I never meant to hurt anyone (look how thoughtful I just was with that ant) and now I've really hurt the Hansons. I've hurt Denise.

Shame was what he should feel. What he felt was something like pride. When it counted, today, he did what he had to do to survive.

Peaceful silence. Then he could identify the hum of cicadas, the far-off thud of some factory noises, traffic probably from the highway that goes west to Kastelli Kissamou. He'd never been to Kastelli. Maybe now. See the Roman mosaics there. Anything could happen now. He listened harder. Leaves rustled. There must be a breeze starting up.

He became aware of a complaining goat. Goats don't usually complain. Not like that. They pretty much do what they want. He had gotten to know the goats grazing around the Rhodopou site. He'd watched them climb up shrubs and small trees, searching for anything tender in the harsh land. When the herders moved them they grumbled a bit, but they never really complained.

Douglas listened more attentively. A child's voice argued with the goat.

He stood up. Sure enough, a boy of about nine years was trying to drag a loudly bleating goat down the road. Boy and goat faced each other, a rope stretched tightly between them. The boy was pulling as hard as he could but the goat had dug its feet into the hard-packed dirt of the roadbed and was not going anywhere. It wasn't a large goat, but a very determined one. The boy had tear tracks down his dusty face. He looked exhausted.

Douglas went over to the road, came up behind the goat and clapped his hands. The goat bolted forward, just missing the boy. It trotted down the road, dragging the boy at the end of the rope. The boy caught up with it and went along briskly beside it. When the boy turned back to Douglas to thank him, the goat stopped again. It pointed its curved horns at the boy's stomach. The boy pushed the goat's head away from him and walked around toward the goat's tail, to drive him forward. The goat swung around and faced him again.

Douglas picked up a fallen eucalyptus branch and signaled the boy to face down the road. The branch was large and full of dry leaves. Douglas shook it at the goat. The goat moved away from it.

29

The procession then continued down the road: boy, goat, shaking branch, and Douglas. He didn't know where they were going, but it didn't matter.

As he went along, shaking the dead leaves at the goat, he thought how simple life must be for this little boy. Goats were exasperating, but they were easy compared to what he'd just experienced. He wished his life could be as simple, at least for a little while—nothing to worry about but moving a goat down the road. No debts, no future plans, just the sunlit summer day and a resistant goat. The simple life!

He wished he knew Greek so he could speak to this boy. Or even that he had his Greek phrase book with him. The procession moved on in silence except for footfalls, hoof sounds, and the rustling leaves. They walked for twenty minutes and approached a settlement. This was not a tourist site, and had no grace. It had no visible taverna, even. Douglas guessed it was just a packing and shipping center for the citrus and avocado farmers of the area. At the center of the town stood several warehouses protected by chain link fencing. Orchards came up to two sides of the fencing. The boy led the goat past three yards filled with produce trucks. No one seemed to be around.

The boy turned off the main street and went down a block to a small meat market. Now, Douglas felt a rush of sympathy for the goat, whose future was no longer in doubt. Boy and goat disappeared through a door in the back of the building and Douglas waited. After a few minutes, the boy reappeared. He folded some multicolored drachma notes into a handkerchief and put them in his back pocket.

As the two left the butcher's, the boy gave a big smile to Douglas. He said something in Greek. Douglas caught the words he thought meant thank you, sas efcharisto. He smiled and nodded. They walked in silence for a bit, heading back toward the eucalyptus trees where they had met. The boy began to chatter in rapid Greek. Douglas waved his hand to stop him, and said, "I'm sorry, I don't speak Greek." He shook his head. "I'm sorry."

The boy said, "No speak Greek?" Then he pointed proudly to himself and said "Speak English!" He smiled, waiting for Douglas to congratulate him.

Douglas obligingly said, "Good for you." Then he asked, "What is your name?"

The boy looked at him, uncomprehending.

"Name? Your name?" Douglas took a new tack. Pointing to his chest, he said, "My name is Douglas Watkins."

The boy still looked puzzled.

"Name. Name. What is your name?" Douglas pointed to a tree. "Name: tree." He pointed to a leaf. "Name: leaf." He pointed to himself. "Name: Douglas."

The boy suddenly understood. He pointed at Douglas. "Daonglos!" He pronounced the name with a Greek sound. "*Me lene Aleko. Eimai tou Panou o yios.*"

Douglas caught the sound of "Aleko." He said, "Your name is Aleko, right?"

The boy nodded happily, "Name, Aleko." He grinned at the achievement. Douglas grinned back.

Just at this moment, a crash in the underbrush behind them announced the arrival of ... who? A man, wearing a black ski-mask came running toward them. He carried a sawed-off shotgun. Aleko dodged to the left and then darted to the right. The man ran after him into the orange grove. He knocked Aleko to the ground and tore open the boy's back pocket, taking the handkerchief of bills.

Douglas didn't stop to think. He ran after the armed man, yelling "No you don't! That's a little kid." He caught up with him and grabbed his left arm. The man spun around. The shotgun barrel slammed into Douglas's arm.

The blow surprised Douglas. He fell to his knees, got up and lurched forward, grabbing the man by the back of the shirt. The robber pulled free. Douglas gave chase, but stumbled when his left wedding shoe came off. He watched the retreating figure. When the robber was about ten meters ahead, he turned and aimed his shotgun at Douglas.

As the gun barrel came up, Douglas faced away and covered his head with his hands. There came the sound. Douglas felt stinging pellets penetrate his right shoulder and upper back. He screamed, in protest more than pain. He dropped to his knees, then to the ground. The robber made off somewhere.

Time slowed. Douglas lay on the ground, listening to the retreating footsteps over the dry earth of the orange grove. Then a

31

huge silence. A bird sang tentatively from some distance. He tried to move, thought better of it, and sank into a curled-up position. He waited.

At last, Douglas heard the sound of small feet approaching. He turned his head to see Aleko peering down at his back. Aleko extended a finger and touched him. The boy's finger came away red with blood. Douglas passed out at the sight.

4

Fr. Dimitrios felt a let-down as he waited for the computer to fire up. He thought, I have nothing to search for this week. I have all the tools I need to remove the whitewash and reveal the paintings. He wondered what else he might need to research. Then he laughed at himself, and went straight to the e-mail program.

He knew there would be an e-mail message from his parents. Sometimes there were notices from his seminary or from Holy Trinity Greek Orthodox Church near his parents' home in San Francisco. Sometimes there was a message from his old girlfriend, Ellen. She stayed in touch. They were engaged but she was never comfortable with the idea of living in his village and she said no just before he took ordination. A married man who becomes an Orthodox priest remains married. A single man who takes ordination may not marry afterwards.

Ellen said she loved him, but she just couldn't be a priest's wife. It was too late to postpone his ordination, and he couldn't go meet some other suitable wife-candidate on such short notice, so there he was. Her choice cost him his sexuality: it committed him to a life of celibacy once he was ordained. He had known full well the price he was paying, but he went ahead with his commitment to a life in the church.

But Ellen remained in his life. She still sent him e-mails every few weeks. She was working for a law firm in Berkeley. She saw his parents often and reported to him how they were. She sent him news of mutual friends. Sometimes he was really glad to hear from her, but sometimes he wished she would leave him alone.

Only one message again this week.

His mother had a cold. His father had gone fishing out of Half Moon Bay with his friend Stelios on Saturday and the two had caught two nice halibut. They barbecued them in Stelios and Sophronia's back yard. They had all talked about how much he would have liked the dinner.

They missed him, they hoped he was well, they sent him much love.

P.S. They had seen Eleni at church. She said she sent him her love and she would write to him soon.

He smiled, until the sentence about Eleni. Then, he sighed. He wrote,

> Dear Mom,
>   I'll bet the halibut was terrific. Did Dad tell the story again about when I thought I'd hooked a shark and it turned out to be a tire? He ALWAYS tells that story. Please say hi to Stelios and Sophronia from me. But I do wish you wouldn't tell me every time you...

He stopped typing and thought for a minute, then pressed the delete button and removed the last sentence. No point in telling his mother that the girl she hoped would be her daughter-in-law should please take her claws out of him. No, he would someday say that directly to Ellen, but he also realized that he was still partly glad to hear from her. He was glad somebody still cared for him in that way.

He paid up his 100 drachmas and went out to his Vespa. No kafe Elleniko today. He wanted to get home to his crumbling wall painting.

34

When he got back to Vraho he changed into his black sweatshirt and work pants and carried his new supplies over to the church. He would do triage to his repair efforts of the past week. Poor Saint Whatever-your-name-will-be, Saint Unknown, your gown is turning to dust and falling at my feet. But I have brought help, dear Saint. All will be well. You'll see.

Fr. Dimitrios stared at the uncovered patch. Within it he could make out part of a pale red robe with a gold border. The figure drifted off to the right, as if it were reclining or falling. Behind the red robe the background was dark, not like the gold leaf behind the saints on portable icons. He looked across at the church's glowing *ikonostasis*, its panel icons festooned with ribbons.

The wall he had started on had a half-dozen pockmarks, and the wall opposite had a cluster of three. Dimitrios avoided them, for now. The painting underneath could not have survived such damage. For now, the whitewash would hold the plaster together in those places until he could reinforce them.

Three new cracks showed in the plaster where he had removed the whitewash. They cut diagonally across the forty cm by forty cm area, parallel to each other. He could see no reason for those cracks to open up because of this work, but there they were.

The cracks were in addition to the half-dozen fingernail-size flakes that lay in a dish. Now, thanks be to God, help was here. In a bottle.

He stood, silently speaking to his grandfather. I am here, Papou, to continue this work, to bring these paintings back into the daylight. He debated whether to use the general confession, but he decided instead to recite the prayer for those being loosed from penance.

Silently, he recited, *I pray for the repose of the soul of the departed servant of God, Dimitrios, Priest and concelebrant, and for the forgiveness of all his errors, both voluntary and involuntary.* He crossed himself.

He studied the instructions, then took out a deep bowl made of blue plastic and measured nine parts of water and one part of the adhesive. He watched it, stirred it, let it rest, thanked it. He drew up solution into the first of his three syringes. In his left hand he had one of the dozen clean soft rags he had gathered. This he held below where his right hand aimed the syringe into the bottom of the first crevice and pressed.

It didn't drip. It didn't clog. It behaved perfectly. Slowly he drew the syringe up the crack, continuing to press on the plunger. When he reached the top, he had filled the inner half of the crack. He paused for a moment to watch it. It didn't run out. It was fine.

He began again at the bottom and placed enough AC33 to nearly fill the crevice. At the top he stopped. He would do a final pass along the crack in two days' time. Then it should be stable. He followed the same procedure with the other two cracks.

The chips were more worrisome. They might disintegrate when he picked them up. He took up a swabstick. On its end he placed a tiny ball of microcrystalline wax. His hand trembled as he approached the first chip. He touched the wax to its painted side.

The chip stuck to the swabstick. He used the syringe to place a drop of Rhoplex on the back. He held it in place where it had once rested. After thirty seconds, he removed the swabstick and wax. The chip held. He realized he had been holding his breath. Now he breathed again. He felt hope this wall could be restored. He'd know for sure when it dried.

You see, Papou? It's going to be all right.

He thought about the last conversation he had with his grandfather. It was November 6th, 1990. He was studying in the Cotsidas-Tonna Library at Holy Cross Seminary in Brookline, Massachusetts, late on a Tuesday night. He was writing a paper that was due on Friday and it was not going well. He'd just come from a long phone conversation with Ellen and something she'd said bothered him, but he couldn't exactly remember what it was. His concentration was divided.

Weekdays the library stayed open until midnight. It was 11:15 now, so he had only another three-quarters of an hour to work and his mind was frozen. He stared across the reading room, past the other students and the half-dozen large lacquered oak tables and the hanging lamps to the book-lined walls. He loved this room. It was a peaceful place to think, but tonight his thoughts were not coming.

A movement in the room caught his eye. Father Zarkos, who taught his church history class, was coming toward him. He smiled.

36

Fr. Zarkos smiled back and when he reached him said, "Dimitrios, your grandfather phoned the office. I said I'd find you. He wants to speak to you right away. It sounded urgent."

Dimitrios stood up and gathered his materials. "It's late. Did he sound all right?"

"I think so. Do you want to call from my office?"

"I don't want to put you out."

"It's no problem. You'll have privacy there."

The two men set out for Cavadas Annex, the faculty office building.

The Massachusetts night was clear and cold. The campus path lights blotted out the stars, but the dome of heaven still felt close. Dimitrios wondered what had made Papou phone him. Papou was not fond of the telephone. Only his love of his grandson made him even say a quick hello on it most times. Dimitrios smiled at the thought of Papou, standing in the hall of their apartment, glaring at the telephone ringing in its wall niche. Or shaking his head in amazement when he saw Dimitrios walking around the apartment talking on the cordless phone. A telephone call from Papou was very unusual.

As they walked across the campus, Fr. Zarkos said, "You know, I'm quite pleased by your progress. Your work is getting really strong. We often find that students who come to us from other fields have a difficult time settling into seminary studies, but you took to it right away. Your degree was in engineering, wasn't it?"

Dimitrios nodded. He told him about his grandfather. "He was a priest on Crete for many years. He spent a lot of time with me as I grew up, and he taught me a little about spiritual matters."

"A spiritual mentor in your own household? That was a blessing, indeed. I hope to meet him one day."

"I'll tell him. He'd be pleased. I know you'd like him."

"Will he come to your ordination?"

"He doesn't like to fly, but I'm sure he'll come for that."

They entered Cavadas Annex. Fr. Zarkos took a large key ring out of the pocket of his cassock and unlocked the door. He turned on the light and revealed a small academic office with papers and

37

books on every surface. He lifted away a stack of papers and found the telephone. He set the papers down on the only chair.

"Here's the phone! Help yourself. I'll leave you. Just turn off the light and make sure the door locks behind you. You all right?"

"Yes. Thanks very much."

Eight-twenty San Francisco time. Not so late. Papou must have known he'd still be up studying. Where were his parents? Dimitrios dialed his home number.

He pictured his grandfather in his mind's eye: frail this year, but still a powerful presence, full beard, long hair caught in a band at his nape. Where in the apartment would he be? Maybe he'd be in the downstairs hallway, standing by the wall niche, gripping the phone firmly. Dimitrios hoped he'd be sitting in the brown chair in his room, warily speaking into the cordless phone. His room would be neat, his narrow bed covered by a red woolen bedspread woven and embroidered on Crete nearly a century ago. Icons on the walls. Panagia. The Trinity. Agyios Phanourios with his sword and candle, his favorite, the one he called Saint Lost and Found. Dimitrios smiled at the memory. Lace on the top of the bureau. Old lace. A shelf of his grandfather's books: *The Bible* of course, and *The Philokalia*, and a large leather-bound book into which he'd written his sermons for thirty years. His other two books were there as well: *The Odyssey* and *Aristotle's Ethics*. A lifetime of thought, of faith, on one small shelf.

Dimitrios thought about the library collection at Holy Cross Seminary and compared the wisdom of all those books to his grandfather's wisdom and his little shelf of books. It's all a matter of degree, he said to himself. We use what we have.

His grandfather answered the telephone. He sounded weak but otherwise all right. They spoke in Cretan Greek.

"Hello, Papou. You called me?"

"Ah, Dimitrios. Well come."

"Well met, Papou. Where are Mom and Dad?"

"They went out. To dinner they went. So, I called thee now."

"How are you? Are you feeling all right, Papou?"

"Poh, poh, not feeling much any more. How goes the school?"

"It's hard, Papou. Lots of studying."

"It was not so hard to become a priest in my day. Too bad. But you are smart. You'll do well. How's Eleni?"

"She's fine, Papou."

"She is a nice girl, but…"

"…but what?"

"…but she will not marry you."

"How can you say that?"

"She is not a *pappadia*."

"She's been with me for a long time now. We are engaged. We love each other. I mean, I think she loves me."

"Ah, Dimitrios. I know she loves you, but she does not love the church. I have listened to her talking. I know this. Watch, Mitso. She will leave thee. Before your ordination, she will leave. She will not marry the church, which is what you are asking her to do. And you? What would you do then?"

"If she left me, which she won't, then if I am ordained as an unmarried priest, I'd be accepting the rule to be celibate for the rest of my life."

"That is right. Yes, exactly. Could you do that?"

"I don't know, Papou, but I don't think it's going to happen."

"Perhaps not. But if it does, do not worry thyself. A celibate life is not a bad one. I've been celibate fifty years, since your grandmother died."

"Did you ever have doubts about going on as a priest after she died?"

"Doubts? No. Why? Life is. We do what we do. We make some of the decisions. Others are made for us and we do with those what we can."

"You make it sound easy. But I think your life was very hard. Lots of losses."

"Dimitrios, you think too much. That comes with all these modern things. Too many magazines. Too many ideas everywhere. Never mind it."

"Yes, Papou."

"Listen to me, dear boy: Losses happen. Blessings happen. We go on."

39

"I'll try. Really. Ah, Papou, what a gift you are to me." Dimitrios started to sit down, then realized there were papers on the chair. He slid down to the floor, cradling the receiver on his shoulder. His fingers went round the shape of the knob on the bottom drawer of Fr. Zarkos's desk.

"You are my treasure. Always." Papou said.

"Will you ever tell me what happened to my grandmother?"

"I will tell you now. It is time. I'll be brief."

Over the telephone, Dimitrios heard his grandfather take a large sigh.

"I have told you stories about the war, when the Germans invaded Crete."

"Yes you have, but you never told me about…"

"I told you strategies, yes?"

"Yes."

"Promises and betrayals. The terrible things that happen in wars."

"Some. But never about your life in the war. Is that when my grandmother died?"

"Shhh. Listen. When the Germans invaded Crete from airplanes by parachute in 1941, the young men of Crete were in the army fighting far off on another frontier. We had few weapons left, few men, no leadership, no plan. We were on our own. We fought every way we could. When they understood they could not just march in and take over Crete, the Germans began terrible reprisals against the villages.

"Fotini and I were married just three years. Your father was a new baby. This time was March 1942. I was a young priest. I took my duties very seriously."

"Yes, Papou."

"Exactly, I did. We heard about the German reprisals. The village of Kandanos, deep in the mountain and west, in the nome of Selino, was destroyed the previous June. More than 150 men there, shot dead.

"My first duty was to serve God, of course, and then my duties were two: to protect my villagers and to defend Crete. I saw no way to do both.

40

"I asked my metropolitan what I should do. All he said was 'Obey the rules of God, my son, as you see them, in this dark time.'

"I found a way both to protect the village and to defend Crete, but it did not win me honors for heroism. I gave the appearance of being neutral. I did not participate in the conversations of the resistance fighters. I avoided their eyes. I looked busy. I would not let the subject of the German invaders come into the church. I preached forgiveness and patience. I did this so if the Germans tracked resistance back to Vraho I could plead for the safety of most of the people. Vraho must not look dangerous, I decided.

"I did not want the Nazis in my country any more than the others did. I made a choice. My first responsibility was to protect my village. It was very difficult for me to remain silent in those days.

"When I was sure I could do so safely, I carried messages from the British on the mountain down to resistance leaders in Chania when I went to visit my metropolitan every week. No one knew I did this."

"If you'd been caught, what would they have done?"

"The Germans? They would have shot me. Did you think they spared priests? No! They killed priests as well as women and children.

"In December of '41 the proethros of Vraho was killed—he'd been working with the Germans and someone found out and killed him. The Germans tried to learn who did it. They couldn't fix blame for it on any of us. One of them said maybe it was a man from Peristeri. Do you remember Peristeri, the next village?"

"I remember hearing about Peristeri. Across the ravine?"

"Three men from Peristeri the Germans killed, to teach a lesson. Those dead men left young families behind. Terrible, terrible."

"So what is this to do with my grandmother?"

"Please. The men of the village found their own ways to fight. My good friend from school, Nikos, and I passed messages, as I told thee. No one ever knew, so no one could betray us. I think Nikos is still alive. I have not heard that he died.

"Even dear Fotini did not know what I was doing. Once, she asked me to take a more active part in the resistance. I was stern with her. Stern I was, only to protect her. She must have no secrets the

41

Germans wanted, I thought. I hated to do it. I still regret it. Poor girl, she was so frightened. I could not comfort her fears.

"Other men in the village went onto the mountain. They became *andartes*. They attacked German patrols; they made mischief; they annoyed the angry Germans. Many times I told them that to do this was dangerous. I said, if you are careless and leave a trail, you'll bring the Germans to Vraho. They ignored me, thinking I was lazy, doing nothing. Only neutral.

"One of the andartes was a show-off. The villagers were fooled. They all thought he was brave, a true *pallikari*, a mountain hero. One night he attacked a German patrol. He killed all but one of them. That man followed him back to Vraho. That man then returned to their quarters and brought a large patrol to our village the next day." The old man's voice cracked. "This is one of the two terrible torments of my life. You must know it and there is not much time left.

"The other one you will find after I am gone."

"O, Papou."

"The Germans came on motorcycles. Some of them had sidecars. They tore up the ancient trails, the *kaldirimia*. Dug them up with their spinning tires. Never will I forget the sound of their machines.

"They demanded to see the proethros. We told them he was dead. They already knew that. Then they demanded to see me. I came forward. They asked me to tell who among us had attacked them last night. I said I knew nothing. This was true. They took me into the taverna and beat me…"

"O, Papou."

"Many of us were beaten. Never mind it. Me they beat, but I had no information to give them. They took me outside. Fotini saw me with my blood. She ran over to help me. They shot her there, in front of all of us. Then they shot two others. When they found that some women and children had hidden themselves inside the church, they tried to ram open the doors, but they were barred from inside and wouldn't give. One of the soldiers threw a grenade at the doors. It tore open the right side. The Germans went to the opening and fired into the church.

"We heard screams from the women and the cries of children. They fired and fired and then there were no more screams. The soldiers went inside the church. There were a few more shots. They came out. One of them went back inside and shot out the four colored glass windows. Then he came out and they all got on their motorcycles and left.

"Thirty-four of our village died that day." His voice faded away. Softly, he said, "Now you know."

Dimitrios could say nothing.

"When we cleaned up the church, after we had given burial to all the people who died, there were bloodstains on the stone floor and bullet holes in the wall paintings. The women of the village took turns scrubbing the floors. It took months, but we cleaned up the blood. There was no way to fix the holes. The people wept whenever they entered the church. The paintings would not let us forget the massacre. One day, I filled the holes and covered the walls over with whitewash. I decided it would be better to start fresh.

"Recently, I have come to know that unless we own all of our histories, bad and good, we are not safe from our fears. The paintings must be uncovered. The beauty of the old paintings and the horror of the German bullets must both be seen. Both are our history. They are who we are.

"You need to know this: I had an enemy after that. I found out who had been careless and had led them back to Vraho. It was a man named Alexandros Kiriakis. I spoke to him. I told him he was responsible for those deaths. He called me a coward in a skirt. After that, he moved out of the village. He fought well on the mountainside with the British commandos. He made no other mistakes in the war. But he and I...we never spoke again."

"Is Alexandros still alive?"

"No, he died. But his son is still in Vraho. Spiros Kiriakis. I have heard he is proethros now. His father hated me after that—because he would not take his blame, and I knew it."

43

"Thank you for telling me, Papou. Now, what was the other terrible thing?"

"Dimitrios, I must ask something of you."

"Something serious?"

"The most serious I ever asked and I must do so now. I want your word that you will follow my directions exactly."

"I will follow your directions exactly."

"Do you know my wooden chest, here in my room?"

"The one under the window? It's been there forever."

"I am going to mail the only key to you. That key unlocks the drawer inside the chest. Do not lose it."

"I won't, Papou. But you always told me that key was lost. That drawer couldn't be opened ever again."

"You were young and would not have understood then. But listen. The drawer must not be opened until after I am gone."

"Why are you sending me the key now, Papou?"

"We never know, do we? Open that drawer when I am dead and gone. Only then. Agreed?"

"Yes, Papou."

"After I'm dead, I want you, by yourself, to open that lock and remove what is there. Follow the instructions on it. Do not share it with anyone else, not even your parents."

"You've got a treasure buried somewhere, Papou?"

"Not a treasure. A secret. A black-hearted secret. I need your help."

"I give you my word. But Papou…" he stopped. He spoke again, "Don't die. I'll be home at Christmastime."

"I will be gone by then."

"Then I will come home now to see you again."

"Do as you wish, Dimitrios, but I do not want it. I think you would be foolish to come."

A small panic rose in Dimitrios's chest. "Let me decide, please, Papou."

"You decide. I am not afraid. Now, go back to your studies. When does the library close?"

"It's closing now. It's nearly midnight here. There's tomorrow for the library. And then I'll arrange a ticket home to see you."

"I am always happy to see you."

"I'll be there before you know it. Good night, Papou. I'll see you soon. I love you."

"I know. I love you. Good night, Dimitrios."

The old priest died that night. His son, Christos, found an envelope lying on the nightstand next to the body. It was addressed to young Dimitrios, stamped, and ready to mail. He put it in his desk drawer for safe-keeping, and then phoned his son to come home for his grandfather's funeral.

When Dimitrios arrived at San Francisco International Airport the next afternoon, his father met his flight. They embraced, held on to each other harder and longer than usual, then went to the baggage area and on to the carpark.

"How's Mom?" asked Dimitrios.

"Bearing up. Sometimes I think she loved him even more than we did."

"She loved him a lot. And he loved her, too."

Christos nodded agreement. They walked in silence, broken only by the sound of their steps echoing off the anonymous concrete surfaces of the parking structure.

As they went along 101 North, Dimitrios looked out across the bay. The warm light of the setting sun made the silhouette of the Oakland hills rosy, with sparkles as lights came on. It looked beautiful to him, but strange. Not familiar any more.

When they reached the house and Dimitrios had embraced his mother, almost the first question he asked was about an envelope from Papou. At first, his father couldn't remember what he'd done with it. The two of them rummaged through the drawers in the upstairs room where the old man had lived. Then Christos remembered, found it in his own desk drawer, and gave it to his son. Dimitrios excused himself and went out to the back steps where he had spent so many hours sitting with Papou, listening to his stories. He opened the envelope. Inside was a small key, taped to a piece of cardboard. And a note, "I bind you by honor to keep your silence."

He put the key back in the envelope, put that in his pocket, half-bowed to the memories that hovered around that old staircase, and went back inside. When he returned to the living room, his father looked at him questioningly but did not ask what was in the envelope.

There were subjects that weren't discussed any more in the Papadakis family. Mostly they had to do with Crete. It was a raw point

45

between them. When young Dimitrios was six years old, Christos brought them all to America to start over. He wanted them all to belong, wanted his son to play basketball, join the scouts, have a paper route, to be part of the new life.

The old priest grieved for Crete every day he lived in America, but he knew he could not bear to live without his family, so he came, too. He talked endlessly about Crete and its mysteries. He bewitched his grandson with those old stories.

The stories Christos feared most were the ones about the times of World War II, when he was a baby, when his mother died, when other dark things happened in the village. Christos had a great respect for secrets, especially those, and he did not want his father or his son to disturb them by poking around. He feared for all of them, for their spirits, if those secrets got out.

Young Dimitrios tried to please his parents, tried to belong to America, half-heartedly tried scouting and sports, but his imagination was fed by his time on the back steps listening to his grandfather. He took a degree in engineering to please his parents, then realized he couldn't live that life. When he started at Holy Cross Seminary, he knew he had found the path for him and there was no turning back. His parents watched, sadly.

5

The Greek-American community near Daly City, south of San Francisco, almost filled Holy Trinity Church for Papou's funeral. Flowers flooded the cathedral—white chrysanthemums, red roses, white lilies, wreaths on tripod stands with ribbons forming great bows. A cascade of white and purple roses spilled over the lower half of the open casket. The church glittered with the flames of the candles. The scent of burning incense filled the air. The always-grand building seemed to be especially splendid for this occasion.

The funeral was long and elaborate. The Divine Liturgy was celebrated first. Ireneus, the Metropolitan of San Francisco, conducted the service. Three priests assisted him. One was a priest Old Fr. Dimitrios had never met. He would have been pleased, his grandson thought. Dimitrios sat in the front row with his father, his father's friend Stelios, and the other pallbearers. His mother sat behind them. He watched as the priests celebrated his grandfather's simple life with the traditional words, chants, and gestures. Then the time came when the metropolitan announced, "It is usual for a eulogy to be delivered by me but Reverend Father Dimitrios has a grandson, his namesake," he nodded to Dimitrios who was now making his way forward, "who is a seminarian at Holy Cross School of Theology, studying to become a priest. So it seems very right that he deliver the eulogy for his grandfather." He stepped aside to make room for Dimitrios.

His throat felt dry as he moved to the front of the church, but when he began to speak, he found his voice.

"Thank you for coming here today to honor the life of my grandfather, Father Dimitrios Papadakis. He lived in this country for twenty-two years, but his life, his heroic life, was lived on his beloved Crete. He was a village priest there, one who worked in the *kampos* alongside his neighbors, one who cared for his people as a shepherd guides his flock. My grandfather had a true faith and trust in God and he passed those great gifts on to me, along with the rich heritage of the stories of the Minoan and Greek traditions. His world was large though his village, Vraho, was small. I take comfort that my grandfather's world lives on in the rich legacy I received from him." He paused to glance at the open casket within which he could see Papou's face.

"He died on Tuesday night, by himself, after speaking to me on the telephone, while my parents were out on a rare dinner date. He made no fuss, demanded no special attention. It was as if he just packed his bags and left. Something he said on the telephone made me think he knew his end was near, though he wasn't suffering any disease we knew of. I offered to come home to be with him to help him die and he said, no, he could manage it himself, and he did.

"Let me tell you what I know of his village, Vraho. I lived there until I was six, but my memories of Vraho are through his eyes, his stories, not mine.

"The village is halfway up Lefka Ori, the White Mountains that crown the western end of Crete. Some of its citizens move up into the higher pastures with their flocks each summer, living in *mitati* and making cheese from the rich sheep's milk—traditional *graviera* and the soft cheeses, so fragile and perfect they can't be exported. He himself farmed a plot of land, so he remained in the village all year, near his church and his people. On the festival of St. John the Baptist, though, he and the villagers would go up the mountain each year to the small chapel dedicated to Agyios Ioannis, where the shepherds joined them and they all celebrated, first with reverence and then with revelry on the bare rock of the great Lefka Ori. I remember those celebrations.

"In World War II, as you all know, the Germans occupied Crete. My grandfather was priest then, and…"

Dimitrios was interrupted by a loud series of coughs, followed by a gasp of air, then another chain of coughs. He looked out into the congregation and saw his father's back hurrying up the aisle. The coughing moved out to the narthex, and Dimitrios continued his eulogy.

"…he told me tales of the courageous actions of the villagers, heroic men, women, and children. I know that he personally paid a great price in the war. His wife, my grandmother, was one of the villagers killed by the Germans.

"I remember very little about Vraho, but I remember being in that church with him, when I was small. It seemed the most holy place I have ever been in.

"Many of you know I am studying to become a priest, like my grandfather, though I only pray I can be one tenth as good a priest and a man as he was. It is my wish, no, it is my goal, and I say it aloud for the first time here today, to serve as priest in his village, in Vraho. I will do that to honor the loving figure in my life who taught me the invisible values of faith, virtue, and honor.

"Thank you, Grandfather, for your teachings. I carry them in my heart."

Dimitrios stepped down and a priest began the dismissal, "Glory to you, O God, our hope, glory to You…May your memory be eternal, our ever-blessed and ever memorable brother." The people responded, "Memory eternal, memory eternal, may his memory be eternal."

49

Dimitrios and the other pallbearers approached the open casket. The priest who had just given the dismissal reached into the casket and removed Reverend Father Dimitrios's large gold pectoral cross and its chain (which had not been fastened behind his neck), kissed it, then handed it to Dimitrios, who also kissed it and received it. It would be his pectoral cross when he was ordained.

The priest closed the casket and the pallbearers carried it down the front steps of the church and set it into the hearse. The mourners were all greeted by name, kissed on each cheek, and thanked.

Dimitrios's mother slipped her hand into his and whispered, "Try not to talk about going to Crete, or World War II, Mitso. You know it upsets your father so." She moved away and smiled.

The funeral home had supplied two black sedans to drive in formation out to the Greek Orthodox Memorial Park in Colma. Dimitrios and Ellen rode in the second one, behind his parents' sedan. They rode in silence much of the way. At last she spoke. "When did you decide you want to live in Vraho?"

"Today, as I spoke. Just then."

"Where do you see me in that picture?"

"I don't know. I guess I hadn't gotten that far." Dimitrios looked at her. "I'm sorry. I'm presuming to decide your life, too, aren't I?" He put his hand on her knee in a gesture meant to be reassuring.

She moved away. "You have an idealistic dream, Mitso, and maybe you'll do it, serve the village and then come back to the world of hot running water and washing machines. Maybe not. But if you're expecting I will live in prehistoric conditions with the villagers of your poor Vraho, I have a right to think about that long and hard."

Dimitrios looked at the driver's back. There was no sign that he could hear their conversation.

"Do you want to break up?"

"No, I don't think so, but I'm howling a protest. You're making plans that threaten to drag my life off its track and you haven't given me a choice in the matter."

"You have a choice. I didn't think about how hard it might be for you when I took that vow just now, but I see it is asking a lot of you."

"A lot? Delivering babies without medical aid? Caring for donkeys and goats and chickens? Speaking only Cretan Greek? I'm from here. I was born in San Francisco. I barely speak Greek, let alone the Cretan dialect. I never kept an animal besides a dog who died when I was four. What would I do on Crete?"

"Learn?"

"Learn what? How to serve God from a life of poverty? How to move backwards many centuries? How to give up all the things my education has prepared me for? So that I can be a helpmate to you? Faithful wife, good servant to the man who serves the people? Maybe if I'd chosen to be a priest myself I wouldn't mind the poverty involved."

"Women aren't priests..."

"I know, I know. Women are just women there. To be held back, shushed up, not listened to. Just like always. I have to give this some serious thought, Mitso. Serious thought."

"I'm sorry. Of course you do."

Silence settled over the car. Dimitrios could feel her eyes studying him. He thought, she will, or she won't, choose to go with me. I hope she does. What more can I do? I feel my destiny finally. I've been waiting for it to show itself for a long time. I don't think I can give it up to keep her.

After some miles, Ellen said, "Mitso, I love you. Truly I do. It's just—this is a new idea for me and I need some time to think about what I want. Right now, I think I want you, whatever the cost, but today the cost just went up. Now, it includes Crete. I'm just not sure I can be me in that life."

He reached over and touched her cheek. "I love you, Ellen. And I do believe that you love me. I am sorry I didn't have a chance to tell you before I announced it, but the weird thing is, I never thought of it before I said it in Papou's eulogy. He said he had some unfinished business in Vraho. I need to do this. I don't seem to have any other path to take. But you'll have to decide what you want. Ellen, I'm as shaken by this as you are."

She shifted her body away from him. She drew up into a smaller space. They rode in silence toward the burial.

Dimitrios felt the floor of his life drop another notch further away from him. Out through the car window, strip malls and car dealerships slid past, offering an air of cheeriness. The thin, acidic sunlight of California in November made the cheeriness look foolish. A sadness rose in him.

Then he heard his grandfather's voice. "I told you she would not marry you. She is not meant to be a priest's wife."

Dimitrios made himself watch the road. He was grateful he wasn't driving. There are a dozen cemeteries in Colma, for different religious groups. He would have gotten lost. Laid Papou to rest with the Lutherans. The silence in the limo grew larger and larger. Dimitrios tried to break it, but there was nothing to say.

The burial ceremony went smoothly. Afterwards, the limousine took them back to the house for a huge *makaria* with family friends. After a funeral, the Meal of Blessedness is always a fish dinner, to remember that Christ shared in a meal of fish after His resurrection. The diners share in the resurrected life of the *makariti*, the beloved deceased.

After a suitable time, Ellen said goodnight to everyone and left.

The day after Papou's funeral, both his parents went to work and Dimitrios was alone in the house. The place seemed so lifeless. He ached for the overhead shuffling footsteps of Papou. He went up into his grandfather's room and opened the chest under the window. He found the tiny lock and opened it with the key Papou had left him. Inside the drawer was a note wrapped around a silver key. The note said,

> So long as I live I am forbidden to tell anyone my great sin. I am still living as I write this, so I can only point you to another trunk, in Vraho, stored in the old house. The new priest, Fr. Theodoros, lives there now. Maybe someday you can be assigned there and have the house back. Even if not, beg him permission to look for that chest. Do not open it in his presence.
>
> I want you to learn my secret and, if you can, pray that I be forgiven. This is a large thing to ask. You are my inheritor, my namesake, the son of my son. I give you my guilt to release. Please. In the name of God the Father, the Son, and the Holy Ghost.
>
> I have no possessions to leave you but those of my priesthood: my books and my cross. I leave you my love, and my hope for my release. I have nothing else.
>
> With love,
> Papou.

Dimitrios stood for a long moment, holding the letter, then he said, quietly, "What could you have done to merit such suffering, Papou? I promise I will learn your secret and forgive you then, when I know the worst thing in your life."

He tore the paper into very small pieces and left the empty drawer unlocked. He strung the silver key onto the chain he always wore around his neck, next to his baptismal cross. Then he left his grandfather's room.

He had already begun to list contacts who could help him arrange the assignment to Vraho.

6

Aleko ran for help. The boy's house was only about three kilometers away, in lower Vraho, but his mother wasn't there. He ran to the Sunshine Beach Taverna, where she worked.

The Sunshine Beach Taverna was a dingy concrete building at the end of a street in Nea Hora, the newer part of Chania, to the west of the Venetian fortifications. The taverna was across from an unappealing beach, so unless the main beaches were packed with tourists, it was usually quiet. The phalanx of turquoise beach chairs rarely had more than three sunbathers using them.

Sunshine Beach Taverna had an open dining area with seating for forty guests. On the two floors above, it offered six guest rooms to travelers on a budget. Because of its location, it was busy only in summer. This was August and Aleko's mother was working every day, cleaning the kitchen in the early morning before the day's cooking began, and then cleaning the guest rooms that had been occupied. She also did the laundry and ironing. She usually started at six in the morning and finished by four in time to go home and take care of the afternoon chores and cook dinner for herself and Aleko. She was cleaning the third bedroom when Aleko ran up to her, crying and speaking so fast she couldn't understand what he was saying.

"Slow down, Aleko. Speak slowly," she said. He blubbered out a story of a robbery and somebody shot. His arms were going in circles and he shifted from foot to foot.

She gave one last rub to the taps of the sink in front of her, wrung out the rag and put it in her bucket, wiped her hands, and untied her apron. She took the bucket to Dimosthenes, the taverna owner, and said, "I must go. There has been an accident."

"Another one? Kyria, your life is full of accidents." Dimosthenes sighed. "Go if you must. But who will finish cleaning?" Muttering, he went off to look for his wife.

Aleko and his mother went quickly to where Douglas lay. On the way, Aleko told his mother the day's events: the trouble with the goat, the help from a stranger, the robbery, the shooting, the blood.

As they neared the site of the robbery, Aleko broke into a run.

Douglas heard him cry out, "Daonglos!" He started to turn toward him to respond. The birdshot stopped him. He moaned. Dust covered his clothes and his face. He could feel the dust working its way into the wounds on his back. The shirt, sticky with blood, grew dry and stiff against his skin.

Aleko knelt beside Douglas. He lay his hand on Douglas's forehead, then turned back and gestured to someone with him. Douglas looked up to see a woman walking toward him. She nodded to him, and then surveyed the area of bloody punctures. Aleko watched.

After some minutes, the woman said something to Aleko, who ran off toward the road. She then spoke gently in Greek to Douglas. He found the sound of her voice comforting but he couldn't understand what she was saying. He tried to release the tension in his shoulders, but couldn't. He imagined what she might be saying to him.

Aleko's mother smiled at Douglas. He could see she was a kind-looking woman in her late thirties. In spite of the heat, she wore a black sweater over a black skirt and blouse. She was all in black. A black cotton scarf held back her shoulder-length dark hair. She wore a wedding ring on her right hand and no other jewelry. Her face was narrow, her eyes light grey, her look was calm.

55

Aleko returned with a stranger, a villager from up-mountain who happened to be driving past. The man greeted Aleko's mother and the two adults discussed in Greek how to move Douglas to the man's pickup truck. Aleko squatted beside Douglas and peered at him without touching him.

"O.-K.?" he asked.

Douglas looked up at him. "Okay," he managed.

Aleko smiled. "O.-K.," and patted his leg.

The passerby apologized for the dirt and trash in his truckbed. He said he used the truck and his dog to drive his goats ahead of him down the road from his village to his fields every day. The truckbed was filled with blocks of wood, rocks, shovels, tools, and lots of plastic sheeting. And the dog.

The two adults helped Douglas stand up, walk to the truck, and climb into the back. The dog made room for him, watching its owner for instructions. Douglas barely noticed the dog. His pain was blinding. The truck driver brought a blanket from the cab and spread it over the plastic bags. Aleko's mother climbed in behind him and Aleko got in the cab with the driver to direct him to their house.

Douglas smiled at her. He tried to look over his shoulder to see the extent of his injuries, but the pain stopped him. He leaned back and fidgeted, searching out a comfortable position on the old, dirty blanket, for the bumpy ride to wherever they were taking him.

Douglas said, "Efcharisto. Thank you for your help."

The woman nodded and smiled. He carefully extended his hand to shake hers. "Douglas Watkins." She touched his fingers in the most fleeting of handshakes.

"Vassilia Andreadaki. *Hero poli*," and she smiled.

"Thank you."

She spoke to him. He couldn't make out any of the words. His eyes shut against the pain.

The road bumped and curved. The motor coughed and caught again. Exhaust fumes rose to make the air thick. The chain holding the tailgate shut rattled against the truck with each pothole.

Douglas was facing the rear of the truck. He couldn't twist enough to see where they were going, but he watched where they'd just been. The road was beginning to climb the mountain. Plane trees and olive groves replaced the receding orange groves. A small stream cut deep into the hill alongside them.

They passed through the olive grove zone into open maquis, low shrubs stunted for millennia by goats and sheep. Trails cut across the scrub in purposeful lines. How old? he wondered. How old are those tracks?

They drove through a village. Douglas watched it recede, waiting for a sign saying Welcome to... and its name. At last, a sign said Therisso in Greek and Roman letters. He made a note to remember Therisso, like Hansel and Gretel dropping bread crumbs.

The paving ended and the road became rocky and rutted. He thought once that he could see the sea, but his eyes closed and he gave up. The dog panted. Pain numbed him. The truck bounced on.

At last the truck stopped, its motor idling. Aleko hopped out and opened a sagging wire and aluminum gate in a half-ruined stone wall. The truck drove in and parked. Aleko closed the gate.

A rectangular house, flat-roofed, part plastered, part exposed stone, was backed into the hillside and surrounded by a derelict farmyard. Three goats concentrated on a few weeds. A fourth goat watched the humans from the roof. It had climbed there from the hillside behind the house. A primitive three-wheeled truck of the type known as *mikani* gave shelter to several skinny chickens. Other chickens were taking dust baths in hollows in the hard ground.

The surrounding stone wall lay on the ground in several places. Still, someone had painstakingly filled the gaps in the stone with rusty chicken-wire to keep the chickens and goats home. The rest of the scene was bare dust over hard-packed earth, shaded only by an ancient fig tree under which a weather-beaten table and three chairs stood.

The woman, Vassilia, and the truck driver each took one of Douglas's arms and got him out of the truck. They led him past three whitewashed gasoline tins planted with tomatoes, and into the house. The fresh paint on the light blue door made the surrounding elements look even more pathetic.

Moving was difficult. The pain Douglas had felt as he lay flat in the jiggling truckbed was nothing compared to the pain when he stood up and walked.

57

They handed him into the house. His eyes grew accustomed to the low light inside. He looked around. Light entered the space around his silhouette in the open doorway and through two small windows in the same wall. They had entered at the midpoint of the long side of a stone rectangle.

To distract himself from his pain, Douglas forced himself to take an interest in the interior. A large dressed-stone arch ran across his view, the length of the house. Between the arched wall and the perimeter walls, three-meter lengths of raw wood formed the ceiling surface. Douglas wondered at the need for the elaborate and expensive arch, then remembered hearing at Big Kostas's taverna that during the four centuries they ruled Crete, the Venetians had cut down all the tall cypress trees for export to Venice. If that was true, there was no tall timber left on the island and they would need an arch to support a roof.

There were no closed-off rooms. He could see everywhere from where he stood. The center wall extended beyond the open archway by about two meters on each end to the short sides of the building. These fins formed four corner spaces that were darker than the open area where he was. Aleko ran for a chair and set it in the middle of the room, under the arch. Douglas sat down and slumped against its carved back. The pain of the chairback against his wounds moved him forward again quickly. Vassilia and the truckdriver examined his wounds and discussed their care in rapid Greek. She went into her kitchen area.

The space between the wall to his right and the front of the house was the kitchen, with no sign of running water. A bare lightbulb dangled on its cord alongside two oil lamps on chains. Vassilia took down one of the oil lamps, filled it with oil, trimmed the wick, and lit it with a Bic lighter. She made no attempt to turn on the lightbulb.

Douglas's attention now grew into fascination with the building. The other three corners had ladders leading to shoulder-height platforms. One platform was filled with shocked hay and cotton sacks of grain, winter feed for the goats and chickens. The other two platforms were made up as beds. Under them were storage areas, filled with boxes and wooden trunks. Next to the kitchen stood four tall *pithoi,* storage jars, exactly the shape and size of those Douglas had helped excavate this summer at the Rhodopou site.

A masonry hood covered two firestones, rectangular slabs of stone with the center carved away. One of the firestones had remnants of a recent wood fire. In the other sat a portable gas cooker. She lit it now, and handed her son a lightweight aluminum saucepan. He took it outside—Douglas assumed to a cistern. He returned and decanted some water into a cast iron pot which he put on the gas cooker.

Several pans hung on the wall behind the firestones. There was no oven. Plates stood in a rack on the wall. A niche built into the stone held a vessel for salt. Bundled herbs and a braid of garlic hung from hooks. Vassilia pulled out several herbs and added them to the pan of water.

Douglas was delighted. Except for the arch, which hadn't been invented yet, the Minoan house he'd excavated this summer, which was built on this island 4,000 years ago, was identical to this. At that time they must have had access to long timbers, so their center roof-support was one long wooden beam supported at the third-points by tree-trunk columns. The Minoans stood them upside down so they were wider at the top than the base. It was a distinctive feature of their architecture. How is this house possible? he wondered. Even the kitchen was like the Minoan reconstructions he'd seen. He wanted to show Professor Ducor. Then his mood darkened as he remembered he had probably cut himself off forever from his previous life, including the professor.

Douglas's energy faded from what seemed a trivial injury, but, he thought, in fairness, he had never been shot before. It was draining his strength. He felt very sorry for himself. He wondered if he was in shock.

While he'd been examining the house, he hadn't noticed Aleko pull a small table out to the center of the room, near where he was sitting. Now the boy covered it with an embroidered cloth. Three more carved straight-back chairs with rush seats appeared from somewhere.

The driver sat down opposite him and smiled at him. Douglas smiled back. There was nothing to say.

He went back to looking around.

59

Douglas saw several areas of vivid color, mostly red, around the otherwise drab house. Bright embroidery and weavings in reds, yellows, and blues caught his eye. They helped him forget his pain. He wanted to get up and touch them but he knew he shouldn't for two reasons. First, because he'd probably fall on his face, and second, these were real dowry weavings and deserved respect. Museum-like respect. White cotton gloves or don't touch.

Douglas had seen a few examples of dowry weavings in Chania in that upstairs folk museum next to the Archaeology Museum, but these textiles were in actual use. This was a real example of living vernacular architecture. If he hadn't been shot by that robber, he might never have seen this. He was momentarily grateful for the injury that had given him this visit.

On the rear wall, across from the door, hung a red and black striped weaving, a rhythm in the stripes, not just A-B-A-B. These stripes were saying something, dancing stripes of black on red, or was it red on black, his mind was slipping. He closed his eyes and waited for things to stop spinning.

When they stopped, he took another look. The length of the wooden bench below the red and black was covered with a brightly colored floral embroidery. Maybe a Tree of Life. Beautiful. Want to see them up close. Later, maybe.

Aleko went outside and returned with his arms full of spindly logs. He set them next to the empty firestone. He arranged three small branches and a handful of dried leaves and lit them.

Then, he dipped a small bowl into one of the pithoi and drew out olives, beautiful, wrinkled, dark, and fragrant. From somewhere else he got a half-dozen walnuts. The bottle of tsikoudia came to the table, and three small glasses.

Douglas eyed the clear liquid and thought, There's that stuff Kostas called brain solvent. I wonder if it will numb my pain.

He remembered the three times he'd tried it at Big Kostas's taverna. There'd been a price the next morning. He decided he didn't care. He'd been shot and maybe some strong alcohol would make him feel better.

The house had a somber feeling. The embroidered curtains that flanked its two windows were stiff with black paint. Their embroidery showed only as a faint change of texture. Was this recent? Was it a sign of mourning? Douglas wondered. He looked at the black garments the boy's mother wore, and realized she was a widow. He felt stupid for not noticing that before, and wondered how long ago the boy's father had died.

Two wreaths of dried flowers bound by faded ribbons lay below the icon of the *Panagia*, the Mother of God, on a small table near the door. He wondered what the wreaths meant. They looked quite old.

The herbs steeped. Vassilia came to the table. They made a toast and drank their tsikoudia. The driver rose to leave. Aleko's mother reached into her skirt-pocket and took out a coin purse. She opened it but the driver raised his hand to stop her and said, "*Oshi, oshi, parakalo.*" She put the purse back in her pocket and shook the man's hand. Aleko also shook his hand and said "Efcharisto," many times. Then the driver came over to Douglas and put a friendly callused hand on his left shoulder and said, "*Ya sas.*" Douglas said, "Thank you very much for your help." Then he remembered the Greek word Aleko had just said. "Efcharisto." The driver nodded, smiled, and left.

Vassilia opened a small chest among the pithoi under the sleeping platform next to the kitchen and returned holding folded cloths and a long dagger. Douglas had never seen its like. Aleko pointed to it, and said, "My father. His knife. *Passalis.*" Douglas looked at it carefully. It rested in a dark leather scabbard from whose tip hung three amulets. When the boy's mother took hold of its ivory hilt and removed it from the scabbard, the hammered steel blade shone, even in the dimly lit room. It was a weapon to be respected.

She set it down on the table carefully, then gathered up the clean cloths, drew a bowl of hot herb-infused water from the pot on the fire, ran the knife blade through the flame to sterilize it, and brought the bowl and the dagger to the table. She also brought a small bottle of something. She gestured to Douglas to get up. He did and she turned his chair so that it faced away from the table, with its front edge facing the door. She asked Aleko to open the door, and indicated that Douglas was to sit facing the chairback. His back was lit by daylight through the doorway. Standing behind him, she began to cut away his

61

torn shirt, carefully peeling the stuck parts off the bloody wounds. When the damp pieces were removed, all that remained of his shirt was the front, the yoke, and the sleeves. She helped Douglas take them off. Then she sponged off the dried blood with the warm herb-water and started to dig pellets out of his back with the dagger. Lucky! She showed him the first shot. Just birdshot. Small pellets. None had gone deeper than a quarter of an inch.

Aleko watched the procedure for awhile, then went off to draw water for the goats and chickens.

Vassilia muttered as she worked. Douglas could feel her grow frustrated as the number of pellets in the small dish on the table grew.

He tried not to make her work more difficult by showing his pain but his hands gripped the back of his chair until they felt like fused wooden knurls. Sweat stood on his face and his jaw was fused, too.

Each time she removed a pellet, she placed a balm of fragrant oil from the small bottle on the wound. After what seemed like hours, she stood up and said, "*Arketo.*" Enough. She put the knife down on the table and walked outside. He turned to see where she'd gone. She stood in the yard, put her hands on her hips, and flexed her back. She bowed her head to stretch her neck. Then she returned to examine his back for any pellets she might have missed. When she was sure no shot was hiding in his back, she draped a double cloth over his entire back and taped it in place with adhesive tape.

"*Skagia*," she said, naming the pellets in the dish.

"Skagia," repeated Douglas.

She lifted the dish and offered it to him. Did he want them for souvenirs?

He shook his head, but then asked to see the dish. He counted the pellets: thirty-seven. When he returned the dish to her, she went outside and threw the lead pellets over the fence, safe from the scavenging chickens.

Vassilia pulled another small chest out from under the same sleeping-platform. She returned, cradling a white shirt in her arms. She handed it to him. It was a man's shirt, of much-laundered, soft cotton. He tried it on. The sleeves were short for his long arms, so he rolled them up. Otherwise, it fit. He thanked her for it. She waved her hand across her face, brushing away his thanks as if they were flies.

Douglas rose, but as he stood his vision blurred and he sat down again, hard.

Vassilia nodded, and pointed to a sleeping platform in the corner opposite the kitchen. Douglas shook his head, declining the offer. Vassilia called Aleko in and said something to him. He said to Douglas, "You here..." His hand waved around as he looked for the word. "friend. Sleep Aleko bed."

Douglas started to decline the offer, thought about it, realized he wasn't strong enough to walk away. He had no idea where he'd go, anyway. Just now, lying down was probably best for his beat-up body, so he nodded "Okay," and allowed himself to be guided over to the bed. He climbed up the ladder and lay down. Vassilia unfolded a sheet to cover him. Aleko pulled a curtain across, closing Douglas off from a view of the rest of the house.

They left. Douglas was alone in the boy's bed-area. He looked around, briefly, at the strange surroundings. Pain and tsikoudia took over and his eyes closed.

Some time passed. He woke, disoriented, to the nearby sound of a man's voice raised in anger. Outside the door? He lifted his head, felt dizzy, sank back. Ah, yes. The day's events came rolling over him. He turned his focus again to the angry voice.

At that moment, somebody burst through the front door, strode across the room, and yanked back the curtain. It was a burly man, dressed all in black, from his Cretan leather boots and baggy pants to a well-tailored shirt. A fierce mustache and a fringed *sariki* tied around his head gave him a dangerous look. In his wake came a pimply teen-aged boy. Vassilia and Aleko followed.

The black-clad figure shouted, in English, "Who are you? Why you are here? What you are doing?" and, after a pause too brief to allow an answer, "Why don't you answer me?" He reached in and grabbed Douglas by the shirt, pulling him toward him. Douglas winced as the shirt came tight across his wounds. He yelled, "Let go of me!" The man released the shirt and stepped back, a small step.

63

Douglas swung his legs over the edge of the platform and sat up, holding his right arm with his left hand. Soreness and swelling were setting in. His back throbbed.

He climbed down the ladder, carefully. The action hurt each of his wounds. He straightened up, and, at 5'11" he stood three inches taller than the Cretan powerhouse.

Douglas rearranged his shirt. He spoke slowly. "I'm Douglas Watkins. I am here because I've been hurt by a robber while I was with Aleko. And who are you?" he asked with a frown.

"Show me your hurt," the man said. Before he could pull the shirt again, Douglas waved him back and undid the buttons. Then he slid his wounded shoulder out of the shirt and turned his back toward the man, who lifted a corner of the makeshift bandage and satisfied himself that there were indeed wounds underneath. The sullen teenager leaned in to look, too.

Douglas buttoned his shirt coolly and repeated, "Now, again, who are you?"

"I am Spiros Kiriakis, proethros of this village. This woman is sister of my wife. You cannot stay here. It looks bad to the villagers. I heard about you at the taverna from the man who drove you. Very bad. You must go."

Douglas turned to Vassilia and nodded, saying, "Efcharisto." He started walking unsteadily toward the door.

Vassilia moved to bar his way. She turned on Spiros and spoke fiercely to him.

Aleko whispered to Douglas, "You stay. "

Douglas watched the faces around him to see what he should do. He figured he was going to offend somebody, no matter what he did. He waited.

Spiros insisted again that Douglas leave. Vassilia moved closer to Spiros's face and glared. Then she spat on her own clean floor. Spiros's face froze. He turned and left the house. The teenager glared at Aleko and trailed out behind his father.

The sound of their truck faded as they drove away. In the ensuing silence, Vassilia and Aleko shared a look. She put her arm around his shoulders and leaned down to kiss his hair. He hugged her back. They parted and looked at Douglas, then looked away.

He tipped his head at the departing sedan. "His son?"

"My....mother sister son, Manolis," said Aleko. He tried to explain, "My uncle want we pay for mikani," pointing at the broken farm vehicle the chickens had taken over. "Can no pay now. Money gone. Very engry, he. I sell other goat tomorrow. Sorry." He looked frightened.

Douglas remembered to speak slowly. "I am sorry, too. Can I help you take the other goat to sell?"

Aleko looked at his mother and translated Douglas's offer. Vassilia paused for a moment, then nodded. She seemed pleased.

Douglas reached for the back of a chair as the room began to go rubbery. Aleko asked, "To bed?" but Douglas sat down in the chair and leaned on the table for support.

Vassilia and Aleko began preparations for supper. Aleko took down a basket and went outside, returning with two tomatoes and three zucchinis. His mother dug two onions out of a basket in the kitchen and sliced them. While Aleko laid the table, Vassilia fried the sliced onions in olive oil then chopped the tomatoes and squash into them. When they were cooked, she added four beaten eggs. Aleko set out a dish with feta cheese and more of the fragrant olives.

The meal was delicious. Douglas thought he had never tasted food before. And maybe he hadn't. Maybe his senses had been as numbed as his feelings.

Sweet, sour, bitter, salt. He could taste the sun-baked richness of the zucchinis and the tomatoes. The goat on the roof had contributed milk for this feta. He sensed the garden, the sunlight, the day's labor with each bite of his food.

He understood saying grace before eating, although it had not been the custom in his life. He wanted to say a blessing on this food, which had been blessed already by the labor of Vassilia and Aleko to produce it.

Gratitude rose in him, the color of amber. It moved like a slow liquid. Like honey.

65

Afterwards, Douglas picked up his plate to carry to the kitchen. Once standing, he remembered there was no water there. Vassilia waved his plate back onto the table, he sat down again, and Aleko took the three plates out into the yard to wash. After a few minutes, Douglas gratefully returned to the boy's bed. As his mind flooded toward sleep he thought how wonderfully basic this life was, and how he envied them their family, their community, their simple life. Even with that grumpy uncle.

With half-opened eyes, he watched Aleko prepare a bed of goatskins for himself on the floor. Aleko smiled and waved as he wrapped himself in a blanket.

"O.-K.?" the boy asked.

"Okay!" Douglas answered.

Vassilia snuffed the lamps and carried a candlestick to her sleeping platform. When she was in bed she blew it out and the house was dark. The three slept. The only sounds in the night were a sheep's bell and the murmur of an owl.

7

A boy wears his history in his bones, behind his eyes, woven into his spirit. He may not ever speak this history, but he bears it, will or no. Aleko's history was dark, shot with a weft of large joy and larger rage. It began fourteen years before his birth.

On May 12th, 1976, Spiros Kiriakis first saw Vassilia Grivaki and fell in love with her. She was fifteen, with a fresh beauty that stopped hearts wherever she went. They had grown up in the same village; he should have known who she was, but until that moment he had not noticed her. His life had been his own.

At eighteen, Spiros was the most powerful boy in the village. He was the only son of Alexandros Kiriakis, the pallikari, that brave resistance fighter. During World War II, Alexandros left the village to live on the mountain. He watched where the Germans moved, attacked their squads, and then disappeared again into the mountainside. The Germans put a price on his head, but he was lucky and no one betrayed him. He was a legend. For the rest of his life, the villagers treated him with great respect. His exploits were retold in *mantinades*, over drinks, by the old men who fought with him.

There were many Cretan mantinades that were sung, unchanged, for centuries, but sometimes they were made up on the spot. One mantinada about Alexandros went like this:

Alexandros was a wasp, stinging the Germans in their beds.
He came in the dark of night and chased sleep out of their heads.

Alexandros doted on his only son, Spiros. He made the mistake of many well-meaning parents: he gave Spiros all the advantages he himself never had. Spiros grew up selfish. Alexandros wanted him to have an education. He saw him as a teacher in the village school. It would be an honorable life, a job with a salary and more future than goat herding. Spiros was raised with encouragement and praise as if he were a brilliant student, in the hope that he might become one. He even took English lessons after school so that he could go on to an international school.

Spiros had other plans. He admired the generals of the postwar government in Athens. He wanted their kind of power—a respect that came from fear. The villagers viewed his father with gratitude. He thought gratitude was weak.

He wanted to be a politician or a police chief, but he did not say this to his father. He took the education that was offered. It was nicer to sit in a classroom and cheat on math tests than to follow his father's goats on the mountainside all day.

Spiros's plans took a turn the day he fell in love with Vassilia. She became his obsession. He wanted her for his own. There was an obstacle. She was engaged to Panos Andreadakis, a nice young man from the next village with vacant blue eyes, a pleasant singing voice, and a white smile.

This did not stop Spiros. He laid siege to the couple. He stole three of Panos's sheep, including the bellwether. He slaughtered them, hung them in an olive tree, and left them to rot. Panos found their carcasses, and knew the bellwether's body by its collar.

In Crete, it's not unknown to steal a sheep because you are hungry. It's a young man's game to steal a sheep now and then. But it is an insult to steal one and waste it. Panos's family did not have sheep to spare. The villagers gossiped, wondering who would hate Panos so. He, himself, had no idea.

Panos was not bright and he was certainly not devious. He was no match for Spiros's ambition, desire, and spite. Spiros made a fool of him many different ways. But the more Spiros made fun of Panos, the more Vassilia loved Panos and despised Spiros.

Panos was not ambitious, but he was loving and handsome, and when he was happy, he sang. Vassilia was enchanted by his looks and his joy. They laughed and talked together endlessly. She could not imagine a life without him.

An engagement in Crete is a serious commitment. Vassilia was promised to Panos, which suited her well. She loved him. Her family approved of him. They had celebrated their betrothal with a ceremony the whole village attended. She wore a ring on her left hand. When they would marry, the ring would move to her right hand. According to tradition, Panos came to live with her and her parents. Betrothed couples were not seen in public without an escort, but they spent their private time getting to know one another and, in this case, falling more and more in love.

Panos's parents were invalids, cared for by his three older brothers. They worked hard to keep the family fields going, trying to help each other along. They all had wives and were beginning families. Their land barely fed them all. The brothers and old parents wished Panos well and sent him off. Then the old ones died, the lands were sold for debts, the brothers and their families emigrated, and Vassilia's parents and sister became Panos's new family.

Spiros glowered. He lurked around, glaring at Panos and Vassilia. He took their betrothal as an insult. It robbed him of what he thought should rightfully be his.

He hovered in places he should not have been, watching for Vassilia. He sat up in a big holm oak tree and waited for her on her way home from the kampos. Sundays, he followed her to church.

One night he got drunk on tsikoudia and beer. He went to where he thought Panos might be, found him, and beat him up. Panos kept asking, "Why?" Spiros howled with rage and hit him again and again. The men from the taverna heard the fight and came to break it up. By then, Panos was bleeding from his nose, he had a black eye, and his good shirt was torn.

69

He was not angry. He only said, "Why are you so mad at me, Spiros? I have never hurt you."

At this, Spiros wept tears of frustration and tried to break free of the arms that restrained him.

Panos forgave Spiros, because he blamed the event on the alcohol.

Over the next two years, as their wedding approached, Vassilia warned Panos to be careful not to offend Spiros. They did not hold hands in public. They were discreet in their affection for each other. They acted friendly but distant toward Spiros. But his desire for her did not lessen. His heart swam in a red sea of rage.

On the day of their wedding, August 22nd, 1978, Panos and Vassilia were both seventeen years old. The joy they felt was only slightly eroded by worry about Spiros and his dark moods. They thought he might try to mar the day in some slight way, but they were not prepared for what happened.

The wedding took place in Agyios Yeorgeos, the stone church in Ano Vraho. Some of the guests stood out in the *platia* because the church could not hold them all.

The bride and her sister, who was her *koumbara,* both wore white skirts over trousers and white blouses with black vests. The bride had a red embroidered apron, and the koumbara's was green. They looked like a pair of fluttering doves as they whispered and paced, waiting for the ceremony to begin.

Panos was never so handsome as that day. He had grown a small, elegant moustache for the wedding. His black vest, *stifania,* and boots set off his blue eyes and his smile. He looked dazed with happiness.

The two koumbari, Sofia and a friend of Panos's, carried the *stefana,* a pair of wreaths of tiny dried flowers. The wreaths were connected by long satin ribbons. They held them over the heads of the bride and groom. During the ceremony the wreaths were exchanged.

Everyone said it was a beautiful wedding.

Spiros fortified himself for the insulting experience of seeing his true love marry another man by drinking a great deal of tsikoudia. Wearing black as deep as his mood, he arrived at the church, very drunk. He stayed near the door, hearing Fr. Theodoros conduct the service he hated so. Once, he elbowed through guests to see the proceedings. Then, shaking his head, he turned away and moaned. The guests nearby looked at him anxiously. One of his father's friends put an arm around his shoulder and tried to lead him out of the church. He threw the arm off with a loud curse.

Fr. Theodoros paused in the ceremony. Heads turned toward Spiros. The older man managed to lead him out of the church and back to the taverna where he bought him another tsikoudia and stayed with him until the ceremony was over.

The villagers were uneasy as they gathered in the platia to celebrate the marriage. A feast spread across long tables to the side, and there was music to dance away the night. Friends played the wedding dances of Crete. One man had the three-stringed *lyra* standing on his knee, and another played the *lauto*. When the first hour of the party passed and Spiros didn't return, people relaxed and their laughter began to fill the platia. They went through the traditional wedding dances: first, the gentle *soysta* with its small, playful steps, then the five step *dozali*, the leap on the fifth step a reminder that it was a war dance in olden days, and then, at last, it was time for the *syrto*.

The hesitant, elegant syrto began slowly. Only Vassilia and Panos were dancing. Three steps right, three left, three forward, three back. Again and again, slowly. In her right hand Vassilia held a handkerchief, a celebratory flag. The guests watched in approving silence. After some minutes, Panos stepped back and the men of the village took turns one by one dancing with Vassilia. More people took hands and the line of the dance grew.

Spiros arrived and joined the end of the dancing line farthest from Vassilia. After a minute, however, he grew agitated and moved to the head of the line. Vassilia was dancing with old Spyridon, the postman. Spiros went to the dancing pair and pushed the old man aside. He put his arms around Vassilia. She struggled to remove herself from his embrace. She looked over her shoulder for help. Spiros held her tightly and danced with more and more abandon. Vassilia twisted out of his arms and her father and Panos pulled her to them.

71

Spiros drew a pistol out of his belt and fired into the sky three times, laughing. The crowd gasped and ran for cover from bullets in free-fall. Two older men tried to take Spiros's gun away from him, but he pointed it in the direction of the bridal party and, waving it wildly, said, "I wish you no joy of this marriage. You were meant to be mine, Vassilia, and one day you will be mine!" And he ran from the circle of villagers.

Women shrieked. The bride's mother fainted. Panos and three other men ran after Spiros until he pointed his gun at them and said, "I'll kill you. I don't care if I do." Believing him, they dropped back and let him run away. He was not seen again for a week.

Fr. Theodoros moved through the wedding guests to the shaken bride and groom. "My dears, tomorrow I will come to your house and we will perform a *paraclesis* to remove this curse from you and your wedding. It will be all right. We must forgive Spiros Kiriakis in our hearts, for he has sinned gravely."

Even after the paraclesis, Vassilia was depressed. She feared the marriage would be cursed, and that she would be barren. Panos tried to console her, but her mood was dark in those early days.

Two weeks later, Spiros abducted Vassilia's sister, Sofia. The village was shocked. The girl's parents hid their faces in shame as they passed their neighbors in their daily tasks.

Sofia Grivaki was fifteen years old, nearly as lovely as her older sister. She had a slight limp, the result of polio when she was young. Now as she was growing into adolescence, her parents hovered over her, worrying about her. Her handicap prevented her from dancing, and she was sure no one would ever love her as Panos loved her sister. But in spite of those insecurities, she was a happy young woman, if a bit timid.

Spiros caught her. He stepped out from behind the holm oak tree and grabbed her arms as she walked past, pushed her and dragged her around the corner to his truck, made her get in, and threatened her with his gun. She was terrified. He took her up Lefka Ori, up the mountain. He drove to the end of a road, told her to get out and walk in front of his gun to a *mitatos,* a stone shepherd's hut, where he raped her. He kept her there for three days. Then he let her go. She found her way home, weeping. Her father, maddened by the disgrace, wanted to shut the door on her, but her mother prevailed and Sofia was admitted, shame and all, to the house.

It is not surprising that the shame for this abduction fell on poor Sofia, not on Spiros. Her future was much altered. It looked as if the only life open to her was to become a nun, since no man would marry a tainted woman and the family could not support her for the rest of her life. Tears flowed in the Grivakis home.

Then, a week after her return to her home, Spiros's father, Alexandros the war-hero, knocked on the Grivakis' door. Irene Grivaki was shocked to see him there, and her first instinct was to slam the door and hide. But she knew her manners and she invited him inside.

She served him a kafe Elleniko and a plate of almond *kourabiedhez*, and went to get her husband. When they returned, Alexandros Kiriakis said, "Please, sit down. I know this is a difficult time for you, but I have come with a way to restore your daughter's good name. I have spoken with my son and he has agreed to lift the disgrace from your family. He will marry Sofia, even though she is no longer a virgin."

Sofia's father burst out of his chair. "It was your son who made her that way!" he bellowed. Kyria Grivaki put her hand up to restrain him.

Alexandros Kiriakis said, "Well, that may be. Do you want her to marry? Because now no one else will have her. Or is she to have a life in the church?"

Irene said, "Kyrie, we need to discuss your offer. Will you excuse us, please?" He nodded, and the girl's parents left the room. When they returned, pale and tight-lipped, they agreed to the marriage. Sofia was not asked.

A modest dowry was assembled and the marriage arranged quickly. There was no betrothal ceremony. The guests at the wedding were subdued.

During the small reception, Spiros caught a moment to whisper to Vassilia, "Now you and I are family, eh?" He grinned and slid his fingers up her back and across her neck. She flinched, ducked out of his grasp, and moved away from him.

73

8

The two sisters built lives for themselves and their new families. Three years after their wedding, Sofia gave birth to a son. Manolis was an awkward child, unhappy and unlovely, though both couples made much of him—that is, until the arrival of Aleko, Panos and Vassilia's son, who was born when Manolis was nine years old.

Aleko was a beautiful child. He had his father's blue eyes, an intelligent and generous face, and a smile that melted the hearts of everyone who saw him. Manolis didn't like him.

On two occasions, Sofia took her son and left her marriage house, returning to her parents' home. Both times, her father brought her back to Spiros. Sofia's mood grew somber, she spoke less, but after the second return she did not attempt to leave again.

Spiros became more and more prosperous. He owned olive groves and vineyards and greenhouses for tomatoes. He owned water systems and gas stations. Sofia surrounded herself with the comforts of material possessions. She was rich.

Vassilia was rich, too. Her house was simple, her table meager, but her home was lit by pleasure. Her husband sang when he was happy, and he sang most of the time. Bouquets of wildflowers in glass jars brightened the room, daily gifts from her husband and son.

Panos loved his family, and he worked as hard as anyone who lived off that hard land. Things were going all right for him but there were times when money ran short. In the winter of 1992, the roof of their house leaked and there was no money to buy the materials to fix it. Panos stared gloomily at the buckets that caught the drips.

The next winter, a cold spell made them wear their coats inside the house because they ran low on fuel for the fire.

Mostly, though, when he knew that his family had enough to eat, he asked nothing more of life. As long as the chickens laid eggs, they had something for their table.

Everything went well for the next five years. The family thrived; there was enough work. 1997 brought a chain of disasters. Aleko caught a serious case of the measles. Vassilia suffered a miscarriage, and nearly died. Their illnesses ate their small savings.

Panos looked around for another source of income. Vassilia's mother talked to them one evening and said sternly that it was time that Panos should go work down the mountain in the packing plant. Give up herding sheep and goats. Get a job. Panos and Vassilia were angry at her for a few days. To work in a plant, for a man of Lefka Ori, was a defeat.

Help appeared from a surprising source. One day, Spiros came over to the small metal table at the kafenion where Panos was drinking a coffee with Tasos, the fix-it man. Tasos excused himself and moved across the room. Spiros and Panos exchanged pleasantries, cautious on Panos's side. Then Spiros sat down, ordered himself a kafe Elleniko, and said, "I see you struggling to get by. You need to get modern, Panos. You need a vehicle. You need a mikani."

Panos answered, "How could I afford one?"

Spiros said, "Maybe I can help you. I have one I don't use. With a mikani you can move your flock to farther fields. You can move loads for other people. You can get paid in cash. I will sell it to you at a good price, and you can pay me back slowly."

Panos said, "Thank you, Spiros, for the offer, but I can't accept it."

Spiros said, "Then you are a fool!" He leaned back in his chair and looked appraisingly at Panos, as if fixing this label well and truly.

The words stung Panos. He counted out the drachmas for both coffees and placed the bills on the counter. He left.

He walked up Lefka Ori for half an hour and found a rock to sit on. He thought about Spiros's offer. Was he a fool? Did he want to become indebted to Spiros? Would Vassilia forgive him if he did? What should he do?

Spiros had never done anything kind for them before. But the money was gone. His wife and son needed to eat lots of meat to recover their health, and meat was not easy to get. He hated to see hunger in the eyes of his beloved wife and son. He wanted to believe Spiros.

He did not ask Vassilia her opinion. First, because it was unmanly not to handle such problems alone. Second, because he knew what she would say. She would not choose to be indebted to Spiros for anything, ever.

He went home, silent. Vassilia was still very weak. Aleko was listless, recovering from his measles. The house was very quiet. Panos remembered the happy times, when his son had been well and the smells of chicken and garlic, cheeses and pastries had filled their home.

After dinner, he walked the two kilometers to Spiros's house. Sofia seemed surprised to see him. He asked her if he might see Spiros. She brought him in to their darkly elegant salon. He stood in the archway of the room. Light from between the drawn curtains played through crystals hanging from a lampshade. The room was very still. Sofia went to fetch Spiros.

"You want to see the truck? Come. I'll drive us."

Spiros ushered Panos out to his big, dark blue sedan car and drove to the large, fenced *kipos* where he kept his equipment.

He parked the car away from the tall grasses and any mud puddles that might soil it. The two men walked across to a mikani parked near a fence.

This small, three-wheeled truck had been designed for wartime. It and its brothers were still working all over the developing world. This one had a faded canvas awning over the driver's seat. The awning fabric was once printed with big red roses, but now they were almost invisible. The back was an open truckbed with wooden railings on the sides. The metal framework was tan, and the engine was exposed. Panos had seen such trucks passing on the roadways, carrying large boulders or whole flocks of sheep. A mikani was an admirable machine, he thought.

"I bought this. I don't use it. I could sell it to anyone. I thought it might help you. I will give a good interest rate on the loan to pay for it. You pay me every month. It will help you earn more than it costs by ten times! At least!" Spiros named figures for the loan and the monthly payments.

Panos calculated the payments' impact on his present income. But, if Spiros spoke true and his income would go up by ten times with the truck, he could pay for it easily.

They shook hands. Spiros said, "Do you drive?"

"No," said Panos.

Spiros said, "You can pay off the license examiner. I'll lend you the money. You don't need lessons. Any fool can drive one of these." He patted the three-wheeled truck.

The deal was struck. Panos walked around his possession and wondered how to start it. He left it at Spiros's kipos so Vassilia would not know. He didn't tell her anything about the purchase. It was the first time he had kept anything from her.

The next day, he bought a driver's license. Thanks to Spiros's friend, he didn't have to pass a test. He just paid for the license with cash he borrowed from Spiros.

He knew he had to drive the truck to make the money to pay for it and to provide for his loved ones. License in his pocket, he climbed into his truck and turned the key in the ignition. The truck wheezed, roared, lurched, and stopped.

Panos's heart pounded. He studied the controls—levers and pedals and wheels. He took the key out and walked homeward. He

77

detoured to the taverna and bought a tsikoudia. He sat in a corner and nursed it.

Old Tasos came over to him and invited himself to sit down. He said, "So you bought Spiros's old mikani."

Panos nodded.

"Need help?" he asked. "I could drive and you could load and unload and we'd both get rich, eh?"

"You know how?" asked Panos.

"Yeah, sure. I drove myself here all the way from Agyia Irini two years ago. Don't you remember?"

So Panos and Tasos went up to the kipos where the mikani was parked and Tasos started it up, and they drove to show Vassilia how they could get rich. Panos watched what Tasos did with all those levers. It seemed complicated.

When they arrived at the house, Vassilia did not smile. She watched as Tasos drove to the center of the yard, scattering chickens. He shut down the mikani with a grand flourish. Vassilia still did not smile. After she had walked all around the mikani, she went back into the house. Panos followed her inside, talking fast, trying to convince her of the wisdom of this purchase.

Tasos knew when it was time to disappear. He went off into the evening.

Panos suffered from Vassilia's silent disapproval of his mikani. He knew he had to prove the wisdom of his purchase, but even he wasn't so convinced of its wisdom any more. Little was said in the house that evening. Panos slept fitfully.

The next day, he walked over to Spiros's house again. Spiros came to the door, smiling.

"What's the matter, little brother?" he asked Panos.

Panos said, "I don't want this truck. I want to return it."

Spiros said, "No, no, no. I don't take it back. You bought it. You enjoy it."

"Please, take it back."

"We have an agreement, and we keep it. You owe me the money and the truck is yours." And he closed the door.

At the sound of the door closing, Sofia looked up at Spiros from where she sat on the velvet sofa in the salon. She said, "Who was that? And why are you smiling like that?"

Spiros didn't answer.

9

The mikani was killing Panos. It had caused the first rift between him and his wife. Four months had passed and he still couldn't drive it. He had to depend on Tasos's help, which meant that if he earned any money, he gave half to Tasos.

He'd had a few driving lessons, but by the time Tasos finished his fancy explanations about the clutch and the gears, it was clear to both of them he'd always need Tasos to drive the thing.

He barely earned enough to make the payments to Spiros. He worked harder and had less, thanks to the mikani. He didn't sing any more.

Vassilia said nothing about the mikani. Nothing. Her silence filled Panos's mind with more elaborate arguments against the truck than she could ever have spoken. He felt shamed.

One day in August, Tasos came by saying, "Great news! I heard of someone who needs to move a load of rocks and no one else will drive them for him. The job is ours!"

"Rocks?" Panos asked. "How big?"

Tasos said, "Rocks are rocks. Let's go see."

So Tasos drove and Panos sat next to him, watching him shift gears and move pedals.

The mikani coughed and sputtered its way up the Lefka Ori toward the south coast.

"Why won't anyone else do this job?" said Panos, as they drove slowly through the narrow street of a small village. They paused while a young man guided his flock of goats into a kipos. Then they drove on.

Tasos didn't answer at first. Then he said. "Don't know." Panos thought he did know. They climbed slowly, on paved roads up to the ridge and then, when they could see the Libyan Sea below them, they turned onto rutted dirt roads, and finally onto rough track. In the distance they could see a red car and a man with a camera on a tripod, looking down the mountain.

"What's that man doing there? Another archaeologist, I bet," said Tasos. Panos nodded, but he kept his eye on the dirt track. Even a mikani wasn't meant for this road. They dodged melon-sized rocks. Twice, Panos jumped out and moved rocks aside. The empty mikani labored up the next hill.

A man flagged them down just when they neared the top of the grade. They stopped and waited as he crossed over runnels and boulders to reach them.

He explained the job. He needed to drive his flock across a very deep gully every day. He wanted the gully filled with some large rocks so that his goats could cross.

Panos thought the rocks would probably wash out with the first big rain but a job was a job. They'd driven a long way, and he needed the money. He thought too many rocks at one time could destroy the mikani, and wondered if that was why no one else would do the job.

The scree was a hundred meters from the gully. The rocks the man wanted to use were large, up to half a meter in diameter. Impossible to pick up by hand. Tasos figured it out. There was an embankment below the rocks. There was a ditch in front of it, so they wouldn't back up all the way. They would back the mikani up to the edge of the ditch, make a ramp of some heavy wood they had in the mikani, and then lever the rocks onto the truckbed, drive them over to the gully, and push them off the truck. Easy.

81

They discussed how to back the mikani up to the rocks. Then Tasos started it up, and Panos stood behind it to direct him. The shepherd watched from the side.

Tasos had never actually backed the mikani before. He wasn't sure where reverse gear was. He tried one gear after another. He slipped the clutch. The mikani lurched forward a bit each time. Finally he found the reverse gear, but his foot slid off the clutch as his other foot pressed the gas pedal down.

The mikani jumped back, slipped into the ditch, picked up Panos, and pinned him against the embankment. Panos couldn't even scream. His lungs had no air. Everything stopped while he waited for Tasos to release him. Tasos, not knowing what he had done, shut off the engine and got out of the mikani.

The shepherd ran toward Panos, yelling as he ran.

When he heard the man scream, Tasos went to look at the back end of the mikani. He saw Panos pinned between the truck and the embankment. The mikani was over the edge into the side of the ditch. The front wheel was off the ground. Tasos ran back to the truck. He turned the key and lifted his foot off the clutch. The truck backed up just a bit more, and the rear wheels slid, spinning, down the side of the ditch, until Panos's body would give way no more. Tasos shifted the gears hurriedly but the mikani just spun its wheels. The shepherd pushed the mikani forward and at last Panos slumped to the ground. The mikani slid back into the ditch, covering him over.

The shepherd and Tasos pulled and pushed Panos's body out from under the mikani. They had to drag him in front of the rear axle and it was hard work because Panos didn't help them at all. He just lay there, letting them drag him along.

82

Tasos knew things were bad when Panos wasn't even mad at him. Panos's eyes were glazed. His face took on an odd lack of color. His breathing was fast and noisy. Tasos tried to pick him up, but Panos sagged, like a slaughtered sheep.

Tasos remembered the man they'd seen when they drove in. He yelled across the mountainside. The archaeologist looked up. Tasos waved his arms. From across the ridge, the archaeologist folded up his camera equipment, got into his car, and drove toward them. He had to double back to drive around a ravine, and then cross over another ridge before he could get to where they were. It took a long time.

While they waited, Tasos said to the shepherd, "You saw what happened. The truck got stuck. It wasn't my fault. You're my witness. It wasn't my fault. Was it?" Then he yelled at Panos, "Get up. Get up. Come on."

Panos didn't respond.

The archaeologist's car pulled up. The mikani wasn't going anywhere. It had merged with the ditch in one interlocked knot of steel and rock. The archaeologist was from Sweden and his Greek was limited, but somehow he communicated that he would drive Panos to hospital.

The three of them dragged him to his feet and somehow got him pushed into the archaeologist's car. Tasos slid into the front seat beside him, and dragged Panos's body onto his own lap to cushion it. The Swedish archaeologist started the car and they set off for Chania, as fast as they could go. The drive took nearly two hours, over the same twisting mountain roads they had crossed that morning.

Panos didn't speak. He moaned a few times. He seemed to drift in and out of consciousness. He frightened Tasos, who kept saying, "Hang on. Hang on, Panos. We'll be there soon."

The Swedish archaeologist didn't understand Tasos's directions to the hospital, and once in the city of Chania they had problems with left turns, right turns, traffic jams, and general comprehension. Tasos began yelling at cars and dogs that got in their way. Also yelling at the Swedish archaeologist. Panos just lay there, moaning intermittently.

Finally, they saw the hospital ahead.

They went to the clinic next to the big hospital entrance for visitors and doctors. Panos was pale, almost white. He was admitted, diagnosed with internal injuries (nature unknown), and strapped to a gurney, where, while he waited for x-rays, he died.

Tasos was standing next to the gurney with his hand on Panos's arm when Panos died.

He realized something had changed. He shook Panos. He leaned his head down to Panos's chest to listen for a heartbeat. Then he

83

howled. The nurses hurried over and moved the gurney with Panos's body into a curtained area away from public view.

The archaeologist drove Tasos to Panos's house to tell Vassilia and Aleko the news. Tasos rehearsed his story so it would make Panos a hero instead of sounding like Tasos himself was a novice driver who couldn't back up the mikani.

Vassilia and Aleko were gathering eggs. They both put them in a blue bowl she was holding. Vassilia looked up at the unfamiliar car coming in the yard with Tasos as a passenger. She guessed that something bad had happened. She put the bowl of eggs on the ground and rushed over to the car. Aleko stood beside the egg bowl, watching.

"Accident, right? I knew this would happen. Where is Panos?" she cried.

Tasos couldn't speak. His eyes filled with tears. He lowered his head.

In a very tiny voice, she asked, "Is he...dead?"

Tasos nodded.

A moan began from inside her. It grew into a wail. The sound seared Tasos's brain. Aleko ran over to her and threw his arms around her.

Vassilia and Aleko, embracing, sank to their knees in the dust, their howls mingling in a terrible sound.

The scene was even worse than Tasos imagined it might be. The keening was loud and long and very painful to hear, especially if one feels responsible for the person's death. Tasos just stood there, shut out of the process of grief.

Vassilia's howls gradually died down and she grew still. That was worse. Aleko was still weeping loudly. Vassilia looked fiercely at Tasos and said, "Where is he?"

"The hospital," he answered, meekly.

Vassilia released Aleko, got up and began the business of death.

84

10

In the night, Douglas woke. It took him a moment to recognize where he was. He could just make out vague dark shapes of the table and chairs and the windows in the boy's house.

He lay still and thought about what he had done.

His stomach kicked him. This was nuclear damage: He'd blown his career in retail. Yeah, and he had blown it with Denise. She'd forgiven him a lot of his goof-ups, but this one was beyond forgiving. He should feel sorry about it. He should feel bad for hurting her.

He didn't.

It surprised him, a little, not to feel any sadness about the end of his relationship with the only girlfriend he'd ever had.

He thought he should go back to St. Louis. It seemed like the logical thing to do, but then he realized he wouldn't know where to go if he *did* go back there. His clothes and books were all at the Hansons', in the servants' quarters above the garage, where he'd been living. Besides, his jobs and all his contacts were Hanson-connected.

His life had been intertwined with the Hansons, all right. Now he'd blown the whole package.

Why?

And why did it feel so good?

Douglas couldn't remember ever asking himself why anything. He'd always gone along with other people's plans—mostly, the Hansons' plans—and it had worked out well for him, until now.

Mr. Hanson was right. He had been late sometimes. But this time was different. The hole in the paving wasn't his fault. The truck broke its axle. He couldn't get back any faster, could he?

It wasn't fair. His whole future went up in smoke because of the Chania Highway Department's lack of barriers.

Well, he thought, he could have gone around it, onto the shoulder, but they should have marked it. It looked like a puddle.

Douglas felt a wave of hollowness. What would he do with his days? Even the routines of the summer digging schedule were gone. He lay in the dark, looking for some sign of his new life, some ritual, some task. He remembered, he could brush his teeth. No, he had no toothbrush.

Nothing needed him and he couldn't name his own needs, beyond food and sleep.

He made himself think about the Hansons. It was inconvenient for them that they'd come all this way and then there'd been no wedding. They could afford it, but still, he recognized that it wasn't nice for them.

Yeah, especially poor Denise. She'd be embarrassed back home. Douglas felt a chill of unease, but an idea brightened his self-image: If he was going to run away, she was just lucky he didn't run away from that big church wedding with all the friends present. She should be grateful.

No, she shouldn't.

Theoretically, he felt sorry for them. Mostly, his view of the Hansons—as he lay here in the dark—was of giant waves in a consuming ocean, seen safely from behind a thick glass window. They couldn't get him now.

He thought about that: they wanted him to be one of them, just like them. Well-dressed, socially smooth, able to step into the business and the social life, able to keep Denise looking good in St. Louis.

He'd tried to be what they wanted, but it was always a personality he put on from the outside. His real self was curled up in a tiny space somewhere else.

So now what? His mind searched the blank wall of the situation for a door, a latch, any way to move beyond this blank. He was still alive. There would be more to his life, but what it would be was a complete unknown.

His shoulder throbbed. The boy's bed was surprisingly comfortable, or maybe he was just so desperately tired that he could sleep anywhere. He lay still, listening to the sounds of the house.

The boy stirred in his sleep. Outside, a night bird sang. The leaves of the fig tree rustled. Beyond that, there was a huge comforting silence. No city noise. No sounds of man. No sixty-cycle hum.

These people didn't have electric service!

Douglas had never gone camping. He couldn't remember sleeping in a place without electricity. It felt good. Maybe he didn't need all the surrounding luxuries he'd been used to. He felt a glimmer of new thought.

He fell back to sleep.

11

There were relatives to tell, arrangements to make, but first, Vassilia had to get to the hospital and bring Panos's body home. The archaeologist drove her and Aleko over to Sofia and Spiros's house.

Only Aunt Sofia was home when they got there. She heard their news, hugged her sister and then her nephew, saying, "I am so sorry. I am so sorry."

Since Spiros had taken his blue sedan, the only vehicle remaining was his big truck. Sofia couldn't reach the floor pedals in it, but she had learned to slide down in the seat, depress the clutch, start the engine, set it in second gear, and move back into the seat. She rolled through stop signs. She used the handbrake to slow down. She couldn't drive very fast this way, and she couldn't back up, but she managed. Spiros said she was making problems where none existed, but if she slid down the seat to reach the pedals, she couldn't see over the dash board. Sometimes she just took the bus instead. Today she drove them in the truck.

Sofia had always envied Vassilia's life. She felt Vassilia had been blessed and she had not, first, because Vassilia hadn't had polio and didn't have a limp. Then because Vassilia's son was happy and beautiful, while her son carried the scars of his father's explosive rage. Manolis was a moody boy, not given to laughter. Third, Vassilia's marriage had been one of loving friendship, while hers was a bad business from its beginning. She tried to be generous in her spirit, but envy invaded her sleep.

Now the envy weakened and Sofia felt genuinely sorry for all of them. She wondered how they would live without Panos to support them.

At the hospital, people were kind. The priest who was chaplain in the hospital came to them and recited the *Trisayio* over Panos. Orderlies helped move his body into a coffin. They wheeled it out on a gurney and put it into the back of the truck for the ride home. They brought out rope and tied the coffin down in the truckbed, because the tailgate wouldn't close.

Sofia drove home very carefully. Aleko sat on his heels and faced backwards out the cab window, to make sure his father's coffin stayed in the truck. No one could see his tears that way.

Tasos brought two men from the lower village to help move the coffin indoors. Panos looked pale, but there was no blood on him. He was still beautiful, even with his blue eyes closed.

The men removed his body from the coffin, and laid it on the bed. Vassilia began the process of undressing, bathing, and preparing the body. Aleko watched her until he could bear it no longer, then he ran outside and returned with a cloth full of summer wildflower blossoms: tansy, summer daisies, and sweet-smelling honeysuckle, though the smell of the tansy was stronger. He scattered the flowers in the bottom of the coffin, a blessing for his dear father.

His mother dressed his father's body in his church clothes. Black shirt, stifania, and wide belt. She tore strips from a sheet and used one to bind his jaw shut. She crossed his hands across his chest, and bound them with another strip. A neighbor woman from the lower village brought a white shroud, with which Vassilia covered the lower half of Panos's body. On it, she placed their icon of the Blessed Virgin. She put a large white candle between Panos's hands. Then she kissed his mouth and turned away to hide her tears from him, in case he could still see her.

89

Other women from the village, even from the upper village, appeared, and took over the preparations for the funeral. Someone went up the mountain and notified Fr. Dimitrios. They knew that, because the bell of the church began to toll, slowly, as was fitting for grief.

They set about to make *kollyva* for the funeral guests. They cooked wheatberries in a tub of water, added sugar, sesame seeds, walnuts, raisins, parsley, basil, and cinnamon. They placed lace doilies on a large board and spread the kollyva out on it, mounding it slightly at the center. Then they dusted it with lots of sugar. They used pomegranate seeds and almonds to pick out the shape of a Greek Cross and the letters P and A. For Panos Andreadakis.

The men took the coffin lid outside and set it next to the front door, a sign that friends and neighbors were welcome to pay their respects to the dead man. The women covered the mirrors in the house with black cloth. They draped black cloth around the shrine where the wedding wreaths rested.

Vassilia and Sofia silently regarded the still beautiful form of Panos. They began to sing the same lament their grandmother sang when their grandfather died:

The tree is felled, as all trees must someday be.
It lies in sorrow beside us, broken, on the hard ground.

They wept. Friends came to say goodbye. They murmured, "God forgive him. *O Theos na ton sihorisi.*" They lit candles and set them on the floor near Panos's body. Some placed coins on his chest. They kissed his forehead and the icon on his legs.

Aleko gathered small bouquets of yellow henbane, blue forget-me-nots, and more honeysuckle from the fields nearby. He put them in jars to decorate the house. He covered the jars with black paper and tape. He made garlands of ivy, tied them with black crepe paper that someone had brought, and draped them everywhere he could.

When Fr. Dimitrios arrived at the house, the lamenting stopped and everyone stood up. The priest held a lit candle in one hand and a censer in the other. He said the Trisayio over Panos. Then the men promptly lifted Panos's body and set it back into the coffin.

The sun set and the neighbor women went to their homes to feed their families. Sofia reluctantly left to return to her own house. Spiros was home then and she told him the sad news about Panos's death. Spiros asked, incredulously, "The mikani killed him?" She explained the details to him a second time. He seemed fascinated by the idea that the truck was the instrument of Panos's death.

The funeral was held the next day, on August 4th, 1998, at three o'clock, at Agyios Yeorgeos, the same church as their wedding twenty years earlier. Fr. Theodoros, the priest who married them, came back to the village for the funeral. He had retired because of his diabetes and had moved to Chania. Sofia telephoned him to come.

Some of the villagers thought their new priest, Fr. Dimitrios, was an odd one, even though he came from the Papadakis family, people who had lived in Vraho for many centuries. His parents had emigrated to America. He grew up in San Francisco. He was part American now.

This Fr. Dimitrios Papadakis kept suggesting advanced ideas for things. Spiros, as proethros, and Sofia, as his wife, had opposed the choice of this young foreigner. In the end the elders of the village who remembered his grandfather had agreed to have him as their next priest. Still, change is hard, and they missed Fr. Theodoros and the old ways.

Sofia had to admit that, young or not, this Fr. Dimitrios knew how to honor the dead. Panos's funeral was formal, dignified, and very sad.

Panos was only thirty-seven years old.

The day was overcast. As the day wore on, the clouds lowered and darkened. Whenever Aleko asked to help with the preparations, his mother seemed distracted and his Aunt Sofia said he was underfoot and sent him outside. He threw pebbles at the stone wall.

The entire family—uncles, cousins, second cousins, distant cousins, godparents, friends—all assembled. Everyone wore black. Only Fr. Dimitrios wore white vestments. More villagers were at Panos's funeral than had attended his wedding to Vassilia.

They loaded the coffin into the back of Spiros's truck which was swagged with Aleko's ivy garlands and black crepe paper.

91

Vassilia took Aleko's hand. They went to their position behind the truck. The two of them began to walk, slowly, followed by the rest of the family and their friends from the village. Aleko felt scared. He thought his mother looked as if nothing on earth could reach her ever again.

Spiros drove the truck slowly to the church, followed by the mourners. The whole village shut down. Windows in houses were shuttered. All businesses were closed. The life of the community paused. The air grew damp. The women's pale faces contrasted with their black head scarves and garments. Finally, a light rain fell on the procession. Umbrellas came out.

At the funeral, Spiros was jovial among the mourners. He had a jumpy energy. He joked with the old drinkers from the taverna. They moved away from him. He followed them, slapped their backs, and told loud jokes. He began singing. Lambros came over to him and led him away.

12

Spiros woke up in an awfully good mood the day after Panos's funeral. For him, the day was full of promise. He hummed to himself as he dressed. He was going to re-claim his mikani, that obedient servant of his most secret wishes, the instrument of the death of his rival. It would be his again, as well as the money Panos had paid him for it. Good business, he thought. You can't cheat the dead.

He left the house early. He patted the winch on his truck as he walked around it. He drove over to the taverna, which wasn't open yet. He parked his truck and waited, at first patiently, then with growing agitation, until three minutes later, when Tasos showed up at the top of the path from Kato Vraho.

"Kalimera," said Tasos, in a high voice. It sounded like a question.

"Ya sas," answered Spiros, casually, as he backed the truck up onto the platia and turned around to head up-mountain. Spiros sensed Tasos's unease. The buffoon couldn't drive. Anyone knew that. Tasos could try to blame the mikani, but it wouldn't stick. Crushing someone with their own truck weighs heavy on one's conscience.

Tasos tried several times to make conversation, but Spiros barely answered him. They drove in silence then, until they came to the turnoff onto the first dirt road. From that point, Tasos gave him directions to the site of the accident. After the last turn, from way down the road they could see the mikani resting on its rear wheels and undercarriage, its nose pointing skyward, its lone front wheel useless in the air.

Spiros drove his truck so its nose was pointing toward the front of the mikani. Tasos dismounted, released the winch hook, and drew the cable out enough to reach the mikani. Spiros came around his truck to supervise.

A mikani doesn't have a heavy frame to hook a winch cable onto. In fact, there's not much of its frame that will support a winch hook. The two men studied the problem. They both walked all around the mikani. They tried pushing it from behind. It rocked back and forth but they couldn't push it out of the ditch.

Spiros said, "Run the cable through something on the frame and hook it to itself. But make sure it doesn't pull apart." Tasos studied the mikani and found a gap in the welded frame that supported engine and driver. He said a silent prayer as he threaded the cable through and hooked it to itself.

"Please look, Spiros. I want you to check it. If it pulls apart, it's not my fault," he said. "I want you to check it."

"Yeah, yeah, not your fault." Spiros looked at him. "What is your fault, Taso the fix-it man?"

Tasos did not look up at what Spiros said. His face reddened.

"You know what the village calls you? Taso Mastrohalastis. Taso Master fix-it-wreck-it. Let's hope you've got it right this time, Taso Mastrohalastis."

94

Spiros got back in his truck and pulled the winch cable tight. Tasos held his breath. He thought the mikani was going to pull apart, but then, slowly, the back wheels lifted, rolled up the bank of the ditch, the front wheel came back to earth, and the whole vehicle rolled free.

It coasted toward Spiros's truck, gaining speed as it went.

"Stop it!" yelled Spiros.

Tasos ran to the mikani and grabbed hold of it. It dragged him for a few steps, then stopped before it hit the truck. Spiros used a nearby rock for a chock. Tasos unhooked the cable.

"Start it up, Taso. You have the key?"

Tasos patted his pockets, then looked inside the truck. He looked apologetically at Spiros, then got into the mikani and turned the key which had been left in the ignition for the two days since the accident.

"You forgot to take the key? You are lucky it wasn't stolen, Taso."

Tasos's jaw rippled with the effort of clenching his teeth. He drove the mikani down the mountain with Spiros following him in the truck. When he turned in to the road to Ano Vraho, Spiros shouted, "No, I changed my mind. We take it to Vassilia's house."

Tasos drove on into town to the platia to turn around. Spiros followed him and said, "What's the problem? Afraid of reverse?" He snorted a laugh.

Tasos said nothing. He drove the mikani slowly and cautiously down the mountain to Vassilia's house. Spiros followed him.

When they approached Vassilia's sagging gate, Tasos got out to open it. Spiros leaned on his horn. Aleko appeared. Spiros indicated the gate with his head. Aleko and Tasos opened it together. Tasos drove the mikani in, Spiros followed with his truck, and Aleko shut the gate.

"Kalimera, Uncle Spiros."

"Where's your mother?"

"She's inside. She's resting." He paused and looked at his uncle. "Shall I get her?"

"Get her."

Aleko went into the house and returned. "She's coming."

"I'll wait."

A moment later Vassilia appeared in the doorway. Spiros thought she looked different than before the accident. He tried to name how she had changed. She looked transparent, now. Fragile. Weak, even. The change in her didn't dampen his ardor. He still found her beauty intoxicating. He allowed his eyes to travel over her face and body, and

95

told himself that now he had the way to make her his. The indebted widow.

"Kalimera, Spiros," she said, without meeting his eyes. He hated when she did that—when she looked anywhere but into his eyes. She did that often.

"Lovely sister, I have brought back your mikani."

"I don't want it here. I don't want it." She looked at him, pleadingly. "Please sell it for me, Spiros."

"No, no, I can't do that. It's yours. Maybe you can learn to drive it. Or rent it out. You'll think of something. And by the way, you still owe money on it."

Her look of disbelief changed to stoicism. "How much do I owe?"

He named a figure, about the cost of one goat, on the fifteenth of each month for twenty-one months. He walked around her house and counted her goats. He came back, standing near her, speaking softly so Aleko and Tasos couldn't hear him. "Only seventeen goats. Well, I'll tell you how you can pay for the mikani each month after the goats are all gone."

She called Aleko to her, put her arm around her son's shoulders, turned on her heel and went into the house. She shut the door and slid the bolt.

13

After the wedding party had disintegrated, Roland Ducor went back to his grand office in the George Hanson Institute for Minoan Archaeology. He had a sure sense that trouble was about to hit him. That George Hanson was one tough businessman and sooner or later he knew Hanson would get him. He hoped it wasn't now.

He knelt down to unlock the ground-level deadbolt on the large glass double doors. Beyond them was his elegant foyer. His assistant's office was the glass-enclosed rectangle to his right. His own office was through the grand carved doors that were once on the outside of the building. The doors were magnificent.

He loved his office. It was grand. It was historic. It was impressive. It was big.

It was also a mistake. He'd taken the entire ground floor of a Venetian palace on the crown of Kastelli Hill overlooking the arsenali and the inner harbor of Old Chania. He had momentarily succumbed to greed when the real estate agent showed him these offices. He wanted to show his former classmates and faculty at Louvain that when Roland Ducor bounces back from ignominy, he does so in an elegant set of offices. The best offices in Chania. It was a way of thumbing his nose at his own failed past.

For seventeen long years after he graduated from the Universite Catholique de Louvain in 1975, he taught at a private boys' school in his home-town of Tournai, near Brussels. He lived with his parents and saved every franc to raise the money to continue his studies toward a doctorate in Minoan archaeology. At forty-one years of age, he returned to Louvain and began working for his degree.

He should have had his Ph.D. by now except that his thesis was controversial. No one on the faculty had faith in his theory that the undiscovered great Minoan palace of Western Crete (if indeed there was an undiscovered palace in the west) lay on the Rhodopou Peninsula.

A number of scholars had suggested that there must have been a palace at the west end of Crete. Some Minoan ruins were uncovered in downtown Chania (Roland could see them from the Institute doorway, in fact), but they were obviously part of the Minoan town of Kydonia—not a palace. A Swedish and Greek team still worked there. And in the far west of Crete, there were Minoan ruins at Falasarna, but that was a small settlement near a port.

Ducor's theory was based loosely on references to theories proposed by scholars as major as Spyridon Marinatos, but he had taken it further than they had. He had named a site on the Rhodopou peninsula as the location of his palace. The site was not far from the Neolithic cave-site mentioned by J.D.S. Pendlebury: Ellenospilo, north of Moni Gonia and beyond Afrata, on Cape Spadha. He pictured in his mind the palace standing secure on a flat hilltop overlooking the cape. Never mind that the other palaces were back farther from the coast. He was convinced.

Many times, he took the bus out to Kolimbari and walked over the land. He studied its geology. Once he met a shepherd running goats over it. The man thought it very odd that he was walking around this hard, rocky scrub. He gave Ducor the name of the owner of the land.

Ducor made an appointment and went to visit him, asking permission to sink a sample core. He promised he would refill it, would do no damage to the land. The owner refused. What's more, his faculty declined to help him acquire the rights.

He worked on his theory of the Rhodopou palace site for four brutal years. Tenacious to a fault, as his mother always said, he had stuck by his theory through a bungled defense of an unsupported dissertation. He had been denied his degree. He left Louvain with no certificate for his wall, no letters behind his name—nothing.

He returned to Tournai, an overeducated failure. All he could see ahead was a long life of teaching Latin to spotty boys. He slept a great part of each day.

His mother worried about him. It was a month before he confessed to her the details of his defeat. Undaunted, she talked to her sister, who talked to her children, until someone came up with a way to save poor Roland.

The sister had a son, Roland's first cousin, who was a wheeler-dealer. Roland had never trusted or liked him, even when they were children. Pierre Dalmour once stole six of the handmade petits-fours Roland's mother had made for a friend's wedding. He ate them and then put the pleated paper they had rested on in Roland's bedroom for his mother to find. Pierre was quick and not held back by scruples.

Now this man, Pierre, was to be the instrument of his salvation.

Pierre Dalmour had gone to America and taken the exams for a license to sell real estate. He said it was really a license to steal. He'd made a lot of money in the four years he'd been doing that, the same years Roland had been pursuing his Minoan dream on Crete. Pierre was rich, with contacts, with favors to call in.

Pierre spoke to someone named Les Hanson, Dean of Laronwood University outside of St. Louis and his *sub rosa* business partner on a land development scheme close to the as-yet-unannounced new location for the college. It was a murky business the two of them were into, but it was going to make both of them really rich.

Les Hanson had ambitions for his little school. When Pierre suggested that his cousin, a European professor, was available to teach archaeology and anthropology and wouldn't mind also teaching sociology and perhaps statistics as well, and no, he didn't exactly have a Ph.D., in Europe they have other degrees, you know, but he's really bright and quite a catch and I think I can pull it off for you, Les

Hanson said, "Why, thank you. That sounds good. I'd like a European on our faculty. Laronwood: World-Class University, eh?"

So Roland Ducor arrived at Laronwood University in 1994, and began the journey that led him to this uneasy glory in Crete.

The George Hanson Institute would fund his attempt to prove that he was right about the palace on Rhodopou. It wasn't exactly a gift from George Hanson, brother to Les Hanson, his dean. It was more in the nature of a bribe.

His first classes at Laronwood were lecture classes. Art History 101, from prehistory to the Renaissance in twelve weeks, and two sections of Intro to Anthropology. He assigned topics and spent long hours reading the student papers that resulted. Of these, one stood out. A freshman named Douglas Watkins added finely detailed drawings of a Mayan fragment. While it was true he'd drawn them from a photograph in a catalog in the library, the drawing was detailed and clear. Ducor called Douglas in for a conference, told him his drawing was excellent, and asked if he'd be interested in illustrating some academic articles for him. The young man seemed pleased to be asked but declined, saying he was a business major and he supposed he'd better put most of his effort into that.

Nonetheless, over the next four years, Douglas and his girlfriend, Denise Hanson, niece of the dean, took nearly every class that Ducor taught. Douglas always earned an A, and the girl always scraped by with a B- or a C. You'd think she'd try harder just to uphold her uncle's name.

Funny, he thought, how their hunger to learn could be so opposite (she seemed to have none) and they be so apparently devoted to each other. But since his own experience with women was very limited, he dismissed it as the way things were.

100   Laronwood University required each graduating student to have a baccalaureate advisor, and to write a large research paper for that advisor. Ducor was pleased when, in their senior year, both Douglas and Denise chose him for their advisor. He assigned them topics, met with them during the spring semester, and waited to receive their papers. Douglas's paper came in on time and was as fine as Ducor expected. Denise's early drafts had been missing, or sketchy.

He waited for her finished paper. On the final day, it arrived, neatly typed and in a new cover. Ducor was surprised. Her previous papers had been sloppier than this. He opened it and an uneasiness came over him. He recognized pages, not just phrases or even sentences, but pages, taken directly from books he had lived with in school. He looked further. There were no typos, also unusual for Denise. The grammar was good. The paper was too perfect. He went to the library and took down the books he recognized. He found large chunks of text that had been lifted word for word.

Ducor knew when he saw the plagiarized paper that he had a big problem on his hands. Denise was, after all, the child of Dean Hanson's brother. Ducor's ethics were pitted against his very employment. On first thought, it seemed that if he lost this first teaching job because he stood up for WHAT WAS RIGHT, that was all right. Leaving over a principled issue would probably even look good on his CV. Virtue was the most important thing, without which life is a meaningless exercise. He really believed that.

He called Denise into his office. He explained the concept of plagiarism to her, slowly, yet she looked at him uncomprehendingly. Then he showed her sections of text in two books and the identical sections in her paper. She looked at him with fierce eyes and said, "That's not my fault. I paid good money. They didn't say they'd stolen it from somewhere else."

"You bought this paper?"

"Yes. What of it?"

"You've just failed your baccalaureate thesis."

"What! Why? Because the website sold me a lemon? Come on, Professor. Everybody buys papers on-line these days."

"Then everybody deserves to fail their baccalaureate thesis."

Her face registered not so much as a flicker. What is called in the films a cool blonde, Ducor thought. She just looked back at him. Then she said, "You'll be sorry," and she left, like a cool cucumber, like Veronica Lake, like a beautiful criminal in a Sam Spade movie, sliding out the door, leaving Ducor with the decided feeling that perhaps he *would* be sorry. He was amazed. No tears. Just that threat.

He sat back and waited for the next stage of the drama, whatever it would be. He felt nervous, almost excited, waiting for the coming battle.

First came a phone call from her father. George Hanson was a big power in St. Louis. He had some sort of clothing business.

Hanson reached Ducor in his little academic cubicle, the walls lined with his books and dog-eared posters of Greek treasures from the National Archaeological Museum in Athens.

Hanson pere harrumphed a bit and said, "Can't we do something about this?"

Ducor held to his principles. He felt dangerously superior to this prosperous businessman. "No, I'm afraid we can't. Only your daughter could have avoided this problem by doing her own work. Now it is too late. The deadline is past and she is stuck with the consequences. I'm sorry. There's nothing to discuss."

Ducor experienced the transient but seductive power of the barely powerful over the extremely powerful. Only even then he knew, it wouldn't last.

After he hung up, Ducor stared around at his office. He felt less safe there. A chill seemed to have dropped over him. The light was cooler. Something had changed. He opened his thermos and poured himself a cup of lukewarm milky coffee from this morning, masquerading as cafe au lait. He stared at the telephone. It sat there, silent, for nine full minutes according to the wall clock.

Her uncle, what would he do? Lester Hanson, the academic dean who hired him, was a former coach somehow promoted through the ranks. He was a fund-raiser person who told many jokes, mostly not funny ones. Ducor held the secret theory that Les Hanson could not spell his own name without help. But he was grateful for the job. Teaching jobs, even in the States, for failed Ph.D. candidates were not easily come by.

Dean Hanson phoned next. "See here, Professor, I know this is awkward, and publicly I have to support your position, (I hope this never gets public, of course. It won't, will it?) but my brother is my biggest fund-raiser. It's his daughter we're talking about here. Why don't we just write a letter noting the occurrence and put it in her file. That way, if it happens again, she'll be punished. How would that be?"

"That's not going to work, Dean Hanson. She would have to hurry to get in trouble again. She is scheduled to graduate in a few weeks."

"Oh, that's right. Yes, of course. Well. It's all very awkward for me, don't you see? Can't we find some wiggle room here?"

"Wiggle room? I'm sorry. I do not know that word." Ducor pulled himself up as tall as possible, looked sternly at the telephone receiver, and held on tight to his claim of ignorance of an unethical English word. A smile tugged at the corner of his lips but he controlled it so it wouldn't show in his voice.

"Does the college not have a guidelines for ethics? Did you not give me a red book with rules of academic ethics when you hired me? I believe I have it here. Yes." He looked across his cubicle at the red notebook of ethics which sat, untouched, where it had landed when he first arrived four years ago.

He listened to a long pause on the other end of the phone, then a murmured retreat. Ducor congratulated himself on his position. He had stood by his ethics. He had refused to compromise with his employer. For that principled moment, he left himself open to the devil's handiwork.

These phone calls came in quick succession, because grades were due in three days and the computers would lock in the grades. Without the thesis scored, and kindly scored, too, Denise would not graduate with her class. For this slim moment, Ducor held all the cards.

At dinnertime, he had a phone call from Pierre, who sounded very excited. "You will be so pleased with me, cousin, that you will look for ways to thank me forever."

"What do you mean?" said Ducor.

"You will see. And you can thank me oh so very much! You will see how loyal I am to you," and Pierre Dalmour hung up the telephone.

For several hours, nothing happened. Ducor washed his dishes and then tried to finish reading a journal article about antipositivistic approaches on method in archaeology, but his eye kept drifting over to the mute telephone.

A second call came from George Hanson late that evening. This time, he sounded stern. He said, "Meet me at my club."

"Which club is that, may I ask?" said Ducor.

"Pebble Beach Golf and Tennis Club, near the college," answered Hanson.

"I'm sorry? Pebble Beach? Is not that in California?"

"No. It's...I mean, there's one here. It's on Blackhawk Road."

"But I am not a member of such a club."

"You don't have to be a member...never mind." Hanson named a coffee shop on the other side of Grangeville, a suburb well outside the city. "Meet me at ten o'clock tomorrow morning."

George Hanson was standing next to his SUV in the parking lot when Ducor drove up. No trouble recognizing him. He looked just like his brother, but with a grim expression. He was a big man and Ducor had to look up to meet his eye.

They went into the coffee shop, past a number of empty booths separated by partitions of pressed plastic in translucent tones of amber and orange. They slid into the orange naugahyde benches of a booth in the corner and ordered coffee. Two coffees. Cream. No sugar.

While they waited for the waitress to bring their coffees, Hanson looked at him curiously. "What do you want?" he asked.

"Me? I want only to do my job, to instruct young people in my area of expertise, anthropology and archaeology, and teach them to write and to think."

The coffee came. It was the worst he'd ever tasted in America. It must have been boiled for a week. These people, they have no taste, he thought. His eyes wandered across the wood-grained plastic of the table top.

104

"My daughter has learned her lesson, Professor. She will never buy a term-paper again. She will write her own. Now," he said plaintively, "can you please call off your high-minded dogs?"

"How can I do that? I don't see an original paper from her yet. And if I had one, it would be late so it would lower her grade to F anyway. What has she learned, that I should see?"

Hanson shifted gears. He leaned forward and smiled at Ducor. "What do you want most in life?"

"Nothing. I am perfectly content with my life." He again felt the dangerous rush of power over the powerful.

"Now, Dr.—, No, it's Mr., isn't it? Mr. Ducor, I know that's not true. I've heard you have unfinished research and that if you had funding you'd go to it in a flash." He leaned back, away from the table, and waited for Ducor's answer.

Ducor sat perfectly still. Ah, Pierre!

Hanson continued, "Your field is Greece, no, Crete, isn't it? Those early people? What are they called?...Minoans, right? How would you like to head up a small, adequately funded expedition to do this research?"

"I am shocked!" said Ducor. He sat bolt upright on his naugahyde banquette. "I cannot be bought by such an offer." A vision of the rocky Rhodopou peninsula rose in his mind, but he sent it packing. These were principles, here.

Hanson seemed impressed by his virtuous response. He leaned in again. He spoke intensely and eye to eye with the small Belgian archaeologist, "You are a tough bargainer, Professor." There was surprise in his voice. Even, Ducor thought, respect. Hanson bent closer yet, glancing around to see that no one was nearby. "Listen, I will offer you the directorship of an institute of archaeology in Crete for a term of three years," He looked at Ducor's eyes, which were glazing over, "...renewable for another five, funded by The Safari Collection, to be called..." he leaned back and smiled, "the George Hanson Institute of Minoan Archaeology."

Ducor's eyes cleared at the sound of that. Nonetheless, the hook was set. Even the Hanson name in the title could not dull the attractiveness of an institute of archaeology with himself as director. The image of such an institute dawned before him.

105

This is maybe a nice guy after all, he thought. This institute, it could be going to be a good thing. I'll prove I was right about the missing Minoan palace in Western Crete—there must have been a palace on that end of the island—and then I'll be at the top of my field. The next Marinatos! Supernova of archaeology! I could teach anywhere. Anywhere! I could write! Travel! Retire to Crete.

Ducor looked over at George Hanson and said, quietly, "When would this be?" Both men pushed their cups and napkins aside and got their elbows on the table, the better to talk.

Denise got a B on her thesis and graduated with her class, full of smiles. Ducor was named founding director of the George Hanson Institute of Minoan Archaeology. Fate smiled on him. One of the three American permits to dig in Greece that year came to him when the director of another site was seriously injured in a car crash.

It was the redline of his life. Success, or at least an institute to give him the chance of success, brought him no joy. His self-respect became hollow, a pretense, like those repoussé Vaphio golden cups beaten too thin, that look like they would crumble in your hands if you picked them up. He grew brittle, arrogant, mildly dictatorial to his staff. He felt George Hanson's shadow over him always. His cousin Pierre didn't need to say anything to remind him of the gratitude owed him. Ducor spent more than he could afford on Swiss watches and alpaca golf sweaters to Pierre for Christmas.

Ducor loved his institute, but even now the thought of it gave him pleasure tainted with an uncomfortable feeling across his body. He sat in his empty office and looked around at the splendor of the space and knew he was in trouble. Douglas's surprising actions were going to come back to him. He knew it.

He heard a key in the outer door and pulled himself together. He straightened his bow tie, ran his hand across his short hair, prepared for someone. Athina, his assistant, poked her head in his door.

"I thought...I wanted to see how your asthma is now. Are you better?"

"Oh, yes. Yes. I'm fine now. Thanks."

"What were you doing? There's no work to do right now, is there?"

"No. I was just thinking. That's all. But thank you for asking about me."

"Very well. I'll be going then," she said, but paused as if waiting for him to say something. Then she left.

Ducor reached in his drawer for his keys and prepared to lock up and go home. It had been a long day. The heat had broken and the sun was disappearing behind the western end of Lefka Ori. As he ambled through the streets of Old Chania, he felt great love for the place; for its old and new sections, for its worn areas still in use, for the gypsy children tossing small stones into finger-traced figures in the soft dirt, for the lumpy widow in faded black who stopped sweeping to smile at him. He loved these people. He loved this place. He grieved in advance for the loss he felt was coming.

14

Next morning, Douglas woke up stiffer than he imagined a body could be. He could feel pain on his face, bunching his eyebrows. He took in a deep breath and blew it out, willing the pain to lift. He pushed back the curtain and looked out into the room.

Vassilia and Aleko were already up and dressed. They smiled at him and gestured to the table where a small bowl of yogurt with a puddle of honey in the center waited for him. Douglas had a fleeting vision of a plate mounded high with bacon and eggs, but he replaced the vision with thanks for what he had been given and he climbed down the ladder and sat down at the table. He tasted the yogurt. Smooth, and the honey smelled of thyme. Vassilia made a tiny cup of kafe Elleniko for him. Aleko came over and peered into his face to see how he was.

"You come goat today?" asked Aleko.

Douglas winced as he turned toward Aleko. "I think so," he said. "Let me move first." And he stretched.

Aleko said, "O.-K.!" and looked relieved.

He drank the coffee much too quickly and ended up with a mouthful of silt from the bottom of the cup.

When he stood up from the table, Aleko danced around him.

"We take goat!" he chirped.

Douglas reassured him, "We'll both go."

Vassilia asked Douglas to show her his wounds, which she dressed with another layer of salve. Then she, Douglas, and Aleko went to the yard. Vassilia counted the goats and chose one. She went over to it and quickly wrapped a piece of heavy twine around its horns. She handed the other end to Aleko. The goat complained loudly as Aleko pulled and Vassilia and Douglas pushed it out the gate.

The trip to the butcher was much like the previous one. Douglas picked up a fallen branch of dried leaves and rattled it behind the goat who trotted obediently beside Aleko. They made good time and the goat was delivered and paid for before noon.

From the butcher's they headed toward the Sunshine Beach Taverna, where Vassilia would be waiting for them. She would keep the money safe until it could be paid to Spiros. The two tried to look nonchalant, but their eyes scanned their surroundings watching for a repeat encounter with the robber.

As they neared the city, Aleko reached in his pocket and brought out the dagger his mother had used to remove the pellets. He held it out to Douglas, who didn't recognize it at first in its leather sheath with the three amulets at the tip.

"*Parakalo.* Please. You take."

Douglas stared at the dagger. "Where did you get this?"

Aleko tried to put it into Douglas's hand. Douglas drew back.

"Whose knife is this?"

"Father knife."

Douglas looked at the elegant and savage object. Aleko pleaded, "Not use. Just have. Safe with you. O.-K.?"

Douglas gave in, nodded and said. "Not use. Just have. Okay." He put the dagger through his belt and smiled at Aleko. Poor scared kid, he thought. They resumed their walk.

The pressure of the dagger against his shirt made him nervous, though. It was safer with him than with Aleko, but not much safer.

109

He wished for an uneventful trip to Vassilia's taverna. He looked around. Nea Hora was near where he had lived, but he'd never turned west when he reached the seawall. Never seen any of this.

Now they came onto the smell of the sea. Aleko turned down an alley shortcut. A gap between two buildings showed a glimpse of blue. They both looked at it. At that moment a figure in black jumped out at them and yelled. Aleko screamed and fell back.

A wall of red fury rose and filled Douglas. Outrage at the pain and injustice of the last robbery drove his hand, which reached for the dagger, unsheathed it and resheathed it into the body of the robber. The knife slid between two ribs, its hilt hit the body's surface, and it stopped. The fury receded and Douglas realized he had just stabbed someone, and had meant to. The red was replaced by a hollowing-out sensation. All his strength fled. He let go of the dagger and the black-clad body pitched forward slowly onto the ground.

It was peculiar how the dagger grew out of the black shirt. The robber coughed. Bright red blood with air bubbles in it rose through the ski-mask and spread out on the paving. Douglas looked at Aleko. The little boy seemed as stunned as he.

Then Aleko pushed him several feet down the street, yelling, "Go. Go. Go…to my home!" He pointed toward the Lefka Ori. Douglas turned and ran, leaving Aleko to return to the bleeding robber. At the corner, he turned back to look at the little boy.

"You okay?" he asked.

"O.-K.!" answered Aleko and nodded. "Go."

15

When Fr. Dimitrios first arrived at Vrahos three years ago, he set out to win the trust of his parishioners, especially the skeptical ones who remembered him as a small boy. He's still working on that.

His second task was to fulfill his grandfather's request—to find the chest whose key hung next to his baptismal cross, to learn the dark secret, and to seek forgiveness for Papou's deed, whatever it was.

He'd been in Vraho less than a month. He had just written a particularly difficult sermon, bringing the touchy lessons of forgiveness into the context of the villagers, without naming names, hoping to calm some flared tempers over an issue of water rights.

Water determines the placement of a village. Ano Vraho was a spring-line village, built along a rock fracture where a series of springs surfaced. Kato Vraho, the lower village, was less desirable. Water had to be carried from some distance to reach it, part of the way by irrigation ditches and the rest by bucket. Sometimes people were careless or greedy about their time allotment on the irrigation system. It caused fights. Resentments over water could last for generations.

It was evening time. He had worked hard, thinking and then writing the sermon, so he took a break and went over to the taverna for a kafe Elleniko.

The public buildings of the village—the church, the mini-market, and the taverna—were all in Ano Vraho, the upper village. They clustered around the platia, with its enormous plane tree in the center. At the front of the platia, the public water fountain dripped. The ground around it was always muddy. The church bordered the platia on the east side. The taverna was across the road, to the west, hanging over the edge of the plateau the village stood on. The unpaved road, impassable after storms, wound down the mountain to paved Therisso, where the bus route began, where the tourists stopped. Just a few backpackers ever came to Vraho.

As Fr. Dimitrios crossed the platia and approached the taverna, he could hear someone singing a plaintive mantinada,

I suffer alone for love, while even birds with their lovers fly.
She has fluttered off with my heart, leaving me here to die.

The singer was weaving where he stood. As he finished his mantinada, he tossed back a glass of tsikoudia. The other men there laughed and applauded. Shot glasses of tsikoudia stood all over the half-dozen outside tables. Some were empty and some soon would be. Periodically, Lambros, the taverna owner, appeared with a new bottle.

From the shadows near the building another voice sang,

Vaggelis thinks no one else felt pain before now.
Women are hard to please, but some of us know how!

112

"Tell us about it, Stephanos! You have such luck with the ladies!" and they all laughed. From the dark, a lauto and a lyra came out, and the mantinades, with accompaniment, were set to be sung for a long evening. Laughter greeted each new verse. The songs compared the merits of women of Vraho and Peristeri. Vraho, off the highway, had pure, virtuous, and beautiful women. Peristeri women were beautiful, too, but everyone said their virtue was tainted by all the tourists who stopped there.

The heartsick Vaggelis forgot his misery in the camaraderie.

Lambros's taverna had been around for a long time. It was a big white landmark on the mountain. Even in World War II, it had been a taverna. Some stray German bullets had gouged holes out of its concrete exterior and shattered the windows. The building was repaired after the war, and repaired again in 1988, but since then it had been left to decline into comfortable decay.

The taverna didn't get whitewashed this Lent, or last Lent either. It was grey. Black streaks ran down the walls from the rain. Two red geraniums in clay pots by the door bravely tried to bloom, with no help from Lambros. They were a gesture from his wife, and even she didn't invest much hope in their success.

As Fr. Dimitrios approached, the singing died out and a dozen pairs of eyes watched him come up to the taverna. He smiled in greeting. He knew their names and he said "kalispera!" to each of them. They murmured acknowledgment.

Is their silence because of me or the cassock? he wondered. And if it is me, how long will it take before they discover that I love this village and all that is in it; that it is my home and my chosen destiny? He smiled to himself and went inside. After the door had closed behind him, the singing began again, cautiously at first and then again into oblivious merriment.

In the corner, near a lamp, two men concentrated on a game of *tavli*. The young priest nodded to them. Aside from the tavli-players and a very old man sitting by himself in the corner eating a meal of roast chicken and potatoes, the inside of the taverna was deserted. Lambros himself stood behind the counter, wiping it down. Fr. Dimitrios thought that counter must be the cleanest place on Crete. Lambros was always wiping it down.

Lambros smiled at Fr. Dimitrios.

"Don't take it to heart, *Patera*. You are something new to them. Can I buy you a tsikoudia?"

Fr. Dimitrios said, "I still have work to do. I'll settle for a kafe Elleniko and accept your tsikoudia at a later time, if I may."

"The usual, metrio?"

113

"Please." And Fr. Dimitrios sat on a stool near the counter to watch Lambros prepare his kafe Elleniko metrio. Fr. Dimitrios could make his own kafe Elleniko at home, but he liked to drop by at least twice a week to see Lambros, whom he judged to be a good and trustworthy man. Kyria Ariadne agreed with his judgment. She was not easily convinced about people, so her approval of Lambros was significant.

He watched Lambros assemble his coffee. Into the *briki* he put one measure of sugar, grounds, and water. He brought it to a boil three times, and poured it into the small cup.

They heard mantinades through the window. More lovelorn verse and general kidding, sung in the old way, in rhyming couplets. Lambros delivered the small cup with a flourish. The coffee steamed up, its fragrance so pleasant, the anticipation of the taste even more pleasant. Fr. Dimitrios smiled, and said, "Lambros, I've had an idea."

Lambros laughed, "One month here! You have more ideas than anyone I've ever seen. And all of them chicken-brained. What is it this time? A clinic for broken-hearted mantinada-singers?"

"You know that empty building across the parking lot from here? Let's make it a tourist museum about World War II. Put up photos of the pallikaria from Vraho! The tourists will come and eat at the taverna. It'll bring business to the village."

Lambros looked at him. "No. Just no. Trust me: this one is a very bad idea."

The old man sitting near the open window called out, "He speaks true! The village will not love you for baring its secrets."

Fr. Dimitrios turned to look at the figure by the window. Old Nikos wore a worn and stained beret, once dark red, now showing only small bits of red among layers of dust and sweat. He wore a tweed jacket over a sweater vest and a once-white shirt, and he leaned forward and squinted at the young priest.

"Why? What are you telling me?"

"Please. Sit down."

Fr. Dimitrios slid into the opposite chair and said, "I don't think we've met. I'm Father Dimitrios." They shook hands.

"You look like him, too. Your grandfather, the other Fr. Dimitrios, I mean. But you are more in face like his brother."

"Pardon me? My grandfather had no brother. What do you mean?"

The old man laughed and addressed Lambros. "Did you ever hear about Old Fr. Dimitrios's brother?"

Lambros glared at him and said, "Watch out, Nikos."

Young Dimitrios said, "I never heard about a brother."

"He died in the war. I should know. I went to school with him. Philipos. He was the proethros, village president. A rising power in our village. A real comet."

"Are you sure he was the brother of my grandfather, Fr. Dimitrios, the priest before Fr. Theodoros?"

"Yes, yes, yes. I know who you are. I know all about you." The old man drained his tsikoudia glass.

Fr. Dimitrios said, "Lambros, please pour Nikos another glass."

"Ah, yes—to loosen my tongue. You are Cretan, after all. You know about *kerasma*."

"My pleasure. I am happy to buy your drink, Nikos."

Lambros did not look happy as he came over with the bottle but he refilled the old man's glass. Fr. Dimitrios took a billfold out of his cassock pocket and paid for the drink. Lambros said, "Old Nikos, your fee has been paid. Now you owe this man some good stories." He paused. "Just make sure they're the truth!" He returned to the bar.

"Does your grandfather still live?" Old Nikos asked.

"He died in 1990."

"He was a good man. I always thought him honest. Do you miss him?"

"Yes, I do. Did you know him well?"

Old Nikos laughed. "We were best friends. We grew up together. He was two years behind me. I was born in 1913, the very year Crete joined Greece. He was born in 1915. His brother, Philipos, was a year older than I was. Born 1912 that would be."

"What happened to the brother?" Fr. Dimitrios moved his chair closer to the table. The chair squeaked, its glue loosened from dozens of taverna disagreements.

115

"I told you, he died in the war."

"Was he a hero?"

Old Nikos laughed. "Surely not. You did not hear about him because Philipos was a Nazi collaborator."

The room fell silent. Fr. Dimitrios was aware that the tavli players were now listening to what Old Nikos had to say. He was also aware that his ears were ringing as if he'd sustained a blow to the head.

"How do you know that he was a..." Fr. Dimitrios choked on the words, "...Nazi collaborator?"

"Because," said Old Nikos, proud of his memory. "Because after he was killed, the Germans killed three men in Peristeri—in retaliation. You see, it seems someone from Peristeri had killed him."

"You mean *that* Peristeri? The village to the west?" Fr. Dimitrios gestured westward.

"Over the ridge, there. Half an hour's walk." He looked closely at Fr. Dimitrios. "Your grandfather never spoke of his brother, at all?"

"I never heard any of this."

"I do not think he was proud of Philipos, was he?"

"I guess not. I mean, I don't know. I have to think about this."

Nikos finished his tsikoudia and said, "I'm here every day. You shall ask me anything about Vraho history. I know it all. I should be schoolmaster, but I'm too old to put up with those noisy children. I know it all, though. I'll be right here."

The interview with Old Nikos was over.

Fr. Dimitrios nodded to Lambros, and walked, as steadily as he could, drunk from information, out of the taverna, past the singers, and back toward his house.

The information etched its way through the ganglia and synapses in his brain. His grandfather's brother, Philipos, working for the Germans against his own people? It wasn't possible. Maybe it wasn't his grandfather's brother. Must have been someone else's brother.

Sitting out on the back steps of the apartment in San Francisco, Papou had told him thousands of stories of his life in Vraho. He wouldn't leave out something like that. Or would he? Old Nikos is very old. Maybe his memory is slipping.

116

Fr. Dimitrios pushed the possibility of this news as far from himself as he could. He went home without seeing the village as he passed through it.

He looked around his house, his grandfather's house. Then he took a chair off its hook on the wall and sat down at the small drop-leaf table near the door. He took the telephone off its shelf. Nine hours earlier in San Francisco. It would be early afternoon there. He dialed his parents' number.

His mother answered the phone. He asked how she was, the usual, then he asked her if she knew anything about Papou having a brother. He thought he heard a quick intake of breath before she answered, "Just a minute, Mitso. I'll get your father."

His father came on the line and said, "What's this? Who? What are you asking now?"

Fr. Dimitrios said carefully, "Did Papou have a brother who died in the war?"

There was silence across the phone line for a moment, then Christos said, "Yes, he did. I don't remember him. I was a baby then. He died in the war. Damn! I knew it was a bad idea for you to go back to Vraho. Son, leave that story alone. Don't look into family ghosts. You don't want to know. Please, give me your word."

"Dad, I can't give you that promise. I need to know all of it."

His father moaned.

"I'm sorry, Dad. But I have to know."

"Mitso, this can only bring pain to all of us. Whatever you find out…don't tell me. Don't tell your mother, either. I don't want to know."

"All right, Dad. I'm sorry to open wounds for you."

"It's not my wound. There are secrets that aren't your responsibility. Or mine. Or your mother's. I wish you'd leave them alone. You don't need to know."

"I'm truly sorry, but I do. I promised Papou."

"Promised him what?"

"I can't tell you. Thanks for understanding."

"I wish I did. Goodbye, son."

"Goodbye, Dad. I love you."

117

"I know. I love you, too."

Fr. Dimitrios sat staring at the telephone receiver before he replaced it into its cradle. He felt as if he were standing on liquefied earth, like after an earthquake. Like after the Loma Prieta quake, when everything went liquid under them all, when the city melted down. Now things were melting down under him again.

What secret was his beloved grandfather asking him to find? His mind leapt to possibilities, each more terrible than the other. He felt naive for telling his grandfather's spirit that he forgave him without knowing what he would be asked to forgive. Then he felt disloyal for admitting doubts without knowing what was true of this new disclosure. Feeling stupid, clumsy, and disloyal, he lay down on his bed. He knew he faced a tortured night's sleep.

His clock battered him with the sound of its ticks. He tried meditating, but his thoughts forbade it. He lay flat, a victim of doubt, for what seemed like months. At last, he slept.

Morning came, and still he slept. Noon, then early afternoon. He dragged himself out of bed at two-fifteen. Feeling like sludge, he dressed and made himself a dry rusk topped with graviera. He told himself the sooner he began this task the sooner it would be over. Knowledge would replace this awful doubt. Then he started to tear apart the storage area under his bed, looking for the chest whose key now burned on the chain around his neck.

He went to the shoulder-height clay vase at the front of the space under his sleeping platform. It was the one Ariadne drew olives out of. He pushed on it. It was stuck. He pushed on the other one, next to the first. Also stuck. He looked at the floor to see if something had leaked and dried to stick them. No, they looked swept clean and freshly moved. He tried again to push the first one. He couldn't get it to move more than one centimeter.

Forget that, he thought. He looked at the crates and sacks that filled the space alongside the two great vases. He pulled them out into the room until there was no space to walk between them. None was locked, and as he looked inside them, none contained anything he could call a dark secret. Some had winter squash and pumpkins. Two were filled with potatoes. A box contained candles for the church.

Another had plastic-wrapped printed icons and prayers for church holidays, for baptisms, for weddings. It's good to know what's here, thought Fr. Dimitrios. But it's not what I'm looking for. In the house, you said, Papou. Right? In the house?

No answer came. Earlier he had been able to create, imagine, hear what his grandfather would tell him in certain circumstances, but now that voice, whatever it was, was silent.

Fr. Dimitrios went for a flashlight, then crawled back farther into the storage space, but there was nothing there but an empty mouse nest. He crawled back out and returned with a broom to remove it.

Kyria Ariadne brought his dinner, as every day. She knocked on his door, then opened it. She looked around at the floor, covered with the wooden crates and plastic sacks that usually lived under the bed. Fr. Dimitrios's head appeared from under the bed.

"I don't think God will mind if you don't wear your cassock all the time," Ariadne said. "What are you doing?"

Fr. Dimitrios crawled out into the tangle of boxes and removed his dusty black cassock. He wore jeans and a t-shirt underneath. He gave the cassock to Ariadne, who took it as if taking a wounded child.

"I'm looking for a chest my grandfather left here. Do you know anything about a chest of his?"

Ariadne stood in the bright sunlight of the doorway, examining the cassock for injuries. She spoke as she picked at one spot with great seriousness. "No, and I clean that space out twice a year. I did it just before you came. Those are things for the church, for holidays and weddings and funerals. What chest?"

"I don't know. It's not here, anyway. I'll put these things back."

Ariadne hung the cassock on a wall peg and headed toward the storage cave. "I know where everything was. I'll put them back in order."

Fr. Dimitrios moved there first. "Why don't you tell me where to put them? I took them out. I'll go under there again." He crawled into the dark space, dragging the nearest box behind him. Ariadne directed him to replace the crates and sacks in the order they had been.

The dinner she brought sat on the little table. Chicken cooked with oregano, lemon juice, and olive oil. Alongside it, two little pies filled with something, probably cheese, maybe greens, maybe both. Ariadne said, "You don't look well. Please. Eat. This food will make you stronger." While he ate, she took the cassock back off its hook and out to the well. She sponged water on a recalcitrant spot, then brought it back into the house and hung it carefully again on its wall peg. "There." she said.

Fr. Dimitrios smiled an apology at her.

On most days he would have been delighted with one of Ariadne's dinners. Today, he just picked at it. Since Papou's death he had carried the sense that Papou was with him, had moved into his head. Now, he felt an absence.

After he'd eaten and cleaned up his dishes (it surprised Ariadne that he insisted on washing up after his meals. Neither his grandfather nor Fr. Theodoros had ever offered to wash up. It was another of his American strangenesses), he resolved to do something, take some action, to move closer to the truth, whatever it might be.

He went back to the taverna, but Old Nikos wasn't there. No guests were there. It was dinnertime. Lambros was upstairs, eating with his family, and the taverna stood empty and unlocked.

Fr. Dimitrios was undecided as he returned to his house. He couldn't think of anyone else who might know something about that time. Nikos seemed to be the oldest person in the village. Kyria Ariadne was only a couple of years older than his father, but maybe she had heard something. There was some relationship, some deep connection there. Was she a cousin? Fr. Dimitrios didn't know for sure. He went to her door and knocked.

The door swung open, revealing Ariadne and her son, eating their dinner.

"Oh, I'm sorry. Please excuse me."

"Father, please come in. Was your dinner to your liking?"

"Yes, it was delicious. Thank you."

She looked at him, waiting for him to say something else. Her son, twenty-year-old Stamatis, looked at him as well.

"I'm sorry. I shouldn't have come at your dinnertime. I'll come back another time."

He shut her door and went home. He felt foolish, he felt uneasy, he felt out of place, over his head, out of control.

What, he asked the no longer tangible spirit of his grandfather, what, in God's name, and I really mean that, have you gotten me into?

He reviewed what his grandfather had told him of the war.

Earlier, Papou had told him stories of the actions of the pallikaria, the warriors of Crete, and their bravery against the German occupying forces; entire villages resisting the invaders and all the men being massacred; village women hiding wounded British soldiers right under the nose of the Germans. These were heroic stories of the courage of the entire island. They were not stories about himself.

On the night he died, on the telephone, he'd said there was a massacre in his church the same day his wife had been shot in the platia. The German attack was brought on by a raid by Spiros Kiriakis's father, a pallikari.

Even then, at the very end of his life, he hadn't mentioned having a brother. Why would he keep a brother a secret from his own grandson? Maybe Old Nikos was wrong. He didn't sound wrong, though.

Fr. Dimitrios jumped at a knock at his door. He opened it and said, "Please come in, Kyria Ariadne."

"You looked ill when you came to my house. I came by to see what help you need."

"Nothing. I was wrong to come. I'm sorry to have bothered you."

"May I sit?" she asked.

"Please," said Fr. Dimitrios. He took another chair off its peg on the wall and set it down for her.

"I have heard from my neighbor, Ekaterini, that that old fool Nikos has been worrying you."

"News gets around."

"Yes, it does. Nikos means no harm. He fought in the war. He still lives in those times. That old hat of his: some British officer gave it to him as he was leaving Kriti. He's worn it for fifty years. Do you want to know what I know?"

"Please." He returned with a bottle of tsikoudia and two glasses.

Ariadne waved them away. "No, thank you."

He put them away again.

"You want to know about your grandfather's brother."

Fr. Dimitrios nodded.

Kyria Ariadne adjusted herself in the stiff-backed chair until she was comfortable. Then she told him what she remembered about the wartime and Philipos.

"After the Germans had been here for a few months, some people began to think that we might never get rid of them. The Germans were punishing villages that resisted. They usually shot the proethros first, as an example to the others. To take away the leader. Philipos was our proethros. He was the one they'd kill if they found Vraho was not behaving.

"Who knows what anyone else thinks? If I had been him, I could see where it might seem a good idea to make friends with the conquerors, especially if they were going to be around for a long time."

"So?"

"Well, I don't know. I mean, he died before anyone accused him directly, but the Germans came around after he was dead and wanted to know who killed him. I remember the adults talking about it, years later. I don't think anyone knows for sure. But it seemed to me that he must have been working for the Germans.

"The same night he was stabbed on the mountainside, a German officer fell to his death off the trail. We never knew who did it. Not even to this day.

"After the war we tried to forget about those among us who chose the wrong side. Philipos was safely dead anyway. I don't think anyone thought your grandfather was a German sympathizer, though. He was a good man. Most of the villagers loved him very much."

She shifted in her chair.

"Who didn't love him?" asked Fr. Dimitrios.

"Oh, I don't know." Ariadne studied her fingertips.

"Please."

She looked straight at Fr. Dimitrios.

"Alexandros Kiriakis. I never knew why, but Alexandros Kiriakis hated him. He's dead now, too. His son, Spiros, doesn't like you, but that's just family matters, because his father hated your grandfather. Watch out for him, though. He's not your friend."

"Thank you for telling me. I will be careful."

"Shall I tell you what I know about your grandmother and how she died?"

The light was fading in the house. Ariadne got up and trimmed and lit an oil lamp. She set it on the table.

"I was three years old. This was March of 1942. Philipos was already dead. I will tell you what I remember. It may not be true. Just true for me. It was night. The Germans came up the *kaldirimia,* the donkey trails. There were no roads to Vraho then. Not like now. Their machines made a horrible sound. I still hear them in my sleep sometimes.

"My mother led me up the hill behind the village. There were other children already there, at that rocky place with the one tree, you know the one?"

"That really old olive tree with the thick trunk?"

"That one. Just when my mother and I got there, Fotini came with her baby, your father, who was about six months old. He was crying. I held him and told him to be quiet and he did."

"Fotini went back to the village, leaving us with my mother. We couldn't see what was happening, but we heard shots and screams. We waited at the old olive tree for a long time.

"Finally my mother took me and your father to an old man's barn, away from the village. I don't know whose it was. I could never find it again. We were given milk to drink and we slept there that night.

"In the morning, someone came to tell us that Fotini was one of the dead. She and the others were shot."

"I heard about this from Papou," said Fr. Dimitrios.

"Good. After that day your father lived with us. Your grandfather was our priest. He couldn't also be a mother to a baby. He was a good man. He came to our house nearly every day to see his son."

"So you and my father were like brother and sister."

"I raised him. My mother and I raised him."

"Thank you. Thank you for raising him, and thank you for telling me."

123

Ariadne rose to go. "Can you sleep now?"

"Thank you again."

She closed the door as she left.

Dreams filled Fr. Dimitrios's sleep with shadowy figures, German, Cretan, British, fighting for their lives, their homeland, their duty, their honor. Through the fighting men wandered the tall, stately silhouette of Papou, in cassock and kalimavki, doing what? saying what? Fr. Dimitrios couldn't make out the words.

He woke in the dark. A bird was singing very close to his bedroom. He felt jumpy and ragged. He fingered the chain around his neck and followed it to his baptismal cross and the small key that hung next to it. Soon, maybe today, he would use it.

No reason to lie around waiting. He got up and put his cassock and pectoral cross and chain over his work clothes, added his kalimavki, and went over to the church. The sun broke over the ridge that went from the peaks of Lefka Ori down toward Aptera. He unlocked the big door and let himself in. He stood in the narthex.

The morning light illuminated the narrow windows flanking the apse. Fr. Dimitrios made the sign of the cross toward the ikonostasis. The strips of light across the patterned stone floor reassured him. This floor was the oldest unchanged part of the building. It had survived two attacks during the Turkish rule and the German one of 1942. The walls gleamed back at him white and anonymous.

He looked around the interior of the church. Opposite the narthex was the ikonostasis. Nothing was behind the ikonostasis but the usual three stations: the prothesis, the diakonikon, and the holy table, all used weekly for the service. No secrets from him there.

He thought about the exterior shape of the church. The building was a Greek cross. Its outside surged in and out exactly where its interior did. There was no space for a closet or storeroom anywhere in it. The chest he wanted was not in the church. He crossed himself again and left, locking the large wooden doors behind him.

The ossuary stood a short distance from the church. It was a small stone building where the bones of the dead were moved after they had spent their three years resting in the graveyard. No, he thought. Papou would never hide something so that I would have to disturb the bones of the dead to find it. He returned to his house.

124

Along the way, he saw the bent figure of Old Nikos, his ancient beret perched at a dangerous tilt. He increased his stride and caught up to the old man.

"Good morning to you."

"And to you, Patera. I was on my way to your house right now. Even without the favor of a drink, I have something to tell you. I think it may be important."

"Please, come to my home. Perhaps I can find something for your thirst."

"No need. No need. but if you had some, it would be welcome."

The two entered the young priest's house and Fr. Dimitrios arranged table and chairs to make their conversation comfortable. Old Nikos sat down and waited until a small glass and the desired bottle appeared in front of him on the table. He smiled.

"Now, this is what I have been thinking. I have been thinking that Philipos was one of our citizens, and though he was known all over the mountainside—he was widespread in his activities. I mean, he stole sheep from everyone. They all knew him—nonetheless, it occurs to me that, in spite of what the Germans thought, it just might be that Philipos's death was not caused by the men of the village of Peristeri. Maybe, I am thinking, maybe one of us killed him."

"You? Are you saying you killed him?"

"Use your head. If I'd killed him I would have known it."

"Who do you think, then?"

"Who do *you* think?"

Fr. Dimitrios just stared at him.

"Your grandfather left a chest behind and it was in Fr. Theodoros's way. It was stored under there," he pointed toward the freshly organized space under Fr. Dimitrios's bed, "so I took it to my house and put it with my things. Do you want it now?"

125

"Have you opened it?"

"Certainly not. It was locked and I had a feeling he would come back for it one day. Now he's dead, so I can stop guarding it for him. I can pass it on to you."

"I will gladly take it from you."

"I have a price."

"What is your price, old man?"

"I want to know. I want to know what you find inside. More than fifty years I have wondered and I want to know."

"My grandfather asked me to open it alone. I gave my word."

"Can you give me a nod yes or no?"

"Let me think about it, please. My word to my dead grandfather means a lot to me."

"Of course. I can see you are a man of honor, just like him. Just like your dear grandfather, my friend, Dimitrios. Yes, of course."

The glass of tsikoudia was quickly drunk and the two men went over to Old Nikos's house. It required navigating uphill on a rocky narrow path made by and for goats. The old man knew the ideal pattern for his feet, and after stumbling a few times, Fr. Dimitrios fell in behind him and imitated his feet. They stopped twice along the way for Old Nikos to catch his breath.

Old Nikos's house was a wreck. The door sagged on its hinges, almost all the pale blue paint on the shutters had flaked off, but the shutters still closed, the door closed, the stone held the weather out, and the old man was proud of his home. "It has withstood 103 winters, two wars, heavy snows, earthquakes, and me living in it eighty-three years now. I was born here," Old Nikos said, proudly.

"It is a fine house, Nikos. Truly fine. It has a happy feeling to it."

"Come inside, please." Old Nikos climbed up a rustic ladder to a sleeping platform less tidily made up than Fr. Dimitrios's. He rummaged through blankets and goat skins, and made a great deal of noise banging and clanking. Then he crawled backwards to the ladder and came back down to the floor. He held a wooden chest, the size of a small suitcase, locked with a padlock. His hands were shaking.

126

He handed it to Fr. Dimitrios, whose hands also began to shake. Then Old Nikos said, "I'll wait outside. Open it alone. I'll be out here, waiting," and he left Fr. Dimitrios alone with the chest.

Fr. Dimitrios looked at it and wondered if it was the right one. He thought it might be larger, somehow. He asked his grandfather's voice if this was the chest, but again, there was only silence. He reached inside the throat of his cassock and took out his small baptismal cross and the key. He slipped the chain over his head and slowly moved the key toward the lock.

Maybe it won't fit. Maybe it's not the chest. Maybe…he thought.

The key slid into the lock as by a force greater than Fr. Dimitrios's hand. The lock sprang open and the hasp popped up. It remained only for Fr. Dimitrios to lift the lid of the chest.

He closed his eyes and murmured the prayer, *I pray for the repose of the soul of the departed servant of God, Dimitrios, Priest and concelebrant, and for the forgiveness of all his errors, both voluntary and involuntary.* He crossed himself, and then lifted the lid.

He saw folded black wool serge. He lifted it out of the chest. It was a cassock, like his own, but much older. He held it up to him. Something was odd about it. Stains. There were stains of dark stiffness down the very front of the cassock. He scratched a stain and smelled it. Nothing. He looked at the flakes. Then he looked back at the chest. Inside was another object, wrapped in paper. He unwrapped it. It was a Cretan dagger, a passalis, with a silver sheath and two amulets hanging from the tip.

Old Nikos coughed outside.

"Soon, soon I'm coming. Please wait," answered Fr. Dimitrios.

"Of course, of course. Take your time."

Fr. Dimitrios refolded the cassock and replaced it in the chest, putting the paper-wrapped dagger on the top instead of the bottom. He locked the chest again and returned his baptismal cross and key to the safety of the inside of his cassock. He went outside, holding the chest.

Nikos said, "You need say nothing to me, young man. Your face tells me what I already knew. You have not broken your word to your grandfather."

Fr. Dimitrios said, "I am taking the chest to my house now. I bid you goodbye and thank you. Forgive me, but I wish to be alone for awhile."

"Of course. I understand." And Old Nikos went into his house, leaving Fr. Dimitrios to find his own way carrying the chest down the narrow goat path.

127

16

In 1940, Dimitrios Papadakis received the appointment as priest of his home village of Vraho. He was twenty-five years old. He and his wife, Fotini, had a newborn son they named Christos. Their lives seemed full of blessings, and they were very happy. His desire was to shepherd his flock of parishioners as he had herded sheep on Lefka Ori as a youth. He felt empowered by the trust of his office, and determined to serve his people well. He prayed daily for the guidance and strength to do just that.

Fr. Dimitrios had an older brother—Philipos. Three years older. Philipos was quick, facile, a man of slippery thinking. He was not married. He was a dangerous sheep-thief, a badge of honor in those days. The villagers, and people from nearby villages, knew who he was and respected him. He was proethros of Vraho.

In the village tradition, before Dimitrios and Fotini married, he built her a house, next door to his brother's house.

Philipos said he loved his brother Dimitrios, but he always teased him for not thinking on his feet like a good thief. He was disgusted by Dimitrios's decision to go into the church. He wanted him to share his sheep business, even just the herding part of it. For years, every day, whenever they met, he invited him to join him on the mountain. Philipos continued to offer this partnership even after Dimitrios was ordained. By that time, Dimitrios treated his brother's offer as a joke, and laughed it off.

In late October 1940, Mussolini ordered his troops to attack Greece from their position in Albania. The King of Greece with his government ministers and their top British allies retreated from Athens to Crete. The Italian attack on the north was a failure. The Greek military met them there and beat them back. With all its young men on the frontier facing Albania, Greece was under-defended elsewhere.

The botched Italian campaign in Greece made Il Duce look foolish. Hitler and his generals took back control of the campaign for the eastern Mediterranean. They determined to drive a wedge through the Middle East, to reach the oil fields of Saudi Arabia and, equally, to isolate the forces of Russia and Britain. Crete became a strategic necessity.

When the Germans began their invasion of Crete from the air in May 1941, the King of Greece escaped, together with his ministers. Allied forces from Cairo tried to evacuate the stranded British, Australian, and New Zealand forces, but many of them surrendered to the Germans as prisoners of war. Others made it into the mountains of the island and were guided across to the Libyan Sea to wait for passage to Cairo. Their guides were the andartes, the mountain men of Crete.

While it was an occupied territory, Crete had three main fighting groups: the Germans, who controlled the lowlands; the Allied troops hiding in the uplands of the island, who worked to aid the Cretans in their resistance efforts; and the Cretan people, who fought fiercely against the invading forces in spite of terrible reprisals from the Germans.

Fr. Dimitrios was caught in a bind. He thought hard about what he should do. Some priests were taking up guns and going to the hills with the andartes. Part of him longed to join them, but Fr. Dimitrios

129

felt he needed to protect his village. To do so, he decided he must appear neutral, so if the Germans came, he could talk them out of hurting his flock. There are times when the hardest thing to do is to do nothing.

Fr. Dimitrios searched his soul, made his choice, and stayed true to it. He gave the appearance of neutrality, almost disinterest. Once a week, on Thursdays, as was the usual procedure for young priests, he rode his donkey to Chania to meet with his metropolitan. In the early days of the occupation, the Germans gave him safe passage.

Nikos, his friend from schooldays, didn't join the andartes, either. "Why do I want to go hunting for Germans at night? They'll come here soon enough," he said. And he appeared simply to go on with his everyday life. But Nikos and Fr. Dimitrios, together, began passing messages for the British. Nikos brought down papers left in a hiding place on the mountain. He gave them to Fr. Dimitrios who hid them in his cassock when he went to Chania each week.

The andartes, especially young Alexandros Kiriakis, knew nothing about their message delivery. They complained that the priest was too soft and wasn't helping in the fight against the Nazis. They were disgusted that whenever he spoke to them he urged them to use caution, to protect the village.

"Caution!" they snorted. "We'll all be killed anyway." They didn't listen to him.

One day in mid-summer, his brother Philipos caught up to him on the street and said, "People at the taverna are saying you're a coward, but I think you're smart not to join up with those bumblers. You know, you should get off your sanctified ass and help me."

Fr. Dimitrios said, "No sheep-stealing, Philipos. I'm a priest now." He gestured to his cassock.

His brother leaned near his ear and said, quietly, "Not sheep."

"What, then?"

Philipos winked and said, "Come on, little brother. You know what I mean."

When Fr. Dimitrios protested that he did not understand, Philipos told him that the best way to preserve the village was to dance to the music being played.

The priest pretended to be as dumb as his brother thought him.

Philipos whispered, so no one would hear. "There are favors to be gained from helping these Germans."

Fr. Dimitrios was shocked. He remembered seeing those landings: silky blossoms of evil floating down, bringing German invaders to poor Crete. What's more, these Germans were killing and burning and torturing Cretans.

His brother continued, "You know the Germans are not ever leaving. Not in our lifetimes anyway. When this war is over, I'll be the real power around here, and I want to help you, too, little brother. The war can't last forever, can it? Come join me."

"What are you talking about?"

Philipos winked and said, "You're dumb, little brother, but not *that* dumb. See me when you're ready to join me. I love you." He slapped him gently on the side of the face.

For a flicker, Fr. Dimitrios was flattered by his older brother's generosity toward him, but he knew that his honor as a Cretan and a man lay in defending Crete's independence to his death.

The British began using Vraho for a supply stop as they transported troops across Crete to Sphakia to be shipped to Cairo. Allied soldiers arrived in the night, guided by the andartes. Mostly they slept on the mountain, in caves, but occasionally they slept in barns, in storage sheds, and once, even, they slept in the church, but without Fr. Dimitrios's knowledge. His hands were clean. The key to the church was left in a niche. He told his metropolitan where the niche was, and the metropolitan gave the information to the British. Fr. Dimitrios could not be accused of participating in the war. He could protect his people.

Fotini didn't know about his secret activities. She asked him, twice, hesitantly, if he thought he shouldn't do something to help the andartes. The second time she mentioned it, he had snapped at her, saying his duty was to God and the church, not to the folly of mankind. She had wept at his angry tone and after that she never mentioned it. He was sorry he made her cry. He wished she could know and respect him for his position, but he told himself her ignorance was for her own safety.

131

The Germans were learning things they should not have known. Fr. Dimitrios watched his brother. He saw that the others in the village were watching each other. No one knew who to believe. Mistrust sprang up between old friends. The village was coming apart because of suspicion.

The day came when he knew he had to choose his loyalty, to brother or to country. He approached Philipos and said, "What would you have me do to join you?"

"Ah, now you are waking up. Let me offer your services to my friends. I'll come back to you with information day after tomorrow."

"Well, then. Let me know how I can help."

The next night, Fr. Dimitrios slipped out of his house in the dark. He waited at the rock outcropping above the village, watching all the sleeping houses. A figure came out of his brother's house and went to the west of the village, up mountain. Fr. Dimitrios watched the figure disappear. After some minutes, at a point farther along, he saw a light flicker, then go out.

The next day, his brother said, "I will have an assignment for you in two more days. We must be patient."

Fr. Dimitrios answered, "Very well," and waited.

That night, some New Zealanders and their Vrahiot guides were attacked by a German patrol waiting for them half way between Vraho and Peristeri. They were unarmed. They ran for cover. One New Zealander was killed. Never before had the Germans patrolled this part of the island. How had they known about that dangerous and unmarked path? The partisans worried. Fr. Dimitrios kept his patience.

The next day, his brother dropped by his home. He was very cheery. He smiled and patted Fr. Dimitrios on the shoulder. "Good times coming, dear brother," he said. Fr. Dimitrios nodded and said "When will I hear from them?"

His brother said, "Tomorrow, I told you. Tomorrow."

The next day he was in the church, preparing the decorations for the week-long *Panygiri*, the celebration of the Dormition of the Virgin, when his brother came to him and said, "I have to talk to you right now, little brother."

132

Fr. Dimitrios said, "Not here," and led him out of the church.

"Weren't you alone in the church? Do you think God will overhear us?" said Philipos, looking annoyed.

Fr. Dimitrios shrugged. "Why take chances?"

"You astonish me, little brother." By now, they were standing in the middle of the platia, with no one around them. They were visible, two brothers speaking, no problem. No one could hear what they said. Philipos spoke softly. "Listen! The oberleutnant would like to meet you. He feels you can be very useful to them."

"Where? Where would he like to meet me?"

"In Chania, of course. You go down there every week to see your metropolitan. Next time, you will go to this address and present this note and they will clear you. Then you can carry messages." He handed his brother a folded piece of paper.

Fr. Dimitrios put it in the pocket of his cassock and said, "I go every Thursday."

"That's soon enough. On Wednesday night you'll have to meet my contact, Herr Hartwig. We'll meet on the ridge across from the stone face. Just walk away from your house after dinner and come up there. Then he'll be there when you go to the oberleutnant's office in Chania on Thursday so he can confirm your identity. Don't worry. This is the usual way. Wednesday, nine o'clock."

"Nine o'clock, then."

Wednesday night he reached into the bottom of his clothing chest and drew out his father's passalis. Its silver hilt gleamed above its silver scabbard, with the two amulets dangling from its dragon-head tip. He remembered his father's pride in the knife and the honor it had been when he gave it to him. He looked at it for a long time, then slipped it into the pocket of his cassock.

He went out of his house, past the church, and down the center road of the village. He walked slowly. He greeted people normally. When he reached the end of the village, he drifted casually to the path up-mountain and then disappeared into the brush. He circled back in the other direction, toward the meeting place. Once safely out of the village and up on the mountain, he moved the knife. He put it through the wide leather belt he wore over his cassock. When

133

he approached the meeting place, he paused and watched. No one was there. He proceeded past it, beyond the ridge, toward Chania.

The new moon cast indistinct shadows down the mountain. He caught sight of a movement on the far side of a ravine. As he watched, it grew into a man in a light colored uniform, four dark buttons down the chest, soft cap projecting in front of the man's brow. German. The soldier made his way cautiously toward the meeting place. Until that moment, Fr. Dimitrios had not known what he would do. Now he knew.

He removed the knife from its scabbard and waited until the German passed him on the goat trail just below where he hid. He stepped down onto the trail, knocked the man's hat forward, grabbed his hair, pulled his head back, and quickly sliced his neck, severing the carotid arteries on both sides as well as the windpipe. A good kill. Like a sheep. The man coughed once and was dead before he hit the ground. Fr. Dimitrios looked longingly at the German's polished boots. The andartes needed boots, but a barefoot German would put the lie to the appearance of an accidental fall.

He pushed the body off the trail into a deep ravine. It landed face down. Lucky, he thought. It would look like the man slipped and fell and no one was likely to go down that sheer face to retrieve him.

Very sad about the boots, though. Someone could have used them.

He returned to the appointed meeting place and waited until his brother arrived.

Philipos said, "Ah, you're on time. Good. Have you seen anyone else? My friend should be here any moment."

Fr. Dimitrios moved next to his brother, swung the passalis into his brother's midsection three inches above the navel, and pulled up and forward with force. The knife tore through the diaphragm and found the heart. Philipos barely had time to look surprised before the light went out of his eyes. Fr. Dimitrios had trouble removing the passalis. He had to put his foot on his brother's body, next to it, and pull hard to get it out. Then he wiped it off on his brother's pants leg and restored it to its scabbard.

He made the sign of the cross over Philipos's body.

What bothered Fr. Dimitrios for the rest of his life was that his brother never knew why he killed him. He wished he could have talked to him first. He wanted to tell him, to ask his forgiveness, which, of course, was impossible. But it haunted him—the surprised look on the trusting, traitorous face of his own brother.

It was odd. Growing up on Lefka Ori, he had killed many sheep, but he had never thought to kill a person. Now he had killed Philipos. If it were not wartime, Philipos would not have had the choice to be a traitor. So circumstance had forced this act. But he knew he was going to pay for this sin. He only wondered in how many ways he would pay.

The night was dark. The moon-sliver had set. He returned to Vraho by a different set of paths. The bodies would be found tomorrow by shepherds. Or maybe Friday.

He stopped at the public fountain. He rinsed the passalis and his hands first in the muddy overflow, then, when he thought the blood was off them, in the water of the fountain itself. He shook them dry. When he got to his house, he reached inside the door for the hidden nail where he kept his own key to the church.

He let himself inside the dark church and stood still facing the ikonostasis. He was surprised at himself that he did not weep. Some part of himself had been sacrificed on that mountain, too.

He returned to the house and undressed, folding his blood-spattered clothes around the passalis and putting them in the bottom of his trunk. He placed his other clothing on top. In a day or two he would do something about those blood-stained things, but for now they were safe there. He lay down beside Fotini. She stirred in her sleep, but did not wake.

Fr. Dimitrios went to Chania the next day as he did on all Thursdays. He met his metropolitan in his office, and after they had done their usual business, he presented him with the folded paper his brother had given him. The metropolitan read it and said, "Who gave you this? And where are they now?"

Fr. Dimitrios said, "Your Eminence, I received this from my brother."

He told his story. The metropolitan listened in silence. After he was done, the metropolitan looked stern and, at the same time, deeply

135

sad. He said, "If the Church knew what you have done, they would have you defrocked at once, but these are desperate times. What you have done is between you and God. I have not heard you say anything today." He paused. "But no one else must ever hear you say what you have done. So long as you live, you must keep silent about this."

The bodies were discovered while he was in town. The village was very agitated. Everyone waited to know who did it, but no one stepped forward.

They brought Philipos's body to his home and laid it out there overnight. Since the dead man had no wife, village women came to prepare the body. The laments seemed half-hearted.

A German patrol came to the village the next morning. They were looking for a missing officer. When they saw a coffin lid standing by the door and three women going into Philipos's house, they followed them in. They saw his body and talked among themselves in fast, crisp German. In Greek, one of them demanded to know who had killed Philipos.

The women said, "He is one of ours, our proethros. Why are you asking who killed him? Maybe your missing officer killed him."

"Fools! He was going to meet with our officer. Who found the body? Where was it?"

The villagers told them where the body had lain on the trail.

The feldwebel snapped at them, "We will go now to search for the missing officer. But we will be back. Someone must pay for this death."

The village people were horrified to discover that their proethros was a traitor. Fr. Dimitrios felt that some of them were watching him, to see if his loyalties lay where his brother's had.

After the Germans left, some people asked whether Philipos the traitor, *o prodotis*, should be buried in consecrated ground. Fr. Dimitrios silenced the talkers, saying "Judgment is left to God. Philipos was a member of the church."

On Friday morning, Fr. Dimitrios said the *trisagion* and the body was moved to the church that same day, in a solemn procession. Fr. Dimitrios walked in front, carrying the censer. Vaggelis-the-chanter followed with a beeswax taper.

They set Philipos's coffin down in the narthex of the church. The service continued, but it was spoken much more quickly than usual.

Fr. Dimitrios said, "...Do you, Lord, give rest to the soul of your servant, Philipos, who has fallen asleep, in a place of light, a place of green pasture, a place of refreshment..." all very fast, and then the coffin was taken back out of the church and set beside a fresh-dug grave in the cemetery.

Fr. Dimitrios poured the blessed oil from the lamp onto his brother's body. The coffin was lowered into the grave. Fr. Dimitrios picked up a shovel and scattered dirt in the form of the cross over his brother, saying "The earth is the Lord's, and its fullness; the world and all who dwell on it." He covered Philipos's face with the shroud and closed the coffin. The pallbearers began to fill in the grave. No one wept. It was like a funeral attended by sleepwalkers. The only sound was Fr. Dimitrios speaking the service, and his voice sounded hollow, as if he were speaking from a long way off.

The Rite of the Dead ended with "Eternal your memory, our brother, worthy of blessedness and ever-remembered." Fr. Dimitrios's voice grew unsteady as he said those words.

And then the service was over. He walked away quickly, not offering comfort to anyone, since he was the only direct family-member of the deceased. His wife Fotini followed him. The others dispersed quietly.

The villagers later said they observed that Fr. Dimitrios seemed to want to get this over in haste, not to be associated with his traitor-brother's death. Opinion turned to favor his loyalty again.

The story of his grandfather's action came together for Fr. Dimitrios in a nightmare revelation. His mind connected the links between the details he'd learned from Nikos and from Kyria Ariadne. Facts fell into place and the magnitude of the old priest's deed emerged. First Fr. Dimitrios felt horror, then an overwhelming pity for Papou, then an admiration for the courage it took to commit— he hesitated and waited for the word to rise to meet him—fratricide, in order to protect his parish and his village. Then the horror filled him again.

He spent his free hours alone at the rocky place near the old olive tree, the place where Kyria Ariadne had witnessed the massacre of his grandmother and the other villagers. He remained still and let his feelings rise and recede.

He never discussed it again with either Kyria Ariadne or Nikos, nor did they speak to each other about it, yet all three knew.

For weeks, the deed rolled around in his mind, casting other thoughts aside. To choose between loyalty to his brother or to his country and his parish. What a terrible choice to be asked to make.

He said, "Papou, I am sorry you spent all those years with that secret shut up in your heart. When I was little, I thought you were perfect and I loved you perfectly. Now that I know your dark secret, I love you more because you are human, too.

"Thank you for trusting me and loving me so much that you asked me to find the evidence and learn your secret. I think I love you more even than I did before. I love you because I know now what an unbearable burden you took on yourself. I'm not sure that I would ever have the courage to do what you did then. Your action was done knowing that it would cause you pain forever. It's one thing to be brave in a moment, but quite another to know what you must do, know the cost, and still stand and do it.

"I must remember that you did not ask me to forgive you. You asked me to seek forgiveness for you. Your act shocks me, but it is not mine to forgive. We humans wander around judging and forgiving each other and truly the power is not in our hands. God has you with Him now, as He has your brother, too. All I can do is ask for forgiveness for you. How shall I?"

He asked the *Theotokos*, the Holy Mother of God, to pray for his grandfather's soul. He prayed, *With the saints give rest, O Christ, to the soul of thy servant, Dimitrios, where there is neither sickness, nor sorrow, nor sighing, but life everlasting.* He read through his prayer books, looking for other appropriate prayers.

Then one morning he woke, remembering his grandfather's concern for the icons under the whitewash.

"Papou, let it be that I will clear the whitewash from those icons, reveal the saints, return them to the light. This will be my act of expiation for you."

When he had made that vow, he'd felt lighter. The next day he started looking for how to do it without damaging the paintings.

Now, after three years, he could at last start to fulfill his pledge. Today he had begun, and his morning's labor showed that the method would work. He repeated silent prayers asking for forgiveness for Papou as he picked at the flaking whitewash.

17

George Hanson went down to breakfast at nine, hoping no one would be singing in the streets outside. He needed quiet.

They were staying at Hotel Minos. Douglas had chosen it. He said it was the nicest one in Chania, but it stood right in the middle of the oldest part of town—historic, he called it—with narrow little streets paved with sloping steps. Mrs. Hanson had already tripped on them several times.

Shopkeepers yelled to each other down the street. Young people in doorways sometimes sang Greek songs. George thought they did this probably just to get tips from tourists.

Hotel Minos was built in the mid-1980s. It was shaped like the neighboring merchant houses of the Venetian period, but unlike the real ones, the hotel's plaster was perfect and its color constant. The closed courtyard where George went for his breakfast was paved with amber-colored Italian tiles that blended with the walls, which were discreetly decorated with well-mannered grape vines.

Breakfast extended across a buffet table covered with stiffly starched white linen, behind which stood a handsome young Greek in a starched white jacket, ready to construct kafe Elleniko. There were dully-gleaming hotel-silver pots filled with kafe Amerikaniko (*real* coffee to George Hanson) and Earl Grey tea. George eyed a crystal pitcher of freshly squeezed orange juice, a warming tray filled with bacon and sausage, another with fluffy, orange scrambled eggs, a third with chicken livers grilled in butter, and, at the end, two large silver trays covered with tesserae of sliced cheese and salami. Then pastries with jams. He wished he were hungrier.

The fruit compote looked just like the Sunday buffet at the Country Club back home—the same safe fruit.

He made a plate for himself, took a glass of juice and some real coffee, and sat down. He felt brutalized by his women's emotions. The morning sun stroked his tight shoulder muscles and invited them to relax, but he knew he had to return to the room of furious women with a breakfast tray for them. His shoulders couldn't relax.

Damn that Douglas! Mostly, he hated seeing his Denise so unhappy. Second, he hated the wasted money. They'd come to this steaming dump in the middle of tourist season, for Pete's sake. And third, he knew he was going to have to hear about the public humiliation of being stood up at the altar for a long, long time. Damn!

The guests eating at the other tables in the courtyard nodded and smiled at him and returned to their conversations. He could tell they were all from Europe. Probably didn't even speak English, any of them. George felt like an odd fish.

At home, he was powerful. Knew the ropes. Had connections. Here, he'd been treated badly by that damned boy and there wasn't much he could do about it. His mind searched for possible weapons in Chania that he could bring against Douglas. He didn't taste his food.

141

Afterwards, he made up plates of fruit and sweet rolls for Denise and her mother, juice for both, coffee for Denise and tea for the missus. He asked the waiter for a tray, and carried it himself upstairs and back to the room. Rooms, actually. They had two connecting bedrooms with a sitting room between. All three rooms had large windows opening out on the Chania harbor and the promenading lowlife tourists out there in their strange clothes, dancing 'til all hours. George longed to be home.

His tray of food was greeted with howls of protest. Couldn't he see they were both in such pain that eating was impossible? One had a headache and the other was swiftly orbiting the room, too wound up to sit. He put the tray down on the coffee table.

"Daddy, can't you do something?"

"Yes, George, can't you go to the police or something?" His wife held a damp towel to her brow.

With great effort, he answered, "What would I ask at the police station? You want him arrested?"

His wife said, "There must be some crime here."

Denise said, "That bastard! Find him."

"All right, I'll try, but I think he's slipped the noose. We've all been trying to make him into the perfect boyfriend since eighth grade and it didn't work out. If you get him back now, you won't want him. He's broken."

"What do you mean, broken?"

"Douglas has never had an idea of his own before now. Didn't you ever notice that he took whatever we offered? Sometimes he made a little effort to please, but not much. I used to wonder if he had the balls to run The Safari Collection. When he took off yesterday, he finally showed some gumption. He wasn't following anyone else's orders for once."

Denise picked up the room service menu and threw it at the wall. Her father kept his eye on her while he picked it up and put it back on the desk.

He continued, "If he came back now, things would never be the same."

Mrs. Hanson said, in a hopeful tone, "But he might be better at running Safari Collection, right, George?"

George gave his wife an exasperated look. Denise threw her hands in the air.

"What are you saying, then?" Mrs. Hanson asked. "Are you saying that the Douglas we knew died yesterday?"

George eyed them both. "I'm saying he can't come back into my life. Denise can do what she wants."

Denise hurled herself down onto the sofa.

His wife continued, "Now who will take over the business when you retire?"

George didn't answer. He picked up Denise's untouched cup of coffee, now cold, and drank it. Denise looked at the tray. There was no more coffee. She glared at her father.

Mrs. Hanson said, "Does this mean you can't retire until Denise gets another boyfriend and you teach him all you know?"

"Oh, MuTHER. All you think about is yourself. What about me?"

George said, "I'm going out for a walk."

He went to the hotel desk. The clerk looked up brightly and handed George an envelope from the mayor's office. George opened it and found a bill for damages to three crystal paperweights. George threw the bill into a nearby wastebasket.

He asked the desk clerk, "Where's the police station?"

"Police. Yes. Go down to the harbor, turn away from the water, walk up Odos Halidon and cross Odos Yianari. When you get to Odos Kidonias, turn left and go to Odos Karaiskaki. You can't miss it."

George was not convinced. "Can you draw me a map?" The clerk did, and George set off with the piece of paper.

When he got to the end of the map, he saw a storefront with the words TOURIST POLICE in many languages on the plate glass window. Inside, people milled about. They looked like tourists, all right. To George, they looked European. Funny clothes. He pulled himself up tall and opened the door.

He took a plastic number card from a hook and looked at the number in lights on the wall above the uniformed men behind the counter. Twenty-one people before him. Balls! He went outside again and looked for someplace to get a coffee.

143

An officer followed him out and said, "Please don't take our numbers out of the office. They cost very much and it is difficult to get new ones."

George looked at the plastic number in his hand and at the officer. He said, "I want to file a missing persons report." He followed the officer back into the waiting area.

"You must wait your turn."

"But, am I in the right place?"

"I cannot tell you until it is your turn."

George debated walking out again, with the number, but he decided against it and stood near some seats filled with tourists, waiting his turn. When one of the seated tourists got up, he took her seat and continued to wait.

He watched the traffic and pedestrians through the venetian blinds until his eyes saw horizontal stripes when he looked away. After a very long time, his number came up. He got up from his sticky plastic chair and went to the available officer.

"I want to file a missing persons report."

" Oh, no, no, no. Not here. That is a police matter. We are the Tourist Police. Police station is on the inner harbor. Go there."

"I knew you'd say that," said George.

He retraced his steps until he came to the harbor, then went around the corner past the Mosque of the Janissaries and found the real police station. He went in. There was no crowd. He went up to the desk sergeant.

"Do you speak English?" he said, in a loud, slow voice.

"Of course." The man barely looked up from his paperwork.

"I want to report a missing person."

"Is the missing person a tourist?"

"Yes. He's a tourist. But I've been to the Tourist Police. They sent me here. So now, can you take the report?"

"We don't have missing persons reports."

"What do people do when people are missing?"

"They find them. What is the problem? Are you declaring a kidnapping? A crime?"

"Not exactly."

144

"Well, what then?"

George drew on the last patience he had to explain, "My daughter's fiancé ran away, I mean, he left the wedding, and hasn't been seen since yesterday."

The officer barely hid a smirk. "He what? He ran away? And you want us to find him?"

George had nothing to say.

"Mr. American Tourist, we are real police. We do real work. We don't look for missing...how do you call them, bridegrooms?"

"You won't take a report?"

"Your daughter is so angry you must do something, is it? You must bring her a form. Very well. Here is a crime report. Fill it out and I'll give you a copy and she will be happy. But we are not going to do anything, you understand? This is not a police matter."

George nodded in a humble way, and took the form over to a small table where he filled it out. He felt frustrated, helpless, foreign. He hated this place. He imagined a flight back to Athens. When he had filled in the blanks, guessing what some of the lines were asking for, he returned it to the desk.

The original sergeant took it from him, folded it, and put it in his desk drawer. George said, "No, I need a copy." He held his hand out. The sergeant handed him back the original. George said, "Copy...Please."

The sergeant got up from his desk and went to a small copy-machine. He made a copy and handed it to George. Then he folded up the original and added it to the detritus in his desk drawer.

"Thank you," muttered George. He went back out onto the promenade next to the inner harbor and made a loop through the Old City. He found himself peering at the faces of the tourists sitting in the open air kafenions. He wanted to make sure Douglas wasn't out there having a nice time while the three of them were suffering.

As he walked through the network of narrow alleys, his thoughts were of reprisals. But what? If Douglas was hiding somewhere, he couldn't do anything directly to him. He hoped that bastard was hiding somewhere really uncomfortable. He looked in at happy, tanned tourists drinking beers or tsikoudias or eating *boureki* or ice cream sundaes. Douglas wasn't among them. He wondered where he was.

145

He passed a shop with a huge poster of a man in black clothing and boots, with a big moustache and a turban. No, it wasn't a turban. It had fringe, just like the rack of fluttering black nylon scarves below the poster. He stopped to look at them.

"*Sariki*," said the shopkeeper. "Cretan men wear them. For fighting. Keeps the sweat out of their eyes. Also scares enemy. Is traditional, see?" and he took one of the little nylon ones and twisted it and held it across his brow. It looked silly because it was half the size of the one in the poster. "Like this." He looked momentarily fierce. "You want one?"

George knew he would never wear a fringed nylon cloth around his head, but the idea of buying the fighting power of this place appealed to him. Besides, later he could give it to Denise who might wear it around her throat and think it was lacy and pretty.

He bought the nylon totem and put it in his pocket.

It took a good angry thirty minutes to work his way through the happy vacationers along the harborside. Their pleasure made him madder. He reached the east end of the harbor, near the arsenali, a row of old warehouses the Venetians had built. He turned absently toward them. A tourist bar on his right brandished a large sign saying, "Welcome Inn" in English and as near as he could determine, in Danish, Finnish, German, and something else. He could see a dazzlement of bottles reflected in the mirror behind the bar. Lots of bottles. Scotch and bourbon. Real stuff. Not just beer and that tsikoudia. His feet found their way right inside. He sat down and ordered up a Manhattan.

Just like home. Manhattans taste the same the world over, he thought. The alcohol began to dissolve the edges of his rage. It didn't diminish, but it changed form. He sat in the dark shade of the interior bar and peered out past the sidewalk tables and happy Scandinavians. He dared Douglas to walk past.

After that drink and two more, George stood up, pulled some drachmas from his wallet, and put them down on the counter. He turned and went bravely back into the daylight. He still didn't have a plan and he still felt dangerous.

He worked his way past those 400-year-old warehouses and turned right, past some shells of stone buildings, never rebuilt in the fifty years since the Nazis bombed the city. Birds flew through their windows and landed on full-grown trees inside their walls. George wanted a bomb. He wanted to cause real pain.

He turned another corner and was abruptly lost. He cursed and after another block, he found a passageway between two buildings, came out in a small square he hadn't seen before, turned another corner and was surprised to find himself at the Venetian headquarters of the George Hanson Institute of Minoan Archaeology. He admired the sign for a moment, then he knew what he was going to do. He climbed the steps and opened the door to the Institute.

The elegant marble floor received his footsteps with a respectful clicking sound. That woman Athena, only she pronounced it differently, AthinAH, and certainly didn't look like Athena-the-goddess, tall and armored, since this one was short and pale and easy to ignore, came out of her glass-box office to see what he wanted.

"I'm going to see Mr. Ducor, my dear," Hanson said in a don't-mess-with-me voice.

"I'll tell him you're coming." Athina said and retreated toward her telephone, but before she had time to buzz, George Hanson let himself into Ducor's damned, elegant office. He closed the door behind him and stood, looking at Ducor, who was first surprised then alarmed to see George Hanson before him with a very red face. He thought perhaps the man was ill, except that electric charges seemed to be flashing from Hanson's eyes. Ducor was frightened but tried not to show it. He stood up and walked around his desk, then gestured to the other chair in his office, inviting Hanson to sit down.

Hanson shook his head. "Pack your bags, Professor. You're finished here!"

"What are you saying, please?" Ducor's voice cracked.

"Pack up. I'm shutting you down. This Institute is over. You've had all summer and you've just found a bunch of little pieces of crockery and some walls."

"Pottery. Sherds of pottery. But they tell us a lot."

"They don't tell me much, and it's my Institute. How do the politicians say it? Someone serves at the pleasure of the President. In this case, you serve at my pleasure, and I'm not pleased!"

"But what did I do?"

Hanson's body was weaving forward and backward, and his voice grew louder as he continued.

147

"I just told you. You're too slow. No results. No payoff on my investment. No headlines saying, Great Discovery in Western Crete on that peninsula whatever-it's-called Rodhosomething...Rodho-Nothing! You were expecting a lifetime assignment, weren't you? Well, it's over."

"Mr. Hanson, this is our first season—an exploratory season. We did well. You said three years, renewable another five maybe. Remember, we have had only four trained workers from Crete, and then just volunteer labor from college students on holiday, and not enough of them. We had five student-workers to start with, and of those, two were useless: they just wanted to get suntans and drink beer. Then another one went home early with a broken foot. How do you expect me to excavate a whole palace in one summer with two students and four workers? At Troy, Schliemann had crews of hundreds of workers, and many foremen—I have only poor Efthikas for a foreman, and then Athina and myself."

"I'll look into this fellow Schliemann. Maybe he's available."

"Mr. Hanson, he's dead. He discovered Troy in 1873."

There was a long, out-of-focus moment as Hanson thought about Schliemann.

"How'm I supposed to know that?" He glared even harder at Ducor. He added, "Don't you make fun of me."

"I promise I am not making fun of you, Mr. Hanson. And look, Troy is being re-excavated in the present day. The Daimler-funded UNESCO dig there has had as many as seventy experts working at any one time—in each aspect of archaeology. We have had just me."

"So now I'm not generous enough? Well, I'm not Daimler. I funded you and you promised results. Where are they?"

"Mr. Hanson, they are in boxes in the storeroom at the Archaeological Museum. There are many nice sherds of coarseware from our site."

"And they all look like bits of flowerpot. Besides, they don't have any designs on them. I wanted designs so I could copyright them and use them on textiles. These pieces are just blank. Useless!"

"That's because they are utilitarian. We have found a storeroom, probably filled with pithoi used for storing oil. Those pieces will probably be the least valuable ones we find, but they tell us we have a good chance of being on the edge of the Minoan palace."

"Why not start with the royal treasury? Dig there first. Why begin with the store room? You're wasting my money and time."

"But," howled Ducor, "you are asking the impossible!"

"Get out. Close up shop and go home. And not back to Laronwood, either. Go back to Europe. I don't want to bump into you by accident at the Galleria or under the arch or someplace. I'll tell my brother you've resigned."

"Mr. Hanson, let's talk about this another day, when you are not so upset about your daughter being jilted."

"Damn you! No! I'm freezing the assets today. The Institute is closed. Get out. Fire the staff. Turn in your key." He held out his hand.

"If I give you the key now, how shall I lock the building when I leave it?"

"Oh. Right." Hanson dropped his hand. "You have til noon tomorrow. Who do we rent this building from? Turn the key in to him." Hanson left, slamming the door behind him.

Ducor's breath came in short, desperate gasps. He followed Hanson out to the marble corridor. Athina saw him, through her glass walls. He stumbled over to a leather bench, grasped it, and slid to the floor. He lay there, a beached fish, gasping, unable to tell her his horrible news. When the puffer did not help, Athina called paramedics.

His lips turned blue. When the medical crew arrived, they moved Ducor onto a stretcher, hooked him up to an oxygen tank, and drove him off to hospital.

Athina borrowed a motor scooter from a friendly jeweler nearby. She followed the ambulance. She told herself that because Professor Ducor had no family, it was her job to go. In truth, she loved him, and hoped one day he would notice that she did.

She pulled up at the parking area of the hospital in time to see the ambulance back up to a double door, attendants pull the stretcher bearing the professor out of the vehicle, and everybody go into the building. By the time she reached the doors, they had shut

149

and locked. A red sign on them said AMBULANCE STAFF ONLY/ NO ADMITTANCE. She ran around to the front entrance. The receptionist did not look up when she ran in. Four people stood in line waiting for the receptionist's attention. Athina stood behind the fourth for about fifteen seconds, then burst past the lineup, past the desk, and through doors marked HOSPITAL STAFF ONLY, into the inner sanctum of the hospital. She ran to a nurses' station, asked a young woman where Emergency was, followed her gesture and ran on down the hall. No one tried to stop her.

The corridor ended. She looked to the right, saw a door marked EMERGENCY, and pushed it open. She saw Professor Ducor being lifted from the stretcher onto a gurney and the gurney raised to bed height. He was then wheeled into a curtained section of the room, and several people rushed around doing things. She could not see what they were doing. She watched their feet under the drape.

At last, the pace slowed. A man in green scrubs saw her there and came over to her. "Are you his wife?" he asked.

"His secretary," she said.

"You want a report on his condition, though."

"Yes, I do."

"Well, he had a bad asthma attack. Even now, his vital signs are agitated. Did he have a great shock?"

"I don't know. Maybe." Athina remembered the gray color of Ducor's face as he followed Mr. Hanson out of his office. What had happened between them?

"He'll have to stay here for several hours, until he stabilizes."

"Will he be all right?"

"I think so. It'll be a while before he can talk to you. Why don't you wait over there?"

He gestured to a dozen straight-backed chairs upholstered in red naugahyde, lined up in a corridor. She followed his directions, sat, and watched the minutes pass on the wall clock.

18

Aleko walked back to the injured robber slowly, giving Douglas time to get away. The robber moaned. Aleko tucked himself into a doorway and watched. Passersby stopped and then went over to the fallen man. They were puzzled by his ski-mask and the blood. Nobody touched him.

Someone ran to a nearby taverna to call for a policeman and an ambulance. The policeman arrived first. He pushed through the cluster of people and knelt over the stabbing victim. Aleko re-joined the crowd.

The policeman put his hand on the back of the ski mask and gently pulled it forward, revealing the face of the wounded man.

Aleko gasped, "Manolis!"

The robber coughed more blood, opened his eyes, looked at Aleko. Then his eyes glazed and seemed to roll up. Just the whites showed. The eyes closed and his head slumped down.

The policeman turned to Aleko and said, "Manolis who? Son, who is this man?"

Aleko said, "I don't know. I thought I knew. Maybe I'm wrong."

The policeman gave him a quizzical look, then said, "Well, he has to go to hospital quickly or he'll die."

Aleko said again, "I'm wrong. I don't know him." But he couldn't help staring at the stabbed man.

The policeman gestured to the onlookers to back up and make room for the arriving ambulance to back into the alley. The ambulance paused while two attendants got out. Then it continued to back up.

The attendants ran over and knelt near the body. They pulled Manolis's chin up and stuck something black into his mouth. Then they wiped blood from his nose and chin and put a plastic cover over his lower face. It had a skinny hose that went over to something like a fire extinguisher.

Aleko could see the knife. All that showed was the handle. The blade was all the way in. Then it was hard to see what was happening because the ambulance men were moving all around. They lifted the robber up and onto a stretcher, and he wasn't moving at all. Aleko was pretty sure he was dead.

He watched as they put a fat band around his arm. They stuck a needle into his other arm and then taped the arm to a stiff thing. They hooked the needle to a hose that went up to a bag of something.

They did something with the knife but didn't take it out. Then they picked up the stretcher and put it in the ambulance. They took off fast with the siren going. Aleko thought if Manolis was already dead, they wouldn't use the siren. He felt a little bit better about that.

The policeman wanted information from Aleko. He didn't answer the policeman's questions. He didn't know what he should say. Family honor was at stake. He shouldn't say anything about Manolis the robber to the police, but then, there was Manolis maybe dying, and then again, Douglas stabbed him, he didn't have to do that, and the knife was his own father's, *Mbaba's*, and after all, Manolis was being mean, and what was he supposed to do? He didn't say anything, but he began to cry.

The policeman was patient with him. He waited. When Aleko's tears slowed down, he asked where Aleko was going when this happened. Aleko said he was going to see his mother at work. So the policeman, fishing for information and hoping the mother would give the boy permission to tell something, offered to drive him to his mother's work place. Aleko nodded.

He ran up the steps of the taverna calling out for his mother. She opened the door to the room she was cleaning and he ran into her arms and began talking a mile a minute. He stopped, and pulled the 20,000 drachmas out of his pocket and gave them to her. Then he continued his tale of the second robbery. She nodded gravely until he reported whose face was under the ski-mask. Then she gasped and said, "Are you sure?"

"*Mana mou*, I am sure. But I didn't want to tell. Did I do right? What do we do?"

"We go to the hospital and see if it is Manolis. Where is Daonglos?"

"He ran."

"Oh dear," said Vassilia. "It looks very bad for him. Why did he run?" She put away her cleaning tools.

Aleko followed his mother downstairs. He didn't tell her that he had told Daonglos to run.

Vassilia took off her apron and handed it to Dimosthenes, who said, "Who's going to help me now? Where are you going?" As she headed toward the door, he said, "Wait! When will you come back?"

Vassilia turned and answered, "I don't know when I'll be back. This is a family matter."

Dimosthenes said, "That's it. Too much family matter. You don't have a job here anymore."

She walked past him and down the steps to the sandy sidewalk. Aleko was now really scared. He led his mother to the policeman, who held the door open for them to climb into the patrol car. As the policeman drove to the hospital, he tried to get some information about Manolis, who might be the stabbed man. He learned nothing from Vassilia, either.

At the hospital, the policeman went inside with them. He disappeared into some offices there. Vassilia and Aleko sat on stiff red chairs with chrome arms and legs. They waited. The stabbed man was in surgery.

Vassilia asked Aleko again how he knew it was Manolis. Did he have any idea why Manolis would rob him? No, he didn't.

Vassilia asked at the reception desk if someone would dial a phone number for her. She called Sofia and, in a soft voice, told her it might be a good idea for her to come to the hospital right away.

When Sofia arrived, they all went outside the waiting room and out to the street, so that they could speak freely. Sofia said to Aleko, "Tell us what you know, please."

Aleko told them about the two robberies. His mother confirmed his account of the first robbery and the pellets in the American's back. He told his aunt he knew it was the same robber who jumped out of a doorway at them today. Then Daonglos stabbed him and ran away. When the policeman came and pulled off the ski-mask, the face underneath was Manolis.

Sofia asked a lot of questions to try to make it not true, but Aleko stuck to his story. He was convinced it was Manolis. She looked at her sister and said, "Oh, what do I do?"

"I am here, little sister," said Vassilia.

The two women hugged, then they sat on a concrete retaining wall and stared off at the Lefka Ori. Aleko began to walk along the top of the wall they were sitting on. After awhile, they went back to the waiting room to wait.

19

Dr. Gavalas went down to the ER to wait for the arriving stab victim. The ambulance radio said knife wound to the left chest. Coming in from Nea Hora.

Would this be one of the regular muggers from that area? he wondered.

When the gurney rolled in, though, Dr. Gavalas hadn't seen the boy before.

The young man was unconscious. Fresh blood was welling around a black rubber airway. He was cyanotic and respirations were shallow. Knife still in place.

"What's that between his ankles?"

The driver said, "Ski mask he had on."

"Robbery?"

"Don't know."

"How long was he down?"

"We were eleven minutes at the scene and another ten getting back here. Police were already there." The driver read from a clipboard. "Pulse weak and thready, 90. Blood pressure 70 over 45."

"Do we know who he is?"

"Police are looking into it."

Dr. Gavalas slipped on gloves and cut the t-shirt away from the knife. He studied the knife's angle of entrance. Straight to the lower lobe, likely missing the spleen and stomach. Could be worse. He wrapped a towel around the knife handle, leaned his hip against the table, and pulled hard. He dropped the knife into a plastic bag.

A rush of blood followed the knife. A nurse packed gauze against the bleeding wound and placed a piece of tape tightly across it.

"We can't wait for an ID and consent. Let's go."

Dr. Gavalas held the elevator door open while a nurse rolled the gurney in. They went up to the second floor operating room.

The assistant surgeon had scrubbed up and was waiting. Dr. Gavalas scrubbed up while the anesthesiologist put the patient on oxygen and anesthesia. He and a nurse turned Manolis onto his right side and placed a pillow between his bent legs. They taped his arm to a frame that hung over the top of the operating table.

Dr. Gavalas incised along the fifth intercostal space from the sternum in front almost to the spine in back. He pulled the muscle layers aside.

"Rib spreader, please."

He ratcheted the jaws until the ribs were ten centimeters apart.

The assistant surgeon held two clamps on the pleura while Dr. Gavalas incised between them, mindful not to cut the lung.

"That was a wicked knife. A real passalis."

Dr. Gavalas answered, "My father had one like that. He said they were used for sheep slaughter up Lefka Ori a long time ago."

"For fights between andartes, I'll bet. I wonder where he got it?"

"No idea."

156

The exposed lung was barely moving. It'd be a waste of effort if he expired now. Dr. Gavalas asked, "Vitals?"

"He's pinking up. Heart rate, 80. BP, 80 over 50. Blood's coming now."

Dr. Gavalas found the cut in the lung. The suturing was a straight-forward job. The nurse handed him a syringe to irrigate the wound. They sewed the pleura back together.

Then, Dr. Gavalas went one rib below and made an incision in the skin. He pulled a chest tube through the incision and positioned it close to the lung. When the tube was set, he attached it to a suction system. Several bags of blood arrived just then.

"How could he have been stabbed from that low angle? I can't figure how the stabber was standing."

"Later. Take out the spreader and let's pull these ribs back together."

They watched Manolis's bones move back into position. Dr. Gavalas closed him up.

"He's lucky to be alive."

They moved him to a hospital bed and rolled him to the recovery room. Dr. Gavalas made sure his green scrub suit was blood-free, and went out to see if the boy had been ID'd and his family found.

20

Douglas ran, at first in an adrenaline-powered dash, then he settled into a steady pace as the momentary shock faded.

Yesterday, escaping from his wedding, he had run toward Lefka Ori. He was in trouble because he was late, not even his fault. Now, a day later, he'd probably killed a man. So here he was again, heading toward the same mountains. He didn't stop to wonder how many people in Crete's long history had gone to Lefka Ori for protection. He went toward the mountain on instinct.

Several passing drivers slowed down at the sight of a foreigner running up the road, but since he didn't signal for a ride, they all drove on. Douglas felt a lump in his throat, of frustration, anger, and, mostly, fear. He slowed to a walk, trying to catch his breath.

By now he had cleared the outskirts of greater Chania and was moving along the dirt shoulder of a narrow paved road. To his right, a dusty windbreak of cane screened a field of potatoes. He ducked through the windbreak and bent over, holding his knees and breathing deeply. His sweat stung his pellet wounds. He kicked out his leg cramps and when his pulse and respiration had returned to normal, he sat down in the shade, out of sight of the road. He was thirsty.

A mouse in the dry cane leaves startled him as it moved away. The image of the ski-mask spilling blood rose before him like a remembered scene from a movie. He shuddered. He had never killed anything before. It seemed so quick, so easy. He wondered, was this how people felt who killed for a living?

He went cold when he remembered the feeling of the knife hesitating at the surface of that man's body. The blade broke through his shirt, and then slid through skin and flesh to its full extent, to the very hilt. It was easy. He felt two things at once. He was repelled by the violence, and he felt excited, proud of the deed.

When he could step back from the sense-memory of it, a new thought came: well, he could at least congratulate himself on having felt rage enough to do it. Felt something for once in his life. Felt real rage. He thought, Now I am not just a watcher, but a do-er.

Then revulsion rolled over him again and he tried to erase the repeating image of the blood through the ski-mask and the strange and alarming rise of pleasure that came with the memory of the penetrating dagger.

So now I am wet by the sea of sin, an observer no longer. I am just like everyone else, driven by passions, too, only I've never met these feelings in myself before. I didn't really think I had them. Emotions were always Denise's territory. She felt them for both of us.

How do I learn to live with these feelings? They're like wild horses and I don't know how to hold on to the reins.

He tried to settle down, but he couldn't. He sprang back to his feet, went out onto the road again, and took up the ground-eating stride of his high school track days.

His stomach hurt. His running grew erratic. Again, he slowed to a walk. "Stab and run," said the rhythm in his head. He tried to turn it off. His skin felt cold. Clammy. Like snakeskin laid wet onto his cold flesh.

Aleko said go to the house. He would do that and wait there for the boy and his mother to come home.

The mountain had changed in the early afternoon. Shadows cut into the shape of rocks and knolls. None of it looked familiar. But he was confident he could find the boy's house. How hard could that be?

He tried to reconstruct the landmarks he had seen retreating from his position in the back of the pickup truck the day before. He even turned around and walked backwards for a few steps at a time trying to remember the plane-trees, any outcropping of rocks, and the distant views from the road. They all blended into a dusty image of shade-scarred hot countryside. He longed for a drink of water.

He remembered the truck passing through a village. Two villages, in fact. But one of them ought to be right around here and there was nothing here but dusty fields and olive groves bound in by stone and wire fences along the roadside ditch. There was water in the ditch, but it was slimy in places and it didn't look safe to drink.

He came back to the problem at hand. Aleko's house. Where was it? Had there been a turn-off? To the left? Right? His head began to hurt.

A police car drove up the road. Douglas paused to stare off at the distant landscape. He made an earnest study of goats that seemed only tiny spots on a carpet of tweed scrub. He watched them with as much interest as he could muster. He listened carefully to hear if the car slowed down, but it drove directly past, as if it wasn't looking for a runaway American murderer at this time. When the police car was out of sight, he resumed his walk.

It seemed curious to him that when he ran away yesterday he had no goal and didn't need one. Now, twenty-four hours later, he needed these barely-known peasants with their simple life. He felt lost until he could find them again.

It was all very strange. He thought, how can I care about these strangers as if they were my family when I don't feel that much about people back home? What do I have in common with Aleko and his mother, anyway?

Yeah, but what do I have in common with the Hansons or anyone else in my life?

Another wave of questions rose. Where did his anger come from? He'd never allowed himself to be angry, really angry, in his whole life.

160

Yet there he was, fighting like an animal. Who was this animal within him? And where had it been hiding all his life?

Physically, too, he was miserable. His wounds stung where sweat dripped into them. The bandage was sticking and the tape pulled. The leather shoes reminded his feet each step that they were meant for a wedding, not a hike. They rubbed his toes and the bones on his heel. Red raw spots were blossoming into blisters. Mostly, he was thirsty, damn it.

There! A six-inch length of white PVC pipe stuck out of the hillside above a stone retaining wall. Water trickled out of the pipe. There was no formal fountain around it, and it certainly wasn't in a village, but it might be an artesian well, running fresh, cold, spring water, just for him. He went over to it, bent over it, and sniffed. He determined that it wasn't sewage. Must be potable water. He closed his eyes and moved his mouth into the line of water.

It didn't taste exactly like the bottled so-called spring water from the office cooler in Chania, but it was water and it seemed to be natural. He drank until he wanted no more. He thought about the vivid pleasure of simple things. That fresh food at Aleko's house. Now this water.

He looked about, hoping for a landmark to direct him to Aleko's but he saw nothing familiar. Time to change plans. He thought he was probably above the turnoff he meant to take. So the idea would be to go to the next village, ask directions from someone—if he could find anyone who spoke English—and then go down-mountain in the right direction. Easy solution. By the time he got to Aleko's, the boy would probably be home to meet him.

There wasn't a village around the next curve, nor the one after that. The day grew hotter and the light glaring off the dust-polished paving hurt Douglas's eyes. He began to think about a drink of cold water again, and then about food.

This seemed like a very harsh punishment he was suffering. After all, he hadn't planned to stab the robber who attacked him. Aleko had given him the knife. Without the knife, he wouldn't have killed the guy. Socked him, maybe, but not killed.

161

Poor Douglas. Injustice moved right into his head, bringing self-pity along for company. He felt really picked on by the time he arrived at the next village. He thought it was probably a good four kilometers above where he wanted to go. It would be a long walk back.

A yellow dog approached, stiff-legged, head down, to sniff him. Douglas held his hand out, palm down. The dog sniffed the hand, raised his head and wagged his tail slowly. First challenge passed.

Douglas was annoyed at the village. That is, he was annoyed and the village was there. He hobbled in on his very sore feet and looked around for the fountain. Every village has a fountain. This one stood in a muddy place. He had to wait while an old woman filled up a liter-size blue and buff stoneware pitcher and then another one. He shifted from foot to foot as he waited. When she finished, she smiled at him as she left. He attempted a smile in return. He drank.

Douglas went up three tall concrete steps into the village's mini-market and looked at the food there. Plastic-wrapped cakes and sandwiches, boxed juices, colas and cans of beer in a cooler, sausages and cheese beckoned to him. He went slowly past the displays, full of choices he couldn't afford. He had not one drachma. There was nothing he could buy. These foods tormented him. He deserved to be treated better than this. He picked up a package of Mizithra cheese and nonchalantly slipped it into his pocket. He casually walked out of the shop.

His foot hadn't even touched the second concrete step when a voice said, in American English, "Put the cheese back."

Douglas kept going down the steps, telling himself he had heard no such voice.

A hand on his arm stopped him. He turned around. A Greek Orthodox priest, with a full black beard and a long black cassock glared at him. "These people are not here for you to steal from. They work hard and deserve respect. Put the cheese back or pay for it." He held on tightly to Douglas's arm.

Douglas wondered if all Greek Orthodox priests on Crete spoke English. Then shame worked its way up his body, pushing the hungry self-pity aside. This shame filled him. He stood perfectly still. He reached in his pocket, removed the packaged cheese, and handed it to the priest. "I can't pay for it. I have no money."

"That's not their fault. You can just go back to your hotel and get some more money. Then come back and buy food like everyone else does."

"I wish I could." Douglas tried to leave, but even without the cheese, his arm was still clamped by the large, strong hand of the American-sounding priest.

"Return the cheese to the shopkeeper and apologize to him for what you have done."

"You're treating me like a naughty six-year-old."

"That's the way you've behaved. Go on. Back inside."

Douglas called down lightning on himself, but none came.

He climbed back up the steps into the shop. The priest handed him the stolen cheese, and he presented it to the shopkeeper and said, "I took this and I am sorry. I have no money to buy it from you but I should not have taken it." Then he glared at the priest and said, "Can I go now?"

The shopkeeper looked to the priest for his cue. He was prepared either to act angry or to give the poor man the cheese. The priest shook his head and said, "This man is Kyrios Varasulakis. He owns this shop. Respectfully address him when you apologize…and don't steal again from anyone on the island. Your kind are destroying their livelihoods."

Douglas pulled together all his remaining strength and looked the shopkeeper in the eye. "I am sorry, Kyrios Varasulakis. I will not steal food again. Please forgive me."

"*Then pirazi.*" said the shopkeeper. "Is good, Pappa Dimitri." He nodded and the priest released his hold on Douglas.

"Now, do you really have no money?"

"None."

"Do you have a place to go?"

"Yes, I'm staying with a little boy named Aleko and his mother."

"Really?"

"Yes. Do you know them?"

"The ones I know couldn't be the ones you're looking for. Why do you look familiar?"

"I don't know. No reason, I think."

"You aren't dressed like a tourist."

"I've been working on a dig all summer."

163

"You don't look like an archaeologist, either."

"I guess not. Anyway, I think I've come too far up the mountain. So, thanks, I'll go now."

Douglas turned down-mountain out of the village. He wondered what he had thanked the priest for. Maybe permission to leave the scene of his shame.

He, too, had the feeling they'd met before.

He went over the crest of a hill, and started down the mountain, on a road that was now dirt, if it ever had been paved. Crete was riddled with remnants of Roman roads and even older ones. Sometimes they only showed up from an airplane or in an infrared photograph, but this old road was still in use.

Once he could no longer see the village of his disgrace, or it see him, he began to feel better. He weighed the relative value of hunger and shame. Hunger only bothered the body. Shame climbed into his head, or heart, or wherever it was the spirit might reside. He'd never thought about where that was, but shame shot straight there and it made him feel awful.

He determined he'd rather be hungry.

Now there were two places he could not go back to in Crete: Chania for fear of Denise and her parents, and this nameless village, for fear of running into that strange priest who spoke English like an American.

Where else was he no longer welcome? he wondered. A wave of unsettled dis-belonging hit him again. He dis-belonged everywhere. He wondered if he would ever belong to other people. He trudged on, his feet hurting. He had the intention of returning to Aleko's place but with no clear idea where that might be. A large buzzard soared past on an updraft. Douglas stopped to watch it, to envy it that it belonged here and he seemed to belong nowhere.

The sound of a motor made him turn around. A plume of dust followed closely behind a small motorbike. The priest was riding it. He waved when Douglas turned around.

"Wait. You still haven't eaten. Come back with me and you can earn your lunch by helping me do something." The priest gestured to Douglas to get on the pillion behind him and the Vespa labored back up the dirt road.

21

Athina waited in agony in the corridor. She couldn't see anything through the open doorway to the ER except a short wall of particle board with notices stapled to it. She could hear things, though.

She heard things rolling—she imagined those tall steel racks that hold bottles of medicines to drip down tubes into people through needles.

She heard things clicking—she imagined heart-starting apparatus like she'd seen on TV. She hoped the dear professor didn't need to have that treatment!

She heard muffled voices. She listened hard but she couldn't make out the words. She tried to read the tone of voice to see if this was routine treatment or if her beloved was in trouble.

She said the word to herself again. Her beloved. She sat back in the uncomfortable chair. A broken spring pushed her forward, so she sat with her elbows on her knees and closed her eyes to listen.

Beloved. She tasted the word. He was her beloved, all right. And if he died, she would grieve terribly. She reminded herself, if he walked out of the emergency room right now he would probably be surprised to see her there.

Athina was not a beauty. She was of middling height, a little plump, with hair that used to be streaked blond when she was young and out in the sunlight. Now it was a nameless color. Her features were pleasant but only if one took the time to notice them.

She was an old maid and she knew it. She might have married Nikolaos Loukakis when she was seventeen. She had chosen university instead of marriage then, although her parents had warned her that by twenty she'd be too old for any Cretan man to wish to marry. And it was true. Now she was thirty-four, and her days were spent doing work in support of the field she loved, and writing I love you on memo pads while thinking about Professor Roland Ducor and then tearing up the evidence of her devotion before anyone could see it.

Back then she had believed the optimistic view that it was possible for a modern woman on Crete to have a career and marriage. She'd gone to the University of Crete in Rethimnon, begun the archaeology curriculum, was doing fine, but then the fates stepped on her plans. Both her parents got sick. There was no one else to care for them. Of course she quit school. After they died, she sold their house to pay the costs of their last illnesses. Soon the money was all gone. She was left with no parents, no money, no husband, no degree, and no prospects, so she took a job selling tourist trinkets and went to secretarial school. Then she applied for work in every office with any connection to her former field of archaeology. If she couldn't study it, at least she could help others and be around talk of it. It was an onlooker's life and she had grown accustomed to it. She asked nothing more.

166 The first office she had worked in was for an American team of archaeologists and geologists. She found them brusque.

Then a British study group from a university—she honestly couldn't remember which—hired her. They were funny, joking all the time, but they joked past her and she felt belittled.

Her third job was with Professor Ducor. In her first week he surprised her by asking her opinion about the arrangement of the office. In fact, by the end of that first week he left the entire management of the office in her hands. Ever since, he had treated her with respect. She was grateful.

Please don't die, she thought. Please. You have no idea how deeply I will grieve if you die. Please!

She opened her eyes and stared at the floor. She could conjure his face even there. She remembered the scent of his aftershave. The sight of his handwriting gave her a flutter. She adored the wrinkles in his khaki suit. She ached for him to live, without any hope for herself that he would ever love her. Or even really notice her.

As Athina sat there, awash with loving fears, a nine-year-old boy came into the corridor area and sat on a chair across from her. He got up and moved to another, turned around on it and looked out the window behind it, turned back and sat down again. He brought his feet up to the chair seat and hugged his knees.

Athina felt his presence like a coiled spring. After half a minute, he jumped up again and walked quickly down the hall.

Athina returned to her reverie. She began to list what she was prepared to offer to God if He would just spare the Professor, just spare Roland. In her daydreams he was "my Roland." She would sacrifice her future, her health, yes, even her life, if Roland would live.

The boy came back. He again took the chair across from her. He crossed his arms and grabbed his shoulders with the opposite hands—he hugged himself.

She looked at him this time. He was a dark-haired boy with sky-blue eyes. He looked firmly past her at the wall behind her. His lip trembled. He breathed several sighs, then sank deeper into the chair.

Athina watched in silence until she could bear his pain no longer. She said, "Would you like to talk?"

The boy looked at her. "No," he said and was silent. But something had changed in the air in the room. His isolation was broken. Athina waited.

The boy cleared his throat, then said, "My cousin got stabbed. He may die."

"Why was he stabbed?"

167

The boy buried his face in his hands. Athina moved across the corridor and sat in the chair next to him.

He said, "It is my fault," and sank weeping onto her lap. She stroked the thin shoulders and waited.

Presently, he sat up and looked at her. "I took my father's passalis and gave it to Daonglos, so we wouldn't get robbed again today, but Daonglos stabbed him."

"Your cousin? This Daonglos stabbed your cousin?"

"Yes. Manolis. The robber."

"Your cousin was trying to rob you?"

"Yes. I don't know why. He has some money. I am not his enemy. Why did he do this? And why did Daonglos stab him? I don't understand anything," and he fell to sobs again.

Athina sat still, holding his shoulder, breathing slowly to calm him. There was no comfort to offer. She just held on.

A woman, the boy's mother she guessed, came to the door and saw them. She held her finger to her lips and gestured to Athina that she'd be in the waiting room on the left. Athina nodded and did not move.

Vassilia and Sofia told the receptionist that they believed Sofia's son was the knife victim in surgery. She took their names and they sat down in the waiting room near the post-op recovery room. They settled in to wait to hear if Manolis would live.

One hour and twenty minutes later, a nurse came out to the receptionist, who pointed to Sofia and Vassilia. The nurse reported to them that the knife had gone in between two ribs and punctured the left lung, but recovery looked good. They would be able to identify him in ICU after the surgery.

After that, the minutes stretched flat and horrible while the doctors kept working on him.

Vassilia looked around for Aleko. When she couldn't see him, she got up and went down each of the corridors that led off the waiting room. She found him in one, his face in his hands, sobs shaking his frame, comforted by a stranger, a woman who seemed willing to be bothered by an unhappy boy.

She gestured to the unknown woman to show where she'd be, then she returned to her sister, to wait to see the patient. The two sisters didn't say anything until after they went to the ICU and identified Manolis.

Vassilia asked, "What will you tell Spiros?"

"What can I say?"

"What will he do?" Vassilia spoke in a whisper.

"Beat him, I think. I never know what he'll do. Maybe he'll praise him. He mustn't think he has a reason to beat Manolis. He'd kill him."

"He doesn't have to know about the robbery part."

"That policeman knows. He was the one who pulled off that head thing."

"Will Spiros check with the police? Maybe he won't ask."

"He'll ask. Would you know that policeman? If you saw him again, I mean."

"I'd know him."

Sofia said, "Then let's talk to him and tell him Manolis made a bad joke and the blame is all the American's. He's gone now, and we don't know him."

"Spiros will find out some day."

"If he does, it will be old news and Manolis will have healed."

"Then I am afraid for your safety, little sister," said Vassilia.

"Because of the lie? He has never hit me. He only hits the boy."

22

The Vespa pulled up in front of the stone facade of Agyios Yeorgeos. Fr. Dimitrios led the way to the church doors, unlocked them, and stepped aside.

Douglas found himself in an empty room, a formal space, mostly square, with a polished stone floor. Across the room was a step leading to an elaborate free-standing screen hung with painted figures on gold backgrounds. There were no pews.

The ceiling was a dome, thirty feet wide. He sensed its volume, felt it first, then looked up. Sunlight through two small windows high in the south wall shone across the room, struck the floor, and reflected light into the rest of the room. Along that wall, four straight-backed chairs stood. He noticed a faint smell of candle wax and incense. It was clearly a sacred space, but unlike any church Douglas had seen before.

Fr. Dimitrios faced the painted screen and crossed himself. Douglas walked toward the screen, to admire what he recognized as the Annunciation—figures of the archangel Gabriel and the Virgin

Mary—on a pair of doors in the center. He stopped a respectful distance away and looked at the other figures across the screen.

"Is that your altar?"

Fr. Dimitrios said, "That's an ikonostasis. Ever seen one?"

"I saw Byzantine icons in an art history class, but not something like this."

"The altar is behind it, in a sacred space where only the priest and his acolytes go." Fr. Dimitrios walked over to the north wall. "The paintings I'm trying to uncover will be in a similar style to those icons—Cretan style—but older. Much older."

"Paintings?" Douglas followed him and saw dropcloths over the stone floor. Some small tools lay across a rough stool near the wall. Alongside were a blue plastic bowl and a bottle. The dirty-white wall was missing in an area above the stool. In its place, a section of pale red and dark forms showed through.

"I'm rescuing icons from whitewash."

"How are you doing it?"

"Look here. I flake it off and then patch the pieces that come loose from the painting underneath with this stuff." He handed Douglas the bottle of Rhoplex AC33.

"What do you want me to do?" Douglas read the label on the bottle.

"I was hoping you'd say, 'Oh, I've removed lots of whitewash. Let me show you an easier way' and then show me how to do it faster."

"I'm no use. Never done it. I know nothing about it—but that looks like a backbreaking job. If you show me what I need to know, I'll pick for awhile for you."

"Great!" Fr. Dimitrios disappeared and came back with a second stool. He demonstrated the technique he'd developed for flaking off bits of whitewash. As they worked, the two sat in silence. After some time, Douglas spoke.

"I don't usually steal food, you know."

"I didn't think so. How did you come to be without your wallet?"

"It made a bulge in my suit so I left it in my room."

"Where was that?"

171

"Chania."

They worked on in silence. Then Douglas said, "Why do I still feel so bad?"

"Is it because you stole? or because you were caught?"

"Both, I guess."

"The apology you gave Kyrios Varasulakis frees you from blame. What you lay on yourself is shame. He's not angry at you. He has excused the whole thing."

"He has?"

"Sure. You are not in disgrace with the community here. Only with yourself, it seems. Do you know where the healing of confession comes from?"

Douglas shook his head.

"It incorporates the act of accountability and the balm of forgiveness."

Douglas nodded absently. He tried to explain himself. "I'm not used to..."

"...to what?"

"...to doing things that break through the safe mold of my life. I always avoided trouble by doing what I was supposed to. Amazing how well it worked, too. Now I'm on new ground—not safe anymore—and I'm not sure what I'm doing."

"I don't think I follow what you're saying."

Douglas told the young priest about running from his wedding the day before. He described helping Aleko and getting shot. He told of spending the night at Aleko's house, and of Vassilia's kindness.

He failed to mention the second robbery that had happened that day. Or the fact that he had stabbed someone. He skated past that, saying he was supposed to meet Aleko back at the house and he'd taken a wrong turning and had no money and had taken the cheese because he was hungry.

"The cheese! And you still haven't eaten. I'm sorry. Let me go get you some food." Fr. Dimitrios left him picking at the whitewash while he went to Kyria Ariadne's house and asked her to prepare something for a guest. He returned with two small cheese pies and a plum. Douglas ate them gratefully.

Fr. Dimitrios took a look at the itchy pellet wounds. "I'm not a doctor, but they look fine to me. Not inflamed. I think you're okay."

Over lunch, they talked about home and belonging. Douglas said he knew he no longer belonged where he had grown up. He certainly wasn't part of the culture of Crete. He had no idea where he belonged. He said, "I'm in exile now, but from what? And where will I end up?"

Fr. Dimitrios thought for a moment. "Exile," he said, "is too grand a word to apply to either of us, but I know what you mean. We have left the safe places of our childhood."

"Yes, even if those places weren't as safe as we thought, we had a home there."

"Exactly." Fr. Dimitrios said, "My exile is a different kind. I was born here but spent my school years living in San Francisco. Whichever place I am, I ache for the other. I am always in a kind of exile."

"I see," said Douglas. "Sure, I can see that." But he honestly didn't see it. How is it possible to ache for a place? He envied the priest. The envy surprised him, too. Feelings were bouncing off everything that was happening to him. New feelings. Now, envy.

They picked at the wall for some time. Then Fr. Dimitrios stood up and stretched. He said, "You've more than earned your lunch. I wish I could have your help every day on this long process, but you can go now."

Douglas stretched, too, and thanked Fr. Dimitrios for the food. He asked again for directions to Aleko's house.

Fr. Dimitrios said, "I'll show you. Wait a moment." He went off and came back with a white plastic bag containing three plums, three cheese pies wrapped in waxed paper, three hard-cooked eggs, and a tomato. "Here. I think Kyria Andreadaki will be pleased to have these. Now, let me show you how to get there faster."

Douglas found himself outside the church, holding his bag of provisions. The bag said Chania Music Centre on it, in English, Greek, German, Finnish and Swedish. He remembered that store, in the city. It was on the way to the Institute. They played the theme from *The Mission* on the street speaker. Yo-Yo Ma. Not very Greek, but he was always happy to hear it. He had that CD back home.

The priest said, "You want to go to the lower village. The road winds around quite a bit. I'll show you a shortcut and you'll save some time." He pointed to a rutted dirt alley. "Take this road about 500 meters and you'll see a path through a field. It's not much of a path, actually. I'd better show you." So he took off with Douglas down the rutted road.

"You're looking for Kato Vraho. Someone there can direct you to the Andreadakis house. I'm assuming that's the Aleko you met up with. Nine years old, with a widowed mother, no other family."

Douglas nodded. "Thanks. If I can find the village I can find the house. I know it."

"Well, then. Here's the path." The priest indicated a stretch of hillside covered by a lumpy carpet of woody plants. Most had bluegreen foliage. A few still had late yellow blossoms. Only the toughest plants could afford a bloom in August. The fragrance of Jerusalem Sage hung heavy, like sour dust. Douglas tried to ignore the smell. A network of narrow pathways worked its way through the plants.

"You'll come to the lower village in a kilometer or so. Watch out for herders' dogs and don't trust the billys. They can both attack. I've learned to respect the dogs of Crete. And billygoats are unpredictable. Put a few rocks in your pocket."

"Thanks for the warning. And for the food."

Douglas climbed up a sandy bank and stepped into the landscape.

He turned down a narrow path which led him first right then left. He tried not to tread on the plants, but the smell of oregano rose from some of the leaves he stepped on.

He thought, I was shamed over that cheese thing, but it's past. It's all right now. I apologized, suffered the humiliation, said—and meant—that I wouldn't do it again and I feel free of the event. I paid the price in shame, not money. I don't owe it any more.

He realized he had been separated from his American identity for two days now. He thought, I am not dependent any more. Off the tether. Wandering free.

He felt huge.

Present time seemed only an illusion. The olive trees on the ridge ahead were outlined with halation, and his thoughts seemed newly large. He saw his progress as timeless, resonant, brilliant. He stopped and abruptly wondered if this was a sign of infection. He touched his wounds, but they felt all right.

Life was perfect. He had food, he had a plan, no one was out to get him…and then a knot of fire dropped into his stomach. He thought of the blood coming through the robber's ski-mask. What about the police? Were they looking for him yet? Aleko was the only witness. Maybe. He wondered if that man had died. Likely so, he thought. The police will have come. They will have filed a report. What could Aleko and his mother say to protect him? And why should they? He wondered if it was a good idea to go to their house after all. Maybe he was walking into an ambush.

No place to go. No friends. He came to a stop. Then he turned around and retraced his steps to the church. He would confide in this priest, and ask what to do.

When he knocked on the door, no one came. He called out, but he heard no answer. The door was locked.

He felt foolish and went back out to the path Fr. Dimitrios had sent him to.

Forty-five minutes later he hadn't gotten far. The going was possible only if he stayed on the very narrow twisting paths trampled by the goats picking their way through the thorny, brutalized plants. Mediterranean scrub. He'd heard the name for it. Maquis. Garigue. Something like that.

These goats eat the landscape. It's amazing anything can survive Cretan goats, and for millennia, too. He caught glimpses of the sea to the north of Crete.

What was Aleko's mother's name? Douglas wished he'd paid more attention. He wasn't good with remembering names. It was like that first time Denise took him home and he'd tried to be chummy with her father and he'd called him Joe when his name was George. Dumb! And George had spared no effort in telling him that! Afterwards,

175

he'd called him Mr. Hanson even up to—when was it? Yesterday! The wedding.

The enormity of it all spilled over him. He had run away from the very people who had taken him in, treated him like a son, prepared him to be a worthy husband to their daughter and to take over the family business. He should have felt grateful. He knew that's what he should have felt. But when it came down to the actual moment of commitment, of marrying into the Hanson family, he couldn't do it. How could he have been so selfish?

But wait. They just gave him stuff. They had more stuff. They could replace the stuff. What they were asking from him was the only life he had. The price was too high. Really.

He felt better. Not solidly better, but better. He'd think about all this later.

He looked around for guard dogs or billygoats, but saw none. No one seemed to be using this piece of land, at least not now. He came to a clearing. It looked like a scene from a cowboy movie—an arroyo. It was a scooped-out bowl, about ten meters across and just red sand, no plants. He slid down it, feeling like a kid. At least he could walk in a straight line across it. He was getting tired of weaving in and out between those stiff plants. The earth felt springy under his feet.

Then it gave way.

Douglas fell. He landed, hard, on cold damp rock. He lay there for what seemed like hours, trying to make sense of what had happened. The only light came from the hole he'd fallen through.

He ran an inventory over his body. Nothing seemed to be broken. He'd landed on his feet and then gone down to his knees, then hands and knees. He dusted off his hands.

He knew Crete was riddled with caves. He had probably walked on top of lots of them before now, but this was the first time he'd been inside one. What's more, it looked like no one had fallen in here before him. He was the first human to be in this space.

Maybe he was the first human since Minoan times. 5,000 years. What could he find in here? He thought about the wonderful archaeological treasures people had found in other caves. A vision rose of a huge store of ornamented ceramics, in the style of Kamares ware. Great piles of it. That was supplanted by the thought of an enormous votive bronze, perhaps of Zeus himself, who, after all, had been born only a few mountain peaks away in a cave in Mount Ida. Who knows what could be in here? If only he could see.

He peered into the darkness beyond the pool of daylight below the hole in the ceiling.

That would be perfect, he thought. The easy solution. Leave one life and fall into a better one. He imagined headlines: Brilliant Young Archaeologist Scores Great Find. Douglas Watkins, discoverer of giant Cretan bronze, will join staff of museum…or will teach at Harvard…or will lead expeditions on Crete. The possibilities were endless.

He stood up. The floor of the cave felt pillowed, a series of round bumps with dips between and all of it silt over something harder. It sloped in all directions. Standing up was not easy. Walking was nearly impossible. He walked carefully to the edge of the light and tried to see into the cave.

The darkness beyond was darker than he could imagine. Black didn't describe it. He turned back to where the daylight came through. He could dimly see the plastic food bag. Good. It would be a landmark for him.

The cave was cool and smelled stale, like old laundry. The ceiling he'd broken through was probably forty cm. thick at the break. Clods of red sandstone were still falling. The opening was about a meter across, with crumbling edges.

He reached up. His hand was nowhere near the edge of the hole. His heart thumped. He sure as hell wasn't going to get out the way he got in. How could he announce the great discovery if he couldn't see and if he couldn't get out again. New headlines came up for him: Young Archaeologist Found Dead Near Treasure in Cave. He pushed the idea away.

177

The darkness had weight to it. The air in the cave physically pressed him to the wet ground. He got it: all the water on Crete was hiding inside the mountains. None was on the surface.

His body felt like someone else's. Nothing felt usual. He couldn't find a baseline for any sensation.

Sounds in the cave rose to frighten him. What were they? Water drips, but where? And what else? What living things might be down here with him?

Up and down seemed arbitrary. He felt dizzy. Vertigo. Is this what blindness is like? He didn't understand what he sensed. None of it.

He felt a slight air-movement from his left. He decided to walk toward it, into the dark, slowly because of the bumpy surface. His plastic bag would be his visual anchor. As long as he could see it, he was not lost.

He moved forward awkwardly and lost his balance. His knees took the blow. From a kneeling position, he yelled to see what the echo pattern would be, but he didn't learn anything from the returning sound. He wondered how large the chamber was and if there was a passageway to the surface somewhere. He scanned his dark horizon in hopes of finding a light-glimmer. He realized he no longer knew if his eyes were even open, except when he looked back at the plastic bag. But when he did, he had to dark-adapt his eyes again. Better not to look for the bag.

He wished for a flashlight, a candle, a match even. The notion of a great Minoan discovery no longer seemed interesting. He wanted out of here. Empty-handed would be fine.

The darkness changed when he blinked. He saw red explosions within it, about two meters away. Was there something out there? A bear staring back at him? There were no bears on Crete. He knew that for a fact. He couldn't see any movement. The red pops stopped. Just darkness, which seemed to be coming closer. He couldn't penetrate it with his eyes.

His shoulder hurt. The bandage was stuck to the wounds and the fall had pulled it loose at the edge. No time for that. Bigger trouble now.

He heard a sound somewhere around him. It sounded like a rat, but smaller, a cockroach maybe. He imagined it the size of his fist, with no eyes, a species evolved for living in the dark like this. What would it eat? Flesh from the likes of him, animals and humans who fell in and died. Maybe the cockroach would start eating him while he was still alive.

The sound came again. Douglas could feel his pulse. He made a noise with his leg and the scuttling sound stopped. His mind looked for some new danger to embrace. Nothing else moved.

Douglas felt thoroughly doomed. Fate's victim in every way. His wounds stung. He became aware of the cold. He was losing body heat. Slowly, he stood up.

He moved into the darkness, keeping the white bag just in the corner of his vision. The footing was slick and sloping and he couldn't see where he was putting his feet. He had to take tiny steps. Each step required thinking. It was tedious.

He managed twenty steps. Getting the hang of this. He looked back for the bag. In that moment, his leather-soled shoe slipped out from under him and he skidded down a bulge of slick slumprock. His fall stopped only because he wedged his heel into a vertical groove in the rock. He held himself still, waited to see if he had really stopped his fall. He could no longer see the plastic bag.

He saw no light source at all. He could feel the sides of the groove against his shoe. He tried placing the other foot above it in the same groove, but couldn't find a place that would hold him. He explored with his hands. There was nothing to hold on to. His fingers slid over the surface.

Terror hit him. He opened his mouth and screamed. As he did, his foot slipped another notch. He stopped screaming. He stood still, clinging to the stony ooze, the petrified jellyfish, his fragile hold on life.

He thought he heard a pebble fall for a very long time.

23

George Hanson wandered past the endless shops that lined the alleyways and narrow streets of Old Chania. None of their wares held any interest for him. He was looking only for Douglas. Where could that boy have gone? And how? All his clothes were still in that awful taverna where he'd been working. No one had seen him anywhere around the city.

Shop after shop after shop. Tourists going in, tourists coming out with smiles and purchases. All these customers and they were not his. He thought of his own thriving business. He missed his office at The Safari Collection, where his staff, including Roger, snapped to attention when he rounded a corner or opened a door. He liked that. He missed the respect he got back home. No one noticed him here, or if they did, he felt they were laughing at him. He was homesick.

Damn that Douglas. Bringing Professor Ducor to his knees this afternoon had tempered George's anger a little, but not enough. He needed to see Douglas suffer. And then, he needed to go home to The Safari Collection. Get out of this hot, crowded, foreign place. Go home.

He turned down an alley on his left and found himself at the harbor, face to face with a small black gondola nodding its *ferro di prua* at him, looking almost sinister, waiting for some dumber-than-most tourist to go for a ride. A gondola like in Venice, to remind visitors that Venetian rulers built this harbor, hundreds of years ago.

The surface of the water was dotted with juice boxes and plastic cups blown there off the kafenion tables.

As he passed the row of quayside cafes, he kept looking for Douglas. It was hard to see who was sitting at the back of the awning-covered table area. It was deep shadow back there. These places were all much alike: a tiny kitchen serving maybe forty small tables and a few hundred matching cheap chairs, some filled with tourists and some of them empty. They all had some good-looking guy with his shirt open and his gold chains showing, flirting with all the ladies, young and old, cajoling them into this place instead of that one.

The big awnings flapped when the air was moving. They baked in silence when it was still.

A voice rang out, "Daddy! Over here!"

George peered into the darkness at the back of the awning. Sure enough, Denise and her mother were eating gigantic multicolored ice cream sundaes, enhanced with candies and several tiny umbrellas in each.

George entered and worked his way between tables toward them. "What happened to your diet, Denise?"

"Who cares about being thin? My life is over. I'll eat ice cream before I kill myself."

"That worm isn't worth killing yourself over."

"You didn't used to think he was a worm."

George Hanson didn't answer. He brought over a chair from another table and sat down with them.

181

Denise continued, "Well, did you? You thought he was good enough to take over the business when you retire."

"...because you wanted him, honey. And only if he was a good husband for you."

Mrs. Hanson put a warning hand on his arm. "I think, dear, that today we're feeling real sad, now that we're over being mad."

"So what's next? Mad, sad, glad? If so, I can hardly wait for tomorrow."

"Well, he might have been a good husband for me if you hadn't screwed things up."

Mrs. Hanson glanced at her husband. She perched on her chair, ready to bolt if things got nasty.

George said, "What did I do?"

"If you hadn't threatened to kill him, he might have stayed and married me. Then I'd be in Santorini now, eating ice cream with him in among all those white buildings and steps."

"You were throwing things at him. Remember? The mayor charged us for the damage you did to three of his paperweights. Maybe your attack drove him off more than my threat to kill him."

"You always try to make everything my fault, Daddy."

"You're right. You're right. And really, everything is my fault, right?"

"Throwing a paperweight at someone is not exactly the same as threatening to kill him."

A tall, good-looking waiter came to their table. He smiled broadly and said, "I am Tonio. I am your waiter. I want to serve you. You want menu?"

George shook his head. When Tonio-the-waiter didn't move, George said, "I don't want a menu. Nothing, thanks."

Tonio nodded and cast a long hungry glance at Denise. She didn't seem to notice him.

Mrs. Hanson said, "I think Daddy's right and Douglas isn't coming back. So we need to figure out what we're going to do next."

George said, "We're going home. That's what. I'm going to have Roger get us the next flight back to St. Louis."

"But it's summer. It's hot there. Can't I take the honeymoon cruise anyway? It's already paid for."

George stared at the sherds of sunlight bouncing off the surface of the inner harbor. The gondola bobbed on its tether.

His daughter continued, "Mom could go with me. You could go home."

He stood up. The nylon sariki dangled from his pocket.

"Daddy, wait. What's that?" Denise pulled on the sariki.

"Who'd you get that for?" she said, accusingly.

"Who'd you think I got it for?" he said, and handed it to her. She held it up and examined it: a black nylon lace triangle with fringe on two sides.

Tonio came back to their table and mimed something across his forehead. Denise looked at him, puzzled, then handed him the sariki. He wound it into a strip, then held it across his brow, looking nothing at all like the mountain men of Crete. He smiled a tanned, gorgeous smile and knelt by the table so the Hansons could see him better and would not have to strain their necks.

George pulled the sariki away from him and shook it out. Tonio smiled at Denise and backed off.

Denise examined the sariki carefully and said, "You know, these could be good details for something. Look!" She held the triangular textile, fringed sides down, across her clavicle. "See? You could attach it on a boatneck front and it'd dress up a French tee-shirt. Or..." She began draping the piece across her shoulder, down her sleeve, bunched up by her neck. Ideas were rolling off her like water off a duck.

Her father watched her think.

"So, tell me, Denise. These just come in black. What colors would you use with them?"

"If we bought enough of them they'd come in any color we wanted. But I'd use the black with a strong, dark blue, or again a red-red-orange, maybe linen, or a dark green. Malachite, kind of. Not pale colors. Not white." She sounded authoritative. More than that, she sounded as if she knew what she was doing.

George looked at his daughter as if he'd never seen her before.

He had an idea. Nothing to lose: he decided to run with it.

In his mind, Ducor's fancy office transformed itself into the Chania branch of The Safari Collection. They could spend the summer here, away from the St. Louis heat, although God knows it's hot on Crete, too. But this way, Denise could be away from the embarrassment of inquiring neighbors saying "How was the honeymoon? Where's Douglas?" It was embarrassing for him, too,

183

to have that creep run out on them. They could all be out of the way until they could replace the bad news with some good news.

"Can you draw?" he asked her.

"George, of course she can draw. She made drawings all over her books all through school. Don't you remember?"

Denise looked at him as if he had just hatched from a large egg. He did remember doodles on things around the house. Okay. Let's try this, he thought.

"Could you design clothes like these?" He pointed to a nearby poster of the Minoan bull dancers mural. Three lean young people in scanty outfits were leaping over a large bull.

"Of course I could, Daddy." Denise acted insulted that he should need to ask.

"Come with me," he said and took his daughter's hand. Followed by Mrs. Hanson, they went straight to an art supply shop he had noticed on Odos Halidon. He quickly chose sketchbooks. a dozen drawing pencils, and a sharpener. Denise found a tiny watercolor set for travelers. George bought them all.

Then they went to the bookstore where they had first met Fr. Dimitrios, and Denise bought every guidebook they had for the Minoan collections on Crete.

Back at the hotel, they moved the writing table into Denise's bedroom and set it in front of the window looking out to sea. They brought in a pitcher of lemonade, tuned the TV to a soft audio feed, and left Denise to draw.

George stood in front of the living room window looking out on the Cretan Sea and said the first prayers of his life: *O, Lord, please, puleeze, let Denise have some abilities at design. Let her be the son I've always wanted. Let her be the one to take over the business from me. Let this dumb failed wedding be a gift. O, Please.* He closed his eyes and focused all his strength on this prayer.

24

Aleko doubled back into the waiting area where he had left his mother and aunt. No one was there. He looked around to see where they'd gone.

They called to him from across the large lobby. They were sitting at a table with the policeman who brought them here.

The policeman saw him, too, and waved his arm that Aleko should join them. He walked slowly across the vast and gleaming floor.

The policeman said, *"Ya sas,"* to Aleko, pulled up a chair for him, and introduced himself, "Officer Vrondakis. Hello, Aleko." He smiled at him.

Aleko looked at his mother, who wouldn't meet his eyes.

The officer reached into his briefcase and pulled out a plastic bag containing Panos's *passalis*. It looked the same as always. No blood. Aleko watched his mother's face as she recognized it.

She said, "That is my dead husband's knife. I know it well. The American must have stolen it from my house."

Aunt Sofia said, "Manolis was wearing that mask to make a joke on Aleko. The American was the robber. He's the one!"

Vassilia shot a fast warning look at her son.

Sofia went on. His name was Daonglos. No, they didn't remember the family name but he was about so tall and nice looking. Wore a white shirt.

Aunt Sofia patted Aleko on his head. She said he and Manolis were cousins. They grew up together. Cousins would never rob or hurt each other. Boys play games, don't you know? A prank.

Aleko watched the two most important women in his life dig their way into a mineshaft of lies. His sense of right and wrong was running backwards, away from their story, but he didn't say anything to the policeman. He would not make the two of them lose face.

Yes, they would press charges against the American. They both signed the forms naming Daonglos as the attacker. It was a criminal charge. Now the police would have to find him.

Aleko remembered that he had told Daonglos to go home and wait. He had to get home to warn him about this lie and the police. He had to get home.

His aunt drove horribly slowly up the mountain. Aleko supposed she went so slowly because she didn't want to tell Uncle Spiros about the stabbing. She took a long time to get to their house, and then she came in for a kafe Elleniko. Aleko sat silently on the drive home, and when they got there he hopped out of the car and ran quickly around the property, looking for Daonglos. When he didn't find him he was relieved, but then he began to worry where he might be.

At last, Aunt Sofia left.

Vassilia came outside to where Aleko was sitting. She sat down near him and said, "Sometimes one has to say what is not the truth to protect someone else."

"That's not what you taught me."

"I know it's not. It's a difficult problem, and you must trust me that I did what was needed."

"You blamed Daonglos. Manolis was attacking us. Really. He's the same one as yesterday. He was the robber! I told you. Didn't you believe me?"

"Son, you must trust me. I did it to protect Manolis. Daonglos is not family. Manolis is our relative." She looked unhappy, too.

Aleko felt really terrible. His mother had behaved in a slippery way and didn't seem to know what was right to do anymore. She didn't fight for the truth anymore. His aunt was lying to protect her own son. That was bad, but not so bad as his own mother's lies. His father was dead, and his mother was a liar.

Sofia drove home with trepidation. It was sunset.

"Where've you been?" Spiros asked when she unlocked the door and walked in. He sat in the salon, with no lamps on, in the fading light of dusk.

"Manolis has been hurt. He's in hospital and I've filed a report with the police."

"You could have left a note saying where you were and when you'd be back."

"I'm sorry, Spiros. I didn't know what had happened when I got the phone call from the hospital. I just wasn't thinking clearly."

"I guess you weren't. And you're late for suppertime, too. How is he?"

"I'm very sorry, Spiros. I'll fix something for you to eat right now. Manolis is very bad. He was so bad they would only let me see him for a minute, but the doctor says he's going to live—he's going to be all right." She started to cry. "He was stabbed." She turned to leave the room, but Spiros's voice stopped her.

"What? Stabbed? Who? What's this about the police? Who stabbed him?" Spiros was now up and pacing around the darkening salon. Sofia turned on a light. She was glad she had rehearsed her story.

"Manolis was teasing Aleko, you know, scaring him, and that American you met, Daonglos? Well, he pulled a knife and stabbed Manolis."

"Why?"

It was a good question. Sofia knew that. The weak point in her story. What reason would Daonglos have to stab Manolis? And why was Manolis playing a trick on Aleko? This would seem out of

187

character even to Spiros. Manolis had never willingly played with his cousin, or showed any interest in him at all. It was a stretch to suggest that he was teasing him wearing a ski mask and jumping out, but the police had bought the story and now she was going to have to make it stick with Spiros.

"You'd have to ask that American." She went to the kitchen. Spiros followed her.

"*Malakka!* I knew he was no good. Where is he?"

"Gone. That's all I know. Spiros, I want to ask Fr. Dimitrios to say an *efchelaio* for Manolis's recovery. Do you mind?"

"Of course I mind. I don't want that priest in this house. He is my enemy. My father hated his grandfather-the-coward. And I hate him. No."

"Not even for your son, to pray for his life?"

"No."

"I'll start your supper now, Spiros." As she opened cupboards she heard him stamp around the house for a moment and then go out. She looked out the kitchen window and saw him drive off in the blue sedan.

She continued laying out a supper for whenever he returned.

Spiros drove to Vassilia's house. He parked outside her wire gate, opened it, and let it sag to the ground. Two chickens ran past him right away and the rest got the idea soon after. The goats took longer to amble over to the open gate and out.

He went into her house without knocking.

"Where is that American?"

"I don't know, Spiros. I don't know anything about where he is."

"If you are hiding him, it will not go well for you."

Aleko poked his head around his bed-curtain.

Spiros said, "Do you know where the American is?"

"No," said Aleko in a small voice.

"You'd better be telling the truth. Both of you."

Spiros got back into his blue sedan and backed up onto the road. Aleko went out to shut the gate. In the rearview mirror, Spiros saw the boy trying to bring back the animals.

He drove back to Ano Vraho and went to the taverna. As he got out of his car, he remembered that he'd had a fight there this week and that he owed Lambros for a broken chair. He was not prepared to be teased about that right now. And he sure wasn't ready to pay for it. Lambros could wait.

He got back in the car and drove home to the supper Sofia had by now prepared for him. As he approached the house, he changed his plan, turned around, and headed down to Chania to the hospital.

Spiros drove through the center of the city, cursing the oncoming traffic. His mood was fierce. When he arrived at St. George Hospital, it took him five minutes to find a safe place to park his blue sedan. He parked it at the far end of the parking lot, away from other cars that might open their doors into his.

He locked the car and walked around to the front entrance of the hospital. He'd never been sick, never been to the hospital before, not even to visit someone else, and the large empty lobby was intimidating. He headed across the open space to the nearest door, which had a sign on it: DOCTORS AND STAFF ONLY. He was just about to push the door open when a young man dressed in all-white clothes approached him and said, "You can't go in there, sir."

"My son's in there."

"I don't think your son's in there. That's for staff. Would you like to check in at the information desk?" He gestured all the way across the no-man's-land of the lobby.

Why do they make me come so far into their territory to just speak to them? Spiros wondered. He hated the lobby because it dwarfed him, made him feel unimportant. He hated the young man's uniform because it made him feel his own clothes were not as clean. This place was trying to draw him down and he was not going to take it. He wanted to get Manolis and get out of there!

He crossed the shiny linoleum floor as boldly as he could. At the information desk, a young woman, just a girl really, looked up at him. "May I help you?" she said in a voice that made him feel he was interrupting something important. He pulled himself up bigger and said, "I have come to take my son home."

"What name?"

189

"Manolis Kiriakis."

The girl shuffled carefully through the flaps on an index and stopped at a flap with Manolis's name. She looked up at Spiros.

"Has the doctor released him? Did you get a phone call?" She seemed puzzled.

"He's my son. He's coming home now."

"You'll have to talk to a doctor, sir. We can't release patients without the doctor's consent." She rang a bell and the orderly in white came over to them.

"Kyrios Kiriakis has come to take his son home and I don't have any release orders. His son is in ICU. Can you go with him?"

The man in white nodded, but Spiros saw his eyebrows go up just a bit. Spiros felt these two were conspiring against him in some secret code language. Information about him had been transferred. He felt foolish. His anger grew.

He followed the white uniform over to some very large double doors. The orderly pushed the right side open and held it for him. Beyond the doors were corridors of the same linoleum, shiny and endless. They passed medical people, or at least people in white, standing around and doing nothing. Spiros thought they should be doing something. Manolis belonged at home.

They turned right, then right, then left and there was a sign saying INTENSIVE CARE UNIT. The orderly held open the door and gestured him through. Inside he saw a large room, underlit, with two rows of beds with metal sides along the walls, facing each other. Curtains might have divided them but they were all pulled back, so there was no privacy between the beds. In the middle of one row of beds was a nurse's desk facing a bank of machines with flashing lights. Behind and beside the beds were more machines, hissing and clicking and whirring.

190

He thought it was funny there were no flowers. He had heard that everyone in a hospital had lots of flowers.

Where was Manolis? He wasn't here. These people were just lying around, dying or very sick. He couldn't see anyone who looked remotely like Manolis.

The orderly handed him over to a nurse who led him to a small pile of human flesh lying like a scarecrow with slats on his arms,

THE PALE SURFACE OF THINGS

machines everywhere, and a clear plastic tube across his face, under his nose. He looked at this person for several moments before he could discern signs of Manolis in the face.

"Oh…" escaped his lips.

The dark face didn't move. The nurse said, "He is unconscious. He won't respond if you speak to him."

Spiros felt defeated. He had come to the hospital to bring his son home. He expected he might look pale and even weak, but this body with his son's face, lying in the bed attached to all these tubes, looked nearly lifeless. Obviously, Manolis couldn't walk. Spiros couldn't even imagine how he could pick him up and carry him out of the hospital with all those tubes.

He went to the side of the bed. He touched his boy's immobilized arm.

"Manoli."

There was no response.

Louder. "Manoli."

No response at all. Not even the flicker of an eyelid.

He stepped back, looking uncomprehendingly at the limp and nearly-lifeless form in the bed. How dare Manolis not respond to him? He wanted to take him home today. Hospitals are bad places, places to die. Manolis was not going to die. Sofia said the doctor said so. Manolis should come home and let his mother take care of him. But he could not take this lump home. The lump wouldn't even look at him. Where was Manolis's life? This body was frightening.

The hospital powers had taken his son from him, thwarted his plan, controlled his life, stopped him. He left the ICU and went down several corridors. He couldn't remember where he had made right and left turns on the way in.

He barged through a door he thought he had come through and found himself in the hospital laundry room. A woman in a green uniform with her arms full of wet linens swung around and looked at him. He backed apologetically out the door he had burst through.

After that, he was pleased when he found his car where he'd parked it.

191

25

Douglas felt his body adjust, seeking to balance itself. He could hear his pulse and he thought that each thrum of his heart might be strong enough to overbalance him and pitch him forward and off. His muscles felt useless, but when he thought about them he realized they were stretched taut, holding him motionless.

For how long? he wondered. His mind tried on the idea of the fall he faced. That rock fell for a long time. How many times would he carom off the walls of the cavern before he landed on some semblance of floor? Would he be dead before he landed? He'd heard of that: people jumping or falling off great heights, dying of fear before they ever splashed down.

His arms ached. A sharp cramp stabbed the foot that was wedged in the crack. He couldn't move it. That foot was all that was holding him up. The other leg was shaking. How long could he sustain this position? He couldn't even see where his arms and legs were.

There was no feeling of space, large or small or bottomless. He knew from that rock sound that the cave was terminally deep below him. It felt like being in outer space, or underwater. He couldn't breathe.

He couldn't back up the slumprock. If he moved at all he'd lose his footing and his hands couldn't hold him by themselves. There was no way out of this position but to fall.

He hated waiting. Always had hated waiting. What was he waiting for? The cockroaches weren't going to pull him up to safety. Even if he got back to the level part, he couldn't get out of the cave. There was no other scenario. He had to end the anticipation. He chose death, swift and sure. He ordered his hands to let go of the rock.

His fingers wouldn't release.

Try as he might, he could not will them to let go. They clamped on to the slumprock and paid no heed to his orders. He saw that even here, he had no control over the events of his life.

He hung to that sliprock, unable even to fall to his death. The cold of the cave turned his panic sweat into an unpleasant soak. What a death. In several hours, hypothermia would make his fingers release. Until then he would feel colder and colder and colder.

He noticed he hadn't breathed in awhile, made himself gulp air, then felt dampness on his cheeks. Weeping.

Who am I kidding? he thought. I don't control my life. I've only just moved into living my own life and now I'm going to lose it. What have I learned from all this?

I've learned pain, anger, shame…that humiliation stealing the cheese. But then…Oh yes, I learned something about confession. I can't remember what it was, but it seemed good.

I was learning to think, on my own, not as someone's puppet. Discovering that I have a soul. It wants to live. It feeds on joy. It needs joy to grow. At least I saw that soul. One moment of understanding what life could be. Well, that soul had better get smart then, because I can't get us out of here.

193

He cautiously shifted his hips to the right and found he could move them further back, away from the edge. That shift allowed his leg muscles to change their position. They were grateful for the change. He began to feel comfortable, if that was possible, hanging over his death there.

The thought returned: I can't hold on forever.

He felt a real pull toward release and the drop down the bottomless pit, and a new pull to hang on and not fall.

I want to sit somewhere quietly and find out what my goals are. I want to love what I do. I want to love this poor world. I'd like to love some people. I'd like to taste food as fresh and vibrant as I had at Aleko's house. Water as wonderful as what came from the pipe on the road. Work as uncomplicated as picking off whitewash in a church. A life that is as simple as the one Aleko and his mother have. A life with no big problems. Just daily tasks.

He did think that maybe Aleko and his mother had a few more difficulties than he had seen when he was there. That was worth thinking about, but later.

Life, he realized, is about breathing, drinking clean water, eating fresh food, and being clear and, somehow, honorable, though he wasn't sure what he meant by honorable.

Hanging over that space, Douglas listened to his thoughts.

The memory of stabbing that robber passed fleetingly across his mind, gone before he could touch it.

"Hallooo?" said a voice. "*Einai kanenas eki?*"

An electric light bulb switched on, brilliantly illuminating surfaces of rock several layers removed from where he was, but also casting enough borrowed light on his surroundings that he saw he was less than two feet above a paved path.

He pried his fingers open and stiffly pushed his feet down onto the paving. He held on to the sliprock and stood up. His body went into a fine tremor. His hands retained their clenching position. His fingers burned. He knelt down, slowly, to touch the rough concrete with his fingers, blessing its solidity. His fingertips were extraordinarily sensitive. He welcomed the concrete's roughness.

The light went off.

Douglas yelled again. The light came back on and the voice called out, "Hallooo?"

"I'm here," called Douglas. More lights turned on, more rock showed in layers of illumination, like a stage set. Footsteps grew nearer. A lean man in jeans and a t-shirt carrying a large flashlight appeared at what had seemed the end of the path Douglas was kneeling on. He squinted at Douglas. "Why you here? We are closed today. You have a ticket?"

"Ticket? To this cave? What cave is this?"

"Plativolia. Open to public for summer season only. Admission 5,000 drachmas. How did you come here?"

"I fell in, over there."

"No. You need a ticket."

This struck Douglas as so funny that he laughed until he had trouble breathing. The man watched him, and when the laughter stopped, he said, "Really, need a ticket."

Douglas said "So arrest me. Take me to jail. I fell in to your stupid cave. I wasn't trying to get in here. And I'm not paying for a tour." The man looked confused. Douglas said, "Look." He touched the man's arm and crawled up the now visible slumprock surface to the layer where he had first landed. The man followed. They went to where the plastic bag lay, now in a complex pool of natural and electric light. He pointed to the hole above it. "Look. I fell. Here. This is my food." He opened the plastic bag.

"Then you have no ticket."

"I have no ticket. Now get me out of here. I'm very cold. Please."

They climbed back over the uneven surface to the concrete path. The guide led Douglas out a labyrinth of walkways, turning off light switches as they passed them. When they reached the cave entrance, the man went into the ticket booth and came back out with his own jacket. He offered it to Douglas, who put it on. They stood in the evening light. The amber hue gave an illusion of softness to the mountain slope. A drainage swale in the recently paved parking lot made its own seasonal stream. Near it, opportunistic bindweed and honeysuckle fought for territory. Nettles seized the leftover watershed. Farther on the hillside, thistles and more nettles encroached on the sages. It was a landscape both inviting and unwelcoming.

195

Douglas began to shiver. "Where are we?" he asked.

"I told you. This is Plativolia cave. On the road to Chania."

"Lots of roads to Chania. What else are we near?"

"Some small villages. Nothing for tourists. Where is your car?" He looked at the empty parking lot.

"No car. Are we near…we must be…are we near Vraho?"

"Which one? Ano or Kato? Upper or Lower Vraho?"

Douglas sagged. The man helped him inside the ticket booth, which had been warmed by direct sunlight all day and now was stuffy and warm. Perfect, thought Douglas. He sank into the ticket taker's chair.

"You are very sick, I think. I go for doctor?"

"No money for a doctor. I'm just very cold. From the cave."

"Cave is not so cold."

"I am cold. I think I will be all right if I get warm."

"Where you stay?"

Douglas shook his head.

"You want to sleep here? In office? Warm, nice. I stay here sometimes." The man pointed to a cot in the back of the small room.

Douglas started to decline, then thought about it. He was here, he needn't go anywhere. He had food with him: three tenderized plums, some hard-cooked eggs, a tomato, and those two crushed cheese pies. They looked delicious, even through the waxed paper wrapping. "Do you have drinking water?"

The man pulled a half-filled bottle of grey-tinged liquid out from under the counter. "Fresh this morning. You take it. You sleep here."

The guard pulled blankets out of a cabinet and made up the bed. Then he took a cashbox from the counter and, tucking it under his arm, said, *"kalinikta."* Douglas watched him cross the parking lot, get in a small, dust-covered car, and go left, up the mountain.

Douglas thought fate had taken care of him nicely. He was alone with his clamoring thoughts, no host, no conversation, just him and his thoughts. He drank some water, ate a cheese pie and a plum, then got under the covers.

He slept and woke, sometimes chilled, sometimes hot. He might die but that would be a nicer death than falling down a bottomless cave. He felt his old ideas flaking off him. He no longer needed to be as meek as he had been. He was entitled to no more than any other living creature, but he deserved that much: air, sunlight maybe, an opportunity to earn his food, a way to be useful.

Here he lay, saved again by the hospitality of a stranger. The shivering stopped after awhile and he sank into a deep sleep.

Douglas woke early, feeling clear-headed about a few things. He decided first to find Fr. Dimitrios and confess to the stabbing. He would do whatever it took to get that act forgiven. That robber may not have died after all, he thought by morning's light—I can't possibly have stabbed him that hard.

He stretched, raised his shoulders, and remembered his own pellet wounds. He tried to look over his shoulder but couldn't see anything. The wounds seemed better today.

He explored the plastic bag of food that had been with him through the adventure in the cave. Overnight, ants had gotten to the last cheese pie. He started to crumple it up. It seemed such a waste. How much can ants eat? He shook, brushed, and blew the ants off the cheese pie, and ate it.

He took the hard-cooked egg, the tomato, and two plums, opened the door of the ticket booth, and went out onto the hard earth.

There was no sign of another human, no sound at first, though when he concentrated he could hear chattering birds far off. A machine chugged faintly as someone's work day started. He sat on the ordinary ground and ate the plum.

Funny. I feel free, as if I've slipped out of a suit of plaster clothes that had been cast around me, unmoving, wrinkle-proof, and safe. Now I am only what I am.

An answering thought snorted, and *that's* not much!

But I could be. I could be.

He crossed the empty parking lot and looked over the lower slopes of Lefka Ori and the fertile plain that slid down to the sea.

This was the country of brave Cretan andartes and British commandos crossing those cliffs and fields on moonless nights. Douglas had heard the tales of heroism—a number of times, in

197

fact—in Big Kostas's taverna. Back then, it all sounded like some distant dream. No one could be that brave, except in the movies.

He saw them now, those men, shadows running back and forth, carrying messages, supplies, and human beings to the south coast.

He thought of Aleko's mother.

I wrote her off as a kindly peasant woman. She's more than that. She descended from bravery. Her mother and grandmother probably hid wounded men in their homes.

Their courage made Douglas nervous. They did what was needed, in dangerous times. They were brave. Braver than he could ever be.

A raptor flew past. A kind of falcon, he thought. Out for a morning hunt. This fellow was a descendant of those skeletal birds the Minoans painted, the ones that spread their large wings over the guardian figures on that wall painting at Knossos.

Douglas sat down on a boulder and consumed the last plum.

This land will be here long after me, he thought. But not forever. He had heard that idea before, in his science courses, about the transience of life, human life and even planetary life. Then it had been mildly interesting. Now it was vivid. He thought, as I am transient so even this land is transient. It is heading toward the sea and one day it will be gone. Seashell fossils are carried up in rocks found far from the sea, pushed up from the earth's core, the rocks dissolving and slumping back down. There were other signs, too, that the earth's surface acts like a slow-moving liquid. Glass is a slow-moving liquid, he thought. This rock is like glass, only still slower. He thought that Crete would fall and maybe rise again, undulate again. Crete had a life-span, too; in a way, the land was no more permanent than he was. The idea comforted him obliquely.

In St. Louis, everything had appeared so fixed, so permanent, and so new. Geologically new. Everyone behaved as if they had a contract that said things would stay okay for them for all of their lives. No meteors. No volcanoes. Maybe a bad storm or a flood, maybe a burglary, nothing more.

The island of Crete had supported human life for a long time. It didn't pretend to be permanent. Douglas liked its honesty.

This fresh view of his insignificance made his next step seem easy. He would find the Hansons. He would say he was sorry and accept responsibility. Well, maybe they wouldn't accept his apology. That was their choice. They could stay mad if they wanted to. Denise might stay mad for the rest of her life. She could. She had really loved him all those years they were together.

Hadn't she?

Small doubts came up from somewhere. Never mind.

He felt more alive free-floating across this island—isolated by the lack of language, rootless, useless, but learning and growing by himself—than he had felt in all the years of being at Denise's side.

I will stop running, he thought.

He walked back toward the ticket booth. The clock on its wall said ten o'clock. It may have said that for years.

The cave-attendant's car pulled into the parking lot and parked at the far corner. The man got out, smiling at him. Douglas waved.

"*Kalimera*! You look better," the man said.

"Kalimera to you. Yes, thank you. I am fine now."

The man produced a large bottle of orange soda. "My wife makes this." He thrust it into Douglas's hands.

Orange soda for breakfast was a new experience, but strangers offering him food, sharing what they had, was becoming almost usual in Douglas's experience of Crete.

"How kind of her. Please thank her for me, and thank you, too, for all you did for me. Sas efcharisto."

The ticket man nodded and smiled. "Now where you go?"

"Do you know a Cretan priest with a motor scooter?"

"Father Dimitrios. He is American."

"He told me he was born here."

"Yes, but he has funny ideas that come from America."

"Maybe he's both?"

The man thought about this. "Maybe so."

"Where would I find him?"

"Ano Vraho. Twenty minutes down the road that way," he pointed to the right, away from the direction he had gone last night.

"This road goes straight there?"

199

"Straight there. Yes."

Douglas set off for Upper Vraho to find the good Fr. Dimitrios. He would know what to do next.

Douglas knew he had experienced real happiness, joy even, when he woke this morning. And he knew, for sure, that life was meant to be joyous.

On that road to Vraho he sorted through all the people he could think of, looking for one who knew joy. He couldn't think of anyone except the cellist, Yo-Yo Ma, who seemed full of joy. He'd heard him in person once, a concert at Powell Symphony Hall, with Denise. Ma had come out on stage so happy, carrying his cello by the neck, and he'd played with his eyes closed and a smile on his face that said, I'm not here. I'm inside this music. But I'm giving you the music, too. Douglas had been struck by something he named the generosity of the performance.

But Yo-Yo Ma was some sort of miracle and anyway he didn't really count because Douglas had never actually met him.

If most people never experience joy, what's the use of this life, then?

And yet, he had clung to that cave as if he wanted to keep his life.

He thought again about the Cretan family who had taken him in, shared their food with him, nursed his wounds, the boy had given up his bed for him, the mother had defended him against that angry uncle. They had not asked to know who he was. They had simply given him the comfort he needed.

Of course, he reminded himself, he had helped with the goat, so some gratitude was due him. No, it wasn't. He saw clearly that what he gave and what he got were not at all equal.

Suddenly, he felt so hugely unworthy that if the sky had fallen in on him and crumpled him like trash he would know he deserved it. He'd felt unworthy before but not like this. He was no longer willing to just feel unworthy and stay there. He would take action to become worthy. Yes. He was going to accept responsibility for what he had done.

What is a real man supposed to be? No example came to mind. He remained with the question.

George Hanson? George Hanson never knew doubt. He was always sure of himself. Douglas always wavered about things.

Yeah, but George Hanson wasn't bothered by principles. Not like Professor Ducor. There was a man who was certainly opposite to George Hanson. The professor knew a thing or two about principles and ethics, all right. He had stood up to George Hanson when he caught Denise after she turned in that paper for his class. Douglas had been embarrassed. He knew she didn't write it. He'd tried not to hear or understand exactly what she'd done, but he really knew that she had bought that paper off the Internet. He had stayed loyal to her, of course—one has to stay loyal in a time like that—but he had secretly sided with Ducor in bringing her up short. That was right, wasn't it?

But then, nothing happened. Denise graduated anyway and nothing more was ever said about it. Wait a minute. Douglas struggled to remember that time and he realized he'd never asked how things had been resolved.

He remembered now that Denise's grade had been changed to a B. About that same time, the school had established the Institute with Ducor as its director.

Did George Hanson buy him off? Could he?

Douglas knew the answer. Something got whitewashed over at that time and he had gone right along with the lie. He'd never questioned it. Never looked at it again.

He tried to think of another example of an honorable man, but his thoughts kept returning to Professor Ducor and the sudden creation of the Institute.

26

Professor Ducor watched from behind his large, empty desk as Athina dismantled his world. She took his enormous aerial photograph of Rhodopou Peninsula down from the wall and rolled it up. She moved all the files out of their drawers and into boxes, in order.

She called a furniture rental company. They would pick up the office furniture early this afternoon.

As he watched her, he stroked the arms of his ergonomically-padded desk chair. He felt quite mournful. Never again would he have such a fine office. He had known it was extravagant the moment he signed the lease for the first floor of the Venetian palazzo that crowned Kastelli Hill, but he wanted it. It had given a certain lustre to his little Institute: deep red carpet, marble in the foyer, ochre walls with white baseboard and moldings.

When you come back to a place you've left in defeat, he said to himself, it's important to come back in grand style. He didn't regret it.

The sherds from the site were already safe in the storeroom of the Archaeological Museum of Chania. Every piece was cataloged and registered. They were the property of the Greek government, thank heaven. Even George Hanson himself couldn't get his hands on them.

The file boxes Athina would take to her apartment.

"Why would you do that?" he said softly. He still felt weak from his asthma attack yesterday. "Surely your apartment isn't large enough to store all these boxes."

She gave him a strange look. "I can find room for these files. They must not be lost. You'll need them again."

She stopped pushing on a box and asked, "You look very pale. Is this too strenuous for you?"

"No, no, I'm fine. I'm sorry I can't help you pack up."

She came over to him and knelt next to his chair. "You have just come through a terrible physical and emotional trauma. Packing up this office is a big loss for you."

"I can't even pay you for your time today."

"Don't be absurd." She paused. "We've come so far with this project and we must dismantle it correctly."

Ducor heard her say we even though he no longer had money to give her. His head felt paralyzed from the tranquilizing meds from the hospital.

He tried to clear his vision. The idea was still there. We, she said. What's more, Athina still knelt at his side. Now she was looking into his eyes.

Roland Ducor was not a hot-blooded man. He had lived a quiet, scholarly life. The last time he could remember having entertained even a sexual fantasy was when he was sixteen and it had worked out disastrously.

He had invited the doctor's daughter, Miguette, to a dance. She said yes. He had never dreamed she'd say yes. Then for the next three weeks, waiting for the day of the dance, he dared to dream.

Miguette had red hair like flames, which she wore in braids at school. She would have been attractive but for her eye-distorting glasses. He always felt seasick looking at her eyes through the glasses.

203

For those three weeks, Roland Ducor was a mental Casanova. He imagined wild scenes of ravishment. Sometimes they took place in a forest. Sometimes he had his way with her on the balcony outside the dance. In the end, he settled on the vision of seducing her in his own small bedroom. He imagined his parents out of town. He imagined her parents out of town, too. He even cleaned his room, cleared off the desk, put his rock collection in the closet, made his bed. He suggested to his parents that they might like to go to a movie. He thought they might go.

Miguette's hair would be down, a firefall, and her glasses would be left at home. Her dress would be black, or maybe very dark blue, and it would have little straps over the shoulder and a lot of bare skin. When he touched the dress, it would fall away and reveal virginal flesh. Soft pink skin sprinkled with freckles. The idea was very exciting.

On the evening of the dance her hair was piled high with gardenias pinned in it. Their petals turned brown where she touched them. The smell of the sweet flowers made him queasy.

Her dress was sap green, a color that may look good on new spring leaves but doesn't look good near any human face. The dress had a high neckline with a stiff lace collar. The full skirt was scratchy tulle, with petticoats that made it stand out. He placed his hand on her waist to dance and the dress made his hand itch. It was hard to get near her.

She wore those eyeglasses.

When they danced, she kept kicking his shoe with her toe, because she was leading. She bent him into each turn. He never had a chance to guide her. She pulled him off balance. By the evening's end he didn't even want to kiss her.

204

Since then he had thought of himself as a neuter. He did his work and cooked for himself and caused no inconvenience to anyone. Romance played no part in his plans.

Now he found himself wondering if he was the object of Athina's attentions. Of course not. Yet she was still kneeling next to his chair. Why would she do that?

He remembered other things, too. She waited for him at the hospital yesterday. She waited for hours, and then she took him home on a little motorbike. He remembered the back of her helmet in front of him, her upright back, her decisive way of managing the machine. She'd borrowed that motorbike from someone to follow his ambulance. And then she made him dinner, and she kept looking at him. Looking worried, too. Smiling a lot.

Now here she was, helping him preserve the records of the Institute, storing them in her home. No one can be that devoted to work. He looked at her more closely.

Those were loving glances, all right. What does someone do about this?

Her hand was resting on the arm of his chair. He tentatively reached out his hand and laid it lightly on top of hers. She firmly placed her other hand on top of his.

The realization of this moment left him even weaker than before. Some celestial phenomenon—St. Elmo's Fire—skipped lightly across the surface of his body.

He looked again and she was no longer just a steady worker, reliable helpmate, living furniture. This figure kneeling beside him—he loved it that her name was Athina—was desirable, luscious, and just possibly, attainable.

He slowly leaned forward. He paused to give her the chance to move away. Well. She didn't move. Then he kissed her.

Her sigh encouraged him. Ducor felt abruptly powerful, attractive, desirable. He sat taller in his chair. To have had such an effect on a woman like this, a wonderful, capable woman. She was really quite pretty, he noticed. Nice face. Kind eyes. Soft lips…those especially.

It was his first kiss. He had forgotten about never being kissed for so long that it was a shock to realize he'd just lost that virginity. Many feelings swirled about.

Athina remained kneeling next to his chair.

He asked, "Is it that you love me?"

A smile broke out across her face.

"I had no idea." Ducor said.

205

She laughed. "But now you have. Now you can know it's not because of my job. It's because I see you as an ideal man."

"Why?"

She dropped her gaze and thought for a minute. Then she looked at him again and said, "It's because of your ethics...and your deep love of Minoan archaeology."

Discomfort tinged his delicious mood. "My ethics?"

"Of course. A lesser man would have scurried around trying to please Mr. Hanson, but you always kept your dignity around him."

"I did?"

She kissed him again, lightly. "Come on, dear man. May I call you Roland now?"

He nodded.

"Roland, we must go to a restaurant now and eat. The movers will be here in an hour. You need your strength."

She drew him up out of his chair.

Pale as he knew he was, he felt both powerful and confused. He carefully placed his hands on her waist and kissed her again. The illusion didn't dissolve before him.

Then she gave him a smile that seemed to flow from her eyes and radiate out and fill the whole office. A thread of fear joined with his confusion and pleasure. The three feelings darted around his head as they went out into the usual brilliant day.

Athina said, "Shall we go to that very nice hotel by the water? Not where the Hansons are. The other one. This is an important event."

Ducor couldn't think what hotel she was talking about. It didn't matter. He nodded.

The Venetian stone staircase cascaded elegantly before them. He paused at the top. Athina saw the pause and took his arm. She guided him firmly down the stairs. She smiled at him again.

He gave her the management of his body without a protest. He was grateful. The steps did seem full of treachery today. Descending was dangerous.

He was amazed at the speed with which his whole world shifted.

206

27

Manolis was vaguely aware of someone saying his name. Then he sensed light through his eyelids. He opened his eyes. The focus was blurry, but a woman was moving near him. She wore white. She put her hand lightly on his shoulder. She smiled and said, "Hello, Manoli."

He tried to say something and felt a wall in the way. She said, "Don't try to talk. There's a breathing-tube in your throat. You're all right now. But you have to wait to talk. Can you blink if you understand?"

He blinked. He was puzzled. Where was he? Breathing-tube? He tried to remember the recent past, but nothing came to mind.

He turned his attention to his body. It seemed barely there. He couldn't feel much. He wondered what had been done to him.

He tried to raise his head to look down at his body, but his head wouldn't obey.

The woman continued to speak to him. "Manoli," she said, again.

He looked around for her. He tried to keep his eyes focused on her face.

"You're in Intensive Care in the hospital. You won't be able to move much for awhile, and your arm is held down to a board because of the drip." She gestured to something beyond his range of vision. "Your mother has been here. She'll be back this evening." She leaned in. "Can you make a fist?"

Manolis ordered the fingers of his hand, either hand, to close. He couldn't tell if they did or not.

"All right," she said, as if it really was all right. "When you can control your fingers a little better, I'll give you a call button. But for now, I'll be nearby. Go back to sleep if you wish." She left his view.

He tried to stay awake, to assert his right to choose whether to sleep or not. He let his eyes wander wherever they could. Ceiling. Light in ceiling. Metal railing and curtain. At the very edge of his vision, a plastic sack of something clear was hanging. Something was making things worse. His mother had been here. She shouldn't know. Know what? His stomach flared up with fear. Then things got vague again. His eyes closed.

When they opened next, the woman wasn't in sight. He tried to raise his head, and it obliged with the slightest movement. He started to speak, then remembered he couldn't. His throat felt outraged by a foreign object that held it open. He took a deep breath, but his lung wouldn't take in much air. Then pain came. He panicked. He thought he couldn't breathe at all. He gasped. He moved his splinted arms. The woman came back into his field of vision.

"You are all right. Breathing will feel difficult. You were stabbed in the lung. The doctors repaired it, but there's air outside your lung in your chest so you can't get much air into your lung with each breath. We're trying to get that other air out. That's the sound you're hearing."

Manolis had not noticed any sound before. Now he heard bubbling water. He tried to turn his head and couldn't. He gave up.

She said, "That's a machine sucking out the extra air. It goes through water. You feel like you can't get enough air, but you really can. Trust me."

Trust you? What choice do I have?

The pain began a slow crescendo. The breathing panic came and went. Thinking was impossible. All the effort he could summon went into breathing and meeting the pain. He felt one emotion: love of oxygen. He pursued oxygen. He desired it, craved it, sought it, thought only of it.

He returned his energy to breathing. It was his work, his life-work. He didn't question anything. He struggled with each breath. Just the in-part. It let itself out. Air. Grab air. Grab air. He faded back into unconsciousness.

28

Aleko looked at his mother differently now, since the lie. She was a bad person, not able to stand up for the truth. A bad person to go along with Aunt Sofia's lie. His mother was a truth-betrayer. She had told him to love the truth, but she herself did not.

He had to warn Daonglos that the police were looking for him. The morning after Manolis was stabbed, Aleko began to do his morning chores very busily—he fed and watered the goats and the chickens, he carried water to the tomato plants near the house, he brought in wood for the day's fire—but the moment that his mother went back inside the house, he took off up the mountain toward Ano Vraho. He would find Daonglos.

He didn't know why he headed toward the village like that. Daonglos was supposed to be at the house, but something told him to look in the upper village.

He went up the road about fifty meters then turned into the shortcut across the goat field and up behind the church. He followed the twisty narrow trails with annoyance. Usually he enjoyed their crooked route. Usually he poked along looking for snakes under the bushes. He'd carry a stick and try to whap them on their heads. Now the bushes were slowing him down.

He looked ahead. Something was different on the mountainside. That funny bare bowl of red dirt had a big hole in it. Aleko approached it, curious but cautious. He picked up a rock and threw it into the hole. He heard it hit bottom, so the cave wasn't deep. Another time, he'd come back and explore it. He kept on toward the village. When he reached the village he strolled into the taverna.

Lambros looked up from behind the soft drink machine. It was pulled out from the wall. Tubing and motor parts lay in pieces on the floor around him.

"Hello, Aleko. Do you need anything?"

"I'm just looking."

"For what?" Lambros reached for a pair of pliers on the floor. Aleko handed them to him.

"Not a what. A who. But you wouldn't know him."

"I know everybody."

"He's not from here."

"A stranger? Friend of yours?"

"Sort of. Never mind. What's wrong with it?"

"I don't know. It doesn't cool things anymore."

Aleko nodded in sympathy. "Good you know how to fix it."

"Can I give you a soda? Not cold, though. And you can tell me who you're looking for?"

"No, thanks anyway." He moved toward the door.

"Come back soon."

Thomas the policeman rode up on his motorcycle, parked, and settled in at one of the outside tables. Lambros crawled out from behind the machine, went out to take his order, came back. Aleko watched him make a kafe Elleniko.

Aleko said, "I'll take it out to him."

Lambros gave him the cup to serve to Thomas. He returned to his repair job.

Aleko set the coffee down in front of the policeman and sat down in the opposite chair. He waited for Thomas to take a sip. Then he asked, "Have you arrested anyone today?"

211

"I never arrest anyone. You know that."

"But you might, some day..."

"I'll arrest you, if you like." He took a playful swipe at Aleko.

Aleko slid out of the chair and skittered a few feet away. "For what crime?"

"For interfering with an officer and his coffee!"

"But really, you're not looking for anyone bad are you?"

"Why are you asking, Aleko?"

"No reason."

Thomas took a serious look at the boy. "You worry too much for a boy your age. Leave the worrying to your elders. Look how beautiful the day is."

"All right." Aleko said. If it was true that Thomas wasn't looking for Daonglos, it might mean Daonglos was already in jail, or maybe just the city police down in Chania were looking for him.

He drifted off around the corner of the taverna, past the platia and the church. The church door was open. He went in.

Fr. Dimitrios sat on a low stool, picking at the north wall. He inserted a metal thing under the edge of the white and pulled up until a bit chipped off. The priest was surrounded by tiny chips of white wall. Aleko thought they looked like gulls when they landed on a newly planted field.

"What are you doing, Patera? You're hurting the wall!"

"I'm making it better. See? Underneath the white are some very old paintings." Fr. Dimitrios stopped and stood up to stretch.

The whitewash was gone in two areas. Near the center of the wall was the figure of the Virgin Mary, reclining, with the infant Christ at her side. "Theotokos," Aleko said softly.

"What's that?" Aleko pointed to the other cleared image, a group of two women with a baby. The women were different sizes.

"That's Salome and the midwife bathing the infant Christ."

"But the Mother of God has the baby Jesus, too, right there. Why are there two baby Jesuses?"

"To tell the story." Fr. Dimitrios tilted his head and looked at him. "How's your mother?"

"She's fine, I guess." Aleko looked down at the floor.

"You miss your dad still, don't you?"

Aleko gave a startled look toward the priest, as if he'd been found out.

"If you miss him for the rest of your life that's all right. It's a terrible thing to lose your father."

"Did you lose your father?"

"No, my father is still alive, but he's far away in San Francisco. I miss him and my mother, but that's not the same kind of missing. I lost my grandfather, though, and I miss him every day."

"I know about your grandfather. He was priest before Fr. Theodoros."

"That's right, he was. I hear you and your mother are having a guest."

Aleko looked puzzled. Fr. Dimitrios said, "The American, Douglas. Is he staying with you?"

"Oh. Yes, Daonglos. Yes, he is." Aleko was mystified how Fr. Dimitrios knew about Daonglos. He sidled toward the open door. The sunlight skimming across its carved surface made little stripes of shadow where the soft part of the wood grain had worn away.

He turned back to Fr. Dimitrios.

"Do you know where he is, Patera?"

Fr. Dimitrios looked up. "The American? I haven't seen him today. He left here yesterday. I showed him the shortcut through the goat meadow to your house."

"No. He never came there."

"I wouldn't worry. He'll show up." But Fr. Dimitrios wasn't looking as confident as his answer sounded.

Aleko said, "Well, bye."

"Take care, and drop in anytime you see the door open. I like your company."

"Thank you, Patera."

Aleko went up the street trying to imagine where Daonglos might go, what wrong turning he might take to get back to Aleko's house from the robbery place in Nea Hora. Maybe he took the fork to Peristeri, though that would be a funny wrong turn. No other idea came, though, so Aleko checked into the mini-market—no

213

Daonglos—and then he started across to Peristeri on the old goat path.

The *terra rosa* dust lay thick on the path. He shuffled his feet to stir it up. In a minute, his shoes were covered with red powder. That wasn't as much fun as it used to be, when he was younger, but he still liked to do it. He sighed and concentrated on second-guessing Daonglos.

The path curved down toward an easier place to cross the ravine that separated the two towns. The ravine was the reason there was no road between them. Aleko scanned the lower slope and beyond it, the coastal plain. He saw no sign of a foreign man in a white shirt who might be lost. He crossed the ravine and started back up the path.

A secondary path led off to the right, downhill. He paused and looked at it. Something said he should go that way, though he couldn't figure why Daonglos would be down there.

Aleko turned down onto the new path.

He crossed some fenced kipoi belonging to people from Peristeri, kitchen gardens mostly, though one had a small flock of goats. No houses nearby. A dog guarded the goats. As Aleko walked past the goat fence, the dog rushed at him. He stepped back without thinking. The dog took that for an excuse to attack, jumped and then clambered up the fence, dragged itself over the top, and dropped down. The boy and dog now stood facing each other, four meters apart. The dog's teeth were bared. Its fur stood up along its spine. Its eyes reflected no light—dull, grey eyes.

Aleko backed up and the dog moved forward. Their eyes were locked on each other. Aleko called out, but no owner came to retrieve the dog. Aleko knew not to look away, but he could not find a place of safety if he didn't. He took another step back. The dog advanced several steps. The distance between them narrowed.

Aleko knew there were spells called *hitia* that sheep thieves put on dogs so they would sleep for several days. He wished he knew how they did it.

He stood still and the dog stood still. They stared at each other. It seemed like a week they'd been standing there. He knew he had to look away to find some escape from this dog.

To the west of him, ten meters uphill, stood an old olive tree. He could see it in the corner of his eye. He backed up toward it, off the trail, onto the rough mountainside. The dog followed.

Walking backwards uphill over uneven footing he stumbled, lost his balance, fell. The dog sprang. He raised his arms to cover his face. The dog took a deep bite into his right forearm and held on. Aleko screamed and kicked. The dog released his arm only when Aleko landed a hard knee to its belly. It yelped, retreated a little, and circled to come in again. Aleko scrambled up the tree, above the dog's reach. The dog clawed at the tree, tried to jump up into it, fell back, and then stood, its front legs against the tree, snarling and snapping.

The olive tree was centuries old. Its branches were brittle. Aleko moved carefully, but even so, two branches cracked under his small weight. He worked his way up into the tree as high as he dared, well above the dog but below break-off point on the arms of the tree.

The dog looked disappointed. It lay down on the hard ground and continued to watch Aleko. It seemed to say that time was on its side and eventually Aleko would sleep and fall out of the tree and then it would have leisure to kill him. Aleko held on.

Hours passed.

No one came to take the goats in from the kipos. No one came to feed the dog. Darkness fell. The warmth of the day slid away. Aleko grew cold. He was hungry. He was frightened. His arm hurt. Now that he thought about it, he carefully released his left hand from the tree and turned his right arm over to see how deep the bite was. His skin was stiff with dried blood but it wasn't bleeding any more. He sank back into his position in the tree and tried to close his eyes.

The dog didn't close its eyes at all.

At first light Aleko looked down and there was the dog. He wondered if he dared try to outrun it. He spent an hour devising a plan, then decided it wasn't safe. If he fell, the dog could kill him with one bite to the neck. They both knew it.

Aleko anchored himself in the tree and thought about his father. If his father was still alive, he'd take care of that dog. He'd know how to cast a hitia on the dog, or he'd kick him and hit him and drive him away. He would never have let all this trouble happen. Ever since Mbaba died, things hadn't been safe.

215

29

Twenty minutes after he left the cave's parking lot, Douglas arrived at the beginnings of Ano Vraho. The taverna gleamed dirty white and streaked in the Cretan sunlight. When he passed it he came to the platia and then to the church. The door to the church stood open. Douglas was relieved. He had no idea which house belonged to Fr. Dimitrios.

He went inside the church and found the priest bent over a second area of exposed wall painting, now nearly one meter square. The original area now revealed the Virgin Mary, draped in soft red, lying diagonally, her head to the right. Alongside her, the swaddled infant Jesus lay on a slab of stone. An ox and an ass stood just inside the entrance to a cave behind them.

The new area was to the right and lower, the other place where the whitewash had looked promisingly bubbled.

Fr. Dimitrios was filling a crack in the new area with a needle-less hypodermic full of clear goo. The crack bisected the lower right corner, where the fresh figures of Salome and the midwife bathed the infant Christ.

"Hi," Douglas said.

The priest looked up. "Hi. Where've you been? Aleko was just here looking for you."

"He was? That's good. I'm looking for him. I never got to his house. I followed the trail you sent me on, and there was a place, it looks like a red sandy bowl, do you know it?"

"Yes, sure."

"It felt a little spongy underfoot."

"It *is* spongy. I wondered why that would be."

"I fell through it into a cave."

Fr. Dimitrios straightened up. "Are you all right?"

"I'm okay now, but you need to warn people that place isn't safe."

"How deep was the cave?"

"I fell about 10 feet. It was so dark in the cave I don't know how deep the rest of it is."

"How did you get out?"

Douglas told him about his rescue by the ticket taker of Perivolia and his night in the ticket booth.

"But that's a couple of kilometers from here."

"I know. I just walked back from there. So tell me about Aleko."

"He was worried because you never came to their house. Now I see why."

"Where did he go?"

"Toward the mini-market. I wouldn't worry. He'll be back in awhile."

Douglas looked closely at the exposed wall painting. "You've made good progress."

"What's lucky is that the wall was dirty and smoke stained, so the whitewash didn't bond very well. Except for the cracking, it's not so bad to take off. Are you hungry?"

Douglas shook his head. "The food you gave me for Aleko's mother fed me well. I'm all right, thanks…but, I need to talk to you, professionally."

"What do you mean, professionally?"

"I learned a big lesson from you, about confessing and getting forgiveness about the cheese."

"I'm glad if that helped you."

217

"I have another confession I need to make, and I don't know how to proceed after I've made it."

"Do you want to talk over coffee, informally, or do you want to make it here, in the church?"

"Here. It's a big one."

"Give me a minute." Fr. Dimitrios drained his hypodermic, took it apart and rinsed it, scrutinized the area he'd been patching, and then straightened up and removed the shop apron he was wearing over his cassock. He closed the church doors and barred them.

He picked up the stools he and Douglas had used. He carried them over to the ikonostasis.

"Sit." He gestured to one of the stools.

"Thank you." Douglas sat opposite the priest. The reflective gold surfaces of the ikonostasis put a honeyed light onto Fr. Dimitrios's face.

At first, Douglas's body did not allow him to speak. Then he began. He repeated his story—about leaving his wedding, about the goats and the trips to the butcher and the first robbery. This time he told of the second robbery, too. He described the dagger Aleko had given him.

Fr. Dimitrios nodded, "I know those daggers. They are wicked."

Surprised, Douglas asked, "Do you have one?"

"It was my grandfather's. I certainly don't carry it, but I know what they can do."

"So when the robber jumped us the second time, I don't know, rage filled me and I stabbed him. Hard. The blade went between his ribs, and he fell. Then Aleko said run home, so I ran."

The priest waited.

Douglas continued, "I think I've been running from things all my life and I don't want to run any more. From anything. But I don't know how much trouble I'm in. I mean, did the guy die? Is he okay? He can't be okay. But am I wanted? Should I go to the police? What do I do?"

The priest said, "You must go to the police. What we don't know is whether you need an attorney to go in with you. We need to know what shape the robber is in. Aleko must know more, if he stayed on there after you left. I hope he comes back this way soon.

"Meanwhile, I'll telephone the hospital in Chania and see if I can find out anything." He took his cell-phone out of the pocket of his cassock. Taped to the back of the phone itself was a piece of paper with emergency numbers. The clear tape that held it was peeling back from the corners and the paper was soiled, but he could still read the phone numbers.

He dialed the hospital and asked to speak to admissions.

"Can you tell me the status of a stabbing victim who was brought in yesterday? No, I don't have his name. I'm not asking for his name. I want to know if he survived...I am a priest. I think it may involve someone in my parish...You can't tell me anything over the phone? I understand...If I come to the hospital in person, can you tell me anything? Yes...Yes. I will come to the hospital. Thank you anyway." He returned the telephone to his pocket, and translated the conversation to English for Douglas.

"Our local policeman stops in at the taverna every day around now. Let me go over there and see if he knows anything."

"I'd be grateful." Douglas wrapped his arms around his knees and rested his chin on top of them. He stared at the stone floor. He heard Fr. Dimitrios close the church door behind himself. The door-sounds echoed off the stone walls.

Douglas felt vulnerable, but he knew he was in the hands of a good person. He had begun to absorb the truth of what he'd done—that strange, uncharacteristic act of brute violence.

There was a faint rustling sound in the church. Douglas looked around, but saw only the walls of an unoccupied stone room, much used, much cared for. Worn and polished with ritual. Full of spirit and layers of devotion. He was touched how this simple building could seem so holy to him now.

He looked up into the dome. His eye caught movement there. Bats, he thought. So he wasn't entirely alone.

He hadn't noticed the painting on the dome before. The stern but comforting face of Christ Pantokrator looked back at him from the cavity. He thought there was something about the stony acceptance of the icon faces that reflected the lessons he was learning from the villagers. What was it?

219

It was the idea that bone-less, sentimental love, mostly talk, like the attention he'd gotten from the Hansons, was not as much support as hard acceptance was. The icons and the Cretans he'd met seemed to—he reached for a word—fawn less than the Hansons. They didn't invest themselves in him. They just accepted him the way they accepted all that happened in their lives. Fewer expectations? Maybe. He felt support in the coolness of their attitude.

The door opened and the priest returned.

"Thomas, our policeman, knows nothing about it. He said it was funny I was asking because Aleko asked the same question. There are two systems of police on Crete, and they cooperate, but sometimes there's a delay. I don't want to try by telephone to get through to the right person at the Chania police station. I'm going to go down to the city and speak to them there. Then I'll talk to the hospital in person. If I do this for you, I want your word you won't run away."

"I won't run away. No more running."

"It'll take me a few hours. You'll be all right here, I think."

"I can pick off whitewash while I wait."

"That'd be great. If you do, look, work on the area right of that foot, where there's a red patch starting." He indicated a fresh area that was on the left side of the wall. "I'll leave a note on the church door for Aleko to come in if he comes back this way. Don't worry. We'll figure all this out. While I'm in town, why don't I stop and get your wallet?"

"Great! It's at Big Kostas's taverna, on top of the hill, and my passport is with the secretary at the Institute."

"Write a note and give me the addresses."

The rattle of the Vespa faded away down the mountainslope toward Chania.

220

Douglas settled in near the wall. He picked at the whitewash and slowly enlarged the red patch. He looked along the expanse of the wall and then across at the opposite wall of whitewash. He thought Fr. Dimitrios was nuts to take this job on. He'd never finish it.

He listened for any sound that might be Aleko coming back to the church. The only sound he heard was the rustling of the bats.

30

Three days after she was jilted by that no good sonofabitch, Denise Hanson was up and running. She poured herself into designing clothes with a Minoan theme. She was happy. Her mother was so relieved to see her happy that she was happy.

At first, George thought he was promoting this project to pull Denise out of her rage, but when she showed him her design sketches over dinner, he knew enough about vacation clothing lines to know the designs would sell.

He said as much to Roger back in St. Louis the next day.

Roger said, "Sure, George. If you say so."

When George faxed him some of the sketches, though, even Roger's skepticism dissolved. He said, "This is the first collection of ours that I've liked in four years." George was both pleased and annoyed by the comment. He let it slide.

He bought up 20,000 nylon tourist sarikis and shipped them to Indonesia. Faxes of Denise's designs flew to Roger and to their pattern-maker in Hong Kong.

Roger said, "George, I envy you. I wish my little Caroline was as talented as your Denise."

George glowed.

Denise drew in a frenzy. Her enthusiasm amazed her parents. She had never shown such commitment to a project before.

Over the next few days, she created an entire collection of resort clothing based on ideas from the Minoan frescoes, including an Italian silk overshirt of midnight blue with the Prince of the Lilies in a Minoan Red rectangle on the center of the back, and another of Minoan Red with the blue bird fresco reproduced on its back. They would be manufactured in Asia.

Roger said they should be priced high. The Minoan Line would usher The Safari Collection into the high-end designer market.

With the silk shirts they'd offer tapered cream silk trousers and small silk handbags beaded with Minoan motifs. The bags would hang from a very long gold chain.

The swimsuit collection was unique. The legs would be cut even higher than French-cut legs. They'd go to the waist, bound by a belt of gold, just like the female figures in the Bull-Jumping Fresco in the Iraklion museum. The buckle would be a reproduction of the Phaestos Disk. They'd tag each suit with a card explaining something about the Minoans—in a friendly, non-academic way. They'd come in Goddess Purple, Minoan Red, or Iraklion Blue.

A long straight linen skirt, split to mid-thigh on the left side and sporting a pocket embroidered in a Minoan design on the right side, would go with a cropped jacket, both available in the blue and red colorways. An ochre transparent blouse would go underneath. For more modest patrons, a camisole of ochre would be available, at extra cost.

222   His daughter's idea of the transparent blouse with the option of the wearer's breasts showing excited George's own sense of style. In the museum at Iraklion, he'd been struck by the Minoan figurine called the Snake Goddess. She wore an elaborate bell-shaped skirt and a low-cut vest which left her breasts bare. She wasn't shy about it, either. She had a bird on her head and snakes in her hands, but never mind those. George pointed to a photo of the Snake Goddess

and said, "I dare you to make something of that!" Denise took up the challenge. She was working on it.

Mrs. Hanson and Denise had their arms full of shopping bags. They'd been hunting all morning for local lace and embroideries. Now they were going back to the hotel. One bag contained twenty more of the nylon sarikis, for Denise's samples, to use as black fringed sleeves or collars, or fluttering hemlines on wraparound miniskirts and beach cover-ups. Denise draped these purchases on her patient and flattered mother, and drew more designs.

Walking back to the hotel after lace shopping, Mrs. Hanson squeezed her daughter's arm and said, "Honey, I am just so proud of you. Look at you! A real designer. All these years you were doodling in your schoolbooks and it was all getting ready for this moment. My daughter, the brilliant clothes designer!"

"Mom, if I'd married Douglas I never would have become Daddy's top designer. That tragedy has led me to this success."

"That's such a good way to look at it, honey. Look! There's that priest who wouldn't do the ceremony. He's riding on a motorcycle!"

"Aw, Mama. That's only a scooter. They probably don't let priests ride motorcycles. The power would go to their heads. And what about their skirts? See? He's sitting on that thing almost like a chair."

"I never would have noticed that. You are so clever, honey."

"Thanks, Mom. I'd like to talk to him."

"The priest? What about?"

"I have this idea: I want him to do photos with models of the clothes, on that Zorba beach." Denise ran a few steps, waving her arms. "Oh, Father! Sir! Hello!"

Fr. Dimitrios stopped the Vespa. He seemed surprised to see her. "Hello. Denise, isn't it? How was your wedding?"

"Don't ask. Just don't ask."

Fr. Dimitrios looked over at Mrs. Hanson. Her face told him nothing.

"Well, nice to see you again," he said.

"Wait. I want to ask you a favor. Since you wouldn't do a wedding for me, would you be a model on that Zorba beach when we shoot the stills of my line of Minoan clothing?"

223

"Pardon me? What is it you'd like me to do?"

"Pose, like that, in your, you know, ethnic outfit, with models in my Minoan designs, on that beach."

"I'm awfully sorry. I can't do that. Thanks for thinking of me, though." He restarted the Vespa and rode off.

Denise watched him leave. "Spoil sport," she muttered.

They watched him ride over to the police station and park the Vespa.

"Look!" she said to her mother. "He's going to the police. I bet he's on parole and has to check in every so often. He probably really isn't a priest. It's just a costume. And if he had his photo taken with my clothes, someone might recognize him and arrest him for something. That's why he wouldn't do it, I bet."

"I bet you're right. Aren't we lucky he has nothing to do with our lives?"

They stopped in their favorite quayside kafenion. The sign said Fruits of the Sea, and had drawings of fish and shells with hermit crab arms coming out of them. Today, a wire stretched above the entrance. A line of octopi were drying in the sun. Their tentacles hung down like so many fingers. Denise observed that dead things here didn't even smell bad to her any more. "I must be getting used to Crete."

"Honey, after what you're doing to promote this place, they should make you an honorary citizen!"

"I think I'll have a tuna sandwich."

"Do they have tuna? I don't see it on the menu. You ask the waiter. They probably do. I just want some spaghetti."

31

The Police station was crowded. Officers, pickpockets, and unfortunate bystanders milled about. This week had seen a rash of tourist crimes and it was time to shape up the local unsavory petty-criminals. Most of the pickpockets were not Cretans. They were Albanians or Romanians, of course. *Xeni*. People from Elsewhere. They all got rounded up, along with a few who weren't pickpockets, and now they were being processed.

No one had time for Fr. Dimitrios. He waited at the counter for fifteen minutes, and twice an officer had smiled at him and said, "Be right there!" but they couldn't leave their unhappy prisoners. No one had come to speak to him.

Ah well, he thought. I'll skip this for now. I'll just go to the hospital after I pick up Douglas's things.

He went to Big Kostas's taverna, but Big Kostas wasn't there. Mrs. Big Kostas retrieved Douglas's wallet and gave it to Fr. Dimitrios. She said they worried when he didn't come back to get his things after the wedding. They'd put them in their storeroom. She was pleased to hear that Douglas was all right, and would give the message to her husband.

Then he found the address of the George Hanson Institute of Minoan Archaeology, but there was no sign identifying it. A paper was taped to the glass door. He parked his Vespa away from a large truck that was parked right in front. He went up the steps to read the notice.

As of August 20, the George Hanson Institute is closed. Invoices may be presented to...a postal box address. *Other inquiries may be addressed to Ms. Athina Stavraki,* and the paper gave a telephone number. Fr. Dimitrios wrote everything down.

Just at that moment, the door opened from the inside and George Hanson stood before him.

"I remember you. You're the coffee-drinking priest who wouldn't do the wedding for us."

Fr. Dimitrios said, "That's right." He smiled, pleasantly. "I am looking for Athina Stavraki."

"She doesn't work here any more. Phone her," and he gestured to the note on the door.

"Thank you, I will."

Hanson went past him down the steps to the truck, where two workers were unloading a very large drafting table.

Fr. Dimitrios returned to his Vespa, took his cellphone out of his sakkoula, and dialed Athina's phone number.

When she answered the phone. Fr. Dimitrios introduced himself as priest of Agyios Yeorgeos in Vraho.

"How can I help you, Patera?"

"I have a note from Douglas Watkins. I'd like to get his passport for him. Do you have it?"

Just then a group of five young men, college students from Finland and quite drunk by early afternoon, came down the street, singing loudly,

"Hei vahtimestari! Tule täytä lasini! Vie tyhjät pullot pois!" (Hey janitor! Come and fill my glass! Take away the empty bottles!) They were carrying their empty bottles, holding them high, clinking them together.

226

Fr. Dimitrios turned away from them and pressed his finger to the ear away from the telephone, but he could barely hear Athina's answer.

"From Douglas? Where is he? How is he?"

He guessed at her response, cupped his hand over the cellphone and answered, in a loud voice. "He's all right. Noisy here. Can you speak up? The passport?"

"I have it. Please, are you calling from Chania?"

"Yes."

"Then please come over." She named an address in the Spiantza district of Old Chania.

Fr. Dimitrios rode over to her apartment, a tiny flat with cardboard boxes stacked along one wall.

"Please excuse the boxes. I have brought all the files from the Institute over here until we find a place for them."

"What happened to the Institute?"

"The patron, George Hanson, decided to close it. It was all very sudden. He gave us twenty-four hours to vacate the office."

"I got your telephone number from the notice taped to the door. And now it seems that Mr. Hanson is moving into the offices."

"Is he? What will he do with them?" Athina looked puzzled.

"Wait a minute. His daughter was getting married. And Douglas was working for your institute...was she going to marry Douglas?"

"They'd been engaged for a long time, practically since childhood, I think. Then Douglas ran off, right from the wedding. It was a dramatic thing to do, to run away like that, but it seemed like maybe a touch of nervousness and that he would come back in a little while, and they'd go ahead with it. That's why we were worried when he didn't come back." Athina asked, "Would you like a coffee? Or a soda?"

"Coffee, please," said Fr. Dimitrios.

She spoke to him from the kitchenette.

"Those Hansons! They are very difficult people. Douglas was not like them, but he was going to go into her father's business, so it seemed he knew what they were like."

227

She came back into the room with two cups of kafe Elleniko. She sat down.

"The day after the wedding, yesterday, Mr. Hanson burst in and told the professor to close up the office right then. I thought it was perhaps a punishment to the professor because Douglas ran away, but Roland, the professor, had not run away. It made no sense.

"Professor Ducor was so stressed that he had a terrible asthma attack. I brought him home from the hospital last night. This morning he and I packed up the files and at noon the furniture was taken away."

"Where is Professor Ducor now?"

"He's at his apartment, resting. Poor man, this has been very hard on him. I am quite worried about him. Now the Hansons have broken the lease on his apartment. He must move from there before the first of the month. Such a move could bring on another stress attack. More asthma might kill him."

She disappeared into another room, and returned carrying a manila envelope. "Here is Douglas's passport. How did he manage for so many days without it?" She drew the passport out and handed it to Fr. Dimitrios.

"*Philoxenia*. Cretans are generous to strangers."

"But he has no Greek language."

"I know. He was lucky that the villagers he met spoke a little English."

She smiled. "And then he found you. Is Douglas all right? I mean, really?"

"He is. And now he will have his passport and his wallet—I picked up the wallet, too, from the taverna where he was staying. That reminds me. I must keep moving. I have other stops to make today. I think a member of my parish was stabbed yesterday."

He rose, and handed her the demitasse cup. "Delicious," he said.

Athina said, "I heard something about a stabbing at the hospital yesterday. I was waiting for the professor and I sat near a little boy who was very upset. His cousin had been stabbed and was in surgery. The attacker had used the little boy's father's knife."

"His cousin? Can you remember anything else?"

"The boy felt he was to blame. He was suffering…He had blue eyes."

Fr. Dimitrios said, "Thank you. I think you've given me the identity of the stabbing victim. I will go now to the hospital. I'll give Douglas your phone number. I know he'll want to see you and the professor, as soon as Professor Ducor is well again. Thank you."

He rode his Vespa quickly to the hospital, where he inquired at the information desk for Manolis Kiriakis.

"He's in Intensive Care, Patera. Only family may visit. But of course his priest would be all right, too. An orderly will take you there." A call bell summoned a young man in white. He would lead Fr. Dimitrios to Manolis Kiriakis.

Fr. Dimitrios followed the orderly to Manolis's bed in ICU. He saw what Spiros had seen: a shrunken body resembling Manolis, with a tube down his throat, tubes to his arms, and tape everywhere. Manolis's eyes were closed. Sleeping? Comatose? Fr. Dimitrios couldn't tell. Manolis looked terrible.

On his way out he said to the nurse, "I'll be back again to see this patient." The nurse replied, "You are welcome anytime, Patera."

When Fr. Dimitrios gave Douglas his wallet and passport, Douglas grinned. "All right! Let me stand you to something at the taverna!"

Over their kafes Elleniko, Fr. Dimitrios told Douglas what he had learned. He hadn't been able to speak to the police. He would try later by phone. The robber was still in Intensive Care.

"Who is he?"

"I don't understand this, but it's Aleko's cousin, Manolis."

"A sorry-looking kid with pimples? I saw him at Aleko's house. He was hovering behind his angry father."

"That would be Manolis."

"Why would he rob Aleko?"

"I don't know. There's more news, too. The Institute is closed."

"What?"

"George Hanson was there, moving furniture into the offices. Was that his daughter you were going to marry?"

229

"That's right. Denise." Douglas looked chagrined. "How is she?"

"I didn't see her and he didn't say. Athina and the professor are out of work. She had taken your passport to her home for safekeeping. I went to her apartment to get it. They were worried about you. Athina said to say hello."

"You told them I was all right?"

"I did." They finished their coffees while Douglas absorbed the new information. None of it made sense. Why Aleko's cousin? Why would George Hanson close the Institute and move into the offices? Douglas found the news incomprehensible.

"Now I have something to show you," he said. He led the priest back to the church.

During the time Fr. Dimitrios was gone, Douglas had cleared whitewash from the figure of a man on a galloping white horse. Fr. Dimitrios said, "Wonderful! That must be one of the wise men. There should be two more. Ah, it's coming, isn't it?"

They looked at their wall. Douglas still saw only patches of a story-picture mural, but he began to understand that what Fr. Dimitrios saw was something more. He looked at the images, and at the holes.

"I've been wondering—were those bullet holes?"

"The Germans did those, in World War II."

"Inside the church?"

"There was a massacre here. That's why the paintings were covered over. To forget the massacre."

"And now?"

"It's time to acknowledge all of our past."

While Douglas swept up the whitewash chips, Fr. Dimitrios went over to the taverna. He asked Lambros if he had already rented out both his guest rooms for the night. Lambros said two German backpackers were in one room but the other room was still empty. It was dusk. No more tourists would be coming to Vraho tonight. Fr. Dimitrios asked if he could book it for Douglas.

Lambros said, "Pappa Dimitri, your friend may have it for nothing."

"I don't want that. He must pay for it."

"Very well, if you say so, but I make a little discount for him." And Lambros winked.

Fr. Dimitrios said, seriously, "Do not give it to him. He has some money now."

Douglas finished cleaning up the church and settled in to his room at the taverna. He washed up, then went downstairs to eat a meal. Lambros talked to him while he wolfed down the taverna chicken dinner.

Fr. Dimitrios returned to his house, but on the way he stopped by Kyria Ariadne's house.

She said, "I was just coming over with your supper."

"I'll save you the trip."

"It's not far."

"I know it's not. But I am here."

She smiled. "Very well, then." She said, "You are still an American person. No other priest carried his own food, not even your dear grandfather!"

When he came into his house he raised the dropleaf of his small table and laid the meal out across the surface. Cold roast chicken, cooked greens with lemon and olive oil over them. On the side, a dish made from potato, onion, and cheese. Three *zournadakia* for dessert. Bliss! Little rolls of phyllo pastry around chopped walnuts and almonds. His very favorite sweet. He sighed contentedly. There was a knock on the door.

When he opened it, there stood Vassilia. She was pale and looked very upset.

"Please, come in." he said.

She didn't move. "Patera, I am very worried. Aleko left this morning after feeding the animals, and he still isn't back. He never does such a thing."

"I saw him here, at the church, this morning. He dropped in and we talked for a few minutes. He seemed all right then. Do you think he's run away?"

"I don't know. He's always been a good son. What did he say to you this morning? How was he?"

231

"He seemed all right. He was looking for something. He didn't stay. He went on up the mountain. That was hours ago."

"Something must have happened to him."

"Trust him, Kyria Vassilia. He wouldn't want to worry you. He'll come home soon, I think. He wouldn't stay out overnight on purpose, would he? Please, go back to your house and wait for him. If he doesn't come tonight, come back to me tomorrow morning and I will perform a paraclesis to protect him. All right?"

"Yes, Patera." She started to leave.

"Kyria, wait." She turned back to Fr. Dimitrios.

"Can you tell me anything about the American, Douglas?"

Vassilia started to cry. "I think that's where Aleko went."

"Where?"

"To find him."

"Are we talking about the same person: a young man, white shirt, my height?"

"I gave him one of Panos's shirts. His was torn."

"Douglas is here, in Vraho. He's not lost. If Aleko went to look for him, he will come home tonight. I'm sure of it."

After Vassilia had gone, Fr. Dimitrios went over to the taverna. Douglas was chatting with Lambros over a kafe Elleniko. The priest told him Aleko was missing and might be looking for him.

Douglas said, "The cave!"

Fr. Dimitrios borrowed a flashlight from Lambros and both men ran to the red arroyo with the fresh hole in it. They shone the light down the hole and called "Aleko." There was no answer.

"He wouldn't have fallen into a clearly visible hole like that. It was daylight. He has a mountain kid's respect for caves, I'm sure." Fr. Dimitrios said, but he didn't sound entirely convinced. The cave weighed on them both.

232

"Where else could he have gone to look for you?"

Douglas mentioned the meat packing place down the mountain where they'd sold the two goats. Fr. Dimitrios borrowed a map from Lambros. Douglas found Fournes and marked where the butcher was.

Fr. Dimitrios took off on the Vespa to Fournes to see if he could find the missing boy. The meat packing place was closed when he got there, and he found nothing. Back at the taverna, he knocked on Douglas's door and said, "Aleko and his mother don't have a phone. He's probably back home, but just in case, keep thinking, okay?"

Douglas sat on his bed with the map and tried to plot where Aleko might have thought to look for him. He fell asleep on top of the map. He woke several hours later and put himself to bed.

32

Early the next morning, Vassilia knocked on Fr. Dimitrios's door.

When he saw her face, he knew there was trouble. He said, "Kalimera, Kyria Vassilia. No Aleko yet? Time for a paraclesis, then." He smiled at her. "Will you please go to the bakery and get bread for *prosforo*? Tell people that Aleko is missing and we will have a paraclesis at ten o'clock at your house. I'll get Vaggelis-the-chanter and meet you there."

Fr. Dimitrios assembled what he would need. He opened a chest under his bed and took out a small silk envelope containing his *epitrachelion*, a long stole of silk brocade. He lifted his grandfather's prayer book off its shelf. He put these into his sakkoula, along with his grandfather's favorite, the small icon of Agyios Phanourios, Saint Lost and Found. He put his cell phone in the pocket of his cassock. Vassilia had no phone.

As he took up the sakkoula, he silently thanked Kyria Ariadne once more for making it for him.

He made a notice for the church bulletin board and one for the taverna door. The signs said:

ALEKO ANDREADAKIS IS MISSING.
PARACLESIS 10 AM AT HIS HOUSE, KATO VRAHO.
SEARCH PARTY FOLLOWS.

He rode the Vespa over to the taverna and asked Lambros if he'd seen Douglas yet this morning.

"Not yet. Shall I wake him?"

"I'll put a note under his door. He must be exhausted. Which room?"

"Two."

Fr. Dimitrios went upstairs. He tapped lightly on the door of Room Two. Douglas opened the door. He still needed a shave and his clothing was still dirty and wrinkled, but he had bathed and slept and he seemed much better than the night before. He looked inquiringly at Fr. Dimitrios.

"No Aleko. We will do a service to ask the intercession of the Virgin and saints, for his safety, and then start a search party. You might want to start looking now. Show me what you marked on the map."

Douglas explained where the first and second robberies had been and where he had taken the wrong turn when he ran up-mountain after the second robbery. Fr. Dimitrios marked where there were several paths between the roads and suggested that Douglas try them.

Fr. Dimitrios rode over to the home of Vaggelis-the-chanter. The tiny old man was in bed with a sore throat, but he got up and came with the priest. He rode on the pillion of the Vespa.

When they reached Vassilia's house, no one was there.

Vassilia was crossing the last gully back from Ano Vraho. She walked around the stone wall of her property and came through the drooping gate. She carried two bags of bread from the baker's. Fr. Dimitrios said it was fine for the prosforo. Even though it was not baked especially for the purpose, it would do.

Inside her house, she set up a small table which she draped with a white cotton cloth bordered with bright flowers and red scrollwork. She brought the icons from around her house and Fr. Dimitrios laid

235

them out on the cloth. He put the Theotokos, the Holy Virgin, in the center and St. George to one side. He added his St. Phanourios next to St. George, and then placed the large icon of Christ Pantokrator on the other side of the Theotokos.

Vassilia set seven slender candles into a bowl filled with sand. This she put in front of the icons.

Neighbors began to arrive. Some came from the notices on the church or the taverna. Others Vassilia had invited while she bought the prosforo. Ten villagers came.

Fr. Dimitrios unfolded the sacred epitrachelion and draped it around his neck. He lit the candles and the incense in the censer.

He and Vaggelis-the-chanter then celebrated the supplicatory canon, praying for the intercession of the Mother of God and the other saints to return the lost child, Aleko. The comforting scent of the incense and the sound of chanting filled the room.

As Fr. Dimitrios performed the paraclesis, his thoughts flew. He had interceded, asked God's help, for many requests but never one as vital as this one. Of the children in the village, Aleko was the one who sought knowledge, loved truth, cared about God and the honest life. He was the treasure among treasures.

Fr. Dimitrios silently prayed, *This favor I really ask: return this boy to his mother and I won't ask for insignificant blessings ever again.*

After the service, Fr. Dimitrios removed the epitrachelion from his neck and folded it back into its silk envelope. Vassilia packed up the remaining prosforo bread. She gave it to Fr. Dimitrios to take back to the church to be used in next Sunday's service.

Vassilia's sister Sofia and her husband Spiros were not at the service. Vassilia said they had a relative in hospital. Fr. Dimitrios did not risk showing he knew who it was. His face revealed nothing.

236

In the three years Fr. Dimitrios had lived on Crete, he had witnessed many kinds of human suffering. He thought back to his childhood and adolescence in San Francisco. The only pain he had been aware of then was his own. He had not seen agony like the suffering of this disintegrating family when he was growing up in the Greek community in California. Did they not have these problems? Was he blind then or was it only after he was able to step out of his own pain that he could see the pain of those around him?

Vaggelis looked weak and feverish by the time the service was over. Fr. Dimitrios rode him straight home. At the door, he shook the old man's hand and thanked him for his good work. Vaggelis-the-chanter was very old now, and his voice was not what it once was, but his piety was solid. He was a great asset to the congregation. Fr. Dimitrios was grateful to have him.

He returned to Vassilia's to join the search party.

33

Douglas clutched the map of the area. He'd been lost across much of its surface and underneath some of it, too. Now the task was to find someone else who was lost, and not get lost again himself.

Before now, the boundaries of his life had been his own small world. Those boundaries had changed a lot since he met this little boy, Aleko. On this mountain, people cared for each other. Here, when there was trouble—and they seemed always to live on the edge of trouble—there was support and love. Love as giving, not just love as want.

His first stop was the butcher in Fournes. He'd never actually been inside the building. The two times he'd gone with Aleko and a goat, he had waited outside while the goat was sold. He entered and found a grey-haired man wearing a white apron marked with traces of blood. He asked, in English, if the man had seen Aleko. The butcher spoke no English. Douglas smiled, showed how tall Aleko was, flapped his hands around, and cursed himself that he hadn't learned Greek.

The man listened seriously but uncomprehendingly, then he called out for his helper, who also tried to understand what Douglas was asking. Douglas saw that Aleko wasn't there. He said "Sas efcharisto," that one useful phrase he could remember, and he left.

The houses near Fournes were made of concrete block. Douglas wondered what had happened to the stonework of the older houses like Aleko's? The concrete had a dismal air, like prison blocks. Progress! He shook his head.

Look at you, he said to himself. You'd like them to be living in Minoan houses with no running water, no electricity, nothing. What's picturesque for you is difficult for the people who live in it. There are probably lots of good reasons why concrete block makes better houses than stone does. Don't make judgments because you like the picturesque. Wish them well, and keep looking for Aleko.

The fact that there were only concrete houses in this area brought him a slower thought. He remembered the bullet holes in the church and on the taverna. He wondered if the former stone houses right here might have been destroyed in the war. Maybe the war was the reason for the concrete.

He went back to the site of the first robbery, calling "Aleko" every few steps. A dog or two barked at his cries, but no human answered him. From the robbery site he took the route the pickup truck had driven. When he reached the village below Vraho he consulted the map. Fr. Dimitrios's trails were pretty obvious now that he was here, but they showed no signs of a lost Aleko.

He thought about walking all of the trails and decided the only one Aleko might think he, Douglas, was on was one that stretched from the road to Peristeri. He took it, still calling out "Aleko" every few minutes. The path led along the upper reach of a row of small, fenced fields.

He called "Aleko." This time, he heard something. He called again. "Aleko?"

A small voice came back. "*Voithia.*"

"Aleko."

"*Etho!*"

239

They called to each other and Douglas ran toward the sound. He rounded a corner of stone and greenery and saw Aleko up a tree with a dog below.

Aleko yelled, "Daonglos! Hi!"

"Hi! You okay?"

"O.-K.!" said Aleko, but he didn't sound convincing.

The dog addressed Douglas, its teeth bared, its hackles standing. It stalked him in a menacing manner. Aleko started to get down from the tree.

"No, Aleko! Stay there."

Aleko stayed where he was.

The dog gave a guttural snarl that made the hairs on Douglas's arms stand up. He noticed that he had the symptoms of fear but he wasn't feeling fear—not in his old way of not feeling anything at all, but in a new way: as someone who has felt great fear, has been terrified to the point of being willing to lose everything, and who is free of fear afterwards. He had left fear in the cave.

Keeping eye-contact with the dog, he picked up three rocks, pocketed two of them, and moved forward. The dog stood its ground. When the distance between them was two meters, the dog sprang at his neck. Douglas blocked with his right arm and brought his knee up. It was enough to knock the dog off its trajectory. It landed hard, scrambled to its feet and circled. Douglas threw the first rock at short range. It hit the dog above the right eye.

A yelp and a fall-back. The dog stayed three meters away but circled Douglas. Aleko watched from the tree. He offered warnings, in Greek.

Douglas took the two remaining rocks into his right hand. The dog held its head low, its jaw open in a snarl. Douglas aimed for its teeth.

240

He hit the nose with one rock. The effect was good. The animal curled back and presented its side to Douglas, who threw the last rock at its ribcage. It also connected.

The dog dropped its tail and head. It retreated to its property, fifteen meters away. It lay down, rubbed its head with a forepaw, and eyed Douglas, who said, "Aleko! Go! Now! I'll follow."

Aleko understood. He swung down out of the tree and wobbled for a few steps, then took off running up the path Douglas had just come down. Douglas slowly backed up, still watching the dog, who was now busy guarding the goats.

When he was around the bend in the path and could no longer see the dog, Douglas ran after Aleko. He caught up to him at the road. Aleko was standing at the near berm. His face was tear-streaked and dusty. Douglas picked up the child by his ribs and held him tight. Only then did Aleko cry. Douglas stroked his head and said comforting things, in English.

Aleko and Douglas flagged down a truck and hitched a ride back to Ano Vraho. They saw no one in the village, no one outside the church, no one anywhere. They were going to the taverna to look for Lambros when he came out, saying to them, "You're safe. Oh, thank God!" He went inside again to get his telephone. He dialed Fr. Dimitrios's cellphone number and said, "They're here. Aleko and the American. They are here at the taverna." Then he gestured to a table and made them sit down. "What you want? On the house!"

Douglas ordered a kafe Elleniko and Aleko asked for an ice cream. That was how the search party found them when they returned to the upper village.

Vassilia had been riding in a truck with a neighbor. When she arrived, Aleko flinched, thinking she'd be mad at him for causing trouble. She hugged him and kissed him and said, "Don't ever frighten me like that again, please." He nodded. They had a long conversation, too soft and too rapid for anyone to overhear. Then Vassilia came over to Douglas and shook his hand and said, "Sas efcharisto." Douglas smiled back at her. She gestured to his shoulder and he tapped himself, indicating that it was getting better. She smiled.

241

The others who had been out looking for Aleko drifted in. Soon, there was a celebration outside the taverna. Lambros brought out roasted new potatoes coated in salt and lemon juice, and pitchers of lemon drink and bottles of beer. Everyone came up to Aleko and Douglas and spoke to them. Even Kyrios Varasulakis, whose cheese Douglas had tried to steal, came over and shook Douglas's hand. He said, in English, "Thank you for saving our child. The village thanks you."

Douglas said, "Is Aleko related to you then?"

"Not by blood. But all the children belong to Vraho. They are ours."

That was true.

Lambros brought out salves and bandages. Vassilia dressed Aleko's dog bite.

Fr. Dimitrios called for attention and spoke in Greek, then turned to Douglas and said, "Where did you find him?"

"On the first of those trails you marked on the map."

Fr. Dimitrios spoke to Aleko, who nodded. Then he said more to the assembled people of the village, and turned again to Douglas and said, "We thank you for finding Aleko."

"Please tell them that I thank them for their kindnesses to me, too."

Fr. Dimitrios translated. People smiled. The group began to disperse.

When only Vassilia, Aleko, Fr. Dimitrios, and Douglas remained, Lambros appeared with a tray with plates of chicken and rice for each of them.

Fr. Dimitrios began the unraveling by saying, "So these are the people you stayed with?" Douglas smiled. "And Vassilia picked the birdshot out of your back?"

"She did."

He spoke in Greek to the others, "Who is going to tell me now what happened?" He looked at Aleko, then at Vassilia. They looked at each other. "Let me take the secret out of it. I have seen Manolis in the hospital."

"How did you find out he was there?"

"That's not important. I want to know, now, how he happened to be stabbed."

Tears stood in Aleko's eyes. "Daonglos was not to blame. I stole my father's passalis and gave it to him." Aleko looked over at his mother.

She interrupted, "I saw that it was your father's passalis in the hospital, but I blamed Daonglos for taking it. I thought he stole it. That's why I didn't feel bad about putting the blame on him with the police. Pappa Dimitri," Vassilia turned to Fr. Dimitrios. "We don't know why Manolis was doing these attacks. When we talked to the police, Sofia and I said that the cousins had a game they played, of hiding and scaring each other. That Daonglos was walking with Aleko and he didn't know about the game and he had a knife and he stabbed him."

Fr. Dimitrios said, "There wasn't a game between the cousins, was there?"

"No, Patera. Manolis and Aleko never played games on each other."

"I understand that Douglas went along at Aleko's request, to protect him, and..."

"And I gave him the passalis," said Aleko. "I'm sorry, Mana Mou."

Vassilia said, "Aleko, if you will forgive my lie, and I forgive you for taking the passalis, we can start over to build trust with one another."

He let her hug him.

Fr. Dimitrios continued, "So Douglas wasn't armed until Aleko gave him the knife."

Vassilia agreed.

"We must change the report with the police now, so Douglas is not accused of things he didn't do."

Douglas cleared his throat. He had waited to hear what was being said. He heard his name, but the other words he could not understand.

Fr. Dimitrios turned to him and said, "One minute more and I'll explain."

Vassilia said, "But Sofia must sign it too. She is at the hospital with Manolis."

"You must ask her tonight, then. And tomorrow we will explain the correction to the police."

Vassilia looked uncomfortable.

243

"We can talk to Officer Thomas!" suggested Aleko.

"Yes, to Officer Thomas." Fr. Dimitrios thought for a moment. Then he asked Vassilia "Why did you need to protect Manolis?"

"I may not say. It is a family matter."

"This has gone beyond the family, Kyria Vassilia. Please tell me."

"It is a shame within the family. Sofia and I were afraid that if Spiros learned that Manolis was a robber he would beat him. On top of this stabbing, a beating would kill him. Patera, I do not think that Sofia will change her story with the police. She needs to protect her son."

Douglas watched their faces and listened to the tone of their voices and finally said to Fr. Dimitrios, "Please. What's going on?"

Fr. Dimitrios explained the problem.

Douglas said, "It's simple. *I* will speak to Officer Thomas. I will turn myself in. We can sort out who did what to whom later."

"You may spend time in prison."

"Maybe so. The one thing is, I would like to see Aleko's cousin..." he reached for the name.

"Manolis."

"...Manolis. I want to apologize for the pain I've caused him, and I'll need you there to translate."

"Are you sure? ...We can go as soon as he is conscious."

"Let's find Officer Thomas."

"He'll come here tomorrow. I'll ask Lambros to call me when he comes and then I'll translate for you."

34

Officer Thomas showed up on schedule the next morning for his kafe Elleniko. Lambros greeted him, smiling as usual, took his order, excused himself, and went inside to the telephone. He called Fr. Dimitrios, who came fast across the platia, his cassock snapping against itself.

Fr. Dimitrios greeted the policeman and ordered two kafes Elleniko from Lambros. Then he disappeared up the staircase.

Officer Thomas was surprised by the appearance of the busy priest, but then his coffee arrived and his attention was drawn by the aroma of the small cup before him.

Fr. Dimitrios reappeared, in front of another man coming down stairs. They came to Officer Thomas's table and the priest introduced the American, Douglas Watkins. They sat down with him. The American didn't speak Greek, so the priest spoke for him.

"Douglas is the one who found Aleko after he'd been missing all night."

"That's very good news." Officer Thomas nodded to Douglas. "Good work!"

"Douglas is here to turn himself in to you so you can arrest him."

"What for?"

"For stabbing Manolis Kiriakis three days ago."

Officer Thomas looked very puzzled. "Was a crime report taken? Where did this happen?"

"In Chania. There was a report filed. Don't you have it?"

"No. Nothing." Lambros arrived with a tray holding two more cups of kafe Elleniko.

"Well then, what should he do?"

Lambros set a cup before Douglas and the other cup before Fr. Dimitrios.

"I think he should drink his coffee," said Officer Thomas.

Fr. Dimitrios translated for Douglas, who looked puzzled, but smiled at the officer.

"Now listen, Patera. I have been around longer than you, but I have never had an accused criminal come up to me to turn himself in. Is this American manners? Criminals asking to be arrested? Not what I see on American TV. Where is Manolis now?"

"In hospital for the stab wound."

Officer Thomas sat up straighter in his chair. "So it wasn't just a scratch? He really hurt him?"

"Yes, but Manolis shot him the day before."

"Why? He doesn't even look Greek."

"He's a stranger. Xeno. Manolis was trying to rob Aleko."

"Of what? Aleko doesn't have anything."

"I know, I know. Manolis's mother and aunt filed charges against Douglas. They claimed Manolis was playing a game with Aleko and that Douglas interfered. But that's not the truth."

"If I don't have the report, I don't want to hear this information. Any of it. When Chania is ready to arrest him, I will come to you and you will find him, yes?"

"I will be responsible for him, whenever you're ready for him. It sounds like the charges should be dropped, doesn't it?"

"Dropped? In Greece we can't drop criminal charges. With luck, the judge will dismiss them at his trial. The best you could hope for is that the charges get lost in the desktop papers in Chania and are never processed."

Fr. Dimitrios said, "I will hope for that."

Officer Thomas leaned back in his chair. "Look at this view, Patera! Aren't we lucky to be alive?"

Fr. Dimitrios agreed with Officer Thomas and then explained the situation to Douglas. They finished their coffees and bade Officer Thomas good day. "Kalimera," they all said, and the two men went to the church to continue chipping off whitewash.

When they were again crouched on their stools and attacking the stiff layer of whitewash, Douglas asked, "So tell me, please, what good is it to turn myself in when the act is declined?"

"It means you are no longer running."

Douglas thought about this for a long moment. "So it does."

Then he said, "I'm really no longer running, am I? I mean, now I am where I'm standing. Sorry. This is nonsense."

"Not nonsense. It's good."

Douglas looked around at the church walls beginning to reveal their beautiful secrets, at the dust floating in the light from the windows, at the stillness of the space, at Fr. Dimitrios, the patient American-and-not-American priest. He felt solid. The feeling surprised him.

"Aha, Douglas. Come look at Joseph."

Fr. Dimitrios showed him a disconsolate figure holding his head in his hands.

"Sometimes there are two images of Joseph in a Nativity—like the two images of the infant Christ." He pointed to the swaddled infant next to Mary and the second infant in the lower right of the painting. "If so, Joseph and the angel should be on the other side, over there."

"Why does that foot dangle like that?"

"He's not standing on the same ground we are. Icons don't share our time and space."

Douglas looked puzzled.

Fr. Dimitrios said, "The icons are emblems of figures in another, parallel world to this one of sensation that we are in."

"What do you mean?"

247

"When I see these icons, I am reminded that a hair's breadth from where I am is the fullness of the invisible world of God. The icons are doors between the visible and the invisible worlds."

Douglas walked over to the ikonostasis and looked long and hard at the figures on it.

"When I see them I see a strong style of condensed art, rigidly—forgive me—rigidly traditional. The more I'm around them, the more I like them. They are interesting, but they carry nothing for me of what they carry for you."

Fr. Dimitrios said, "Don't you think our lives create the filters our eyes see through?"

"You mean, we can only see what we have seen before?"

"More than that. I think we see what we are prepared to see. That's what an education does. It gives the student the tools to find and to understand new areas of thought. I see, for example, with the eyes of a Greek Orthodox student and an engineer. I don't see archaeology, even when I probably trip over it."

"And I see it everywhere around Crete. But I don't see the same thing you do in these images. I don't see their history or the message of spirit they carry for you. Am I wrong?"

"Not wrong. These figures are partly like hieroglyphics. Seeing them feels almost like reading them, because they repeat the order of the images of other icons I've seen. They give me an image again. They tell me something I know. They ask me to feel it."

"Do you have the idea of the presence of God and these saints with you always, wherever you are? Are you ever lonely?"

"Not often, no."

"I envy you that." Douglas crossed back to the wall-section he had been working on. He hadn't realized that loneliness was the name of his companion, and further, that it might come from an absence of belief in anything.

He leaned close to examine the finely-striped surface of the painting before him.

"Look at these bits of hatching on the rock of the cave." Tiny curving and diagonal lines accentuated the edge of the cave entrance. "There's a lot of energy in this painting."

248

"Energy, yes..." said Fr. Dimitrios. He stepped back to look at the wall. "The pale or gold hatching on the faces and garments is because light is radiating from within the saints, or here, from the cave itself. I'm told it's because icon painters always lay down the dark colors first and work up to the highlights. To us, it represents that other-worldly light."

They picked away at the whitewash until it was time for lunch.

Douglas felt all morning that he was in the presence of a real friend. Well, it was almost like two friends working together, but he knew they weren't there yet. They were still mentor and student. Douglas could feel that his ideas still sat on the surface, while Fr. Dimitrios lived his: he was a servant to those beliefs.

35

Manolis opened his eyes. His mother sat in a chair beside his bed. He closed his eyes again. When he opened them, she was still there. She smiled at him. Around her were white, soft-looking walls. He was confused. He moved.

"You're awake!" his mother said.

"Where've you been?"

He could speak! He was still attached to machines, to IVs, to a catheter. The tube was out of his throat, though, and he could speak.

His throat was sore.

He could make a fist, and he held the nurse-call-button in his right hand, but his arms were still both strapped to boards for the IVs. He felt like an inflated ghost-version of himself.

"I've been right here for a week now, Manolis, ever since you got out of Intensive Care. You've been sleeping and I didn't want to wake you. Shall I pull back the curtains?" She did so, revealing a four-bed ward with curtains drawn around the other beds.

"Where's my father?"

"He's at home."

"Does he know I'm here?"

"Yes."

Manolis winced.

"Son, I know what you did. I have not told your father."

Manolis looked interested.

"I told him it was Daonglos's fault. That you were playing a trick on Aleko and that Daonglos stabbed you. I also told this to the police. Aunt Vassilia said Daonglos stole the knife from her. So now the police are looking for Daonglos. Your record will be all right."

"Why would Aunt Vassilia lie for me?"

"You are family." She did not tell him that Vassilia was urging her to change her story to the truth, that this was making for an awkwardness between them, this argument over the story to the police. "What were you doing trying to rob poor Aleko, anyway?"

"Nothing." The memory of the failed robbery—can't even do that right—had been coming back to him in fragments over the days and nights of this hospital torment. He still wasn't sure what had happened.

He moved. And moaned.

His mother said, "I'm sorry you hurt so much. Nurse says they can't give you medicine for the pain because it makes the lung lazy and then you couldn't get enough air. So you have to hurt."

"Well, I do. What did they do to me?"

"The knife went in your lung and they sewed it back together. You nearly died." Her voice broke.

"Too bad I didn't."

"Don't say that! My son, I love you. I want you to have a good life." After a moment she said, "Manoli, I have not kept you safe. I see that now. I promise you, your father will never hurt you again. I lied to the police and your father because he would beat you if he knew, and I realize that a beating hurts the spirit even more than it hurts the body.

"Your father is very angry at Daonglos, but he's not angry at you. I protected you this time, and I will again, forever. I give you my word."

251

Manolis sank back into his pillow. A lie had been told on his behalf. To protect him. He was glad she lied. He felt safe.

Then an idea struck him.

"When the police find him? What then? He'll tell what happened."

"If Vassilia will hold to her story, it's Cretans against a foreigner and you'll be safe." The if in her sentence floated in the air over both of them. Manolis didn't feel quite as safe as he had a moment earlier.

His mother looked so sad. He almost felt sorry for her. Then he felt mad. If she'd been a good mother, he wouldn't have been beat up by his father all the time. It was her fault.

His father would beat up anything in his path. Fathers do that. Like Chronos, eating all his children except Zeus. The only reason Zeus survived was because his mother protected him, hid him away inside Mount Ida, here on Crete.

Manolis drifted off, thinking of Zeus. The greatest of the gods, and born on Crete. He liked Zeus best when he learned those stories in school.

When he woke, his mother was dozing in her chair.

36

The telephone by the bed kept ringing. George reached out for the travel-alarm. It said twelve o'clock. George was confused. Midnight twelve o'clock or noon twelve o'clock? He looked toward the window. Blackout drapes were drawn, but he thought he should see an edge of light and he didn't. Dark, then. Must be midnight. He turned on the lamp.

His wife rolled away from the light and didn't wake up. George picked up the receiver.

"Do you have any idea what time it is, Roger?" He snarled in a bear-growl.

"Yes. It's the end of the work day and I have news you want to hear. So wake up."

"What's wrong?"

"Nothing's wrong. We just got the first samples. Just came in. They're wonderful. Denise is a genius! The pattern cutters had a few problems figuring out what she meant on that jacket, you know the one. But they worked it out and it looks good. I hope she doesn't notice we changed it a little."

"Well, you had to make it work. I don't want to stifle her creativity with issues of sewing. Not yet, anyway. It really looks good, eh?"

"George, it's the best collection we've ever had."

"What about the Snake Goddess top?"

"Were you serious about that? I mean, anyone wears that on the street they'll be arrested."

"That's why there's a cape to go with it."

"I don't know, George."

"Just do it. Denise wants it and she keeps asking about the gold bracelets that wind up the arms like the snakes do."

"The bracelets are here. But about the top...I mean, it's your company. If you want it, I'll do it."

"I want it."

"I'll get on it right away. George, the hero of the hour is your daughter. What a gift she has!"

"Yeah, she's making her old man proud. Oh yes, I called in the rental car Ducor was using. No point in running up charges after we've closed."

"All right, but you know you're going to have to find another charity to put that money into, and pronto, or the accounting department will be having fits. The IRS will be on our tail."

"I'll find something we need that could use a boost. Hanson Industries, supporter of Asian embroiderers, or something. Don't worry."

"What ever happened to the bridegroom?"

"Don't know. Don't care. I just pray he stays out of the picture so Denise doesn't stop working."

"Well, work is a cure for a broken heart. Watch out, though. Sooner or later he'll turn up again."

Mrs. Hanson sat up. "Is that Roger? Let me talk to him."

"The Missus wants to say a word."

"Roger?"

"Hello, Mother of the Designer."

"Now Roger, listen to me. I want you to keep your eyes open for a nice young man for Denise. Somebody who will stay put in St. Louis. Someone working his way up through the business, but good-looking, too. Like that nice boy Caroline is seeing. Does he have a brother?"

Roger told her, "No brother. I'll keep my eyes open, but Denise can probably find someone without my help."

Drawn by the sound of her parents' voices, Denise appeared in the doorway. She was wearing a coral-colored nightgown, a gift from her mother, intended for her honeymoon.

"Are you talking to Roger? I need to talk to him." She took the receiver from her mother's hand. "Roger?"

"Nice work, Denise."

"Thanks. Listen: that supplier in Singapore is supposed to duplicate the Cretan embroidery I sent over. I had the samples sent to you for quality control. Have they come?"

"Not yet."

"Goose 'em, will you? We need to get on that. If they can't duplicate them I'll have to go find more in these little shops and they say they're running out of product. Get back to me on this fast, will you?"

"Denise, did you check copyright on the images from the museum there?"

"Copyright expires after a few years. These things are about ten zillion years old. Are you going to bother me with details? You're the legal guy. You can fix it. Here, Dad." She handed the phone back to her father and went to the minibar to look for some pretzels. Then she went back to her bedroom.

"Boy, a regular little executive! She must have been soaking up my talk all the years she was growing up. Makes me want to call the corporation George Hanson and Daughter."

"You watch out, George. Another few months and it'll be Denise Hanson and Father."

George guffawed over the phone, but he was pleased by the idea. Then he had a moment of feeling sorry for poor Roger, with that daughter of his who'd never amount to a hill of beans: Caroline couldn't sing, couldn't act, and couldn't pass dumbbell math in high school.

255

Why did his wife want Roger to find someone for Denise like Caroline's boyfriend? Denise the designer would likely marry someone in the business, textiles big-time, or even politics. An ambassador, maybe. She's moving up in the world, all right.

His smile came back as he thought of his successful designer-daughter. Ah, Denise!

37

"Kalimera. St. George Hospital."

"Spiros Kiriakis here. I want to speak to my son, Manolis Kiriakis."

"Your son is a patient?"

"Yes, but he's not in Intensive Care anymore."

There was a pause. "Here he is. Third floor. One moment." Another pause.

"Third floor nurse's station."

"I want to speak to Manolis Kiriakis. I am his father."

"He's very weak, Kyrie Kiriakis. He'll have to come to the telephone in a wheelchair. We don't have phones in the rooms. It might be easier if you come in to visit him."

"Just get him to the telephone."

"One moment. I'll ask him if he thinks he can come to the telephone."

Time passed. The receiver was uncomfortable against his ear. The nurse came back to the phone.

"We're putting him in a wheelchair. He'll be here soon. Please wait."

Another long silence. Some clanking sounds, then a faint voice on the other end whispered, "Mbaba?"

"What's that? Speak up, boy."

"Kalimera, Mbaba."

"Son, you don't sound like you. Speak up! So, you're better, right?"

"They tell me I'm getting better, yes."

"So come home."

"I don't know if they'll let me yet, Mbaba. We'll have to ask them."

"Since when is such a choice up to 'them'?"

"I will ask them, Mbaba."

"I'll pick you up this afternoon."

The telephone made a loud clunk and then Manolis said, "I'm sorry, Mbaba. I dropped the phone."

"Well, don't do that again. It hurt my ear!"

"I'm sorry, Mbaba."

Then a nurse's voice said, "Mr. Kiriakis, your son is too weak to sit up and talk on the telephone. Why don't you come to visit him instead? It would be better for him. Please come to the hospital instead of phoning. He's on the third floor." She hung up on him.

She hung up on him!

Never had anyone dared hang up on him. He called out for Sofia.

She came quickly to where he stood. "What's wrong?"

"I'm going to the hospital to get Manolis and bring him home."

"Do you think that's wise? Did they say he was strong enough? He's still pretty sick, Spiros. Please. Don't go. Don't do this." She put a restraining hand on his arm. He flung her off and slammed the door on his way out.

He unlocked the blue sedan, got into it and drove down the mountain into Chania. He found a sign marked HOSPITAL PARKING: DOCTORS ONLY. He pulled in and parked. The nearest

258

door was also marked DOCTORS ONLY. He entered there. He found his way to the elevator and then to the third floor nurse's desk.

He waited for the nurse behind the desk to look up at him. When she did not, he slammed his hand down on the counter. She jumped, all right. She jumped quite distinctly.

"Where is Manolis Kiriakis?"

"Are you his father?" Spiros nodded. "Let me call someone to take you to him."

She rang a silly-looking bell at the end of the counter. Spiros thought that a hospital should have a better communications system than that. They need an annoying electric buzzer, for instance. BRAAAAPP! Make those nurses jump. Snap to attention.

Another nurse appeared. The first nurse said, "Please take Kyrios Kiriakis to his son's room, 312. Thank you."

The new nurse led him down linoleum corridors just like those downstairs. Why don't the nurses get lost in this place? All the halls look the same. His authoritative pose weakened. In the face of the labyrinth of corridors, he followed her obediently. When she stopped, he looked where she gestured. He saw Manolis.

"Well, you look better. Much better," he said in a cheery tone, but he was sickened by his son's appearance. Manolis was grey in color and thin, very thin! His pimples were flaming red; his hair was uncombed; he was wearing a green flowered hospital gown. Flowers, on a boy! What were they thinking?

Spiros managed a smile. Manolis tried to smile back, but the result was weak.

"Mbaba, they say I can't leave yet." He paused for breath. "I'm too sick...I'm really sorry."

"Yes, well, you don't look too good. I see that. But if you're just lying around, you can do that at home. Your mother can bring you pills and water. It's a waste to stay here. Where are your clothes?"

"I don't know where my clothes are." His father opened all the drawers and doors in the room. "Mbaba, I can't do it."

"Of course you can."

"I can't"

259

Spiros stopped and looked at his disagreeing son. He straightened up. His voice level rose. "I tell you that you are coming home with me now. End of this."

The boy was shaking. Spiros listened, amazed.

"Mbaba, if you take me home you will be killing me. I will die! I am not well." The invalid was now sitting up, his arms flailing, tubes flapping. He looked like a mad dog.

"You have scared me all my life. You have pushed me and pulled me," Manolis paused for breath, "and beaten me and hurt me. Now I am near enough to dying that I'm not afraid of you any more." He stared fiercely at his father. "I'm not going with you." He pushed the nurse-call-button and then turned his face to the wall. He turned his back on his father.

Spiros was stunned by the insubordination. He went to the foot of his son's hospital bed. He lifted it off the floor and let it drop. Manolis screamed.

Two orderlies came running. They took Spiros by the arms and held him away from the bed.

Manolis, crying now, said, "I was trying to make you love me by hurting Aleko and Aunt Vassilia. I was the robber. Both times. I shot that American."

His father looked at him in amazement.

Manolis continued, "I know you want her not to pay for the truck, so you can screw her. I know. That's why I robbed Aleko. Both times that was me. I did it for you. But you won't ever love me no matter what I do for you. I'd rather have a chance to live my own life than be your slave any more." He paused for breath. "I won't go home with you. I don't ever want to live with you again."

The orderlies heard all this. The shame of it: a father mortified by his son. Now, they were holding him like a common thief. His rage surged, then drained from him. He felt shamed in front of these witnesses to his son's outburst. He pulled his arms from the orderlies' hold. "We'll talk about this later, Manoli," he said. He strode out of the room and down the hall.

When he got to the parking lot, his car had been towed. He had to go through the nuisance of phoning for a taxi and going to the tow-yard to retrieve his car. The tow yard was outside of town toward Rethimnon. Minotaur Tow Yard, for heaven's sake. Everything is Minoan around this place. Just to please the tourists. He focused his hatred on the foreigners on his island.

The taxi raised a large cloud of red dust coming in to the tow yard. The dust settled on Spiros and the man who took his good drachmas in exchange for access to his own car, which was no longer dark blue, but red dust color. The departing taxi raised an even bigger cloud of red dust. Spiros wiped his face with his handkerchief. It came away with red dust, too.

At one side of the fence surrounding the captured cars in the tow yard, Spiros saw a group of damned foreigners doing something scientific with a tripod. He couldn't tell what, but he just knew they were more archaeologists. Damn!

Driving home he was so angry he could only see straight ahead of him. The edges of his vision were all red with rage. He prepared himself to yell at Sofia.

Cars, pedestrians, and dogs fled his path as he drove. He bumped the curb twice in the city and when he reached the country roads he wavered on both sides of the road. He was too angry to care. He pulled up in front of the house and switched off the ignition. He went into the house and demanded, "Sofia!"

She appeared in a doorway, carrying a stack of folded laundry. He thought she looked tired. He didn't care.

He yelled, "That boy is not coming back into this house. Ever! You don't have a son anymore. That's it," and he stamped his dusty feet across the room and lurched into his favorite chair. Red dust rose from his clothes.

"Spiros, tell me. What's happened?"

Spiros snorted. "Pfah! I disown him. He's not my son."

Sofia carefully said, "He is your son. He looks just like you. Everyone says so. And I have not had another lover ever."

"He is not my son after today. After his disobedience to me today. I don't care about blood relations. He is not my son."

When no more information was forthcoming, Sofia asked him, "Would you like a tsikoudia?"

261

"No." Then, "Yes. Yes, I would."

She set down the laundry and brought him a small glass of the clear liquid.

"Bring the bottle."

She brought the bottle to where he sat. He tossed back three successive fillings of the small glass. Then, calmer, he said, "He refused to come back with me."

"But, he's too weak. The doctors said so. I told you that."

"He said he...never mind what he said."

"What did he say?"

"Nothing. Go away. When is dinner?"

"Are you hungry?"

"I don't know. Leave me alone."

She left the room but he knew she was sitting perched on a straight-back chair in the kitchen, waiting for his next command. He felt his power returning.

When Fr. Dimitrios opened the door to Manolis's hospital room he didn't know what to expect. The last time he'd seen him—in Intensive Care—the boy had been tiny, shriveled, and hooked up to machines. What greeted him today was a sullen young man lying on his back staring straight overhead.

"Kalimera, Manoli," said Fr. Dimitrios.

At first there was no answer. Then, slowly Manolis rolled his head over toward the door and looked at his visitor.

"Kalimera, Patera." He went back to looking at the ceiling.

Fr. Dimitrios moved a chair to the side of the bed and sat down. "What are you doing?"

"I'm reading the ceiling."

262   Fr. Dimitrios noticed that tears were flowing from Manolis's eyes. He glanced up at the blank ceiling.

"What does it tell you?"

Manolis looked at the priest. "It tells me I have been a fool, and that there is no hope for me. My father just left."

A patch of strong sunlight made a parallelogram across the white sheet covering Manolis's legs. His upper body was in shadow, from the partly drawn privacy-curtain. Fr. Dimitrios opened it, to let Manolis see out the window.

"He came to take me home so my mother wouldn't spend her time at the hospital with me."

"Where is your mother?"

"She went home to do the wash. I guess he needed clean clothes."

"The hospital won't release you now. You're too weak to go home."

"He was going to drag me out. Pappa Dimitri, I said no to him. I said I won't ever go to his house again."

"It sounds awful. Listen to me, please. You are safe here. The hospital staff won't let him take you out. I will speak to them and ask that they not let him visit you until you are strong."

"Parakalo, Patera." More silent tears flowed down the patient's face.

"All this can be solved, Manoli. I will speak to your parents."

Manolis looked alarmed.

"To both of them, and we will find some other solution. Maybe your grandparents could take care of you after you come out of hospital."

Now Manolis looked straight at Fr. Dimitrios. "When I get out of here I'll go to jail."

"You are not charged with anything. The charges are all filed against Douglas, the American man you shot, the one who stabbed you."

"My mother told me. But the police won't believe her story when they hear from him. He didn't start anything. It was all my fault."

"Would you sign a confession saying that? That it was your fault?"

"What would you do with the paper? I'm not going to put myself in jail."

263

"Is it right that Douglas goes to jail instead?"

"Nothing's right, Patera."

"There are some things we humans can do that make things more right. Do you hear me, Manoli?"

"I'm not going to jail. He can take care of himself."

"Suppose I bring him here to meet you?"

"He'd never come."

"He wants to come."

"Why would he do that?"

"For forgiveness."

"No."

Fr. Dimitrios tried another line. "Can you tell me what you wanted to gain by robbing Aleko?"

"I can't tell you, Patera."

"If you change your mind, I can listen. Whatever you tell to me is confidential."

A nurse came into the room, replaced the plastic bag on Manolis's IV stand, smiled, and left. Fr. Dimitrios paused until she was gone.

"See, a nurse might hear."

"We'll stop speaking if a nurse comes in."

"How is Daonglos?"

"His wounds are getting better. He wants to see you."

"No."

"Manoli, please think about it. I believe if you asked forgiveness of each other, you would both heal faster."

"He couldn't come here anyway. He'd be arrested."

"If you confessed, he'd be released. He is willing to risk it. May I tell him that if he came here, you would see him?"

Somewhere in the hospital a bell was ringing insistently.

"I guess so. But I'm not signing anything."

"I hope you'll re-think that. You're looking stronger already. You have some color in your face now. I'll bring Douglas soon."

Manolis muttered, "...not signing anything."

38

At last Denise understood. Since the eighth grade—from the very beginning—she had done all the work of her relationship with Douglas. After all those years, instead of being grateful (as he should have been) for her hard work, he had run away from her. First she was enraged. Then she was puzzled. Why wouldn't he want to let her do all the planning and organizing for his career and his life? She was good at it.

Her first big step toward getting over it came just now, when she began to design clothes for her father's company. Everyone seemed really happy with her. She saw that she could create her own success instead of working through a puppet like Douglas. She felt the power of the freshly liberated. Funny, she hadn't thought she was oppressed before.

The next surprise was that someone would pursue her. She knew that she had chosen Douglas and he had not put up much resistance. But now...she found herself watched intently by a very, very handsome man. Never mind he was only a waiter at the seafood kafenion on the quay.

Tonio the Albanian was just what Denise needed. He was gorgeous. He was attentive. He was hot-blooded.

Besides waiting tables, he danced at the kafenion whenever things got dull there. His dancing was slow, sexual, solo dancing, with his arms raised, his eyes closed, his head thrown back. It was enough to stop tourists walking by and to draw more customers into the kafenion, so the owner encouraged him to do it.

Suddenly Denise was aware that Tonio was focusing on her, pouring energy into her. She didn't have to do anything at all, just be there, and he would shower her with looks. She noticed he brought an extra pastry and didn't charge her. Every day now he'd smile, and step back and just watch her. At first he made her uncomfortable, but then she began to like the attention.

He told her his story. It was so sad. She listened, wide-eyed, to his troubles.

He brought her a flower pulled from the vine that covered the lattice on the sunny side of the tables. He said it was a passion flower, a flower of passion. She examined the complex blossom until its petals crumbled from handling and fell away. She had never noticed the obscene structure of any flower before, but this one made her feel excited, vulnerable, even feel that she was in some danger.

In danger of what? she said to herself. Of being loved? She sat back in her plastic cafe chair and allowed herself to be attended. Then, Tonio danced for her. Only for her.

He pointed to the sariki she wore around her throat. Puzzled, she untied it and gave it to him. He held it in his right hand and nodded to the owner of the kafenion. The music began. The music was Greek. The dance was actually Albanian, but close enough to a Greek one. It was slow, patiently slow, excruciatingly slow. He kept his eyes on her as he danced. The sariki floated from his raised hand.

266

People walking past on the quay stopped to watch him perform. They noticed, too, that the dance was for her benefit.

Denise felt like a newly-crowned queen. She was a desert receiving rain after a decade of drought. She released the self-pity she had been feeling. Her father was right. Douglas had been hard work and now he was broken. But this man, this Tonio, this exotic creature without a passport, smuggled into Greece across a border, almost a political refugee, living a shadow life…was so beautiful! He was a wonderful sight with his tan, his white shirt open maybe a little too low, his teeth flashing when he smiled, which was often. This man was a treasure.

They went for a stroll. On the seawall, he taught her to dance. There, caressed by the cool breeze off the Cretan Sea, they kissed.

Denise felt like the star of a movie.

39

Spiros sat in his chair embracing his rage. Adrenaline coursed through his veins. He could see his pulse marking time on his view of the darkened room. It was dusk. The light was going.

He knew Sofia was still sitting in the kitchen waiting for his next command. He also knew she'd rather be down at the hospital with Manolis. The thought of the hospital and Manolis released a new wave of adrenaline. Hot anger tingling through him.

When a man produces only one son and that son is weak and whiny like Manolis, it is a disgrace. Spiros should have had a tribe of strong young men for sons. Manolis was Sofia's fault. All her fault.

Tsikoudia was a comfort tonight. But even with his friend, tsikoudia, he felt strange. Something was changing in his body. This made him madder. He called out for Sofia. She came quickly into the room.

He started to say, "Get dinner started," but to his horror no words came out. Spiros's body changed. His vision blurred, his tongue felt thick, his body tingled in a strange and frightening way. A headache erupted behind his left eye. He lurched out of his chair and tried to walk. He stumbled. One side of his body would not obey his commands. He fell. He felt himself drool and thrash. Fear washed over him. He could no longer hear Sofia's voice. He tried to speak and could not. Tears fell from his eyes.

Sofia stepped back from Spiros's flailing legs. Was he trying to make a point? She understood that he was really angry. He didn't need to do a performance like this. It was a long minute before she realized that he wasn't acting to get her attention. She knelt down beside him, dodging his swinging right arm.

"What's the matter with you, Old Man?" she cried.

He made a sound and turned his blank gaze in her direction.

Sofia ran to the telephone and called the ambulance.

By this time, Spiros lay passively. A pool of urine was soaking into the carpet. His face was pale, drained of blood, and his breathing labored. Sofia was afraid. She feared seeing death happen and his death seemed imminent.

The ambulance arrived. The young driver nodded to Sofia and went over to where Spiros lay. He knelt down, took his pulse, lifted an eyelid and peered in at the eye, and told his companion to bring a stretcher. The other disappeared and reappeared with a bundle of steel and canvas which he proceeded to assemble. The driver fitted a cuff on Spiros's arm and took his blood pressure. He wrote on a metal clipboard.

Sofia looked at him, waiting for an answer.

"Stroke," he said brusquely. "We will take him to St. George Hospital now."

"Will he get better?" asked Sofia. No answer came.

The two young men bound the limp body to the stretcher and made for the ambulance. Sofia followed. When they had loaded him into the vehicle, the driver turned to Sofia.

"You coming?"

269

She nodded. "I know the way." She went back in the house for the keys and drove the blue sedan down to St. George's Hospital.

40

At three o'clock in the afternoon Douglas sat in the shade on the edge of the concrete terrace outside the taverna, waiting for Athina and Ducor.

A breeze lifted the curse from the flaming sunlight, and below, the shadows of wispy cirrus clouds moved across the maquis and the orchards.

He ran his fingers over the stone that rested on the top of his table. Each table had one. They were defense against the Table-Moving Wind. Ordinary wind could slam all the chairs against the building and nothing broke, but the Table-Moving Wind could break a big window with flying furniture. Douglas's stone had ballpoint graffiti in Greek on its flat surface.

Finches babbled. He barely noticed them until they were interrupted by the song of a lark. For that moment, all other sound fell away.

A taxi stopped at the platia. Athina and the professor got out, their clothing wilted in the late August heat. Everyone hugged everyone. Lambros brought a pitcher of lemon drink and three glasses. Douglas poured.

Ducor said, "You look good. Running away agrees with you."

Douglas smiled.

"What will you do now?"

"I don't know. Do you need some help at the Institute?" he smiled. "Oh, wait! Fr. Dimitrios said something about the Institute closing. Is it closed?"

Ducor nodded.

"What happened?"

Athina answered. "Mr. Hanson came in and closed it down. He canceled the lease on Roland's flat, because it was part of the Institute, too. Roland has moved in with me." She patted Ducor's hand. "And now, the car, too. Roland says Mr. Hanson was always threatening to 'pull the plug' if he didn't get his way on things. Finally he did. Office, car, apartment, he pulled all the plugs."

"You have nothing? No severance? No notice?" said Douglas. "I bet he closed you down to punish me."

Ducor shifted in his chair. Athina smiled. "We don't know that for sure, Douglas."

Lambros came over with a dish of olives and some sheep's milk cheese.

Douglas leaned forward. "I need to know something: How did the Institute happen? George didn't care about Minoan Art. Why did he give it to you in the first place?"

Roland Ducor broke into a sweat. The line of shade on the terrace had moved away from him. He slid his chair back into the shade. Then he mopped his face with a handkerchief from his jacket pocket.

"It is all over now, so I think I would feel better if I said it. The Institute was partly a tax exemption for his company, but it was also a...bribe to me..."

"What?" asked Athina, worrying about the sudden redness coming over Ducor's face.

"Because of Denise?" whispered Douglas.

Ducor closed his eyes and nodded his head, slowly. "Denise graduated from Laronwood even though she...bought her thesis from the Internet...and I received the Institute in exchange. I'm sorry, Douglas."

271

Athina said, "What are you saying? You gave an unearned grade and he gave you the Institute?"

"O my dear, you see my ethics are not so pure as you thought." His voice drifted off. He looked at Douglas. "You knew already, didn't you?"

"I figured it out last week."

"Dear Athina, please, look at me."

Athina turned her face toward him slowly. She raised her eyes to meet his and said, "It is a disappointment..." Then she smiled lovingly at him. "...but we can fix it."

"What? How?" said a puzzled Ducor.

"It is the truth that you were a victim of his whim. No one needs to know anything else. And if the other archaeologists on Crete find out about this, we will have to tell them what awful things he did to you. How he made you suffer. Maybe we tell them first."

Douglas said, "I brought this on you. I'll talk to him. I'll apologize and ask him to reinstate you. I know I can offer something to make that trade." His face lost its animation.

Ducor shook his head. "Douglas, don't try to use influence to fix things. That is the currency of the Hansons."

Athina said, "Now I understand why they put terrible pressure on poor Roland. We will rebuild his honor, away from any Hansons. Our lives will be a new life, the two of us together, building a future on what we really are."

"Dear girl," said Ducor, and wiped a tear from his cheek. She kissed his cheek. He took her hand.

"What will you do, then?" asked Douglas.

Athina said, "There are no openings with other archaeologists right now, so Roland hopes to be working with Museum Travel, leading tours to the archaeological sites of Crete and Thera."

"Really? Do you have some tours scheduled?"

"Not yet. But when I'm not leading a tour, I can participate in a dig sometimes..."

"...and I have found a job already," said Athina. "with the Tourist Information Agency."

272

Douglas said, "I have to go talk to George Hanson. You should have been given severance pay. And the car and apartment should have been yours for a month or two at least. I can go right now."

"See him if you must, to make your peace with all of them, but don't do it for me. Please," said Ducor.

After they had finished their lemon drinks and delicious cookies from Lambros's wife, they hailed the taxi driver, who had parked in the shade of the giant plane tree in the platia. He drove over, and all three of them got into the taxi.

Lambros yelled after them, "Don't forget: the last bus home leaves Chania at six o'clock."

Douglas answered, "I won't. Thanks." and waved at him.

In Chania, Ducor and Athina got out at the market hall. Douglas told the driver to go to the Venetian palace on Kastelli hill.

He paid the taxi and went up the stone stairway to the former offices of the Institute. The doors were locked, and a piece of paper on the glass directed invoices and inquiries to Ms. Athina Stavraki, just as Fr. Dimitrios had said. Douglas saw a light in what used to be Ducor's office. He knocked on the door.

After a minute, George Hanson appeared and looked through the locked glass door. He frowned when he saw Douglas. George said, through the glass, "What do you want?"

"I want what's fair," Douglas said. "Let me in, George, or I'll go to the police."

"Ha! You want what's fair? Come in here." He unlocked the door and opened it. "You mean like taking advantage of our kindness to you and then standing up Denise at the altar? Please, tell me about what is fair, Douglas."

"I'm not proud of it, but I did what I had to do to survive."

"Did you really think I was going to kill you?" George led Douglas into Ducor's former office. A huge drafting table stood alone in the center of the room. The wall behind it was paneled with fresh sheets of cork covered with photographs of Minoan murals and fashion sketches. Unopened boxes of computer and electronic gear were stacked along the opposite wall.

273

"You said you would, but that wasn't it. I couldn't let myself take on the life you wanted for me. It wasn't me."

"You couldn't let us know sooner that it *wasn't you*? You little prick."

"I didn't know it until that moment."

"Oh, well, that makes it all right, then," said George. He suddenly swung out and hit Douglas in the stomach. "I want an apology."

Douglas bent over from the blow and stepped back, all the time watching George who was seriously off-balance as a result of the swing.

George said, "I always thought you were chickenshit, but I see you're not," he swung again, "because you know I'm going to knock your face in. Apologize!"

Douglas dodged but lost his footing. He tripped and fell into the boxes. A large box marked FRAGILE skidded to the floor. They heard the sound of glass shattering.

Douglas scrambled back to his feet, stumbling over the fallen boxes. He reached an area of clear floor, planted his feet, and punched George in the ribs. "I apologize, George. Okay?"

"Hey!" said George. "Don't you hit me, you worm." He punched out, but Douglas sidestepped and George fell onto the boxes.

Douglas said, "Stop! Listen to me! You're in real trouble, now. You've got the police to think about. And besides, I don't want to hurt you." He extended his hand to help the older man climb out of the boxes.

George said, "But I want to hurt you." He swung again and connected with Douglas's wounded shoulder.

"Ow. Not there," said Douglas, and slugged him in the midriff.

The blow bent George over. From that position, he roared, "I'll kill you!" He lunged at Douglas, missed, and ran into the table. It slid across the floor and dented the cork wall. One panel of cork fell to the floor.

"You've said that before. Come on and try then. Come on."

George ran at him again and missed. Douglas moved over next to the plateglass window overlooking the inner harbor. "If you miss this time, you'll fly out the window and land on the police station down there."

George got to his feet, his arms swinging vaguely. "What did you say about the police? Earlier, I mean. Why did you come here today? What do you want?"

"I want Ducor's job back."

"Hunh?"

"Ducor and Athina. Their jobs."

"What's that got to do with the police?"

"The George Hanson Institute and Greek law."

"What do you mean? The Institute is closed. Gone. It doesn't exist."

Douglas backed away from Hanson as he spoke. George was unsteady on his feet.

"You're wrong, George. It exists in the files of the Archaeological Service of the Ministry of Culture of Greece. Also the American School of Classical Studies at Athens. Are the pits filled in? Is the fencing removed? No. You haven't shut it down. You've just shut it."

George swung and missed completely. He lost his balance and caught himself with a hand on the wall. "Damn you. Stop it!" he said. He was swaying. Sweat stained his red linen shirt.

"I'll stop it when you pay up. You'll write a voucher to both of them for three months' pay, and you will reinstate the car lease for Ducor and turn the office back over to him. He and Athina will meet you at the bank at noon tomorrow. Then they will go through the proper procedures for you to close down the dig-permit and the Institute. If it takes longer than three months, you'll pay them for all the time it takes. Got it?"

"You're full of shit. I checked this out with Roger."

"Roger is just your man back home. What does he know about Greek law? Nothing. That's not smart, George. You are in violation of all your permits, and you're still on Greek soil. They can detain you. The Greek government doesn't look kindly on people who abuse their dig-permits. I can turn you in today. The police station is right there." Douglas pointed out the plate glass window at the roof of the police station next to the inner harbor.

275

"I know where the police station is!" George looked out the window at the roof of the police station. He knew where every police station in this damned town was. "Ducor never said anything about closing things down."

"Ducor, if you remember, was having trouble breathing when you got through with him. He went to the hospital in an ambulance. Did you know that, George?" Douglas took a step closer. George backed up.

"All right, all right. What are we talking about here?" George was patting his pockets, looking for something to write on.

"We're talking about a cash transfer at the bank tomorrow." Douglas went out into the hall and came back with a chair.

George looked at him oddly. "Boy, you are sure different. What'd you do, grow up in the past few days? Why did you pick today to come back?"

Douglas gestured to George to sit down in the chair, which was next to the table. "I've been busy, George. Where's some paper?"

George made an elaborate gesture of looking for paper. He scanned his empty table top, looked underneath, and then patted his pockets: no paper.

Douglas leaned over him. "You were underpaying both of those people. You're going to give them a raise. Write a promise to pay 3,000,000 drachmas, to each of them." George made a strangling sound from deep in his throat, but otherwise did not react.

"That comes to $2,500/month for the next three months. Does this Greek account have that much money in it? If not, you'll arrange a transfer of funds. And another 200,000 drachmas for the car rental place."

"No paper. Sorry." George didn't look sorry.

Douglas took a piece of paper from his pants' pocket. He studied it, then handed it to George. "You can write on the back of this. It's the receipt for towing the truck."

"What truck? Are those your wedding pants? You've been sleeping in them! Where's the jacket?"

"Gone."

"Look at those pants. I paid for those. You owe me for that suit." He was getting agitated.

"You're right, George. I do."

"And the shoes." He was trying to recognize the sleek Italian shoes intended for the wedding. He saw a disintegrating pair of sodden objects so covered in red dust they looked red.

Douglas also looked at his feet. "And the shoes."

"You have to pay for them."

"I'll pay them off when I can. I owe you that. Write, please."

The only sound in the room was George's ball point pen as he wrote out the promise to pay. When it was written, he pushed it away from himself, toward the edge of the table. Douglas picked it up and read it, carefully.

"Now write another promise on the bottom of the page that the funds will be there, and that you'll continue their wages at this level until the Institute is closed down. Even if it takes longer than three months."

"How do I know," glared George, "that they won't just keep it open to live on Easy Street? "

"I give you my word."

"Hah. What's that worth?"

"It's worth a lot. And it's all you've got. So take it."

"You little shit. You didn't deserve my daughter."

"No, I didn't. Please write the guarantee." George did and handed the towing receipt back to Douglas, who folded it and put it carefully into his pocket.

"Thank you. When will you vacate this office? Because Professor Ducor and Athina will need it back so they can start to close down the Institute."

"You're pushing me, Douglas. Back off."

"Fine. They'll move in here in three days' time. More time than you gave them to get out. And you'll meet them at the bank tomorrow at noon. I'll be there, too."

He went over to the plateglass window and looked out. "What a fine harbor this is. Man-made in a rough sea. Built nearly 800 years ago and still in use for fishing boats as well as pleasure craft. A beautiful thing, indeed."

George glared out the window. He had to admire the guts of this damned no-good who had just beaten him into paying that money. He thought, I taught him too well. And all that time I thought he wasn't learning anything from me.

He felt an edge of pride mingle with his annoyance.

He looked out at the view. A too-bright sun bleached the color out of everything. All he saw was glare off the water. It was broken by a skinny seawall. On the near side of it, too many damned boats. On the far side, nothing at all. Just water. He didn't like the sea any more than he liked Crete.

41

George walked back to the hotel. Each step jarred his bruised ribs. His right hand was swelling. He could feel it growing larger.

Chania, which had never pleased him, now absolutely excluded him from the obvious merriment of the other tourists. He turned right and walked out to the quayside.

Something was different. The gondola was not tied up in its usual place. He looked out into the harbor. A man in a gondolier's costume, striped t-shirt, even a straw hat, poled the gondola around in the middle of the circular harbor. Tourists were sitting in it.

Not tourists. Denise was sitting in it.

Some guy was with her.

George took off his sunglasses to see better. Then he put them back on. Denise was in the gondola, all right. The man with her seemed to be that toothsome waiter.

George went to the edge of the water and stood there. Denise waved to him in a fluttery way.

"Hi, Daddy," she called out.

"Who's that?" called George, pointing to the man she was sitting next to. He couldn't see if they were holding hands, but it looked like they probably were.

"Just a minute!" Denise leaned forward and gave orders to the gondolier. He was pretty toothsome, too, George thought. Amazing he isn't singing to them.

The gondola came over near where George stood.

"Daddy, this is Tonio. He's from Albania," she announced, proudly. "Tonio, this is my father."

Tonio stood and reached across Denise to shake George's hand. The gondola tipped wildly, Denise grabbed the quayside curbing, and Tonio sat down again. He held onto both sides of the boat, his arm across Denise's bust.

The gondolier cursed as he braced himself and the boat. He cursed in Greek, though, not in Italian like a real gondolier.

"Watch out," said George. "You don't want to fall into that filthy water. Like Audrey Hepburn did, in Venice."

Tonio turned to Denise and said, "What he says?"

Denise replied, "Not Audrey, Daddy. Katherine."

Tonio said, "Who?"

Denise explained, "Fell in, in Venice. Katherine Hepburn."

"Get out of that boat, now, Denise, and come with me."

"I'll be up in about half an hour. We still have time on our gondola." She smiled broadly and nodded to the gondolier who poled them away from George and the quay.

In that moment, George no longer cared about his daughter's promising career, or the success of The Safari Collection, or the continued existence of the planet earth. He let go of everything. Let them all go, he thought. Let those with greed, with ambition, with desire, rule this troubled world. I'm through.

He walked slowly up the narrow and colorful roadway to the hotel, watching his feet as if they were no longer part of him, stepping carefully up the shallow steps, feeling neither sadness nor pleasure but a new floating sensation of disengagement. He wondered if his death would be the next event of this trip. He checked. His body seemed to be doing fine.

Maybe this wasn't the end of his life. Maybe he'd just retire and hand everything over to Roger and Denise and let them sink it or not as they chose. Maybe he and the Missus would move to Palm Springs now, and play golf in their declining years. Maybe this was what was supposed to happen in people's lives.

He picked up the key from the desk and climbed the stairs to their rooms.

When he opened the door, his wife looked at him with some concern.

"George? What's happened to you?"

"Nothing. Why?"

"Your face is all red and you're moving funny."

She went to his side, but he brushed her away. He went to the window and looked down on the harbor.

"Do you know where Denise is?" he asked. He watched the tiny gondola drifting purposelessly in circles, a loving pair in the back and a Greek Venetian poling it along nowhere.

"She said she was going out for an ice cream. Why?"

George picked up the telephone and began dialing. "We're going home, Wife."

"We are? George, that's wonderful. But what about Douglas? We can't just leave him here."

"Oh, yes we can."

"But, the Institute office you promised Denise..."

"I'll give her office space at home."

"But the neighbors..."

"Sooner or later she'll have to face them."

"You mean it? Oh, George. Thank you." She kissed him. George winced when she hugged his rib cage, but he was smiling. First time he could remember smiling in a damned long time.

281

By the time Denise came up the stairs from her gondola ride with Tonio, the plans were made. They would fly from Chania to Athens the next afternoon. The next day they'd fly to Zurich, to Chicago, and then St. Louis. The travel agent had personally delivered the tickets. They lay in a blue Olympic Airlines cardboard wallet on the desk, in full sight.

When she heard her father's plan, Denise exploded. She hurled her guidebooks across the room. She pulled the airline tickets from their wallet. She tried to rip them, but they would not tear. Then she bit them. It took both parents to stop her from destroying them.

The hotel manager discreetly tapped on the door and asked if he could be of any assistance. Mrs. Hanson explained, "Our daughter has a rare allergy. This has happened before. We'll tell you if we need a doctor, but for now, we can handle it. Thank you for inquiring." She shut the door.

Loud and serious negotiations went on for an hour and a half. At the end, Denise agreed to go back to St. Louis after four more days in Chania, but only if George guaranteed, in writing, that he would hire an immigration attorney in St. Louis who would make all reasonable efforts (Denise wasn't happy with that limitation, but she finally agreed) to acquire a Greek passport and a visa to the US for Tonio.

George thought there was probably not a chance in hell that any attorney anywhere could get a Greek passport for someone who had crossed into Greece from Albania in the dark of night, but he didn't say so. He agreed to the attorney, and to the extra four days. Denise calmed down at last and they all went to bed.

George didn't sleep well. He held his bruised ribs and thought longingly about his new idea of retirement to Palm Springs. He almost said something about it to his wife, but he wasn't ready yet.

He thought this new plan sounded a lot like death, but maybe that wasn't a bad thing after all. He stroked his sleeping wife's hair, tenderly. It would all be different soon.

In the morning Denise was wild again. She announced that if Tonio didn't get a visa by Christmas she was coming back to spend the holidays with him here. And she just might marry him then.

Her father heard himself say, "Fine. Do it."

He was pleased to see that Denise was shocked. What's more, he realized he meant it.

42

Douglas rode behind Fr. Dimitrios, on the pillion of the old Vespa. They went along the back roads to the hospital. They would be dusty when they got there, but with two riders, the Vespa really wasn't fast enough in traffic on the main roads.

Douglas had an idea now that saying I'm sorry—and meaning it: you had to really mean it—gave some sort of release, like when he got caught palming the cheese and met Fr. Dimitrios. He wanted to stop feeling queasy about what he'd done to this kid with Aleko's father's knife. He thought the kid would feel better, too, if he could say he was sorry for shooting Douglas, even though it was only birdshot and wasn't ever going to kill him. Still, it'd be good to get an apology.

They had each made the other bleed. They had shared blood, sort of. Not like blood brothers, quite...there was some idea of it there—Douglas couldn't quite grasp it. He went back to thinking how good it had felt when he was okay after his cheese theft, when the shopkeeper, Kyrios Varasulakis, had said Then pirazi. Had said, It's all right. That's what he wanted to hear now.

Aleko's cousin! That pimple-faced kid he'd met the night he stayed at Aleko's house. The one who hung behind his father and peered out at him.

The paving on the road was pot-holed and cracked. Douglas felt himself slip to one side of the seat. He held on to Fr. Dimitrios's cassock. He leaned forward and shouted into the priest's ear, "What if he doesn't take my apology?"

"Then it doesn't matter." The wind blew the answer past him.

"It doesn't?"

They bumped on in noisy silence to St. George Hospital in the city. When they went into the hospital, Fr. Dimitrios continued, "This meeting is about owning your own actions. Not about forgiving the other guy."

Douglas said, "But, I want to forgive him. And I need him to hear me. I need him to take my apology."

"If you say so."

"Don't I?"

"You may not get it," Fr. Dimitrios said.

As they passed down the long hospital corridors, their heels sounding on the polished linoleum, Douglas reminded himself that Fr. Dimitrios had already spoken to the boy, had asked his consent for this visit. Surely the boy was as ready to forgive as Douglas was himself. Surely so.

When they reached Manolis's room, Fr. Dimitrios opened the door and stepped back, to let Douglas enter. The room was a maze of white curtains. Four curtained-off areas.

"Which one?" he asked.

Fr. Dimitrios pulled back the far right curtain. Behind it lay a thin, pale, and blotchy version of the young man Douglas had first seen at Aleko's. He was hooked up to an IV. An oxygen tube crossed his face. He was the color of his bedsheets: white.

He was asleep. Fr. Dimitrios touched the sheet covering his knee and said his name softly, "Manoli."

His eyes opened. He looked at the priest, as if trying to identify him.

From somewhere a muffled loudspeaker paged a doctor, over and over again.

284

Fr. Dimitrios brought Douglas forward, into Manolis's range of sight. He said, in Greek, "Manoli, this is Douglas."

If Douglas thought he was going to get a smile from Manolis, he was mistaken. He got a vacant stare. It was hard to feel sympathy for that face. When he looked at the condition of the body attached, he felt sick.

I have done this damage, thought Douglas. In that single moment of rage, I did this much harm.

Fr. Dimitrios drew two chairs up to Manolis's bedside and he and Douglas sat. Fr. Dimitrios said, "I'll translate. What would you like to say?"

Douglas looked at the sheet-white face and couldn't think of anything to say. He mumbled, "I'm sorry, man."

Fr. Dimitrios said a few words to Manolis and turned back to Douglas. "That's all?"

"He looks awful."

"Lung injuries are painful. And scary. It's hard to breathe."

Manolis said something. Fr. Dimitrios leaned forward and asked him to repeat it.

"He says the whole thing was a dumb idea. He says forget it."

"Which whole thing?"

Manolis spoke again. Fr. Dimitrios listened then translated. "Manolis says do you know the police are looking for you."

"Will he testify for me?"

There was some discussion in Greek. Then Fr. Dimitrios said, "If he testifies for you, he can't defend himself from charges of robbery and assault."

"What the heck! I'm supposed to go to jail because he doesn't want to? Can you testify for me, to what you heard him say?"

Fr. Dimitrios shook his head. "I'm his priest."

"Oh, fine. So I come to exchange forgiveness but it's only good between the three of us in this room and I still go away a fugitive for what he did. Right? Who is being responsible here?"

"You are."

Douglas tried to name the look on the boy's face. He was surly, yes, but Douglas also recognized the look of someone totally

285

powerless. He had a good idea what that might feel like. "So this is my big chance to give without receiving."

"To forgive without hope of results from it."

Douglas thought for a moment, then said, "Ask if he knows when they'll let him out of the hospital."

Greek question, Greek answer, English answer. "They said another week to ten days and he could go home. He will stay with his grandparents, because his father is angry at him."

Douglas surprised himself. "Maybe I could help care for him after he's out of here."

Fr. Dimitrios turned and translated for Manolis, who seemed unmoved by the offer. If anything, he looked cross, Douglas thought.

There was an intense exchange of information in Greek between the patient and the priest. Then Fr. Dimitrios said, "He's tired. We've done what we could today."

He lay a hand on top of Manolis's hand, and his other hand on top of Douglas's. He prayed, *Forgive all who hate and mistreat us and Let not one of them perish because of us...* He said it in Greek, then in English.

Douglas strained to hear him, then realized Fr. Dimitrios was not speaking to him.

Manolis was beginning to think he might get out of the hospital soon. His wound site was itching and his sore throat had gone. The food they brought him tasted better each day. He began to make plans.

He would move in with his grandparents until he was well, and then he would go to Iraklion and find work in the city. Not watching his father's sheep on the mountain. A real job. If his mother kept her word and preserved the lie she'd told, he really did have a future. The thought cheered him, though he didn't mention his plan to his mother. She was still staying with him, sitting in an armchair near his bed, fussing over him between the nurses' visits, singing to him, talking to him, loving him. It was pleasant to have her near. It gave him comfort. Sometimes he saw her slumped asleep in her chair. He thought she was probably tired.

The other day she said something about his father being in the hospital too, but he hadn't come by to visit. Manolis did not expect he would, after their last fight, so what was she talking about?

She was gone from his room for hours at a time, and he thought she must be out having lunch with Vassilia.

This morning he didn't want breakfast. His stomach felt odd. He began to feel hot. When his mother woke up in the armchair near the bed, she gave him a funny look, then put her hand on his forehead.

She said, "You are red, Manoli. Do you feel bad?"

Before he could answer, she went off to find a nurse. The nurse took one look, touched his head, then went for a thermometer which she placed under his arm.

Something was swollen under there. His armpit hurt.

His wound hurt all the time, but these days that sharp pain had been changing to itching. Now it gave him both pain and itching. Why?

The nurse watched him and waited for the thermometer to be ready. When she read it she left quickly and returned with a doctor. Nurse and doctor were both wearing surgical masks. What did they think was wrong?

They made him spit into a little cup, and made some adjustment in the stuff that was dripping into his arm. They said, "We're giving you Keflex now. It's a strong medicine. It will help you get well." Then they left, and took his mother with them. He lay there, looking at the drip bag.

Keflex. The word echoed floppily in his head.

Manolis was aware that his lungs were filling up. When he breathed as hard as he could, he rattled. After maybe half an hour his mother came back. She was wearing a green hat, mask, and gown. She looked as if she'd been crying.

"Manoli," she whispered.

He could barely hear her. There was whooshing in his ears. "What? What's happening to me?"

"They don't know yet. They're growing the germs to see what they are."

"Why are you dressed like that?"

"They think maybe it's catching."

287

"Oh."

"Manoli, I can't stay with you now. I'll only be able to come in to you for short visits until you're better. But I'll be here in the hospital."

"Where? Why?" whispered Manolis.

"I'll be with your father. He had a stroke. Remember? I told you that. Maybe you don't remember. He's here, in this hospital. So I'll sit with him, and I'll come see you as often as they say I can. All right?"

Manolis was confused by this information. He saw his mother's worried face, though he realized that he couldn't focus clearly. He said good-bye to her. Then he was alone.

There were no other patients in his room now. The nurses came in and went out in a big hurry.

He coughed again. He couldn't clear his lungs. He thought this was unfair. He'd gone through enough trouble. He didn't need the flu. Make it go away.

When he was lucky, he would drift off to sleep. The bad times were the waking hours when he itched and couldn't scratch, rattled and couldn't cough, blinked but couldn't focus. His lips felt dry and his feverish head couldn't think clearly. He thought his eyes were crossing. He couldn't will them to focus.

He wondered how high his fever was. He felt on fire. The longer it went on, the less he cared how he felt. Doctors and nurses and his mother came and went.

He floated into a state of pleasant detachment from his body. It didn't matter any more that he couldn't breathe. It all seemed good enough.

He floated around the ceiling of his room.

At two o'clock in the morning, after three days, he floated out of his body and out of his life.

43

Manolis's death changed everything. Sofia tried to tell Spiros his son had died, but she couldn't be sure he understood her. There was no reaction, not an eye-blink, nothing.

Vassilia came to the church to tell Fr. Dimitrios. Douglas was with him. They were working on the wall.

When they heard the news, Douglas and Fr. Dimitrios looked at each other in horror.

"Will I be charged with murder, then?" asked Douglas. "What do you think will happen to me?"

"It can't be more than manslaughter, I think. It was self-defense, after all. But that's what I know from California law. We can't wait until Officer Thomas gets an official notice. You need a lawyer now."

They rode the faithful Vespa down to Chania to an appointment with a criminal defense specialist named Michalis Maridakis.

Kyrios Maridakis listened while Fr. Dimitrios explained in Greek all of what had happened. Then he picked up his telephone and called the police headquarters. He asked for the status of Douglas's case.

Fr. Dimitrios translated for Douglas, in a whisper. There was a long wait on the phone and then someone gave him an answer. The lawyer spoke to Douglas in English.

"You have been charged with this man's death, but they'll rewrite that if the autopsy proves he died of a hospital infection. The assault charge will definitely have to go to trial before a judge, who alone has the power to dismiss the charges. It is usually a year before we can get you a court date."

"Will I spend that year in jail?" asked Douglas.

"No. The police will hold your passport, so you will be unable to leave Crete. Have you got money enough to live for a year?"

Douglas said, "No."

"As an American you are not permitted to hold a job in Greece. If you were a citizen of the EU, that would be easier. Maybe Pappa Dimitrios can think of something."

Fr. Dimitrios said, "We'll work something out."

"Where is your passport now?"

Douglas pulled the passport out of his pocket. "Here."

The lawyer declined it. "You must present yourself and your passport to the police. Today. Here's the person to speak to." He wrote the information on a piece of paper and gave it to Douglas. "I'll apply for a trial date and telephone Pappa Dimitrios when it is arranged. Good day to you both," and he showed them to his door.

Douglas and Fr. Dimitrios took the Vespa down Halidon Street and turned right at the quay, toward the police station.

They went slowly because motor scooters are not really supposed to ride on the quay after ten o'clock, but the day was quiet, there were not many tourists, and they were just going a short way. No one would stop a priest who was riding carefully.

As they passed the rows of kafenions, Douglas saw a familiar figure. She was sitting on a tiny table with her feet on the chair next to it and her arms around the neck of a dark-haired young man. She wore sparkling white cotton slacks and a scanty lace-trimmed blouse in light blue. A black nylon sariki tied her hair in a ponytail. Her back was toward him, but he had no doubt. It was Denise.

290

THE PALE SURFACE OF THINGS

He had a flash of his old instinct to flee. Alongside it was the new determination not to flee. He also felt curiosity about the man Denise had draped herself around and a flicker of jealousy, which quickly transformed into the bright hope that Denise had, in fact, found someone new.

Douglas closed his eyes and leaned back: He had met with Manolis. He had faced up to, in fact, he had faced down George Hanson. He would not avoid meeting Denise here and now.

He opened his eyes again and she was looking right at him. There was a certain look on her face. He thought it was a look of triumph.

He tapped Fr. Dimitrios on the shoulder and said, "Can you stop here? I need to see someone."

Fr. Dimitrios pulled the Vespa up to the kafenion and Douglas dismounted.

"I should have known you two would know each other. So that's why you wouldn't pose for my publicity shots!" Denise glared at Fr. Dimitrios.

She disengaged her arms from the neck of the waiter, but he kept his arm protectively around her waist. She slid off the table and stood next to him.

"I knew I'd see you sooner or later, Douglas. This is Tonio. He's Albanian!"

Tonio smiled pleasantly.

"Tonio, this is Douglas."

Tonio's smile broadened and he nodded.

Denise gestured toward Fr. Dimitrios, "And this is his sidekick, Father I-won't-help-you." She glared at the priest.

Fr. Dimitrios introduced himself, "Fr. Dimitrios of Agyios Yeorgeos, Vraho. Ya sas."

Tonio answered, "Kalispera, Patera."

"So, where were you, Douglas?"

"I went up the mountain."

Denise looked disbelieving. "What mountain?"

"That mountain," Douglas gestured toward Lefka Ori.

"You never even wanted to go camping. I don't believe you."

Fr. Dimitrios gave Douglas a high-sign and took the Vespa over to a passageway between buildings, leaving Douglas alone with Denise and Tonio.

Douglas bit the bullet: "I'm glad you hadn't left Crete, Denise. I wanted to say in person that I'm sorry for the pain I caused you."

"Well, you're in luck. We're leaving tomorrow, and as soon as we can get him a visa, Tonio will come, too. So it all worked out in the end, didn't it? I'm designing clothes for Daddy—a Minoan line—and I've met Tonio, and my life looks great. And you've got...what have you got?"

"About what I deserve. And I'm happy."

"Really?" It didn't sound like a question.

"Really. I'll be staying here for awhile."

"Doing what?" Her face scrunched up in disbelief. "What could you possibly want to stay here for?"

"It's a long story, Denise." He held out his hand toward Tonio. "Congratulations. You're a lucky man."

Tonio shook his hand.

"Good-bye, Denise. I'm glad things are going so well for you."

"No thanks to you, but yes, I'm happy now. Goodbye, Douglas."

Fr. Dimitrios and Douglas got back on the Vespa and continued to the police station to hand over Douglas's passport. As the physical distance between him and Denise increased, Douglas felt a weight dissolve. He was free, except for the matter of the trial. Even with a criminal manslaughter charge ahead of him, his world was full of possibilities.

The police station was busy, but a policeman left the interview he was conducting and came over to them. Douglas and Fr. Dimitrios signed several forms and Douglas handed over his passport. He was now officially a prisoner on Crete.

The policeman rummaged in the drawer of the desk. He seemed to be talking to himself. He pulled out a crumpled form.

"Douglas Watkins." He looked at Douglas. "You a missing person? You run away from your wedding?"

Douglas said, "I did. Will you arrest me for that, too?"

"Souvenir." The man smiled and handed him the report. Douglas folded it and put it in his pocket.

Fr. Dimitrios and Douglas rode the scooter slowly up the mountain to Vraho.

44

Spiros came out of the hospital after only three weeks. They said there was nothing else they could do for him. His stroke damage was bilateral: both sides of his body were paralyzed. He could make sounds but no one could interpret what he was trying to say. He drooled. He wore an adult diaper. He sat endless hours in a wheelchair.

The first stroke knocked out his left side. That was bad enough. They had been working to stabilize him from that when Sofia came to tell him that Manolis had died. He didn't believe her. He thought it was some kind of bad joke she was playing on him. It made him so mad he felt that adrenaline surge again and then he felt the same things he felt as the first stroke came on. He dropped the nurse-call-button and he couldn't scream. He just lay there and that stroke came on him and finished off the other side. He was trapped in a body that wouldn't obey him. His mind was fine, except now he was afraid to get angry. He kept checking himself, trying not to have another stroke, although, when he came to think about it, he had no more limbs to lose, no remaining body function to fail, and all he could lose was his life. But he hung on to it. He told himself that he could beat this thing. He would get his body back.

Spiros came home. The house didn't have many steps, and Douglas came over to carry Spiros into the house. Sofia and her sister brought the wheelchair in.

Spiros looked longingly at his big leather chair. No one would be able to get him out of it if they lowered him into it. Douglas and Aleko moved it into Manolis's room to make space for the wheelchair. The hospital arranged for a hospital bed. They set it up in the salon so he could go to bed and lie flat sometimes. That meant moving the rest of the furniture into Manolis's room, too. Now the house looked like the hospital room he just left.

Sometimes Sofia took care of him and sometimes Vassilia took care of him, to give Sofia a break, to let her go spend time at Manolis's grave. He thought at first that having Vassilia care for him would be like a dream, but she treated him roughly, jostled him, spilled a little bit of food down his chin, rolled his wheelchair out into the sun and left him there too long. Flies crawled on his head and he couldn't move to brush them away. He wanted to tell her he still desired her, but the more she did these little things to him, he began to realize that maybe he didn't desire her any more. Maybe he didn't even like her.

Sofia came to him one day and said, "Good news, Spiros. I found a buyer for the mikani. I sold it for Vassilia and gave her the money. Now she can keep her goats."

Spiros watched her face as she told him about the mikani. He saw no sign that Vassilia had told her anything at all. Good, he thought.

One day when Sofia was gone, Vassilia pushed his wheelchair outside, to get some fresh air, she said. A few minutes later, Sofia came home, driving a little yellow car. She was smiling. When she saw him out there, she looked embarrassed. He knew she was embarrassed. He couldn't say anything to her but his eyes went from her face to that car and back.

She said, "You're wondering about the car, aren't you? I didn't want to upset you, Spiros, but the doctor said you won't ever drive again, so I sold the blue sedan and bought a car for me. With automatic gears.

It's a little car, so I can park it. I can reach the brake with my foot. I'm sorry I didn't ask you first. But see? The whole back opens up and we can get the wheelchair inside it. Now I can drive you to the hospital whenever you need to go there. Do you like it?"

He couldn't answer, but Spiros stared at that yellow car all afternoon, until the two women wheeled him back into the house.

In the hospital he'd had a catheter and also during the first week at home, but it was difficult to keep it clean because he was having diarrhea and everything was a mess. Now he was in diapers and they had to be changed nine or ten times a day. He had no feeling, no control, no life in his body at all. All his life was in his head.

Spiros had a new thought. It kept coming to him, surprising him. It was this: Why is Sofia so nice to me?

Incidents flooded his mind—times when he had disregarded her and she had, nonetheless, behaved kindly toward him, been a good wife, a proper wife. Times he had left his work clothes lying on the floor and they were always clean and folded, waiting for him the next morning. Times he had yelled at her for losing things, and then he had found the things where he had put them. Her kitchen was clean. She always kept a neat home, which told others that she was trustworthy and would not stray like those loose women of Peristeri, with their slatternly houses and idle lives.

No, she had brought no disgrace to him in the village.

More than that: Sofia had been above reproach, a fine wife, and he had not noticed her for all those years. Now he wanted to correct that wrong. He wanted to say thank you. He wanted to say you deserved my thanks before this. Now he could only make wet sounds, like gargling.

Unexpressed gratitude rises in the throat, like dark green phlegm. It sits there, choking off all other thoughts. Spiros wanted to write his thanks, speak his thanks, sing his thanks, but all he could manage was tears. He kept watching her. When she saw the tears she wiped them away with a towel and said, "Your eyes are leaking, Spiros. I wonder what that means. Maybe the tear-canals are bad now. I'll tell the doctor tomorrow."

295

Being heard!! Being heard!! Now that he had something real and important to say, no one would ever hear it. The lump in the throat grew intolerably large. It blocked his former lustful delight in seeing Vassilia, now when she came to help care for him. He no longer cared for her. What was she but a pretty face? She had never taken care of him, and even now, when she helped her sister, she was rough. No, she was not worth wasting his whole life—his whole life!—thinking about, dreaming about, aching for, plotting to achieve. She was nothing compared to Sofia who had been so good, so generous to him all those years.

Another tear coursed down his paralyzed and sagging face. He tried again to speak. Again, Sofia said, "Is something wrong? Do you hurt or something? What is it?"

He sank deeper into the wheelchair, despair battling with gratitude.

45

Douglas's trial date was set for July, ten months after his arrest. Without his passport he could not leave Crete—not that he had any desire to leave. Desire implied expansiveness. Douglas came to enjoy the small variations in his daily life.

He made an arrangement with Lambros that he would whitewash the outside of the taverna and in exchange he could stay in Room Two for the winter. It was a winter-long job. The building extended way down the hillside, below the basement by another thirty feet, and it was badly stained. It needed scraping and patching first.

It amused him that in the mornings he put whitewash on a wall and in the afternoons he helped Fr. Dimitrios scrape whitewash off another wall.

He helped Sofia with Spiros. He went to their house every morning to clean Spiros up from the night and move him from his bed to his wheelchair, and then again every evening he moved him back to the bed. At first, Spiros was resistant and hard to move, but over time he seemed to accept Douglas's help. They developed a routine so that while Spiros was still dead-weight, with each month that passed it was easier to move him.

In the evening, Douglas fed Spiros his strained dinner and then stayed to eat dinner with Sofia. Spiros sat with them at the table. They spoke in Greek. Douglas was learning. When he mispronounced a word, Spiros would make a sound, and then Sofia would correct the word for him.

Douglas helped Aleko with his English. Twice a week, he taught English lessons with the teacher, Kyria Aspasia, at the school. And on Wednesday nights, he gave an English class to Lambros and several other men in the taverna.

The best time of his day, though, was from one o'clock 'til dinner when he unpicked the wall paintings with Fr. Dimitrios. He'd had all morning alone on a ladder, hanging over space, painting the taverna, to think about things. In the afternoon he'd bring his ideas out and discuss them with the priest.

One day Douglas said, "Nobody ever said the word 'ethics' when I was growing up. I was taught the Golden Rule, and I learned that if I did what was asked, I'd stay out of trouble. But that's all. Where does one learn ethics? How do you become an ethical person?"

Fr. Dimitrios said, "Aristotle's not a bad place to start. He says virtue of character is a condition of the soul. It causes a man to chose the balanced and wise course of action, called the mean."

"How do you develop virtue then?"

"By learning to find the mean in any situation. You mustn't be so brave that you are foolhardy. Nor cowardly because you're not brave enough. The middle course. It means you have to reason out the consequences to any action."

"But there isn't time to reason things out when you need courage."

"Virtue doesn't only mean courage. It means choosing the right behavior in all kinds of situations."

"So, you have to think in each moment, to be virtuous?"

"Right. You can't just put on a virtuous intention and be done with it." Fr. Dimitrios stood up and stretched his back.

298

Douglas thought that Fr. Dimitrios's back-stretches were like punctuation in a sentence. They occurred with a comforting regularity.

Nearly half of the Nativity icon showed through the whitewash. Douglas worked on an area of sheep and a shepherd, on the right side. Fr. Dimitrios unpicked angels in the upper left.

Douglas asked, "My life now, this life in the village, would Aristotle call it a virtuous life?"

"I'd have to think about that," he answered. "Does it feel virtuous to you?"

"It feels different from my life in St. Louis. Some days it feels small and repetitive and other times it feels huge, linked to the whole universe."

Fr. Dimitrios nodded agreement. "I know what you mean."

"You do?"

"This small village, Vraho, somehow contains every shading of human life. To love this place is to love the world."

"Yes," Douglas said. "I see."

They worked silently for a long time together as the ideas floated around them.

In October, a package arrived for Douglas. It was a kit he'd ordered to make a model Spitfire—the real kind of model, with balsa wood and tissue paper, not a snap-together plastic one.

He showed it to Aleko. Together they went to buy the model glue Douglas had special-ordered from Kyrios Varasulakis's mini-market in the village. Vassilia gave them some of her sewing pins and Fr. Dimitrios gave them the sharpest of the scalpels he used for chipping off whitewash.

Lambros let them push two tables together at the back of the taverna. Tourist season was pretty well over, and they needed table-space to spread out their plans. Thomas the policeman brought them four outdated notices on stiff paper from the police station. They taped them down to protect the tables.

After dinner, Aleko and Douglas studied the instructions and cut the balsa into spars and ribs. They named them as they cut them.

299

Old Nikos supervised. He told them when they were putting a piece on backwards.

He told them what he remembered when there were British airplanes like that at Maleme airfield. The Germans hadn't come yet. Actually, he said, those planes at Maleme were called Hurricanes, not Spitfires, but they looked the same as the picture on the box.

Fr. Dimitrios stopped by to watch. Old Nikos asked him, "Did your grandfather tell you about the Hurricanes at Maleme? When the British were here?"

Fr. Dimitrios said, "He didn't tell me much about the war, Nikos. You tell me, please," and he sat down near them. Lambros brought over lemon drinks because the day had been hot like summer, even in October.

Fr. Dimitrios checked out a book from the library in Chania, with pictures of World War II fighters and bombers. They studied the photos of the Spitfire and the Hurricane, trying to understand the difference. They knew that the Hurricane was much faster, but they loved the Spit because it could maneuver in a dogfight. It could almost stand on its tail, do a chandelle, come back at its pursuer before he knew what was happening.

Douglas showed Aleko that the box said the model was 1/24 scale. He said the real planes were twenty-four times as big as their model would be. Each inch of model was the same as two feet of airplane.

He stopped to explain about inches and feet, and centimeters and meters. He made Aleko figure how big the wing span of a real one was. Theirs would have a wingspan of twenty inches. They paced off forty feet across the platia and tried to imagine wings that big.

Sometimes Old Nikos would tell them long stories, things he remembered from when he ran messages for the British, he and Old Fr. Dimitrios, his friend.

Aleko listened without moving, even though the glue was drying in a lump on his fingertip.

The model came with a plastic propeller with three blades. It was grey plastic, but it would be painted black with yellow tips. Before it could be painted, though, the propeller disappeared off the table. They looked everywhere. A plane with no propeller was useless.

It was missing for several days. Lambros found it where it had fallen under the cold drink machine. After he found it, they spent some time talking about why the Spit needed three blades when some planes only had two.

The kit came with an arrangement for a rubber band to be wound up very tightly to drive the propeller, at least for a little while.

When the plane was complete, nearly perfect, Douglas and Aleko looked at it standing in the middle of the cleared off tabletop. Douglas said, "The box says this model is easy to build and not so easy to fly. Are you sure you want to fly it?"

Aleko looked at the model. "It wants to fly."

"Okay if it breaks?"

"O.-K.," Aleko grinned. On a Saturday morning, they walked the plane, each of them holding a wing, up Lefka Ori to a knoll with no trees around. Old Nikos and Lambros went with them. Fr. Dimitrios said he was going to stay behind and work, but in the end he wanted to see it fly, too, so he came after them.

The wind was perfect that day. A light breeze came up the mountain right at them. The plane would fly into the wind, out over the world, and maybe it would land in the level part of the field below, where goats had eaten everything flat.

Douglas showed Aleko how to stand and how to hold the plane to push it straight away from himself. Aleko practiced the position while Douglas and Old Nikos wound up the propeller. Douglas held the prop steady with his finger and gave the plane to Aleko. He held it high, the propeller pressing against his finger, and then he launched that Spitfire into the skies over Crete.

It soared for four seconds (Nikos counted out loud), then it stalled and dropped, caught the wind, soared, curved right, stalled again, and fell to ground. They all ran to where it lay. The left wing was at a new angle and the prop was missing. Aleko found it under a bush. They went back to the taverna, happily reviewing the flight particulars. If the Spit couldn't be repaired, maybe they'd get a Hurricane model next. But even broken, the Spitfire would be hung in a place of honor near Lambros's soft drink machine. They'd string it up with black sewing thread.

301

46

Douglas and Fr. Dimitrios stripped whitewash several hours every afternoon. By mid-November, the north wall was clear and the scene of the Nativity was exposed. Angels spoke to shepherds. Sheep gazed at the miraculous beam of light shining onto the newborn Babe. An ox and an ass in the cave warmed the infant with their breath. The dismayed Joseph in the lower left of the wall was attended by an old shepherd, but when Joseph appeared on the right side of the wall, an angel reassured him. Wise men galloped their horses toward the cave. Letters near the heads of the figures spelled their names. A deep red border surrounded the painting. Below the border, the bottom meter of wall had diamond shapes of red and black on white plaster. High up, above the painting, two small windows pierced the wall. Fr. Dimitrios thought that later, with a scaffold, he would see what other figures might lie between the windows near the ceiling. For now, the repair of this wall was finished.

The two men cleaned up the work space around the north wall and moved all the equipment out of the church. They organized a special festival for the villagers to welcome back the Nativity of the north wall. For that week, the church was free of dropcloths. Everyone said the wall painting was beautiful. Old Nikos examined the wall slowly and said it was just as he remembered it, from before the war.

After the festival, they brought the dropcloths back and started on the whitewash on the south wall. The work went faster now. They knew what to expect from the plaster.

One day Douglas said, "When we met Denise that day at the harbor, I didn't run but I sure thought about it. So, is courage, then, just standing still when you want to run?"

The priest answered, "In that circumstance it was. Aristotle says that each situation requires a different courageous response. There's an element of judgment: If a rhinoceros is charging you, it's no longer courageous to stand. Then it's foolhardy."

"Are you courageous?"

Fr. Dimitrios thought about this. "I don't know. I don't think my courage has been tested. Not like yours has."

"But I failed, over and over. You haven't run away when things got tough, have you?"

"Running never offered a solution to me, but that doesn't make me courageous."

"How so?"

"If staying wasn't a difficult decision, it didn't require courage. I read somewhere that a famous general said he got credit for being courageous when, in fact, he thought he probably just lacked some physical ingredient that made others scared when bombs blew up."

Over the weeks and months, their conversations ranged over many ideas that Douglas was working on. He came to think he needed his own copy of Aristotle, so he counted the money in his wallet and spent most of it, $21.00, at the bookstore in Chania on a copy of the *Nicomachaean Ethics* in English. He read it carefully and underlined passages on the days when it rained and he couldn't work on the taverna.

"It doesn't seem fair, " he said one day. "I do all the talking here. You never say anything personal. The only thing you have said was your comment about exile: that you missed whichever home you weren't at."

303

Fr. Dimitrios answered, "I am a priest. In a village like Vraho, I'm always on duty. I don't talk about my own personal things."

Douglas said, "I guess married priests have an easier time of it. At least they have their wives to talk to."

An image of Ellen flitted across Fr. Dimitrios's mind. "They have a different life. I think it would be very hard to be a priest's wife. She can't really participate in the women's talk of the village as the others can. But honestly, I don't feel lonely. I love the people of this parish, but I must remember I am always their priest."

Douglas looked embarrassed. "So then I land on your doorstep and start pouring out all these new thoughts. You're so calm."

"Douglas, I may look self-contained and calm to you, but remember: I'm not being tested right now. It's easy to look wise when nothing's going on."

"Yes, but still…" Douglas admired Fr. Dimitrios's steadiness. He hoped he would be like that one day.

47

The next Thursday, Fr. Dimitrios packed his sakkoula and organized himself to ride down to Chania. He would meet with his metropolitan (everything was fine, nothing troublesome to report), pick up his mail, take himself for a kafe Elleniko, look out at the sea, and return, refreshed, to the village to begin another week. It was a meditation of sorts, this weekly ride down-mountain, the stimulation of the city, even without summer tourists, and then the silent-but-for-wind-in-his-ears ride back up the mountain, with time for his thoughts to come up and be heard, back to his home, his work, his place on the planet.

The jolt came at the post office. Among the church mail was an envelope to him in Ellen's handwriting. What could she want to say that she couldn't say in an e-mail?

He put all the mail in his sakkoula and went to the internet place. He found no message from her there. He answered his mother's message with his usual answer, that all was well, but as he left Kafe INTER-NET, he wondered if indeed that was going to be true—after he learned what was in Ellen's letter.

As he sat with his kafe Elleniko under the shade of a canvas roof, at a table among a sea of empty tables, he looked at the light glinting off the water in the harbor and wished for the comfort it usually brought him. He reached into his sakkoula and drew the letter out.

The envelope looked like a wedding invitation. It was heavy creme-colored paper. Was that the news? He felt a sadness rise, and he told it to go away. Whatever was happening in Ellen's life, now, he could only wish her well. His life was here, in the Church, in the village.

He opened the envelope. The stationery was as formal as the envelope, with her name engraved at the top. The note was hand-written. It said,

> Dear Mitso,
>
> I have written and torn up this letter so many times I should apologize to the forests for the trees that went into the paper I've wasted.
>
> I'm sorry for the pain I've caused you. And for the pain I've caused myself. Maybe that more vividly, because I'm still in agony. I made a mistake, Mitso. I should have married you and gone with you wherever you went. I was not thinking clearly. Now what's left in my life is hollow. Yes, I'm a lawyer. I defend some wrongdoers against other wrongdoers, but there's not a lot of principles in the lives of any of them. Or in my own life any more.
>
> I have all the things a young lawyer needs: car, cellphone, clothes, fancy condo, and they all turn to sawdust before me. My mind drifts to you and your village, even when I'm in court and need my mind to be there.
>
> I've sent you casual little e-mail messages. "Keep it light, Ellen," I told myself. But I can't get past missing what might have been. There is no comfort for me.
>
> Without you, I am lost, Dimitrios. Tell me, please, what to do.
>
> I will be in London for work next month. I could fly to Crete and we could talk. Would you allow me that?
>
> your foolish, loving, and agonized friend,
> Ellen.

Fr. Dimitrios put the letter away in his sakkoula. His brain locked into a no-think mode. The kafe Elleniko lost its flavor. The sea had no sparkle.

After some minutes, he left the shade of the open kafenion and moved slowly up the sloping steps of the old town toward the seawall parking lot. He passed Big Kostas's taverna, where he had collected Douglas's passport. Big Kostas's wife smiled and waved to him. He returned the greeting so as not to be rude, but he absolutely couldn't stop to talk to her.

He started up the Vespa and made himself ride slowly and consciously out of the city.

When he got back to Ano Vraho, he went straight to his house. He hoped not to see anybody, but of course Kyria Ariadne was standing just outside his door, talking with Douglas. He greeted them both and excused himself.

"Wait," said Douglas. "I have something wonderful to show you."

He looked at Douglas's empty hands. Show what?

"What? Where?"

"On the south wall."

Fr. Dimitrios hesitated for a moment, wanting to say not now. Then he looked at Douglas's pleased face. He smiled and said, "Show me."

The two went into the church. Afternoon sunlight streamed onto the glowing wall of the Nativity. The wall they were working on now, below the sun-filled windows, was in shadow. Douglas turned on the construction lights that lit the areas they were working on. He aimed the lights at the center of the wall. A newly cleared area showed the lower half of a robed figure, the sandaled feet dangling, standing on a fractured wooden structure that made an X-shape. Random piles of hinges and locks showed below the wood.

307

"Douglas, that's wonderful! This is going to be Christ Descending into Hades. Anastasis. I should have guessed. What a wonderful contrast to the Nativity on the opposite wall."

"Look what's underneath the broken wood. What's the hardware there for?"

"All the locks that bind us have been smashed by Christ's Resurrection."

"So the darker subject uses the darker wall. Because this wall is never in the direct sunlight, it's sort of more mysterious than the well-lit Nativity."

"What a wonderful discovery." Fr. Dimitrios looked directly at his helper. "Douglas, I need something from you," he said. He crossed to the doors and barred them. Douglas looked puzzled.

"There's no one in the village I can confide in, as I've told you. There's really no one else anywhere I could speak to about this. Will you keep what I say confidential?"

"Of course." The two men sat on their work-stools, facing the Nativity wall across the church.

Fr. Dimitrios said, "When I was in school, I was in love with a woman and we planned to marry. Five years ago, after I graduated from seminary and was about to be ordained, we broke up. She did not want to leave her American life to come here, and I was determined to come to Vraho. Because I became a priest as an unmarried man, I may not marry afterwards.

"I made the choice. I could have waited to ordain and maybe I could have met some other woman but it seemed that if it wasn't going to be Ellen, it wasn't going to be anybody. I decided I was meant to be celibate as part of my practice.

"I've heard from Ellen from time to time, by e-mail or greetings passed through my parents. 'Say hello to Mitso.' That sort of thing. She finished law school and seemed to be doing well."

He reached in his sakkoula for the envelope.

"Today I received this letter."

He handed it to Douglas, who read it and said, "What are you going to do?"

"I don't know. I want to tell her not to come. The break-up was her choice. I'm committed to my life here. I can't just leave Vraho and the Church for her. I shouldn't have to help her with the pain she feels from her own decision.

"I say that, then I remember that my role as priest is to help all those who suffer...and I loved her. Still do love her, in some way. So is my duty to tell her to come? To resolve her pain?"

"Is this something to ask your metropolitan?"

"I know what he will say. I must tell her not to come."

"Want some friendly advice here?"

"Yes."

"It sounds like you'd know more about what she wants and maybe what you want if you telephone her. Do you have her phone number?"

"Right. Good idea. What could be gained if she comes? I'll call her."

"Okay."

"Okay, that's what I'll do."

"You're sure."

"I think so."

"I'll go now, so you can phone her."

"Oh, it's too late now."

"It's nine hours earlier there. It's eight in the morning."

"Oh, then, she'll be on her way to work. I'll wait til she's home."

"Set your alarm. Call her early tomorrow morning."

"That's what I'll do. I'll listen to her and offer comfort, but it's a bad idea if she comes. I'll tell her not to come."

The next afternoon, at the usual time, Douglas went to the church to work on the whitewash. He found Fr. Dimitrios there, picking at a flaking piece of lime.

"Hi," Douglas said.

"I called her."

"Did you? Good." Douglas moved his stool to where he had been working before. As he lined up some swab sticks with wax on their tips, he heard Fr. Dimitrios sigh.

"She's coming here in two weeks' time."

"I thought you said you'd tell her not to come."

"I couldn't do it."

Douglas moved his stool near Fr. Dimitrios. "Tell me," he said. Then he listened, carefully, while the other man spoke.

Fr. Dimitrios said, "It was easier to go about my days before she told me she was hurting, too. I told myself I was living with her choice. There was nothing I could do about it."

309

"Are you saying you are considering going back to her?"

"I don't have that choice any more. I am the priest here. I have earned the trust of the village. I am my grandfather's grandson. But I couldn't just say 'don't come' to her. Not for her sake nor for mine."

"You do have that choice. You're still alive. You could leave the church."

"Could I? What sort of life would I have if I did that?" He looked at Douglas. "I said to you that my courage had not been tested. Well, it will be now."

"You want to borrow my Aristotle?"

Fr. Dimitrios laughed out loud. "I have my grandfather's copy, thanks. But I think I should read it again. The part about courage."

"Book Two, somewhere around Chapter Six, I think."

"Right." He put away the scalpels he had been holding, and said, "Let's not work today." He picked up his stool and put it in the corner. "I don't want to damage the wall because my mind is elsewhere. We'll try again tomorrow."

48

Two weeks later, Fr. Dimitrios went down to Souda International Airport to meet Ellen's flight. He left an hour early to allow for missed bus connections. An announcement over the speakers told him her flight would be twenty minutes late. He sat on a plastic chair in a row with departing passengers and he waited.

He wandered over to the newsstand to look for something to read. All the magazines demanded more attention than he could bring to them. He went to the car rental counter and confirmed Ellen's reservation. He checked the board of arriving Olympic Airways flights from Athens. Ellen's flight was at the bottom of the board. Over the next hour it slowly moved up. He measured her journey in lines on the flight arrival board.

Fr. Dimitrios wore his cassock and kalimavki. He always wore his cassock and kalimavki on Crete, but he knew Ellen had never seen him in it. His first worry was that she would feel the clothing of his office was a barrier between them. His second fear was that she would not—that she would embrace him or, worse, kiss him, there, in front of everybody.

He was annoyed at himself for not trusting her behavior in the airport, annoyed at Ellen for wanting to come here, annoyed and angry at the injustice that had caused this situation five years before. He spent that hour and twenty minutes rewriting history with a series of what-ifs. The activity only made the present situation seem more stupid.

He cursed himself that he had not tried harder to reason with her back then, had not offered a time limit on village life so she would have tried it—although that had seemed a dishonest thought at the time. He knew Vraho and he knew himself well enough to know that he didn't want to do a two-year Peace Corps-type stint there. He wanted to stay. Such an offer, a lie really, would have felt—would have been—dishonorable.

He was grateful not to see any faces he knew in the people at the airport.

The door opened and Metropolitan Ioannis of Chania and two of his staff entered, a phalanx of black cassocks through the multicolored clothing of the civilians.

He rose and went to meet his metropolitan. He bowed and kissed the metropolitan's hand. He greeted the other priests. His Eminence introduced him, "This is Fr. Dimitrios from Vraho, as devoted a priest as I hope to meet. Would that I had six more like him."

Fr. Dimitrios felt the heat of the blush sweep up his face.

Ellen's flight finally arrived. Anonymous faces on weary bodies flooded out the arrival gate. One figure moved faster than the rest. It was Ellen. She alone radiated energy. She was smiling. Her eyes were searching for him.

Ellen was even more beautiful than five years ago. Self-assurance showed in her black tunic suit, her large gold jewelry, her sleek hair. Her face was still youthful but powerful, too.

He watched her face register surprise when she saw his cassock and kalimavki. She hesitated, then recovered her smile and came over to him. She stood before him for an instant. She seemed about to throw her arms around him.

Fr. Dimitrios was as still as he could make himself be. Don't, he thought. Please, don't embarrass me here.

312

Ellen took his hand and kissed it, in the correct manner of greeting a priest. She shot him a teasing smile, though.

"You're all dressed up!" She looked up at his kalimavki.

"Hi, Ellen. It's good to see you."

"Thanks. Forgive me for staring. The outfit's a bit retro. It will take some getting used to."

He explained, "This is how priests dress here. Every day."

"I'm searching to find your face under the priest's stuff and the beard."

"It's still me in here." Quick change of subject. "So, tell me about your trip over."

They chatted about airports and travel and other lightweight topics while they waited for her luggage. Ellen signed the papers for the rental car. As they got to the parking lot, the cloud cover broke and a light rain fell.

"It's easier, isn't it, if you drive? You know where things are." Ellen handed him the keys to the car.

The area around the airport was an expanse of low scrub with the promise of coastline over the edge of the peninsula. "Welcome to Crete," said Fr. Dimitrios.

"Life in the village agrees with you."

"Kyria Ariadne's cooking agrees with me. I've put on fifteen pounds in three years."

"I think you look fine."

"So do you. Are you hungry?"

"I'm still on California time. I might be hungry in another hour or so."

"Let me show you the city, then."

They went into the old part of Chania. On foot, they explored the old town. They admired the Venetian port and the arsenali, the twisting alleys and the sudden discoveries of hidden squares.

Ellen stopped before a shell of a building. Through its empty window frames she could see rubble.

"When did this happen?" she asked.

"Bombing damage. World War II."

313

She looked at Fr. Dimitrios. "That was more than fifty years ago. Why doesn't someone fix it?"

Fr. Dimitrios smiled, "I guess someone hasn't gotten around to it yet. There are several ruins like this in the old city. They were Venetian buildings, 400 years old. It would cost a lot to reinforce the old parts, and it would be a pity to pull them down and build concrete boxes, so they wait."

"Half a century?"

He smiled. "It's a different world."

At last they turned a corner and saw a restaurant Fr. Dimitrios had heard good things about. It was just opening for the day, and they seated themselves near a small fireplace. He was pleased that no other guests had arrived yet, so it was a good place to talk.

Fr. Dimitrios apologized for the dismal day. "Crete is very different when the sun is out."

"I didn't come here to see Crete, Mitso. I came to see you."

"We should have raincoats." He glared at the damp street beyond the restaurant door.

"We won't shrink if we get wet. Mitso, look at me, please."

Reluctantly, he brought his gaze to her magnificent eyes. His fear softened when he allowed himself to look right at her.

"I envy your life here, being of service to the people, doing large, generous, spiritual things every day. I miss having you in my life. I miss your laughter and the fun we had together."

The waitress came at that moment to take their order. Fr. Dimitrios realized his appetite had gone. Ellen ordered a sampler plate of mezedes. He stared at the menu waiting for an answer. The waitress waited for his answer, too. Finally, he ordered the first thing his eyes saw, prawns, although he usually didn't like them much.

Ellen continued, "But it's not just that I'm not with you. There is no purpose to my life. Everything seems so meaningless."

"Most people's lives don't have a daily sense of purpose. Mine doesn't either. Some days I just get up in the morning and do what needs doing."

"But what needs doing in your life is caring for the souls of your village, ministering to their needs, acting as intercessor between them and God. That's not meaningless."

314

The waitress brought two small glasses of tsikoudia. Ellen tasted it and made a face.

"What is this stuff?"

"Tsikoudia. It's the local poison. You don't have to drink it. It's strong." He drank his glass. Any source of fortitude cheerfully accepted today. Ellen's words cut through his brain, scattering his own thoughts. He couldn't even come up with an automatic response. He sat there, unmoving.

Ellen said, "Look, Mitso. I don't know what you have thought or felt during these years. You may have been fine with it, no regrets, move on. I mean, you have a vocation that asks for a total commitment. Maybe you didn't miss me." Her face was close before him, beautiful and vulnerable.

He slid his chair back a few inches. "Of course I have missed you, Ellen. There are regrets enough here for both of us."

Their food arrived and the moment was over.

He knew the food in this restaurant was delicious, but he couldn't taste anything.

As they ate, Ellen told him about his parents. They seemed to be fine. They had stayed friendly with her all these years. She thought they missed him a lot, and that was part of why they were so nice to her—as a memory link. His mother was forgetful sometimes. His father was getting heavy and seemed to be tired much of the time, but they really were not bad, all in all. Not bad.

Fr. Dimitrios thought about his declining parents. Next time he spoke to them he would insist that they come to visit him here next year. He thought of the discomfort of the long plane ride. He knew he was better able to travel than they were, but he couldn't see a time when he could leave Vraho.

"Your mother said you were doing something with your church building. She didn't understand what. You're taking off paint?"

315

"I'm taking off the layer of whitewash that Papou put over the original wallpaintings."

"Are you finding the paintings underneath?"

"I'll show you tomorrow."

"You can't show me today?"

"You'll be staying in a village called Peristeri."

"Oh dear. I am an embarrassment to you, aren't I?"

"Of course not. Absolutely not. It's just that the only place to stay in Vraho is over the taverna and it's noisy and the beds sag. I thought you'd sleep better in the place at Peristeri."

"Right."

They finished eating and Ellen said, "Do they take Visa here?"

Fr. Dimitrios began to protest, but Ellen said, "Your parents are taking us to lunch."

He gave in. "All right, then. Thank you, and thanks to them." The waitress went off with the bill and Ellen's credit card.

The light rain had turned into real rain. They ran to the car.

Once in it, they brushed the white-reflecting raindrops off their black garments and laughed.

"So much for the walking tour. How about a car tour of Chania, instead," asked Fr. Dimitrios. "I'll take you to the new Byzantine museum. You'll like it, I think."

She put her hand on his arm. Through the sleeve of his cassock, her touch burned him. "Mitso, no. Can't we just go somewhere and talk?"

He turned off the engine. "Okay. Here?"

"Can we park somewhere by the sea?"

He drove out toward Maleme. He knew a road that dead-ended at a beach. It would be deserted.

The sea was re-taking Crete. The summer people thought the beaches belonged to them but when their backs were turned, the sea made the land-edge its own again. Waves ate away the sandy beach. The rental chairs were gone for the season. The small boats clung to their harbors.

316

Raindrops on the windshield of the rental car distorted the view of the sea. The image looked alarmingly like tears, thought Fr. Dimitrios. He turned off the ignition and slid lower in his seat, prepared to hear whatever she had to say.

Her arm came across his field of vision and her hand landed gently on his neck. She pulled him toward her and kissed him on the lips. The kiss surprised him. He recoiled.

"Don't do that!"

She withdrew the arm. "I'm sorry, Mitso. No witnesses."

"No mortal witnesses, anyway. It's not that I don't love you, but to kiss you like that is a sin for me, now."

Ellen looked embarrassed. "I'm really sorry."

"What is it you want, Ellen? Me? It's not possible."

"Don't act so holy, Mitso. It was just a kiss."

"It was a hungry kiss, and you know it," he said.

He looked at her. She seemed smaller now, young and forlorn. She stared at her own hands as she spoke. "I'm sorry. I have missed you a lot. I started to regret not marrying you almost immediately after you were ordained, but I also saw that the door you had passed through was a one-way door. If you loved the Church so much that you were willing to give up any chance of human love for the rest of your life, you had a love deeper than any I could imagine. I envied you that, and it made me long to be with you."

She looked over at him. "I think I just needed to see that you are all right, that I haven't hurt you so much that you never recover."

"Ellen, I forgive you. Does that help?"

"I shouldn't have come." Her eyes returned to her hands.

Fr. Dimitrios said, "No, that's not true. I think we both need to see each other as we are now, and set aside the fantasies."

"I hate it when you sound all-wise and grown-up. You always did that."

"I'm not any more grown-up than you, Ellen. I'm simply trying to think things through rationally, without getting emotional."

"Are you accusing me of being emotional? Damn!" She opened the car door and got out into the rain. "You always were like this!" She walked down to the shore.

Fr. Dimitrios did not follow her. She stood in the rain for a minute, then returned to the car and got in again.

She was laughing.

"We don't change, do we? Same fight we always had."

"The blessing always was that we could laugh again so quickly afterwards. Shall we go to Peristeri now?" Fr. Dimitrios turned the key in the ignition.

317

49

The village of Peristeri had nearly the same population as Vraho but because the main road over Lefka Ori to the Libyan Sea passed right through it, there were tourist shops along its face. Three separate shops competed to sell postcards, t-shirts, key rings, and other tourist essentials.

Fr. Dimitrios parked in a dirt lot at the south end of the village set aside for bus parking. He showed her the edge of Ano Vraho, across the ravine.

They found the address of the place Lambros had recommended: a concrete building with a large sign that said ROOMS over an open kafenion with a few tables. The girl at the front desk led Ellen to her room. Fr. Dimitrios waited downstairs.

Ellen's room was the best in the house. It had doors onto a roof-garden that looked over toward Vraho. Smells rose from the kitchen below. Cooking grease hung in the air, giving a sweet heaviness to the place. She left her bags in the room, washed her face, and went back downstairs. They went out into Peristeri.

They passed a small square with a fountain, two tavernas, and a small museum to the martyrs of World War II. They stopped at the museum.

Fr. Dimitrios stared in the window at the photos of three young men, their frames touching. The wall behind them was draped in black bunting. A card gave their names and death date: December 20, 1941. These had to be the men Papou had mentioned, the ones who died in reprisal for Papou's brother's death. He said a silent prayer for the repose of their souls and the forgiveness of his grandfather's soul.

He looked more closely at the pictures. The men wore sarikis, white shirts, embroidered vests, and fierce looks, as if, afraid of the camera, they stared it down. They were in their twenties, all of them.

Fr. Dimitrios and Ellen went inside the museum and looked at the other exhibits: One wall was full of framed photos of the village before the war and after. Pieces of military hardware filled the glass cases. There were guns, knives, bullets, pitchforks, apparent scraps of farm equipment. A guest book lay on top of a glass case, next to a jar for donations.

They dropped a clutch of drachmas into the jar.

The next shop sold lace.

"Is this lace made here?" Ellen asked Fr. Dimitrios. They stood on the sidewalk looking at a shopwindow choking in white and ecru froth.

"Probably most is from Peristeri. There may be a few pieces from Vraho. We have lace-makers, too."

"I want to look. Do you mind?" She entered the shop, and Fr. Dimitrios followed her.

Lace hung from every surface. Some of it was over-embroidered by hand. Other pieces seemed to be machine-embroidered. Lace hung from the walls and from plastic-coated line strung across the shop. Even with the high ceiling, there were places where Fr. Dimitrios had to duck to avoid the hanging merchandise.

Four large tables held mountains of lace objects, all folded into clear plastic bags. Ellen sorted through the stacks, then asked for prices on several pieces.

319

Fr. Dimitrios wondered who she was buying lace for. He didn't think she liked lace. He watched her go through a pile of large tablecloths packaged in yellowed plastic bags. The bags crinkled as she moved them from stack to adjacent stack. She finished looking, and said, "Let's go."

"Weren't you going to buy something?"

When they were out on the street she said, "Do you know how long it would take to make a tablecloth like that last one I looked at? It would take most of a year. They were charging $225 for it. After the shop takes its cut, the maker would be lucky to have $100 for her work. How do these women live? It is women who make the lace, isn't it?"

"I think so."

They went slowly back up the street toward the rooming house. In the late afternoon light, the village was emptying out. A bus pulled out of the parking lot and went toward the mountains. Backpackers headed toward the tavernas, or their rooms. In the winter, tourists settle in early. The shops closed their doors for the night.

"Why don't they organize a women's cooperative to market their work?"

"That lace shop is a cooperative. There was a sign behind the counter."

"Well, it's not charging enough for their work."

"It's charging what all the other lace shops on the island charge."

"It's not enough. They aren't getting paid a living wage."

"Most of the world is not getting paid a living wage. You move in heady circles: London, New York, San Francisco, yet even in those places, some people barely get by on what they earn for a day's work. The world is not fair, but it is what we have to work with."

"And our work in this unfair world is to change things for the better. This village seems to be totally dependent on the discretionary drachmas of foreign tourists. What happened to their self-sustaining life? Their dignity?"

"It is a more complicated issue than that, Ellen."

"They're being abused."

"If you say so."

"Have I embarrassed you, Patera?"

Fr. Dimitrios smiled. "I'll come for you tomorrow noon and take you to Vraho for lunch. I have some work I must do in the morning."

"Do you want to take the car?"

"No. I'll walk home now, and back tomorrow. You keep the car here. You might want to go sightseeing in the morning."

"I might want to sleep off the jet lag. But, why don't I drive over to Vraho and meet you there? At the taverna at noon. Does that work? I'll ask directions from downstairs."

"That's fine, then. See you tomorrow noon."

Fr. Dimitrios thought, as he walked across the ravine to Vraho, that perhaps he had left a bit too abruptly. He would try to be more patient tomorrow. Patient with whom? he wondered. He was annoyed with himself as much as with Ellen.

It was a difficult trip along that dark path. He found himself thinking of his grandfather and German soldiers and bodies going over the edge. He watched his footing.

50

Ellen bought a map from the people downstairs. She drove down the mountain to the cutoff to Mournies then back up the mountain to Therisso. She followed the signs for the Malaxa Ridge. Above Therisso, the road became a steep dirt mess with big ruts from the rain. I'm glad it's not my car, she thought. She started up the road, conscious of what a broken axle could mean. Rocks, edges, crumbling hillside above, crumbling hillside below, no time to look at the scenery. Nothing but shallow-breathing driving.

Switchback turns. At least no other vehicle came at her. The road kept going. Vraho seemed to be a zillion miles beyond where she was. Could this be right?

She passed through Kato Vraho without noticing it: a couple of gates and drives, some run-down stone houses, and a few goats. A woman standing outside a doorway watched her go past. The road swung out to a ridge line and curled to the right and up another steep slope.

Then, there it was: a vista of the whole Mediterranean, the shore of Crete, the talus slipping down to it, layers of cloud cast across the sky. The hand of man showed only in a strip of macadam highway near the water's edge.

Ellen stopped the car. What she saw was so enormous and so perfect that she had to remind herself to breathe.

When she could, she drove on toward the village of Ano Vraho. She saw a white block building with the word TAVERNA from several twists away. When she reached it, she saw the platia and then the church. She parked near the taverna. A young man up a ladder was putting a layer of fresh blue paint on the building's fascia. He waved to her.

"Hi. Are you Ellen?" He gathered his bucket and brush and came down to greet her. "I'm Douglas Watkins. Fr. Dimitrios asked me to keep an eye out for you. I'll go tell him you're here."

Before she could say anything, he ran across the road to the church.

Vraho seemed very different from Peristeri. None but the most determined tourist could get here, so the village was probably much like what it had been in World War II, when Mitso's grandfather was priest here.

A power line swagged its way down the main street. She wondered how long ago electricity had come here, and what the village had thought when they first saw TV. She pictured Cretan shepherds in their boots and sarikis watching The Shopping Channel.

Fr. Dimitrios and Douglas came out of the church. Who is this American man, Douglas? wondered Ellen. He moves so much lighter than Mitso. Is it the shoes? Or the burden of the priesthood that has weighed down my friend's walk? The two men were as different as air and rock.

The priest offered his hand. She kissed it. She felt professionally greeted. She was on his work turf. Was there any place that was not his work turf?

He re-introduced her to Douglas, who shook her hand. He must know about me, she thought. He's looking at me with curiosity. Or maybe I'd just be an object of curiosity anyway.

The three of them entered the taverna.

323

Lambros the taverna owner came out to meet them. "Welcome to my taverna, dear lady. Here. You must take this table, near the window." He brought a small vase of dried flowers to the table. "Please, sit here." He held out a chair for her. "Pappa Dimitri said he would bring a guest today, but he did not say she would be so lovely. What do you like to eat? I will get it for you. Anything! Only say what you like."

They ordered his daily special. It was the same every day. They ate chicken roasted with tomatoes and zucchinis. They washed it down with a sweet orange soda. She declined the glass of tsikoudia that appeared in front of her.

Fr. Dimitrios asked Douglas to tell Ellen about the whitewash project.

The young American told her about the process and the materials it required. He told her how they stabilized the plaster after they lifted off the hardened layer of whitewash. He asked if she knew about Byzantine icons.

"Of course," she answered. "I was raised Orthodox. I grew up with those figures looking at me all my life."

"I have asked about them at the Byzantine Museum. They think these paintings probably date to the fourteenth century. They may be by an artist named John Pagomenos. They're a lot like some icons he painted around Selinos, over the mountain. Icons are almost never signed, but he signed eight that still exist. I'm hoping we'll find a signature under what's left of the whitewash." Douglas seemed boyishly pleased.

She looked at Mitso. He was pleased, too, but quietly so. He looked tired.

Lambros drew up a chair and joined them. He was talking now about water. She realized she hadn't been listening. She asked him to repeat.

"Pappa Dimitri helped the village to fix the water system..."

Douglas added, "He brought in a conduit and concrete swales where it used to be mud-covered rock. He designed it and helped the villagers build it."

Lambros said, "We don't have to boil our water anymore. The people can use it as it comes out of the mountain. It is very much better."

"You did? You didn't mention that."

Lambros continued, "He wrote an application to the government. We're asking for money to make a small medical clinic here, and for a scholarship to train someone as a nurse."

She looked at Fr. Dimitrios. "You don't have a clinic in the village?"

"We hope to, soon." Fr. Dimitrios smiled at her, but the smile contained a warning. She shut her mouth, but the thought plagued her, how primitive is this place? No medical help here?

Finally she had to ask, "What do you do if someone has a heart attack?"

"We telephone for an ambulance and the person is taken to hospital in Chania."

"What about when you're sick?"

"You go to bed and get well." Fr. Dimitrios smiled as he slid his chair back from the table.

Lambros said, "We have the balms and tisanes that we have always used, too."

Fr. Dimitrios stood up and said, "Come, I'll show you the walls."

When they reached the church, Fr. Dimitrios opened the door and stood back for Ellen to enter first.

She pushed a bill into the collection box and lit a candle. She set it into a container filled with sand. The flame reached high and turned into a line of smoke, then it filled out and settled down.

She felt disappointed. She had hoped to be struck speechless by the beauty of something majestic, but it was only a village church after all. The wall paintings were dark and large. Diffused, she thought. The icons she grew up with were on gessoed panels. They were small tight images with gold backgrounds. These wallpaintings were very different.

Mitso had been here three years and he'd cleared one and a half walls. Okay, they were important to the village history. Important to Papou . He'd repaired their water system, too, but obviously, the lives of the people hadn't changed much. She didn't mean to let him see her disappointment, but she felt it show on her face.

Fr. Dimitrios said, "What is it, Ellen?"

325

"I thought you would have improved things more by now."

"What did you think I would have done?"

"I don't know—rebuilt their school system, organized a better cooperative venture for the lace-making women, or found a way to bring eco-tourists here...something.

"Forgive me for saying it, Mitso, but all you're doing is making the old ways comfortable for people who are several thousand years behind the times."

"Like what?"

"You're preserving the traditional injustices of the village. Their lives here haven't changed much since you came, have they?"

"I don't know. You'll have to ask them."

"Are fewer women beaten now than before? Does everyone have enough to eat? Are children getting educations that will lead to meaningful employment?"

"Ellen, stop it. I came here to serve them, not to fix them. Change comes gradually."

"Not when it's 4,000 years overdue."

"The changes you are suggesting would break as much as they would mend. And as to technology, I'm not convinced that it's the answer."

"But you're an engineer."

"I'm also a priest. And I became a priest because I believe it's the soul that needs care before the mechanical or economic world. Look! When I first came to Vraho, I was full of ideas for them. I've learned that I am only here to love them and help them find their own changes. That's what I see as God's work for me."

Ellen pulled her coat tighter around herself and stood in the center of the stone church looking at the whispering wall paintings. "I don't know. I don't know what to say."

Dimitrios said, "We have the same goals, Ellen, but nearly opposite methods to reach them. You are dedicated to improving things, and so am I, but the difference is, you slice through opposition and charge straight ahead. I try to improve things slowly, without causing new damage in the process. You are a knife, and I am water."

"Knife and water don't work together, do they?"

He came to her and put his arms around her. "I think you made the right decision, Ellen, for both of us. We are more useful to the world working separately than we would have been working together."

"Dimitrios, I will always love you."

"And I, you."

"I'm glad I came to see you. Now both of us can move on."

"The fishhook of regret is removed."

"Fishhook? Yes. It hurt like that, didn't it? You should have been a poet."

"No, I just like metaphors."

She laughed then.

"Mitso, I'm going to drive to Iraklion and see some more of Crete, and leave you to do your work here, at your own pace. Thank you for talking all this through with me."

"I'm glad you came. I'll walk over to Peristeri and go with you to the airport tomorrow."

"You needn't. I can manage."

"I'd like to take you there."

"Thank you."

Then, only, was it safe to kiss. A gentle, loving, non-desirous kiss, and Ellen drove the rental car back down the dirt road to Therisso. She didn't look back.

51

Douglas and Fr. Dimitrios cleared away the drop cloth and the tools of the project from the south wall. They stood in the center of the church. They looked first at one wall and then the other, admiring the opposing scenes. The sunlight through the high south-facing windows made the wall below, the one with the Descent Into Hades, seem darker. The sun's reflection off the stone floor added more radiance to the Nativity.

The next Sunday after the Divine Liturgy, the people of the village stayed in the church to admire the restored wall-paintings. They touched the bullet holes in the plaster and spoke of their relatives who had lost their lives in the church more than fifty years before. They told stories they'd heard from their grandparents about the images in the paintings that now they could see for themselves.

Two weeks later, the metropolitan of Chania came to re-consecrate the church. After the ceremony, he joined in the feast. The village celebrated for two days with much music and dancing. Douglas helped Sofia bring Spiros to the festival. He sat in his wheelchair on the platia and watched the goings-on.

Men sang mantinades they made up for the occasion, about the paintings and the time of the war. Each couplet built on the one before. They told of the great courage of the pallikaria, of Spiros's father and the others. Then Old Nikos stood and sang one about a brave priest who did secret acts of courage, and afterwards he shouted that the song was true and the priest was Fr. Dimitrios's grandfather, as true a hero as ever lived. Almost everybody cheered to Nikos's song, and raised their glasses to Fr. Dimitrios and his grandfather. Even Spiros seemed to smile, although it's hard to tell when he's smiling, since his stroke.

In December, Douglas visited Professor Ducor and Athina in Chania. They were closing up the Institute office once again, this time because they had completed all the paperwork with the Ministry of Culture.

He asked about the site on Rhodopou. They told him that Efthikas had filled in all the holes. The site was gone.

Douglas wanted to see for himself. He caught the bus to Afrata and walked back out to where the dig had been. In the winter sunlight, its colors were darker and it looked smaller. The place had returned to its natural form, as if no one had touched this land since the Minoans. A light breeze broke up the surface of the sea. Several gulls cruised along the shoreline. No goats grazed there at this time of year. There was no sign that this was where he had dug with such feeling.

This land was the first place he had loved. He had dug in it, uncovered things from it, cared about its secrets. This place was his earth-mother. Here he had been born, changed into someone who loved something. He loved archaeology and he loved this unpromising piece of earth.

329

He thought of the Minoans under the site. He still believed Ducor had been right: there must be a palace there.

He thought how quickly the land had healed, how quickly time closes over an experience, the way sea water closes over a ship that sinks below its surface. He touched a nearby rock and went back up the hill to the bus stop.

After the whitewash project was completed, the times when Douglas and Fr. Dimitrios were together were different. There was a distance between them for awhile. They moved from mentor and needful-one to acquaintances. After that, slowly, they became real friends.

Douglas was pleased not to need mentoring any more. Standing on his own two feet. Born (re-born!) in a cave and raised by a priest, with Aristotle as a godfather. Out on his own now. It all felt very Greek.

Once when he'd borrowed Sofia's truck and gone with Aleko up the mountain to gather firewood to heat the house, he'd slipped into the timelessness of the place. Beyond the edge of the road Douglas saw the entire world—the land meeting the sea meeting the sky. He thought of the myth of Icarus leaving Crete, falling into this very sea, so long ago. He caught himself wishing he'd been there to see it. The myths of Crete seemed as real as its history. He laughed aloud.

Aleko asked, "Why do you laugh?"

"Do you know about Icarus?"

"He flew too high and his wings melted. Teacher said."

"Just now I thought, I wish I'd been here to see it."

"He didn't fall here. He left from here, but he fell near Icaria."

"Is that so?"

"That's why it's named Icaria. Icarus and his father wanted to run away from Crete. King Minos wouldn't let them leave the island and Minos owned all the boats. I don't remember why they had to get away. Why would they want to go? Crete is the best place on earth."

"I guess even Crete can be a prison if you can't leave it."

"Oh. *You* can't leave it. Would you leave Crete now, Daonglos? If you could?"

"I don't know, but I'd like to have the choice." He smiled reassuringly at Aleko. "Not leaving today, though. That's for sure."

"Will you get your passport back after the trial?"

"I hope so."

"But if you didn't, you'd go to jail? That's bad, either way."

"Free to go doesn't mean I'd have to go. Let's see what happens."

330

52

While she was cleaning out Manolis's things, Sofia found a roll of drachmas underneath some clothing. She counted the money and asked Vassilia how much the butcher had paid for the first goat. The amounts matched. She gave the roll of bills to her sister, without either of them saying anything more about it.

When Douglas's trial date was getting near, Fr. Dimitrios asked Sofia if she would consider changing the police charge now, since Manolis was gone and didn't need her protection any more, and Spiros could no longer hurt anyone.

She said no.

Fr. Dimitrios was surprised. "Do you not like Douglas?"

Sofia said, "I like him very much, Patera. He has been very good to me and Spiros. But please know this: when I named Daonglos to the police, it was a gift for my son. Too late in his life, but I did it. It was the last thing that I could give him. Now," she looked uneasy, "if I change the charges, I will have done nothing for him."

Fr. Dimitrios argued that Manolis wouldn't want her to stand by a lie. Sofia listened to all of his arguments. Then she said, "Patera, this is a family matter." The subject was closed.

On Douglas's trial date, he went to court, but not alone. He had Fr. Dimitrios, Aleko, Vassilia, Lambros, and a dozen others from Vraho with him.

Sofia came, too. Kyria Ariadne would take care of Spiros for the day.

In the bus on the way down the mountain, Fr. Dimitrios sat with Sofia. They didn't say much. She looked pale. The others gave them respectful distance.

They arrived too early. The day still felt fresh. The sunlight lay low and the long shadows were cool. The courtroom would not open for another twenty minutes, so they all went to a coffeebar and had kafe Elleniko and pastries. Vassilia stayed close to Sofia, knowing that though this was Douglas's trial, her sister needed support. They had not spoken recently about Douglas's upcoming trial, but she knew that family loyalty butting up against issues of fairness was a painful conflict.

After coffee, they went over to the lawyer's office. Kyrios Maridakis walked with them back to the courthouse. He and Fr. Dimitrios were discussing something.

He showed the priest an affidavit from an orderly in the hospital stating that he had witnessed Manolis tell his father he had committed both robberies and had shot Douglas.

Fr. Dimitrios asked him to hold off, and not to enter the affidavit in the trial. He wanted to give Sofia time to change her mind. They could present the affidavit later if it was needed.

Kyrios Maridakis agreed to wait.

The courthouse was a neoclassical building facing a platia and a small park. The building was formal and grand, built in 1898 for Prince George, son of the Greek king, when he was sent to be high commissioner on Crete. Inside, the courtroom was a stern space. There were wooden benches to sit on. They shifted seats until everyone was sitting near whomever they needed to have near. Douglas and the lawyer sat up front, of course. Aleko sat in front of his mother, near Lambros. Douglas looked to see where Sofia was. She was safely between Fr. Dimitrios, who sat on the aisle, and her sister, Vassilia. Big Kostas was there, too, from the city, and Professor Ducor and Athina. They sat near the back.

The judge was a woman in her forties. She wore a black judge's robe. There was no jury, just as the lawyer Maridakis had told them.

Everyone stood as she entered the courtroom. She nodded acknowledgment to Kyrios Maridakis and to Fr. Dimitrios. Otherwise she did not seem to notice any of them. She studied a sheaf of papers for several minutes. Then she called Douglas's name.

He rose.

She spoke in Greek, most of which now, happily, he could understand. She asked him if he understood the charges against him. He said he did.

She listed the charges. "You are charged with stabbing an unarmed man. Further it is charged that you left that injured man and did not make an effort to get him to medical help, and that subsequently this unarmed man died in hospital. I understand your passport has been confiscated and is held by this court."

"That is correct, Your Honor." answered Douglas.

"How do you plead?"

"I plead not guilty, Your Honor." Douglas was calm as he spoke.

Douglas's lawyer rose and requested permission to answer the charges.

The judge granted that permission.

"Your Honor, the deceased victim did not die of his wound. It has been shown by an autopsy performed by the coroner, that he contracted a nosocomial infection of the variety of staphylococcus known as," he paused and read from a card in his hand, "Methecillin Resistant Staphylococcus Aureus or MRSA. This infection is well known to exist in hospitals and to cause grave illness and death among patients and staff. Therefore, according to *conditio sine qua non*, the accused is not responsible for a death caused by an infection contracted in hospital, even though the injury he acknowledges having caused was the reason the deceased was in the hospital. My client's responsibility does not extend to Manolis Kiriakis's death."

"Yes, counselor, I agree with your finding there. What have you to say about the initial injury?"

"The stabbing, Your Honor, was truly not the initial injury between these two people. The initial injury was a shotgun-load of birdshot which the deceased fired at the accused the day before the

333

stabbing, that is, on August 18th of last year. On that day as on the day following, Manolis Kiriakis, for reasons unknown…"

Sofia began to weep. Vassilia put her arm around her.

"…attempted to rob from Aleko Andreadakis, the son of his mother's sister, his own cousin, 20,000 drachmas which Aleko had just acquired in exchange for the sale of one goat. On the first attempt, he did succeed in obtaining that money. Also on that day, August 18th, he fired a *lupara*, a sawed-off shotgun, at the accused, hitting him in the right shoulder and upper back. That injury to the accused resulted in pain and trauma.

"I direct your attention to Article 308(3) of the Greek Penal Code, which says…" The lawyer took a burgundy leather law book out of his briefcase and opened it to a pre-flagged page. He read, "In the case of simple bodily injuries, the perpetrator may not be punished, if he inflicted the injuries out of indignation and as a result of the victim's earlier behavior.'

"The accused agreed to go with young Aleko Andreadakis the following day to sell another goat and to deliver the proceeds safely to Aleko's mother, Vassilia Andreadaki, so she could pay a debt with the money." Here, he gestured to Vassilia, who nodded to the judge. The judge did not nod back.

Kyrios Maridakis continued, "On the day of the stabbing, the accused did not attempt to arm himself. The passalis was removed from the Andreadakis home by young Aleko, aged nine years at that time," he gestured to Aleko, who gave the judge a righteous gaze, "…because he was fearful that they might be attacked again, carrying so much money. He gave the passalis to the accused after they had left the Andreadakis home and before the second robbery."

"Excuse me, counselor. These two events, the first and second robbery, were one day apart?"

"Yes, Your Honor. On the 18th and 19th of August, last year. One day after he had been shot, the accused accepted the passalis he was offered, because the possibility of another attack existed and he believed the knife was safer in his hands than in the hands of a nine-year-old child."

Douglas watched Kyrios Maridakis's face to see whether he seemed satisfied with the judge's reception of his argument. He couldn't tell.

"Your Honor, my client did not choose to arm himself, but when a weapon was offered in a situation of previous danger and a good possibility of recurring danger, he accepted it. He used it, not in outrage, as Article 308(3) would permit, but only in self-defense and in defense of the rule of law. "

"Is there proof of the victim's involvement in the earlier robbery?" asked the judge.

Kyrios Maridakis paused and looked at Fr. Dimitrios, who slowly shook his head. "There is, but I ask Your Honor's permission to present it at a later time."

"And is the victim's interest represented?" The judge asked, looking around the courtroom.

There was a long minute when no one moved.

Douglas looked over his shoulder at Sofia, sitting between Vassilia and Fr. Dimitrios. Slowly, she stood up.

"Your Honor," she said. "I am the mother of Manolis Kiriakis. It is true he robbed his cousin and shot Daonglos." She sat down again. Vassilia put her hand on her sister's shoulder.

"The defendant was justified in protecting himself the day after such an attack. I see no reason to proceed with this matter. These charges are set aside, the record will be expunged, and the defendant's passport will be returned to him at once. Case closed." The judge rose, and everyone in the room rose as she left.

When the judge left, Professor Ducor and Athina slipped out, leaving Douglas and the others to track down the passport and sign forms and do what one does when one has been exonerated from criminal charges. They went out into the windless heat of Cretan summer, blinked in the bright light, and waited to adapt to the glare.

Ducor extended his hand, palm up, like some Elizabethan courtier. Athina placed her hand on his and he led her across the street to the park beyond the Platia Eleftherios. In the center of the platia, a bronze statue of Crete's hero, the statesman Eleftherios Venizelos, watched over everything.

335

Ducor and Athina waited in the shadow of a large holm oak. They watched the others randomly spilling out of the courtroom building. Once outside, they, too, stood around in silence. Everyone felt an air of honor about this trial.

At last, Douglas came out. His friends from the village closed in on him. The little boy danced around him, shaking his hand in an oversized gesture. Aleko, he was called. Athina thought how much younger he looked now than last summer in the hospital waiting room.

Now Douglas was being hugged by a very large man. He must be the one called Big Kostas, with the taverna in the city.

Douglas went over to the woman who spoke in the trial, the mother of the young man who died. They embraced. All of them were smiling.

The attorney came out of the building, waving a blue passport. He handed it to Douglas with a great flourish.

Athina and Ducor watched as the group dispersed. People left, walking in talkative clusters of three or four. They would go to Big Kostas's place for a celebration.

Still, these two stayed where they were. They sat down on a metal bench near the oak. They were happy in their own company. In their minds they blessed Douglas, but they remained behind, sitting in the shade of the tree.

The sidewalk emptied. Two policemen came out, then a woman they recognized as the judge came out, too. She wore street clothes. Without her robes, she looked smaller. The officers touched visors to her and stepped to one side to let her pass. She nodded to them. They all left.

Just the courthouse in the sunshine. Just that and a feeling of something fine having happened here just now.

336

It was the memory of Douglas, standing in the courtroom, answering the judge's questions in his village Greek, so obviously pleased to be able to speak some Greek, standing proud—no not proud: he was standing there, lit up so fair.

No longer was he the bland young American tangled up with the Hansons, self-centered and numb, jogging instead of thinking. No longer, that kid who ran from his wedding.

The Belgian archaeologist and his Cretan fiancée would talk about the change in Douglas because they were at that time of discovery between a man and a woman when people talk about high-minded thoughts. High-mindedness itself feels more intimate to them then. In their talk, they would go over how the young American seemed changed, but they'd be actually thinking about how all people change or don't change.

In the end, they would come to the notion that what people take for being good is just being brave and doing it alone.

ACKNOWLEDGMENTS

Many thanks are due for the kind assistance of those experts who gave THE PALE SURFACE OF THINGS accuracy and vivid life. Any inaccuracies remaining are mine alone.

My thanks to archaeologists Lucia Nixon, Nancy Bookidis, and Alan Richardson; art restorers Glen Wharton and Jane Hutchins; ikon painter Sophronia Tomaras; philosophy professors Elias Baumgarten and Robert Gibbs; professor of classic languages Diane Johnson; Fr. Michael Pappas, Fr. John Contoravdis, and Irenaeus, Metropolitan of Chania; Alisa Aiken, a surgical nurse who also raises goats; speleologist Dale Chase; airplane model builder Patrick Kennedy; several residents of Crete: Athina Andreadi, Tony Fennymore, and Michalis Manousakis; and Americans or Canadians of Greek ancestry: Niki Mantas and Homer Vasels. Sam Perkins generously shared his knowledge of western Crete and the sites of battles in World War II, and Barbara Rose Shuler, Mary Lee Griswold, Ariane Crawford, Robin Ireland, Anna van Blankenstein, Roberta Pyx Sutherland and Eva Wetzel were patient readers. Keith Moen was a perfect publisher and Claire Sierra was a great help with all the graphics. Carol Bly was my mentor on this project. She guided me well through the perils of plotting and character development. I am endlessly grateful to these and more.

ABOUT THE AUTHOR

Janey Bennett grew up in San Diego, the daughter of an English professor whose love of literature shaped Janey's early life. She graduated from UCLA and has enjoyed colorful and varied careers, from radio announcer to horse trainer and drama critic. She spent five winters teaching English to Buddhist nuns in Thailand. Her writings on architecture have been published in the United States and Finland, where she held a Fulbright research fellowship. She has been writing fiction for eight years.

THE PALE SURFACE OF THINGS is Bennett's first novel, leading her into the study of classical Greek, Byzantine icon painting, geology, botany, the vernacular architecture and sociology of Greek villages, Minoan culture and art, the science of archaeology, World War II on Crete, and criminal law in Greece.

A cellist, freelance editor, and author, Bennett divides her time between Bellingham, WA and Hornby Island, BC.